50
GAY AND LESBIAN
BOOKS EVERYBODY MUST READ

50

GAY AND LESBIAN

Books Everybody Must Read

EDITED AND INTRODUCED BY

RICHARD CANNING

50 Gay and Lesbian Books Everybody Must Read

Published by Alyson Books
245 West 17th Street, Suite 1200, New York, NY 10011
www.alyson.com

ALYSON books

First Alyson Books edition: September 2009

Library of Congress Cataloging-in-Publication data are on file.

ISBN-10: 1-59350-119-6
ISBN-13: 978-1-59350-119-8

10 9 8 7 6 5 4 3 2 1

Cover design by Victor Mingovits
Book interior by Maria Fernandez, Neuwirth & Associates, Inc.

Printed in the United States of America
Distributed by Consortium Book Sales and Distribution
Distribution in the United Kingdom by Turnaround Publisher Services Ltd

Contents

Acknowledgments

"*Memoirs of Hadrian* by Marguerite Yourcenar" by Edmund White is adapted from a review of *Marguerite Yourcenar: Inventing a Life* by Josyane Savignea, which first appeared in the *New York Times Book Review*, October 17th, 1993 and was republished in Edmund White, *The Burning Library: Essays* (New York: Knopf, 1994), edited by David Bergman. "*Eustace Chisholm and the Works* by James Purdy" by Jonathan Franzen is the adapted transcript of an encomium given at Franzen's presentation to Purdy of the New York Mercantile Library's 2005 Clifton Fadiman Medal, honoring a great neglected work of fiction by a living American writer. "*A Boy's Own Story* by Edmund White" by Robert Glück originally appeared in the *Review of Contemporary Fiction*, vol. 16, no. 3 (1996). "*The Wild Boys: a Book of the Dead* (1971) by William Burroughs" is copyright the Literary Estate of Kathy Acker, 2009, to whom I wish to give thanks. All other essays are copyright their respective authors, 2009.

Introduction

Richard Canning

This book is *not* a canon!!!
I had to write that first, having in mind René Magritte's infamous 1929 canvas, *La trahison des images* (*The Treason of Images*): "Ceci n'est pas une pipe." ("This is not a pipe.") The viewer looks and sees a pipe, underneath which these words are written by Magritte. Of course, his point was to distinguish between an object and the image of that object. When pressed, he argued that you could prove the painting wasn't a pipe simply by trying to fill it.

50 Gay and Lesbian Books Everybody Must Read isn't a canonical book. If it were, it wouldn't have a leg to stand on. Consider this: cultural historians today rightly ridicule the longstanding notion—promoted by Edward Gibbon's *The History of the Decline and Fall of the Roman Empire* (1776–88), but not originating with it—that Europe descended into a "Dark Ages" in the fourth century; one that lasted anything up to a millennium. By entire accident, these fifty selections, placed and considered chronologically, might seem to argue for an even longer, and even less probable period of sleep in GLBTQ literature—one stretching from Plato to Horace Walpole, and thus covering almost twenty-two hundred years.

Clearly if this volume were attempting anything "representational" or survey-like, then, it would deserve ridicule. Nobody opted to write about Renaissance authors or texts, or those of the Enlightenment. There's no route here established between Plato and Walpole, only a gulf. But I want to emphasize that the sense of a gulf actually resides between each and every one of these fifty essays, and the leaps, counterstatements, and incongruous emphases among the babble of gathered voices has become—for me, anyway—a quality I have come to cherish.

Unlike Magritte's well-honed work of art, then, *50 Gay and Lesbian Books Everybody Must Read* does not intend to resemble anything, least of all a canon. If it has any relationship to notions of a GLBTQ canon (surely now obsolescent notions, anyhow), it can only be this: fifty diverse authors have each taken a single work of literature and written a brief account of how and why they read it (and, usually, repeatedly reread it), and why others (of any and all sexualities) should do so. Some books and authors may be familiar to you—elements of some more familiar, broader context: "a lauded part of the straight canon," as Maureen Duffy writes of Sappho. Melville and Whitman similarly are invariably grouped among writers of the American Renaissance (though, rather as Leslie Fiedler argued in *Love and Death in the American Novel* [1960], it may just be that the whole or near-whole of American letters is fundamentally queer). In such cases, these essays aim to get you to think again about writing you *think* you know. In other cases, recondite works are chosen: the aim must be to encourage you to consider picking up a book you may have neglected, overlooked, or simply never heard of. (I don't think there's a person on the planet who has read all fifty of these books, and a search on abebooks.com reveals that a fair few of the out-of-print titles are presently very hard to find.)

While it can be hard to define rigorously just what "Queer Theory" has legitimized in the past fifteen years (and what, precisely, it displaced or stood against), it has undoubtedly promoted the valuable idea that facets (sometimes mere traces) of gay, lesbian, bisexual, queer, and transgender experience might be discovered in any and all manner of cultural texts. Moreover, it encouraged a distinct idea—that GLBTQ viewers and readers (and others; anyone, in fact) might bring their own sometimes willfully perverse or subjective readings to works of culture, literature, or art. They would thus "queer" them—in other words, subject them to a "queer reading"; that is, bring out a latent or obscure queer reverberation, or "read against" the text to find something that subverts what the text (and invariably its creator) had meant it to be. In this spirit, the contributors to *50 Gay and Lesbian Books Everybody Must Read* are not defined by their sexuality. And, although each piece argues for GLBTQ resonance in the work in question, there's no cumulative or summative aim. In some cases, titles have been chosen that may seem intentionally eccentric: *Mrs. Dalloway*, for example, over Woolf's *Orlando*; Firbank's novel *The Flower beneath the Foot* over the more obviously gay *Cardinal Pirelli*; Gore Vidal's late memoir, *Palimpsest* as Paul Reidinger's selection, over several possible works of fiction. Not all of the pieces adopt straightforward advocacy either; indeed, one or two argue for the significance of a particular book, whilst reproaching it, and its creator, strongly.

When approaching contributors, I kept to one principle only: that each author selected could feature just once. It seemed unarguable that the wealth of possible subjects made this a legitimate constraint. As it is, you'll doubtless already be drawing up your own list of worthy neglecteds. Again, I can only urge you not to measure the value of this book by what isn't here, but by what is. I too have a list of omissions (which might be somewhat addressed by a second volume, who knows?). Perhaps it overlaps with yours, perhaps not. I can't stop myself from starting to type: Hall, Gide, Stein, Genet, Behn, Shakespeare, Townsend Warner, Forster . . . Yes, they're *all* not here—and nobody means anything by that. Some other presences are phantasmic only. For instance, nobody chose a book by Reinaldo Arenas—but he crops up in several of the essays to "comment" on the text to hand.

As I write, there's a little controversy brewing at London's National Portrait Gallery over a new show entitled "Gay Icons." Ten gay or lesbian celebrities have each named a set of "iconic" figures who have been important to them. Each one of these celebrities is out, but among their choices are not only many figures of the GLBTQ past, but quite a few certifiably heterosexual men and women—and rarely obvious choices (divas are notably in short supply). Over Pride weekend, some gay and lesbian commentators took Elton John in particular to task for selecting for his pantheon not only so many heterosexuals, but, among them, people he had known personally: his friend and librettist Bernie Taupin; John Lennon; even Graham Taylor, the football manager who rescued his own team, Watford FC. Billie Jean King chose members of her own family, and also Nelson Mandela. For some, this wasn't quite in the spirit of the *gay* iconic: which was taken to mean, people whose iconic status somehow illuminated the GLBTQ experience.

Interestingly, the three writers approached—Sarah Waters, Jackie Kay, Alan Hollinghurst—took a relatively conservative line, by contrast, largely using the opportunity to commend, and recommend, overlooked writers and other contributors to culture who can themselves be identified as GLBTQ. Businessman Waheed Alli appears to have had most fun in the selection process, acclaiming a foul-mouthed, Liverpudlian drag character, Lily Savage, as well as the Village People and American porn star Jeff Stryker as foundational influences (though oddly the shot of Joe Orton, another selector's choice—and yet another writer missing from the book in your hands—struck me as infinitely more seductive).

For all the carping, what the National Portrait Gallery has done is a rather unexpected thing; in several senses brave. It has refused to "hive off" gay male and lesbian histories, sensibilities, and subcultures, but dared them to talk to one another and mutually enlighten. With *50 Gay and Lesbian Books Everybody Must Read*, likewise, I was thrilled that so many contributors wanted to write about books concerning and/or written by members of the opposite sex. But this is only one possible way of identifying how often these essays describe the effect of a given book by way of its portrayal of *difference*, or the unfamiliar. So, David McConnell makes sense of the overwhelmingly unfathomable culture of what is probably our oldest GLBTQ text, *Gilgamesh* (though not the first to be written down). Fenton Johnson imagines the vicissitudes of imprisonment and spiritual self-questioning which led Wilde to write his least characteristic work, *De Profundis*. Kathy Acker explores the boy-saturated world of William Burroughs, a world she was erotically immune to but textually beguiled by. Mark Behr documents how *The Color Purple* forced him to reconsider everything he thought he knew of himself erotically, but also everything he thought he believed, in terms of racial politics in apartheid-era South Africa.

Other contributors document the early experience of identification with a literary character or temperament. Even here, it is the often remarkable and enduring note of dissonance or incompleteness that startles, alongside this process of identification. John Weir, then, finds out what he must be, or appears to others to be as a gay boy, by way of an American production of the working-class English drama *A Taste of Honey*. At the same time, the message of the play is confounded by the real-life character of the actor playing Geof, as outrageous and confident offstage as he is required to be tentative and insecure onstage. Tania Katan celebrates what Audre Lorde's *The Cancer Journals* taught her about her own cancer diagnosis; here, the misidentification is a benevolent one: Lorde died; Katan survived, with Lorde's book inspiring her to make art out of her own traumatic past.

Some contributors draw on personal reminiscences of authors they discuss, such as David Bergman's trenchant piece on Allen Ginsberg's *Howl*. Rather more announce a sort of resistance or misidentification with the implied author of the work. Mark Merlis skewers A. E. Housman as "sort of a Log Cabin Republican." Regina Marler follows Terry Castle in considering James's *The Bostonians* "the first 'lesbian novel' written in English." But her essay delightfully outlines how such an interpretation can only stem from an understanding of how the book effectively slipped entirely out of James's control.

Other essays are equally revisionary. Given the tendency to consider Edmund White's novel *A Boy's Own Story* as a rare example of "crossover" gay literature, Robert Glück pointedly argues for the book's radicalism and transgressiveness. Neither Christopher Bram nor Blair Mastbaum shies from outlining disturbing aspects in the portrayal of age-differential relationships in Thomas Mann's *Death in Venice* and Matthew Stadler's *Allan Stein*. Both argue for the force and importance of these works from first principles.

There are, inevitably, many watershed moments claimed across this book. Sometimes, particular titles are celebrated *against* what other, earlier books did or did not do. At their best (and rather often), these essays skillfully and creatively investigate both similarity (influence, tradition) and difference (innovation, individuality)—as when, for example, Matias Viegener identifies both the American literary inheritance embedded in Holleran's *Dancer from the Dance* (Fitzgerald, Twain) and its utter seventies contemporaneity (as the world's only disco novel). *50 Gay and Lesbian Books Everybody Must Read* may appear at a further watershed moment; it opens with Aaron Hamburger's beguiling interpretation of the gay Bible (yes, it is!), with immediate reference to the 2005 film *Brokeback Mountain*. This book makes no attempt to "size literature up" against film, but nor is it blind to the important fact that younger gays and lesbians have a vastly more diverse body of potential sources for the representation of their own kind than five, ten, and certainly twenty years ago. It has been suggested to me already that this fact makes this book a sort of posthumous account, of little present interest and no future relevance. On the one hand, I have more faith in the enduring presence of GLBTQ readers than that perhaps presumptuous judgment implies; on the other, pretending for a minute that the end may indeed be nigh for GLBTQ literature, I decided this made the book all the more timely and vital. To some degree, it may be true: the generation that was hungriest for GLBTQ representation in literary forms may now, to some degree, be being replaced by generations less hungry that way. I feel keener than ever, then, to publish: *50 Gay and Lesbian Books Everybody Must Read* may tell them what they are missing. It's also (note the title) announcing the relevance GLBTQ literature has for all contemporary readers. To many of these, a few "breakthrough" authors may be familiar—Sarah

Waters, Michael Cunningham, Armistead Maupin. But in fact GLBTQ writers, like their straight peers, write as individuals, not units. If nothing else, this book demonstrates that there are not—and never were—schools, protocols, inheritances, or duties. Amen!

A brief note about the principles of ordering and citation: the essays largely proceed in order of date of first publication. In the case of several ancient texts, this is, inevitably, somewhat conjectural. In a couple of other cases, I have given the first publication date of a volume, even though contributors may discuss a later, different edition, version, or translation of substantially the same work (Rimbaud, Cavafy). In the case of letters not published at the time of composition, I have tended to gather according to the last date of the collected correspondence (Walpole, Wilde, Sackville-West). At the end of each essay, there are references to any edition specifically quoted or cited, as well as—wherever relevant—mention of other editions that may readily be bought today.

I'd like to thank all of the contributors for delivering these fine pieces, especially given the none-too-generous conditions and deadlines, as well as Don Weise and Paul Florez at Alyson Books for all their characteristic help, advice, and support.

—London, July 2009

50
GAY AND LESBIAN
BOOKS EVERYBODY MUST READ

1 Samuel and 2 Samuel
(after 960 BC)

Aaron Hamburger

I magine two men embracing in a field, tearfully swearing their undying, secret love. Though this may sound like a plot summary of Ang Lee's film *Brokeback Mountain* (2005), I am in fact describing a scene from the story of Jonathan and David from the Book of Samuel.

At this point, traditionalist readers are horrified. Why, they wonder, must professional homosexuals deliberately misread a story of pure fraternal friendship in order to foist their agenda on an unwilling public? Surely the fact that David and Jonathan express their manly regard for each other with tender kisses and weeping cannot be interpreted as homosexual. Surely the memorable description of Jonathan's love for David from 1 Samuel 20:17—"He loved him; for he loved him as he loved his own soul"—is not love, but "love," just a euphemism for some other feeling, like profound esteem? Surely the fact that contemporary readers would interpret a line like the above to connote homosexual love speaks to the depravity of our culture, in contrast to the more innocent time of the Bible, when people did not succumb to the Freudian illusion that they had sex drives?

To back up their varying readings of the story of David and Jonathan, traditionalist Biblical scholars and their more liberal counterparts engage in a game of textual analysis, always tricky to play in translation. Traditionalists, for example, say that the Hebrew word for "love" has many meanings, or that the phrase "Jonathan greatly delighted in David" is never used in the Old Testament to refer to sexual intimacy. Liberal scholars point out that the word "love" is used in this story in the same way as it is used in other parts of the Bible to describe romantic relationships. Ditto for the phrase "[David] found grace in Jonathan's eyes"—a common Biblical phrase to connote physical and romantic feeling.

It's impossible to fully resolve the issue of intent behind the words because of our temporal, linguistic, and cultural dislocation from the time when they were first set down on sheepskin. Yet I think such discussion misses the real point of the story of David and Jonathan: the profound sense of recognition it inspires in anyone who has experienced love. Because what traditionalists fail to understand about gay people is that their condition is not just a yearning to commit a catalog of sexual acts which may or may not be proscribed by Leviticus. Rather, theirs is that most human of all conditions, the yearning to love and be loved in return.

First, some background. David is the youngest son of a poor shepherd named Jesse. Given his circumstances, David's prospects in life look fairly poor until one day the prophet Samuel comes by, and predicts that this boy shepherd will become King of Israel. This prophecy poses a bit of a problem, since Israel already has a king named Saul, who has three sons to succeed him, one of whom is Jonathan.

Now somehow—and the Bible is a little confusing on this— the lowly David gets a gig playing his harp for King Saul. How? The first explanation is that one of Saul's servants gives David a recommendation, saying "Look, I have seen a son of Jesse the Bethlehemite, who is skillful in playing, a mighty man of valor, a man of war, prudent in speech, and a handsome person; and the Lord is with him" (1 Samuel 16:18). Musical, muscled, witty, cute. Sounds gay to me. But I digress . . .

In the very next chapter, however, the Bible presents a directly contradictory account of the meeting of Saul and David. According to this version, David arrives in the royal camp to bring food from home for his older brothers, who are fighting in Saul's army. The mighty Philistine giant warrior Goliath has posed a one-on-one challenge to the Israelite soldiers, who, for all their experience, are reluctant to meet it. Only small, lowly David—not a mighty man of valor in this chapter—accepts the challenge, and slays Goliath with his slingshot. Saul wants to meet the brave young man and summons him into his presence.

The following chapter begins with the sudden declaration that "When [David] had finished speaking to Saul, the soul of Jonathan was knit to the soul of David, and Jonathan loved him as his own soul" (1 Samuel 18:1). Yes, I suppose that line is a bit ambiguous. Nothing at all to do with homosexual love. Nothing.

Just two verses later, we hear: "Then Jonathan and David made a covenant, because he loved him as his own soul." Some readers hear the word "'covenant" and think, "Gay marriage, anyone?" Traditionalists, however, view this covenant as a simple business deal, an "I'll scratch your back if you scratch mine" agreement.

Either way, the details above give telling clues to the dynamic between these two men. The choice of text in both examples makes clear that Jonathan is the one who is "knit" to David. In the second verse, it's clear that the "he" in "he loved him as his own soul" refers to Jonathan, not David, whose feelings are never mentioned. So far, this is a fairly one-sided relationship.

It's easy to imagine the musical, muscled, witty, cute David waltzing into Jonathan's life, causing Jonathan to fall head over heels. By contrast, David is naturally more focused on his own ambitions to be near power, and perhaps less concerned of the spiritual implications of his attraction to Jonathan. He enters into the covenant with Jonathan, sure. But is this a choice made out of true love, or out of David's desire to reap the rewards of being the BFF of the crown prince of Israel?

"And Jonathan took off the robe that was on him and gave it to David, with his armor, even to his sword and his bow and his belt" (1 Samuel 18:4). Here is what looks like one of the classic benefits of gay relationships: you get to double your wardrobe. And once again, we also see Jonathan doing all the giving while David gets all the benefit.

Meanwhile, the bipolar King Saul vacillates wildly between approval and deep jealousy of David. During one of his fits of goodwill to David, Saul gives him Jonathan's sister Michal as his wife. Yet David doesn't seem to be as excited about Michal-the-woman as he is about gaining position in Saul's court. In fact, here is the only line clarifying his feelings on the matter: "it pleased David well to become the king's son-in-law" (1 Samuel 18:26). Similarly, though Jonathan is married too, we only know this because the Bible mentions later on that he has a son who is lame in both feet. The identity of Jonathan's wife? His feelings about her? A mystery.

Eventually Saul's jealousy gets the better of him and he tells Jonathan he wants to kill David. How does Jonathan react? "But Jonathan, Saul's son, delighted greatly in David." While some readers delight in the word "delight," traditionalist readers warn that in Hebrew "delighted greatly" is a generic term whose meaning depends on context. Whatever these words mean, because of his "great delight" for David, Jonathan warns his friend to go into hiding.

As the two men make a second covenant together (sort of like an old married couple renewing their vows), Jonathan does all the talking about his love and loyalty to David: "Jonathan again caused David to vow, because he loved him; for he loved him as he loved his own soul" (1 Samuel 19:1). Again, the Bible mentions nothing of David's words or feelings.

Jonathan agrees to find out if his father really means to kill David or not. The two friends meet again in a field a few days later, and Jonathan warns David that, yes, the threat is real, and David must leave the kingdom of Israel to save his own life. In response, David "fell on his face to the ground, and bowed three times. And they kissed one another; and they wept together, but David more so" (1 Samuel 20:41). For the first time, the Bible shows us David's feelings for Jonathan, which suggests that until this point, David has never realized how much Jonathan means to him. Now he does so, but tragically too late, as this is the last time they will ever see each other.

Later, Saul and Jonathan are both killed in battle. Upon hearing the news, David begs for confirmation, and then sings of his grief, in one of the most beautiful lamentations in all of literature: "I am distressed for you, my brother Jonathan; you have been very pleasant to me. Your love to me was wonderful, surpassing the love of women" (2 Samuel 1:26).

For any contemporary reader of serious literature, gay-friendly or not, it's hard not to read these descriptions as evidence of same-sex love. And yet traditionalist Biblical readers insist that anyone looking at the David-Jonathan story as homosexual is overreaching. Their arguments seem to run as follows:

1. Words like "love," "delighted in," and "covenant" are used in a variety of contexts in the original Hebrew, often not romantic. The word for "covenant," for example, was never used to refer to marriage in any other context.
2. The culture used to be more expressive. In other words, men used to hug and kiss a lot in those days. Today we know better, which is why men just shake hands, or at most half-hug.
3. There is no other evidence of Biblical sanctioning of homosexual relationships.

My counterarguments are as follows:

1. Traditionalists are so horrified by the thought of Jonathan and David having anal sex that they miss the clear description of a love story between two men, which if not homosexual is at the very least homosocial. Whether or not David and Jonathan created the beast with two backs, they clearly were two men who cared a great deal for each other. And that's pretty gay.
2. Bullshit.
3. Just because the Bible describes something doesn't necessarily mean it's sanctioning it (or conversely that it's forbidding it either). The Bible is a sophisticated work of

literature that portrays its characters engaging in all kinds of activities, having a range of emotions and behaviors common to human beings, not saints. Homosexual love has always existed, and it would be a lie for the Bible to pretend otherwise.

I don't pretend the Bible doesn't condemn certain aspects of gay male sexual behavior (though nothing on female sexual behavior). I think it does. Yet the Bible also condemns a bunch of other stuff that people do all the time these days: eating shrimp, wearing fabric woven of two different materials combined, working on Saturday, etc. The Bible also mandates practices that today we'd find abhorrent, such as slavery or the equation of women to chattel. No one—traditionalist, secular or Martian—follows the original text of the Bible to the letter. Rather, we necessarily pick and choose among the Bible's commandments based on their relevance to our lives today in addition to the Bible's core values of love, respect, and human dignity.

Therefore, the question is not if the Bible condemns homosexuality, but why? (Because God said so is not a good enough reason.) One interpretation I've heard is that homosexual behavior was associated with rituals of idol worship. Another possible reason for the discouragement of homosexuality is that Jews wanted to encourage heterosexual procreation to ensure the perpetuation of their tribe. However, the most likely explanation of the prohibition of homosexuality is also the simplest: the bias against homosexuals is as old as it is pernicious.

Whether or not David and Jonathan were getting it on is a question we'll never resolve. But the influence of their story on later generations is undeniable. Even Oscar Wilde mentioned it in his defense of the love that dare not speak its name.

I was influenced too, while growing up in suburban Detroit—a nervous boy, frightened of the confusing feelings I'd always had and knew I could never share or explain. But then when I turned thirteen and had my bar mitzvah, it turned out that my haftorah portion was the story of David and Jonathan. As I chanted the words of the story I loved so well to my congregation, it felt as if God were sending me a message. Whether He was or not is unimportant; I heard it all the same: "Have patience," it said. "Someday, you will have this kind of love too."

AARON HAMBURGER was awarded the Rome Prize by the American Academy of Arts and Letters for his short-story collection, *The View from Stalin's Head* (2004). His next book, a novel entitled *Faith for Beginners* (2005), was nominated for a Lambda Literary Award. He lives in New York City, and his Web site address is www.aaronhamburger.com. Quotations are taken from the King James Version of the Bible.

GILGAMESH

(between 668 and 627 BC)

DAVID MCCONNELL

In Paris, around 1983, I first read *The Epic of Gilgamesh* in Nancy Sandars's prose version for Penguin. Then already twenty years old, Sandars's work has been supplanted in the Penguin library since 1999 by a far more scholarly and accurate, far less readable and affecting translation by Andrew George.

I remember being happy the book was short. I was trying to rack up as many world classics as possible and was grateful for the ones I found easy, like Boccaccio, Cervantes, Chateaubriand (oddly) . . . and Sandars's *Gilgamesh*. But the purist in me found Sandars a little hard to believe. The "real" *Epic of Gilgamesh* couldn't possibly be so cartoon-like, so fun, so heart breaking, so hallucinatory, so modern.

In fact, because the work is jaw-droppingly ancient (basically, there isn't *anything* older), and because its language (Akkadian) and writing system (cuneiform) are so utterly dead, the idea of a "real" version is laughable. In some ways synopsis is best. Rilke, an ecstatic admirer ("Gilgamesh . . . is the greatest thing one can experience"), was convinced he did a better job telling the story to friends than the poem's early translators had.

Taking too thoroughly into account the unknowable culture, the fragmentary text, the dimly understood prosody, the rhetoric, diction, grammar, and even vocabulary of debatable meaning (to say nothing of nuance), we end up with mazy scholarship, and a version riddled with brackets, ellipses, and footnotes. It has to be done, of course, but *Gilgamesh* deserves to live a little. It's why I loved Sandars, though I plumed myself on being a student of Greek and Latin and preferring all things original.

The real *Gilgamesh* is a series of badly damaged, pillow-shaped clay tablets, covered on both sides with blocks and columns of thorny cuneiform indentations like long pushpins in profile. They were excavated in 1850 from the Royal Library of Ashurbanipal in Nineveh (near modern Mosul in Iraq) by Austen Layard and Hormuzd Rassam. The tablets were made in the seventh century BC, or about a hundred years before the Babylonian captivity of the Jews ended; or, say, during the long folkloric gap between the actual Trojan War and the writing of the Homeric epics. At that time, incredibly, *Gilgamesh* was nearing the end of its first run on earth. It was already ancient. Though the standard version was found in the capital of an Assyrian king, earlier versions of it have come to light in other languages—Hittite, Hurrian, Old Babylonian, Sumerian—snaking back in time and generally southward along the Euphrates from Nineveh to Babylon to Uruk, circa 2300 BC, when oral poems were probably first sung about a king of that city, who may have been real five hundred years before that, but who'd long been deified and worshipped.

As page one of all literature, *Gilgamesh* embodies a few ironies.

The standard version is astonishingly sophisticated, even urbane. *Gilgamesh* isn't a "popular epic," it's a "literary epic." Less *Iliad*, more *Aeneid*, though the author, Sîn-liqe-inninni, seems to have been more Homeric compiler than Augustan poet. The great Assyriologist A. Leo Oppenheim stressed that *Gilgamesh* was never the culturally omnipresent national epic we think of when we think "epic."

A more illuminating comparison might be to Ovid. Like the *Metamorphoses*, *Gilgamesh* was probably a refined take on familiar religious subjects read and recited within a small, literate, leisure class. Despite a great deal of protean grandeur, the poem is full of humor and sexuality, and not just the crude kind familiar from folk tales. It's thrilling and spooky, as well. And finally serious: the great theme of earth's first book is fear of death. Gilgamesh has to reconcile himself to that reality. This isn't just an ironic beginning for literature. It's a topic sentence for all the arts that come afterward.

Gilgamesh begins as a love story between two men. Some find that phrasing too strong—too gay. Enkidu and Gilgamesh are both lustily heterosexual. But to say they form a "friendship" isn't right either. They're in love. Just because contemporary Westerners (straight and gay) have a hard time getting a grip on this relationship, doesn't mean everyone always did, or does. Take away repressive Islam, and any modern Saudi or Yemeni boy would have no trouble understanding Gilgamesh and Enkidu.

A certain amount of sexuality is folded into relationships like this, in the form of extreme tenderness, devoted exclusivity, the occasional witty pretense of being "the woman," and maybe the occasional discreet "release" (not in *Gilgamesh* but in real life). The existence of this special kind of friendship blunts any social imperative to distinguish between the straight-at-heart and the gay-at-heart. The idea of identifying people by sexuality may even strike some historically minded Middle Easterners as bizarre, a pendant to that other modern Western "perversity," the indiscriminate mixing of the sexes.

Understanding the relationship between Gilgamesh and Enkidu is crucial to understanding the story. In Enkidu Gilgamesh has to find the love of his life, not just a friend, because Enkidu's death has to be the greatest loss any person can endure. The lovers also have to be interchangeable in a way a man and a woman can't be. Otherwise the story doesn't make sense. Gilgamesh has to see himself in Enkidu. Patroclus's death in the *Iliad* is the turning point of that poem, and of the war, because it's meaningful to Achilles in exactly the same way. But the amused awareness of sexuality, even homosexuality, which is present in *Gilgamesh,* is missing from the comparatively prudish *Iliad.* It took randy fifth-century Athenians to reinterpret Achilles and Patroclus as icons of homosexual love.

If Athenian homosexuality came to the *Iliad* by a kind of historical accretion, the same process has brought strange, wonderful, and unoriginal attributes to all of humanity's really ancient texts. *Gilgamesh* is something of an exception, because it was missing for most of recorded history. While the Bible and Homeric epics were buried under centuries of interpretation, *Gilgamesh* sat out the ages in the dirt. It comes to us fresh from 1850—or from the 1870s, when the first translations were widely circulated. The poem's paradoxical new-but-unimaginably-ancient aura is one of its most striking attributes. It's hard to exaggerate how powerful an effect that unique aura can have on a reader.

On first going over the lines of the deluge episode in 1872 and recognizing the episode from the story of Noah, the scholar George Smith is said to have crowed about being the first person to read it in two thousand years. He ran around the room in excitement and, for some reason, started taking his clothes off. Those present were shocked.

Smith's reaction makes mysterious sense to me. For some reason nakedness and Gilgamesh go together in my mind. I mentioned that I first read Sandars's *Gilgamesh* in Paris in the eighties. I was specific, because at the same time, in the same city, I was studying another relic of the ancient world—the bath house. Not exactly studying it.

The law and fear of AIDS had all but killed off the gay bath house culture in New York. In Paris Americans got to time-travel back several years. Not that the French were completely unaware of what was starting to happen, but gloom, fatality, desire, fear, sex, misery, and regret were an absinthe-like liqueur suited to the national taste. I got a taste for it too. Plus the bath house was someplace to go during the pit of the night, three and four in the morning, when my thoughts were so glassy and stiff they amounted to nothing.

I preferred a small, dirty place beyond the Gare St. Lazare. Sex was part of it, obviously, but only part. The nakedness was almost more remarkable. Stripping down with the riffraff of off-duty hustlers and bakers, *camionneurs* and nightcrawlers, strolling the pungent, black-painted halls under dim red bulbs, realizing I was just one of an almost medieval miscellany of bodies, gave me the most poignant feeling of anonymity. (In daylight I had a crippling longing to be famous.) It was salutary and scary to "get it" for the first time that I was just a single entry on the roll of all the living and all the dead. Exactly the lesson of *Gilgamesh,* as it happened, with all the language problems and all the fear, fantasy, and aching physicality, besides.

HE WHO SAW INTO THE DEPTHS
A QUICK SUMMARY OF THE WHOLE EPIC OF GILGAMESH

The story opens with the bully king Gilgamesh lording it over his city, Uruk (about halfway between modern Basra and Baghdad in

Iraq). The people complain to the gods about him, so the gods arrange for a rival to be created—Enkidu, a wild man. Enkidu is raised by animals and lives among them, until a hunter spots him one day and immediately notices that he's a match for Gilgamesh. The hunter finds an exceptionally beautiful prostitute, Shamhat, to lure Enkidu from the wild. Meanwhile in Uruk Gilgamesh is pestered by strange dreams about a rock and an axe, which his mother tells him represent a future comrade whom he'll love like a wife.

Enkidu has sex with Shamhat for seven days and nights running. It's literature's greatest case of priapism (the descriptions of Shamhat's breasts and genitals are wonderfully pornographic). Afterward, Enkidu has no choice but to abandon the wild. The scent of Shamhat is on him and drives his animal companions away. He learns the arts of civilization, learns them so well he feels outrage on hearing that Gilgamesh demands sex by *droit de seigneur* from every new bride in Uruk. Disgusted, Enkidu goes to Uruk to confront the king.

The two larger-than-life heroes fight. Enkidu loses to Gilgamesh, but as soon as the fight is over they become bosom friends. In their culture heterosexual desire seems to be something of a screen obscuring and dividing the sexes. The vivid, chaste love the heroes share is a much greater emotion and full of explicit tenderness (with a few narrative winks because any lovers can look a bit like a man and a woman).

Feeling the boldness of youth, Gilgamesh and Enkidu decide to travel to the Forest of Cedar to kill the awesome shape-shifting demon Humbaba. In the course of the long journey, Gilgamesh has terrifying nightly dreams. Enkidu bucks him up. The friends alternate between blowhard vaunting and quaking in their boots. But finally they do confront Humbaba, and Gilgamesh kills him. In thanks and propitiation, Enkidu vows to make a door for a great temple out of a particularly impressive cedar.

Back in Uruk, the goddess Ishtar falls in love with Gilgamesh. Wary of a marriage in which he'd lose all manly independence and self-respect, he rejects her. In a rage she borrows the Bull of Heaven from her father and sends it on a rampage through Uruk. Gilgamesh and Enkidu discover a spot at the base of the animal's skull (a spot used in slaughterhouses to this day for a quick kill) and dispatch the bull. Cheerfully, like schoolboys, they mock Ishtar and brag about their triumph.

Sleeping after the celebration, Enkidu has a dream in which the gods decide he must die. He rages about the temple door that did him no good, about the hunter and Shamhat who lured him from the wild. In a second dream, a spirit of Death drags him into the underworld. As soon as he tells Gilgamesh about the dreams, Enkidu falls sick. Full of regret about his miserable, unwarlike end, he dies.

Gilgamesh mourns Enkidu for days and nights on end. He refuses to surrender Enkidu's body for burial until a maggot drops from the nostril of the corpse. He gathers the richest imaginable assortment of grave goods—and they're catalogued in detail with the typical "epic" fascination for gold, jewels, and anything precious or rare.

Now that he's experienced death so intimately, Gilgamesh becomes obsessed with his own mortality. He thinks of Uta-napishti, the one human being whom the gods made immortal. He begins searching for him and for the secret of eternal life. A Scorpion-man guarding the edge of the world reluctantly lets Gilgamesh pass. The hero then literally outruns the sun. He escapes time itself and ends up in a garden made entirely of jewels.

By a sea beyond the garden, an old goddess warns Gilgamesh against going any further. He must not cross the sea she calls "the waters of death." Stubbornly, Gilgamesh insists, so the goddess tells him where he can find Uta-napishti's old ferryman and a crew of Stone Ones. Gilgamesh rashly assaults the ferryman and smashes the Stone Ones. He has to improvise a way across the waters of death.

When Gilgamesh finds Uta-napishti, he tells the immortal why he came. Uta-napishti lectures Gilgamesh about the inescapability of death. He then recounts how he built an ark and survived the great flood and how the gods rewarded him with immortality. Since Gilgamesh remains determined, Uta-napishti suggests the hero go without sleep for a week. Gilgamesh can't do it. Unable to prevail over sleep, he knows he'll never prevail over death.

Disconsolate, Gilgamesh prepares to return to Uruk. Uta-Napishti's wife makes sure her husband offers Gilgamesh a parting gift. So the immortal tells Gilgamesh where a plant can be found at the bottom of the sea. Gilgamesh dives in and retrieves the plant which is called "Old Man Made Young," because it has the magical power to make one young again.

On his way back to Uruk, escorted by the old ferryman, Gilgamesh bathes in a pool. Carelessly he sets the "Old Man Made Young" on shore, and while he's in the water a snake steals the plant. Gilgamesh is overwhelmed by the loss. He knows he can never again find the place he dived into the sea. All his efforts have been wasted. His dreams are in ruins. In Uruk he shows the ferryman the great city walls—walls he put up himself. The walls will be his only lasting monument.

DAVID MCCONNELL's first novel was *The Firebrat* (2004). His short fiction and journalism have appeared widely in magazines and anthologies. *The Silver Hearted*, his next novel, is due out in February 2010. He lives in New York City. *The Epic of Gilgamesh: an English Version with an Introduction by N.K. Sandars* (London/New York: Penguin, 1960; revised edition 1972) is currently in print, alongside many other translations.

POEMS

(c.600 BC)

by Sappho

MAUREEN DUFFY

Why Sappho? Isn't she already a lauded part of the straight canon, like Oscar Wilde and the ambiguous bard? No real need for rehabilitation then. But we must begin our own canon somewhere, and not just with discovery, exhuming the lost. Reclamation has its place too or we shall be denying ourselves those who did, even if sometimes for the wrong reasons, make it into mainstream acceptance. So Sappho . . .

"Didn't she live on some Greek island with a lot of other Lezzies?"

Yes, and a great many of the modern-day inhabitants don't care for what happened to their geographical description in the nineteenth century. Until then, "Lesbian" was a simple recognition of residency: dwellers on Lesbos, or, curiously, according to the Oxford English Dictionary, an architectural term for a certain kind of decorative molding.

Poets could write perfectly straight verses to their girlfriends as "Lesbia" without a nudge or a wink, along with Cynthia, Phillida, Corinna, Electra, Dianeme, and all the sixth form of Joan Hunter Dunne's foremothers.

Sappho's version of oblivion is that of notoriety. She is known for the appropriation of her name to a supposed sexual orientation—"sapphic," again a nineteenth-century coinage, as if "socratic" were to be a term for male homosexuality instead of a method of teaching philosophy. In other words, the art for which she was revered for hundreds of years, and was reputedly called the tenth muse by Plato, has been overlain by a prurient interest, indeed obsession, with what she got up to with her girlfriends, an interest akin to that expressed in the potboilers about gay women intended for straight males.

Sappho needs some of our tender, loving care to restore her to her place as the tenth muse. The known facts about her are few. She was born between 630 and 612 BC, probably, and everything about her life except her very existence and some of her extant work, is hedged with this caveat, to a wealthy family on the island of Lesbos. The island was a cultural and political center, boasting several active poets, including Sappho's friend Alcaeus, another of the lyricists included in the Greek canon, who described her affectionately as "violet-haired, pure, honey smiling."

Cultural life, as so often, centered on groups of friends and lovers, rather like an early version of The Rhymers Club or Bloomsbury, the difference being that the circles seem to have been monosexual in a society where homosexuality was an acceptable form of erotic expression for both gods and humans, though the jury is still out for some commentators on the degree of physicality involved.

Biographical details based on her work and on later writings suggest that she had both a mother and a daughter called Cleis, a father, Scamandronymous, and three brothers, the youngest of whom she is said by the later memorialist Athenaios to have praised for having the prestigious office of cupbearer to the governors of Mytilene, the capital of the island.

There's no mention of a father for daughter Cleis in any of her poems and even the exact meaning of the possible word for "daughter"—*pais*—has been questioned by some scholars. But later experience suggests that there is nothing unusual in a homosexual or bisexual woman having a child she is devoted to, and it seems to me altogether likely that the "beautiful child who looks like a golden flower, my darling Cleis," who she "would not take all Lydia for," is indeed her daughter. The inference lurking in the unwillingness of some to accept this reading is either of a dried-up unmaternal stereotype or, conversely, a desire to keep Sappho unsullied by any taint of bisexuality.

What is reasonably sure is that she lived in a time of great political upheaval in which her friend Alcaeus was deeply involved. He and his brothers had joined a rebel group led by Pittacus, the so-called Sage of Lesbos, in the overthrow of the aristocratic ruler Melanchros. Alcaeus then joined Pittacus's army fighting the Athenians but retired from the battle of Sigeion and was accused of cowardice. Meanwhile the political vacuum left on the island was filled by one Myrsilus with whom Pittacus allied himself and Alcaeus went into exile, eventually travelling to Egypt while one of his brothers joined the Babylonian army under Nebuchadrezzer III.

All this unrest impinged on Sappho and she too went into exile between 604 and 594 BC, but only to Sicily. A marble bust of her which survives in a Roman copy and is dated to the following century refers to her as "of Eressos," on the eastern side of Lesbos. It shows her with a serious expression on a rather plump face, with her hair formally dressed in the ancient Greek version of cornrows but with two long tresses on either side of her bare neck. She was said to be small, dark, and not beautiful. Other depictions of her on Attic vases, said to be about 570 BC, show her with Alcaeus, both with lyres in their hands, or seated reading to three of her companions, one of whom seems to be accompanying her on the lyre. Poetry was usually performed to music for the next several hundred years from the Mediterranean to Britain. The first extant lines of poetry in Old English written down by Bede as the work of Caedmon (fl. 670 AD) were to be sung or perhaps intoned, rather in the manner of some traditional folk singers.

Sappho's work continued to be read, admired, and imitated at least until the end of the first millennium AD Nine scroll volumes of it were in the great library at Alexandria, and Byzantium carried on the tradition in the Suda, a tenth-century encyclopedia. The reasons given for her later neglect vary from persecution by the Christian church—Gregory of Corinth wrote that the erotic phrases used by Sappho and Alcaeus "flatter the ear shamefully"—to the decline in the use and knowledge of the dialect in which they were written by Roman times, when Attic and Homeric Greek were studied at the expense of Aeolian, which was no longer part of the curriculum—rather like the decline in Anglo-Saxon studies in British universities. However, given the Church's attitude even today to any sex outside marriage, an element of discrimination seems likely. The preservation of much Greek text by Muslim scholarship, after the fall of Byzantium, with its masculine bias might also have been an element in her decline and the loss of so much of her work.

She became increasingly identified with her sexuality. A poem by John Donne at the end of the sixteenth century, "Sappho to Philaenus," exemplifies this trend with its explicit erotic descriptions, and its plea for a recognition of the innocence of love-making between women since it has no embarrassing consequences. Whether the future dean of St. Paul's had ever read any of Sappho's poems it's impossible to say, or whether he had caught their yearning urgency at second hand. But it is quite as powerful as his more famous and anthologized evocations of straight sex.

Again, in the next century, Aphra Behn has no qualms about invoking Sappho or expressing homoerotic feelings herself. In a translation from Cowley's Latin verses, "On Plants," there is a marginal note: "Here the translatress in her own voice speaks." What she lets out is the cry echoed by Keats, hoping he will be "among the English poets after my death," and, much later, by Virginia Woolf, wondering if she will make it into that bastion of male celebrity, the Dictionary of National Biography. Translating the story of Daphne, who was changed into a laurel tree to escape the unwelcome pursuit of Apollo, Behn begs:

And after monarchs, poets claim a share
As the next worthy thy priz'd wreaths to wear . . .
Let me with Sappho and Orinda be,
Oh ever sacred nymph adorned by thee;
And give my verses immortality.

Hostile critics of Behn's work concentrated on her life, accusing her of licentiousness and suggesting that she had the clap, under the soubriquet of "Sappho." But Behn was unfazed by this, taking the mantle on herself and coupling Sappho with Orinda—that is, Katherine Phillips, Behn's poetic predecessor, who had been at the center of a literary circle in Wales and kept her reputation by denying that she wrote for publication and was respectably married, while writing intensely intimate poems to her female friends.

What Sappho expresses in those fragments of her poems that do survive—and "The Hymn to Aphrodite" is the only complete text—is a passionate yearning, often unfulfilled, that attains the ecstasy, the intensity of orgasm. It is the literary equivalent of Bernini's sculpture of St. Teresa pierced by the pretty angel's spear, or the duet from Handel's *Rodelinda, Io te braccio*, when sung by two sopranos:

> When I look at you my speech deserts me
> my tongue is unstrung, a subtle fire
> flushes beneath my skin
> my eyes grow dark, my ears hum
> sweat pours from me, I am green
> as new grass and I seem close to death.

The woman she is looking at in this state of spontaneous orgasm is Anactoria, seen across the room sitting next to a man, who is clearly chatting her up and with whom she flirts so openly that Sappho trembles with jealous desire.

A later tradition has Sappho fall in love with a ferryman called Phaon who cares only about his boat, and kill herself when he rejects her, by jumping off the Leucadian cliffs. While this is not impossible, and sexualities may change in either direction, it seems unlikely that an aristocratic woman and poet would go for what is clearly a bit of rough trade. It's more likely a late invention by one of the comic poets, embodying a strand of male psychology that may resent homosexual women, made explicit in the expression: "All she needs is a good seeing to!"

Cicero recorded that there was a statue of Sappho in the city hall at Syracuse, no doubt recording her stay there during her exile. Like Alcaeus, she eventually returned to Lesbos where her image appeared on the Mytilean coinage. If the dates are right, she would still have been in her twenties or early thirties, which suggests that the bulk of her output was written on Lesbos for her circle. But it also includes several fragments which seem to be from epithalamia, and it looks as if she might have been engaged to sing at weddings. Others suggest the pain of young women forced away—presumably by marriage—and for the loss of their virginity. It would be interesting to know how the poems made their way into the world and down the centuries, to be endlessly quoted, admired, and alluded to. It took Victorian prurience to reduce Sappho's circle to the equivalent of a homoerotic St. Trinians of schoolgirl crushes.

And so to the book. Where can those of us who, like Shakespeare, have no Greek come at her work, which still surfaces on pottery shards or is found—as late as 2001—on mummy wrappings, for us to admire in a more tolerant period? All the known fragments are available in Anne Carson's admirable dual text *If Not, Winter*. In these pages you can come face-to-face with her passion. Let your eye pan through the fragments until it comes up with a nugget of pure gold that evokes not only her circle, the island's flowers and scents, female beauty, and desire but the music of her voice across the millennia. She must never again be buried in the dust heap of neglect and homophobia.

MAUREEN DUFFY is author of over thirty works of poetry, fiction, and nonfiction, as well as plays for stage, television, and radio. Her latest publications are a poetry collection, *Family Values* (2008) and a novel, *The Orpheus Trail* (2009). Duffy lives in London, and her Web site is www.maureenduffy.co.uk. Quotations are taken from Sappho and Anne Carson, *If Not, Winter* (London/New York: Vintage, 2003), which is currently in print.

THE SYMPOSIUM
(c.384 BC)

by Plato

SHAUN LEVIN

On or around June 10th, 2000, I fell in love. It was the kind of love that shook me to the core. An archetypal experience. Like a moment of truth. A moment that left me terrified and exhilarated, wanting to roar and to disappear: it was like birth and it was like death. It was that intense. The first summer of the new millennium was a particularly hot summer in London, and my father had been dead for just six months. I was off work for a while, on a break from teaching English as a second language; it was a kind of holiday. My love for him was an obsessive one, and it thrived in the lush environment of self-doubt and grief and too much free time.

Our relationship lasted for only seven months.

But I miss being in love like that, when he in particular or love in general is the first thought you have when you rise in the morning, your last thought when you go to bed at night. It was religious. I was talking in tongues. And although I loved every minute of it and would do it again (with someone else), I was petrified. Books saved me. Without them, I would have had to wade single handedly through the heartbreaking, flesh-rending, unbearable torment of being in love with a man who went back to his girlfriend at the end of each rare afternoon we spent together. In those months following my father's death, I had found a way to relive, on a daily basis, the sense of abandonment the death of a parent brings into one's life.

I went looking for books about love—Françoise Sagan's *Bonjour tristesse* (1954), Rumi, Marguerite Duras's *The Lover* (*L'Amant*, 1984), Christopher Coe's *Such Times* (1993), Juan Goytisolo's *The Blind Rider* (*Telon de boca*, 2002)—and I arrived, I'm not sure how, at *The Symposium*. Without *The Symposium* I would have left the relationship much earlier. I am good at ending relationships; good not as in I do it well (because I don't), but good as in I do it often. *The Symposium* was my guide for the perplexed. It taught me things I'd known intuitively or through experience but had never put into words: that Poverty and Resource are the parents of Love, that it is our job to educate our lovers, to try to show them what is good and wise (in the world and in us and them). It taught me that love is everything. It made me feel validated and divinely inspired. In his book *Why Read the Classics?* (*Perché leggere i classici*, 1991), Italo Calvino says that a classic is a book "which even when we read it for the first time gives the sense of rereading something we have read before."

The Symposium is a story about a group of men who get together and talk about love. First they have dinner, then, each in turn— Phaedrus, Pausanias, Eryximachus, Aristophanes, Agathon, Socrates, and Alcibiades—gives his "eulogy of Love." They talk about the nature of the god of Love, and about the army of lovers that could conquer the world, about love's courage-inducing qualities. They talk about love between an older man and a younger man, about love between equals, and about love between men who spend their whole lives together. They talk about the crazy things one does in the name of love—going down on your knees, begging, spending the night on the beloved's doorstep—and they say this is good. They say "gods and humans allow lovers every kind of indulgence." They say it is "better to love openly than secretly."

Love, they say, is what makes it possible for us to be friends with each other.

And Aristophanes, the comedy writer, tells the story of how we were punished for attacking the gods: Zeus sliced us in two "as people cut sorb-apples in half before they preserve them or as they cut hard-boiled eggs with hairs." Our genitals, because the gods had pity on us, were moved round to the front, so that we'd stop reproducing on the ground like grasshoppers.

"And don't treat my speech as a comedy," he says.

Every living thing, they tell us, owes its existence to Love. They say that Love seeks out only the beautiful. They say that you desire what you don't have and if you don't have beauty . . . well, yes, love doesn't have beautiful things. Love is not beautiful in itself, but is beautiful because it seeks out beautiful things. And I remember thinking: Yes. I am in love with the most beautiful man I have ever been with. But what was different this time—for I have been lucky when it comes to beautiful men—was that I believed him. When he said he loved me, his words sunk in, were absorbed, and they changed me. Though in the torment of it all, I had no idea this was happening; I was ignorant of the transformation taking place. As far as I was concerned, I was going mad, I was neglected, and I was alone.

My main reassurance in the world was the work of the Sufi poet Rumi and Plato's *The Symposium*. They taught me that people had been feeling like this—demented with desire and blessed with poetic gifts—since . . . forever. My love was part of a tradition. I could be the love-crazed poet. I had been to war and written about it; I had witnessed the passing away of my father and sat at his deathbed taking notes; now I was in my mid-thirties and I was finally able to write about love from within. And what I wrote, bit by bit, grew into my first book, *Seven Sweet Things*.

I started by writing about a particular afternoon, somewhere into the relationship, maybe halfway through, maybe nearer the beginning, when he and I were on a bench in Embankment Gardens drinking tea and eating coconut cookies from the café at the edge of the park. I'd been carrying *The Symposium* around with me for days, and I wanted to show him what I'd discovered.

"Let me read to you," I said. "I want to read something nice to you."

So I read to him from Phaedrus's speech on the army of lovers, and the lover's fear of acting disgracefully in front of his boyfriend. I read to him about the virtue of dying for the one you love.

"You're such a romantic," he said.

"Don't be cynical," I said.

"Love is fickle," he said. "Anyway, how old was this Phaedrus guy?"

I realized then that there was no point in talking about love to a lover. I mean, look how terrified Pausanias was, going on and on about Heavenly Love, afraid his writer-boyfriend Agathon would run off with the aging Socrates. But as far as I was concerned, Phaedrus's words were my own; I'd taken them and put them in a context that wasn't a group of men lounging around, sipping wine from golden goblets, giving praise to love, but just the two of us, me and this man I adored, clinging to each other to ward off all doubt. It was my way of telling him I was gasping for breath on the battlefield.

"What do you like about the book?" he said.

"That it's about love and culture and having time for both," I said.

"You just need a proper job," he said.

"These guys never worried about a job," I said, hiding the book back in my bag.

"Did that woman call you from the English Department?" he said.

"Let's just talk about Alcibiades and Pausanias," I said.

"How are you going to survive if you don't take that job?" he said.

"I'll find something," I said. "I'll go back to baking."

"At least you'll make better cookies than these," he said.

He held out his hand for my wrapper, getting up to go to the bin, and I thought: Let it always be this way, a casual going away and an imminent return, coming towards me on a path through a garden in bloom: pansies and roses and fat pink hydrangeas everywhere. The sky is blue. The late-afternoon traffic along the Embankment is a background hum. My love returned to my side, his fingers brushing against the fabric of my trousers, the surface of my skin alert as if we were naked in bed.

"So," he said, "should I come to yours tomorrow?"

"That would be nice," I said.

"Are you sure you don't need to work?" he said.

A young boy, maybe three or four, moves across the grass towards the flower bed, laughing as his parents call him back to their nest on the blanket—"Come back, Finn. Bring back the water, sweetheart"—and he giggles, then giggles louder, running faster, a perfect response to insincere tenderness, and then positions himself at the edge of the flower bed, the bottle held high above his head, as high as he can reach, and he empties the mineral water onto the row of peonies.

"Yes," I said. "I'm sure."

Now, going back to read *The Symposium* almost ten years later, I worry that the story will be flatter than I remember it, now that my love for him has fizzled out (dulled by disappointment and time). Will the text revert to what I'd imagined it to be before I read it back then (I was in love with him the first time I soaked it up): a remote and demanding classic? But, of course, it's not. Calvino again: "A classic is a book which with each rereading offers as much of a sense of discovery as the first reading."

Ten years later, *The Symposium* isn't about love. It's about friendship and about friends celebrating each other's successes. It's about getting together over food and drink to talk about the things that matter. *The Symposium* is about dinner parties and gossip. It's the story of that one memorable dinner party that went on until morning light, where you shared ideas and beliefs and personal stories while you drank and flirted and joked around. It's that dinner party people keep talking about long after it's over. (If we had time, I'd tell you about the dinner party I hosted in the nineties that turned into an orgy and went on till dawn.)

Rereading *The Symposium* now in the midst of the seven days of Passover, I think about the Seder we had here a few nights ago, about the gathering of friends and how we went around the table from time to time, each of us recounting personal tales of liberation and oppression, and thinking aloud about how we bring light into the world. *The Symposium* is one of my Haggadas, a story to be retold and treasured and imprinted on my memory.

Lest I forget
that Love
is
everything.

SHAUN LEVIN is the author of *A Year of Two Summers* (2005) and *Seven Sweet Things* (2003). His most recent work is "Isaac Rosenberg's Journey to Arras: A Meditation," found in the collection *Desperate Remedies*, edited by Rebekah Lattin-Rawstrone (2008). His stories have appeared in *Between Men, Daddies, I Like It Like That, Boyfriends from Hell*, and *Modern South African Short Stories*, among other anthologies. He is editor of *Chroma: a Queer Literary Journal* and lives in London. Quotations are taken from Plato, *The Symposium*, translated by Christopher Gill (London/New York: Penguin, 2003), which is currently in print.

LETTERS
(1798 and later)

by Horace Walpole

DUNCAN FALLOWELL

At the end of 1764, literature's first horror story, *The Castle of Otranto*, was published in London under disguise. It was an immediate success, despite its fatuousness, and has never since been out of print. It didn't take long before its author was obliged bashfully to step forward: Horace Walpole, man of fashion, antiquarian, member of the House of Commons, unwavering bachelor, and youngest of the five children of Sir Robert Walpole.

Otranto established a genre, the gothic novel, but Horace Walpole had long been delving into spiky realms. In 1747 he had acquired a property outside London overlooking the Thames at Twickenham, a spot already renowned for Pope's villa. Walpole proceeded to turn a plain little house into a glamorous sham castle, pretty vaults within, battlements without. He named it

Strawberry Hill, installed his eccentric collections, and it became one of the sights of Europe, initiating the Georgian phase (known as gothick) of the gothic revival.

Gothic had never died out entirely in Britain but the adoption of its churchy flourishes as a style for the home was quite new. In the nineteenth century it would again be associated with spiritual uplift but Walpole wasn't at all religious—the chapel at Strawberry Hill was a garden folly where he interred his pets (he loved animals, dogs particularly). He invented the word "gloomth," combining "gloomy" and "warmth," to describe the effect he was after; and the taste for witchy gothick, like that for chinoiserie, was a characteristically English response to the domestication of baroque, which is called rococo. The baroque was public and religious; the rococo was paganism in the boudoir.

Walpole's third achievement, his correspondence, some would say was his greatest, since it is in the correspondence that all his aspects are incorporated. The man had plenty to write about. Eighteenth-century politics ran on social connections and, as the son of England's first prime minister, Horace knew the great world from within. He'd always been a celebrity; he lapped it up but paid the price. To the Reverend William Mason he wrote in 1773: "it is not pleasant to read one's private quarrels discussed in magazines and newspapers." Through his relations he was attached to all levels of society, except the lowest: his brother Edward, for example, lived with a milliner's apprentice and had four children by her, one of whom, Horace's niece Maria, married the Duke of Gloucester, brother of George III. In addition he was good to his servants who stayed long in his service.

Walpole's geographical horizons were broad too. As a young man he'd spent nearly three years on the Grand Tour through France and Italy and in later life frequently visited Paris, where his *Essay on Modern Gardening* (1780) was particularly popular. Paris, then as now, was not ageist and Walpole never felt old there. He wrote to George Selwyn of Parisian manners: "The first step towards being in fashion is to lose an eye or a tooth . . . it is charming to totter into vogue." He also made numerous rural tours through an England littered with crumbling monasteries, castles, and other relics of antiquity, overgrown or pillaged for stone, returning to "Strawberry," as he always called it, to mull over what he'd seen and perhaps publish the results on the Strawberry Hill Press. His literary production increased after he retired from Parliament in 1768 and he wrote wearing green spectacles, usually in the intimacy of the Green Closet. By contrast Strawberry's Long Gallery, with its *papier maché* fan-vault and mirrored gothic canopies, was the most theatrical drawing room of the age and used for elaborate cabarets.

But Walpole loved too much the *beau monde* ever to abandon London, the world's largest and richest city. He rose at noon for breakfast before embarking on the merry round and staying late at Vauxhall or Ranelagh pleasure gardens, where more adventurous souls could find sexual partners of any kind as the hours advanced. He always maintained a house in Mayfair, at first in Arlington Street where he was born in 1717 (behind where the Ritz is today); later in Berkeley Square, where he died in 1797.

By the time of his death he had become the fourth and last Earl of Orford, the title passing to him in 1791 from his father via elder brother and nephew. Ennoblement dismayed Horace. It was beyond the perimeter he had made his own. His finances up to this time had been healthy, his indulgences funded partly by family money, partly by sinecures under the Crown arranged by his father: Controller of the Pipe, Clerk of the Estreats, Usher of the Exchequer. The ancestral Walpole estate at Houghton, which now became his responsibility, had been ruined by the insane, profligate nephew, and the ornate house emptied of glory by the sale of its famous picture collection to Catherine the Great of Russia. He took it on, of course, but it wasn't his style; he preferred the smaller things of life.

What of love affairs? Walpole was in his own time regarded as effeminate, not merely foppish, and in 1764 was openly attacked as an hermaphrodite. Homosexual behavior would have been very familiar to anyone who'd attended an English boarding school in the eighteenth century, and a recent biographer presents him as the center of a practicing homosexual network. There is no specific evidence for this. His letters, casually frank as they are, make no reference to personal sexual events. But until recent times homosexuality flourished by virtue of being off-the-record and it's not impossible that Walpole gave himself now and again to something or other. The only item of erotica in his library was a late but telling one, Payne Knight's *Worship of Priapus* (1786). But Walpole would never have gone as far as joining the priapic Tuesday Club, for example, where group masturbation was the order of the day. Since there was no taboo against recording involvements with women, we can be certain there were none and to the world at large Walpole presented himself as one of that species whose existence always amazed the Continentals: the English adult male virgin.

Sentimental attachments were another matter. Single and childless, Walpole is one of the great proponents of friendship. His friendships were cultivated with both sexes and with men, given Walpole's decidedly homosexual temperament, these occasionally became emotional infatuations. The earliest was with the poet Thomas Gray with whom he'd been at Eton and Cambridge. They fell out violently in Italy while on the Grand Tour together and the quarrel clearly involved a homosexual dispute of some kind. Towards the end of his life Walpole took up with a young neighbor, Mary Berry. In between came what has been called the Strawberry Hill set, mostly a circle of well-to-do bachelors, some of them actively heterosexual, supplemented by several women of influence or style: Lady Suffolk for example, George II's one-time mistress, and Catherine Clive, a famous comic actress.

Walpole's intimates were an enlightened, gossipy bunch, not exceptionally gifted, and he gave the groupings catchphrases, for they were rarely one-to-one: the Quadruple Alliance, the Committee of Taste, the Triumvirate. George Selwyn, a member of the last, was famous for being sexually aroused by public executions. John Chute, a member of the second, was an effete bachelor with superb taste who contributed to the designs of Strawberry Hill. Gray, a member of the first, was the only close friend of real distinction; he wrote an ode to Eton College which ends with his most famous lines: "... where ignorance is bliss, 'Tis folly to be wise."

For obvious reasons Walpole's more assiduous correspondence tended to be with those he little saw. Almost a third of surviving letters are to Sir Horace Mann, the British representative in Florence, a skilful diplomat, and like Gray unmarried and identifiably homosexual. Walpole met Mann when in Florence on the Grand Tour and never met him again but their association was long and close. The correspondence with Madame du Deffand in Paris typifies Walpole's predilection for elderly, female aristocrats (though this one made the fatal mistake of falling in love with him). However, his letters to her were destroyed at his own request; he was embarrassed by his imperfect French. Walpole's own mother had died in 1737—many said it was the emotional blow from which he suffered most—and with the passing years Walpole spent more and more time in female company.

Over three thousand letters, written across more than sixty years, have come down to us and the definitive Yale edition

(1937–83), with all the editorial apparatus, extends to over fifty volumes. There is nothing comparable in the whole of the English language. Emile Leognis, professor of English literature at the Sorbonne in the last century, wrote: "He approaches the universality of Voltaire more nearly than any other English letter-writer." Walpole was well aware of narrating the age and often chose correspondents for what they might contribute to the larger scheme: George Montagu and the Countess of Upper Ossory for social anecdote, William Cole for antiquarian matters, Mann for politics, and so on. The project of collating this vast trove began in his lifetime. Walpole kept copies or asked for their return or preservation and a substantial selection was published the year after he died as volumes four and five of his *Works* (1798). Selections have appeared regularly ever since. Occasionally new letters still come to light.

His reputation, however, has fluctuated. Walpole once received a party of French at Strawberry Hill wearing a pair of gigantic embroidered gauntlets that had belonged to James I and a lace cravat carved in wood by Grinling Gibbons. His private collection included Cardinal Wolsey's hat and the spurs of the bisexual William III, "the most precious relics . . . I have seriously kissed each spur devoutly." His medievalism was not deeply rooted; he preferred Chaucer redone by Dryden. He'd never been to Otranto; he saw it on the map and like the sound. All this sort of thing infuriated the Victorians who were entirely guided by the opinion of Thomas Babington Macaulay—he'd written in the *Edinburgh Review* in 1833 that Walpole's "mind was a bundle of inconsistent whims and affectations." No matter that Byron had referred to Walpole's "incomparable letters', or that Walter Scott had called him "the best letter-writer in the English language."

Macaulay's is a prejudice against sense of humor because affectation is far from being one's impression on reading the letters. They are fluent, colloquial, affable, remarkably direct, and unencumbered by Augustan mannerisms. Among other things, Walpole experienced the loss of the American colonies and the successive jolts of the French Revolution and reported seriously on them. In a letter to Thomas Pownall, one-time governor of Massachusetts, in 1783 he wrote "the most heinous part of despotism is that it produces a thousand despots instead of one." Indeed as a Walpole and a Whig, his political views can be downright aggressive. The bloated and offensive arch-Tory Dr. Johnson he loathed and said so, refusing ever to be introduced to him; in return Boswell called on Walpole in 1788 and found him "just the same: genteel, fastidious, priggish." Calling soon after, John Pinkerton, Walpole's first biographer, noticed "not the smallest hauteur." Walpole detested the slave trade, despised Diderot, was entranced by Marie-Antoinette's star quality, and thought Rousseau "a mountebank."

However, the marvels of the letters lie not so much in their judgments as in their authenticity to the range of Walpole's experience and emotions. Never blatantly lewd, they can sometimes be naughty. Recounting his day at George III's coronation, he relates that a special "convenience" was set up for the new Queen Charlotte behind the high altar in Westminster Abbey, but when she retired to use it "what found she but the Duke of Newcastle perked up and in the very act upon the anointed velvet closestool." Music, surprisingly, seems to have been a blind spot.

Macaulay's dismissive attitude persisted. Even Wilde makes no mention of Horace Walpole, though 1890s dandyism prepared the way for his rehabilitation, which was conducted (again in the *Edinburgh Review*, eighty years after Macaulay) by Lytton

Strachey. Strachey still harbored reservations and to Ottoline Morrell he wrote spitefully of Horace that "a more callous fiend never stepped the earth." It was the unlikely figure of Arnold Bennett who noted that Walpole's character often appeared "really noble and distinguished."

Clarity and lightness are what one values in him. Behind even his most robust or skittish observations there is something lyrical, personal, lonely, which touches us. In terms of literary context, he fits well into the rococo or dandy tradition of English literature, which is characterized by stylish intimacy, by metropolitan urbanity infused with airy Arcadian fancies and personal daring. One might trace this tradition from the sonnets of Shakespeare (called by Walpole "the first of writers"), through Aubrey, Rochester, and Congreve, and from Horace Walpole to his emulator William Beckford. Its savor arises in the novels of Peacock; and though Oscar Wilde was a baroque figure, *The Importance of Being Earnest* (1895) is a rococo masterpiece whose offspring include Max Beerbohm, Saki, and Ronald Firbank. The rococo spirit added a brilliant vitality to the modern movement in English literature with the work of the Sitwells, the early novels of Evelyn Waugh and Christopher Isherwood, Cyril Connolly's *The Unquiet Grave* (1944), several crafted books of personal exploration by Norman Douglas and Sybille Bedford, the *jeux d'esprit* of Nancy Mitford and Osbert Lancaster, Hunter Thompson's *Fear and Loathing in Las Vegas* (1972), and Truman Capote's *Answered Prayers* (1987) (unfinished though it was).

Horace Walpole, who would have relished all these writers, has also been called the Proust of eighteenth-century England. Less analytical than Proust, he is just as effective in portraying the doings of an entire milieu and is far more informative, while his sensitive, mischievous personality is both endearing and timeless.

Kenneth Clark argues that Romanticism originated in the conscious harnessing of fear, which he dates from the Lisbon Earthquake in 1755 and the appearance of *The Castle of Otranto* soon after. Bonamy Dobrée, hardly less ambitiously, has described the author of *Otranto* as "perhaps the first surrealist writer." Walpole, who confessed that the novel was inspired by a nightmare, would never have claimed so much for himself. He prized above all what he referred to as his "nothinghood." But there is in his endeavors a magical defiance which implies that earthly delight must and can survive anything that life throws at it. This is the tragi-comic sensibility of rococo.

As for Strawberry Hill, it has never wanted for attention— recently it provided several interiors for Francois Ozon's luxurious film *Angel* (2007)—but it has wanted for care. It was inherited by Anne Damer, a well-known lesbian and the only child of Walpole's beloved but boorish cousin, Henry Conway. From her it passed through several more families before being bought by the Roman Catholic Church, who sold off land for housing development, blocking the river views forever. But finally the building is being restored and, after a two-hundred-fifty-year interruption, set up again as an attraction for the public, as it was in the heyday of its creator. Walpole, a man of so many inadvertent firsts, not only issued tickets of admission but also produced the first-ever illustrated house guide.

DUNCAN FALLOWELL was born in 1948 in London, where he still lives. He is a novelist, travel writer, and cultural commentator, whose books include the novel *A History of Facelifting* (2003) and three works of travel writing: *To Noto, Or, London to Sicily in a Ford* (1991), *One Hot Summer in St. Petersburg* (1995), and *Going as Far as I Can: the Ultimate Travel Book* (2008). His next novel is a ghost story. Quotations are taken from the forty-eight-volume Yale edition of Walpole's *Correspondence*, edited by W. S. Lewis (New Haven/London: Yale University Press, 1937–83).

MOBY DICK
(1851)

by Herman Melville

VESTAL McINTYRE

Celebrity interviews bore me, unless the subject is someone like Courtney Love or Mike Tyson—live wires, people on the verge, who, despite—or because of—being famous, are missing the veil most of us use to hide the turbulence of our passions and fears. These weird stars curse at, then coo to, their interviewers. Every emotion is there to be read in their facial contortions, and it makes me alternately thrill and cringe.

When I first read *Moby Dick*, I expected a classic: emphasis on *class*, with perfectly wrought sentences in a voice subtle and wise: Austen or James, basically; the equivalent of the beautifully composed Nicole Kidman in interview. What I got was Tom Cruise jumping on the couch.

Melville is an unveiled writer. *Moby Dick* is a deeply weird book.

It might be the easiest "classic" to summarize: Ahab, crazy captain, seeks revenge on the great white whale that maimed him. We don't need CliffsNotes to know that Ahab bites it in the end. Yet *Moby Dick* must also be the hardest "classic" to characterize, for this is a story bursting at its seams, assembled and sewn together as roughly as Frankenstein's monster. Melville is a man desperate to write, to convey, to *mean*. He describes whale anatomy with the passion most reserve for romantic love, and he does something strange with adverbs and verbs I haven't encountered elsewhere: within the space of five pages, waves "dazzlingly break" against the whale's forehead, sharks "ripingly withdraw" from their prey, and Ahab "draggingly leans" on one arm. Is that allowed? Is it even grammatically correct? I'm not sure. It seems like the English language, as muscular as it is, still can't convey all Melville wants it to, unless he fashions it some new tools. Correct or not, Melville's adverbial extravagancies make a good case for completely ignoring the writing teacher who told me I should search out words ending in both -*ly* and -*ing*, and cut them out.

The narrative leaps from perspective to perspective; its language scales academic heights, then plunges to the colloquial, often reaching into history, literature, science, and the Bible for comparisons. I've never read such sustained wildness. If you buy into the idea that Joyce and Woolf unbound fiction from the oppressive constraints of the nineteenth century, I give you instead *Moby Dick*. Next to this monster of a book, the experimental novels of recent decades are tame as lapdogs.

Our narrator tells us to call him Ishmael. He is a man "with the problem of the universe revolving in [him]." The watery world he observes is full of symbols. Sky and sea, birds and fish, ships, and nearly every part of a whale from bones to blubber to spout is fetishized into a symbol in the grand scheme of good and evil, hunter and prey. But in this book everything shifts. Symbols are reassigned—again, wildly—just as the roles of hunter and prey are swapped between Ahab and Moby Dick.

Even with all the talk of heaven and hell, you leave this book feeling you've read a psychological allegory, rather than a moral one—or a collection of allegories under the overarching psychodrama of Ahab madly pursuing his mortal foe. At one point, our crew tricks another whaling ship into abandoning the rotting carcass of a whale that they had found. As soon as that ship disappears over the horizon, our men haul in the whale and begin burrowing into its rotten head, searching for ambergris, a hard substance hidden deep in the stinking bodies of sick whales, precious as an ingredient in fine perfume. The psychological parallels could fill a book.

At another point, one of the crew's most endearing members, a young black American named Pip, falls from one of the whale boats. The boat continues its pursuit of the whale, and then returns for Pip, but those few minutes alone in the "heartless immensity" of the ocean has taken an immediate toll. Pip has turned "idiot." A moment at sea, with no one in sight—a moment of true *aloneness*—is enough to unhitch Pip from his sanity. It's the human condition as horror story, and it feels utterly modern. After this instance, Pip and Ahab are inseparable; two poor souls who have separately touched damning truths of life.

But are any of the book's allegories gay? There were rumors even in Melville's time that some of his sexual adventures in the South Pacific involved men. And his smaller masterpiece from later in life, *Billy Budd* (1924), contains a twisted gay crush that has been interpreted musically and camped up by Benjamin Britton and Morrissey.

Very early in *Moby Dick*, Ishmael shares a bed with his new friend Queequeg, a strong, silent Polynesian harpooner covered in tattoos. They share a pipe. Ishmael says: "He seemed to take to me quite as naturally as I to him; and when our smoke was over, he pressed his forehead against mine, clasped me round the waist, and said that henceforth we were married; meaning, in his country's phrase, that we were bosom friends; he would gladly die for me, if need should be."

Later, when it's time for sleep, he says: "in our hearts' honeymoon, lay I and Queequeg—a cosy, loving pair." It's the most tender and compelling moment of physical intimacy in this womanless book, and it's drenched with the kind of playful sexiness of Whitman's "two boys clinging." Like so many moments in *Leaves of Grass* (1855) it makes one wonder how it felt in the days before the erotic lives of gay men were medicalized, then liberated, then theorized almost to death. (*Almost.*)

But I believe that, much more than the small man-to-man moments in the book or in Melville's life, it is the overarching drama that is important to us queers. Lesbians and gays of my generation and before know a little of Ahab's conflict—being irresistibly drawn to what the rest of the world, even members of our "crew," considers dark, dangerous, wrong. The irreconcilability of our desires to our world forced us all into a version of Ahab's monomania, and long before the arrival of HIV there was a sense that this sentence of Melville's could describe us: "Ah! how they still strove through that infinite blueness to seek out the thing that might destroy them."

Of course, if you don't buy my suggestion that Ahab's quest is a gay one, I could follow a crass line to convince you. He is, after all, cruising the world's oceans for a white giant with a blunt head shaped like a "battering ram" that spouts frothy water frequently described as "cream." In their first encounter, this sperm whale nearly split Ahab in two, and shot a white scar down the length of his body, leaving him with a bone for a leg.

But even if you don't believe Ahab is searching for Dick, you can't deny he's a man with an intense passion that no one understands. Like all symbols in this book, the whale shifts in what he represents. There is clear evidence that the whale is Ahab and Ahab is the whale: there is that scar, white to match Moby Dick; Ahab's peg leg is made of whale bone. In this sense, Ahab is searching for Ahab, and it's the darkest journey toward self-discovery I've read, ending in annihilation.

My relationship with *Moby Dick* started years before I opened the book. Back in college, I took a class in eighteenth-century satire. One of my fellow students had a hard time believing that children could be engaged in a novel as challenging as Swift's *Gulliver's Travels* (1726). Our professor responded that of course they could. As evidence, she told us that in grade school in rural Montana, the teacher read *Moby Dick* to her class—read it after recess, as a means to get the kids to come in—and it worked. They would gladly drop their games to hear the next chapter in what is, one tends to forget, an adventure.

My professor's anecdote was still lodged in the back of my mind five years later in 2000 when I read *Moby Dick*. I reacted to the book in my literate, writerly way, and at the same time I tried on reacting as a child would. I read it both as psychodrama and adventure. When I reached the novel's harrowing end, I felt compelled to write a short story about two readers approaching *Moby Dick*—one wise and literary; the other a pure, childish observer, enjoying the adventure, gulping it down. I was wondering what would happen if a bookworm teen read it to a child, or—better—read it to a child with a mental disability. How would an illiterate listener, unfamiliar with the techniques of foreshadowing, react to the tragedy?

I started writing the story, got stuck, and started again. It was an interesting but soulless idea that wasn't metamorphosing into a story at all.

Then came September 11th, 2001. A couple of hours into the horror of that day, my boyfriend and I were glued to CNN, when the ground rumbled and our Lower East Side apartment shook. We looked to each other, and then ran up to the roof for the third time that morning. From our perspective, the twin towers were completely hidden behind a cloud of smoke. "One of them fell," said a neighbor. It couldn't be, I thought—the towers were just burning. Buildings didn't just *fall*. Then a gap in the smoke showed that the neighbor was right; there was only one tower now standing alone. I became a little hysterical. "It can't have fallen," I kept saying. My mind couldn't encompass the fact for several minutes. Or days, maybe—my memories are foggy.

Moby Dick is a novel that continues to shift and develop even after you've read it. It changed for me that day. "The ship! Great God, where is the ship?" cries the crew of one whaleboat when, having lost Ahab, they turn to see that the ship and all their shipmates have been swallowed by the sea. This moment leapt out into my life—my symbol now, as much as Melville's.

On September 18th—I can see on my computer that this was the date the document was created—I started writing my short story again. Now it worked. I finished it, and named it "Foray." Raymond, a smart, bitchy teen reads *Moby Dick* to his cousin Vance, who has Down's syndrome. Vance enjoys the story more fully than Raymond can, and the ending fills him with a genuine horror for the world. Although the World

Trade Center is never mentioned, "Foray" is my September 11th story.

Read *Moby Dick*, if you haven't already—and not an abbreviated version that cuts out those bizarrely fetishistic chapters on cetology. Read the whole crazy thing. Like Moby Dick's ancient ancestor, Jonah's whale, it will swallow you whole and spit you out. It'll have you running in from recess. And its symbols will become yours.

VESTAL MCINTYRE is author of a story collection, *You are not the one* (2004), and a novel, *Lake Overturn* (2009). American-born, McIntyre now lives in London. His Web site is www.vestalmcintyre.com. Herman Melville's *Moby Dick* is available in many unexpurgated editions.

LEAVES OF GRASS

(1855 and later)

by Walt Whitman

PHILIP CLARK

You've got an image problem, Walt Whitman, a severe case of poor first impressions. Your problem is high schools and their English teachers. You were right to mistrust the "learn'd astronomers" and their lectures, dry as the dirt you churn under your boot soles. They're content for you to be Walt of the fuzzy gray beard and kindly mien, shedding tears over Lincoln's death or looking on as that noiseless, patient spider casts its filaments ever outward. If one is daring, you might be allowed to nurse a soldier or two, provided that the emphasis is amputations and not strange vigils, with their visions of responding kisses. A few quiet platitudes about democracy and free verse later, it's on to Miss Emily, with her buzzing flies and bobolinks, and there you are, Walt, still stopped somewhere, waiting for us—while we take an awfully long time to catch up, if we ever do.

There was a time, though, before the teachers neutered you, a time when you *were* Walt Whitman: a rough, a radical, a danger. There were those who came to you, compelled, who looked to you for more, sometimes, than you were able or willing to offer. To understand your *Leaves of Grass*, this is what we must return to: not the academic "Whitman," but the necessary "Walt."

I.

An acquaintance heard that I would write about Walt Whitman. "Oh, I've never appreciated Whitman," she said. "He has too big an ego for me to enjoy him."

This, of course, precisely misses the point. We have been trained toward self-effacement, to avoid the boast. But while the meek may inherit the earth, they do not make particularly compelling reading. Whitman does—by being what William Least Heat-Moon called "the great poet of ego, the one who sings of himself, who promises to 'effuse egotism and show it underlying all.'"

Ralph Waldo Emerson saw the potential virtues in Whitman's individualism, responding in a legendary letter to the first, 1855 edition of *Leaves of Grass*. In part, Emerson told Whitman, "I give you joy of your free and brave thought. I have great joy in it. I find incomparable things said incomparably well, as they must be. I find the courage of treatment which so delights us, and which large perceptions only can inspire."

Emerson had been waiting for a singer for the new and expanding nation. If Whitman was to be that singer, a poet who could unify America culturally, he would have to be brash and bold, a man of "large perceptions" and the ambition to deliver them to the people. He would have to be the sort of man who could declare himself "a mate and companion of people, all just as immortal and fathomless as myself"; one who could use the grass as metaphor, noting it "sprouting alike in broad zones and narrow zones, / Growing among black folks as among white, / Kanuck, Tuckahoe, Congressman, Cuff." He had to be a man who could, in imagining himself one with all others, redeem the vision of American democracy promised by Thomas Jefferson, where all men are created equal.

II.

Of course, Emerson did not know exactly what he was getting in endorsing Walt Whitman. By the edition of 1860, where Whitman first included the forty-five-poem "Calamus" section, careful observers could see that he was making peculiar connections between the existence of fruitful American democracy and the love of man for man. Rich with men hugging, kissing, and sauntering the streets together, "Calamus" also includes poems that prophesy the establishment "in the Mannahatta, and in every city of These States . . . the institution of the dear love of comrades." Whitman makes the grand claim that "the main purport of These States is to found a superb friendship, exalté, previously unknown, / Because I perceive it waits, and has been always waiting, latent in all men."

One of those careful observers was an ocean away. John Addington Symonds, the English classicist and tentative gay activist, corresponded with Whitman over the course of two decades. Symonds had been stunned by *Leaves of Grass* when it was given to him by a classmate at Trinity College, Cambridge, and his letters to Whitman are suffused by a sense of discipleship. Beginning with his second letter to the master, in 1872, they also consistently reference, question, and wonder over the "Calamus" poems. It took nearly twenty years, but in 1890, Symonds finally asked Whitman directly about the homosexual implications of "Calamus," prompting Whitman's famous reply that such "morbid inferences . . . seem damnable" and that he had sired six children. It was virtually the only response Whitman could give; as Symonds's countryman and fellow homosexual rights advocate, Edward Carpenter, observed:

Symonds [was] putting him in a very awkward position. He, Whitman, could hardly with any truthfulness deny any knowledge or contemplation of such inferences; but if on the other hand he took what we might call the reasonable line, and said that, while not advocating abnormal relations in any way, he of course made allowances for possibilities in that direction and the occasional development of such relations, why, he knew that the moment he said such a thing, he would have the whole American Press at his heels, snarling and slandering, and distorting his words in every possible way . . . Personally, having known Whitman fairly intimately, I do not lay great stress on that letter.

Neither was Symonds put off the trail by these disavowals. Letters written to Carpenter express skepticism regarding Whitman's paternity claims and his denials that the "love of comrades" discussed in "Calamus" could include sexual affection. Still, Symonds wrote a conciliatory letter to Whitman, and used cautious and precise language in discussing the issue in his *Walt Whitman: a Study* (1893).

Others had no such compunctions. Less than twenty years after Whitman's death, Edward Irenaeus Prime-Stevenson, writing as "Xavier Mayne," included a lengthy section on Whitman in *The Intersexes* (1908), his compendium of homosexuality and its history. Stevenson unabashedly declared Whitman "one of the prophets and priests of homosexuality. Its atmosphere pervades Whitman's poems: being indeed an almost inevitable concurrent of the neo-Hellenic, platonic democracy of Whitman's philosophic muse." Stevenson included three full pages of excerpts from *Leaves of Grass* to support his point, encompassing not only the "Calamus" poems, but also selections from such sections as "Drum-Taps," Whitman's Civil War verse.

Men who need Walt Whitman have a long history of finding him.

III.

Of course, not every man who has needed Whitman has been gay.

Although no longer well-known or widely read, poet Morris Rosenfeld was a key figure in Yiddish and immigrant literature. Largely self-educated, Rosenfeld came to America in 1886, while still in his early twenties. In the words of Leo Weiner, the English translator for Rosenfeld's *Songs from the Ghetto* (1898), "for many weary years he . . . eked out an existence in the sweat-shops of New York," where "his health gave out, and he had to abandon the shop for the precarious occupation of a Yiddish penny-a-liner."

The poems in *Songs from the Ghetto*, particularly those in the "Songs of Labor" section, derive from Rosenfeld's experiences in the New York garment factories. Poems like "In the Sweat-Shop" focus on the dehumanizing mechanization of the shops, where "the machines . . . roar so wildly that often I forget in the roar that I am; I am lost in the terrible tumult, my ego disappears, I am a machine."

It is evident from Rosenfeld's "Walt Whitman" that he took comfort and sanity from Whitman's poems of the natural world, so different from Rosenfeld's typical environment amid the grime and spiritual violence of the city. Following a litany of nature images called to mind through reading *Leaves of Grass*—sun, moon, stars; "the buds of May," thunder, and the nightingale—Rosenfeld praises Whitman's "overwhelming chant" that helps him feel "the pulse of nature, its omnipotence." It allows him to "kneel / upon the dust, before thy dust, and sing." Through Whitman, Rosenfeld found the power with which to reject the brutalities of factory life, and the inspiration through which he could compose his own songs.

The poet of the ego becomes the poet of the universe becomes the poet of the working man. In Rosenfeld, Whitman finds an ideal reader.

I V.

In some ways, Anne Gilchrist was not an ideal reader for *Leaves of Grass*. Especially not when she packed her bags, her children, and her piano to cross the Atlantic and become Walt Whitman's unasked-for wife. For obvious reasons, this was not going to work. But Gilchrist's passionate response to Whitman's poems was, in another sense, the best that Whitman could hope for; her great love for him and her sensitivity to the worth of *Leaves of Grass* led her to write important essays affirming Whitman's worth to a larger public.

Gilchrist was not the first woman to become enamored. In his masterful book *Worshipping Walt: the Whitman Disciples* (2008), Michael Robertson details several woman readers' responses to *Leaves of Grass*, which often focused on Whitman's body and their desire to bear his children. Walt would have had opportunities to sire the imaginary offspring he presented to John Addington Symonds, had he wanted them.

Still, Anne Gilchrist—an educated and deeply intelligent woman—was not so far off the mark in her reading of Whitman's poetry. Is Whitman not the poet who promises his readers, "Camerado, this is no book, / Who touches this touches a man"? Does he not describe the "love-flesh swelling and deliciously aching; / Limitless limpid jets of love hot and enormous, quivering jelly of love, white-blow and delirious juice; / Bridegroom night of love working surely and softly into the prostrate dawn"? This is surely not discouraging readers who dreamed of being drawn to Whitman by more than just his words.

The sexual expressions in Whitman's poetry were particularly powerful for female readers of the period, trapped by the Victorian purity cult. Never allowed to speak of sexual matters, forbidden from sexual experience before their wedding night, believed by the dominant forces in society to be almost asexual, middle-class women like Anne Gilchrist were ripe for the words of a poet who celebrated the body, who would declare in his 1860 poem "Native Moments": "Give me now libidinous joys only! / Give me the drench of my passions!"

As she discovered on first meeting him, the drench of Whitman's passions did not extend to Anne Gilchrist. But the pair forged an enduring friendship that would transform Whitman into a virtual member of the Gilchrist family. And even if his own erotic attachments lay elsewhere, Whitman's poetry provided an affirming voice for women's sexuality.

When I taught high school students myself, I could not bear to drag out "O Captain! My Captain!" I had to let the lilacs wither in their dooryard and allow you to cross Brooklyn ferry alone, Walt. These are beautiful, clever, crafted poems, and they deserve their place in the Whitman canon, but they also miss so much that has been most intensely valued in your poetry.

Instead, I had my students read "I Sing the Body Electric," the kind of physical poem Anne Gilchrist thrilled to. I hope they felt the same kind of peace and wonder that Morris Rosenfeld might in reading "When I Heard the Learn'd Astronomer." "Vigil Strange I Kept on the Field One Night" and "When I Heard at the Close of Day" showed them—as they did John Addington Symonds and so many other gay men—the intensity of the joys and sorrows to be found in "the love of comrades." And that massive ego, the kind so large it could dream of uniting America beneath the banner of your poetry? Nothing could be more apt to describe it than "Poem of the Heart of the Son of Manhattan Island": "And who has made hymns fit for the earth? For I am mad with devouring ecstasy to make joyous hymns for the whole earth!"

Let your hymns continue, Walt, but only if the whole radical, sexual, prideful mess of your verse is acknowledged. Over a century after your death, you must not be made a cipher.

PHILIP CLARK is a Washington, D.C.–area writer and editor. He has essays forthcoming in the anthologies *The Lost Library: Gay Fiction Rediscovered* and *The Golden Age of Gay Fiction*. *Persistent Voices: an Anthology of Poets Lost to AIDS* (2009), which he coedited, has just appeared. Current projects include research for a book about gay pornographic publisher and First Amendment pioneer H. Lynn Womack. He welcomes correspondence at philipclark@hotmail.com. Quotations are taken from Walt Whitman, *Selected Poems 1855–1892* (New York: St. Martin's Press, 2000), edited by Gary Schmidgall, which is currently in print. Many other editions are available.

A Season in Hell

(Une saison en enfer)

(1873)

by Arthur Rimbaud

Kevin Killian

I n the early eighties, there were two movie stars, one dark and one fair, whom I loved from afar—Michael Paré and Tom Berenger—and for one brief shining instant they played in the same movie, *Eddie and the Cruisers* (1983). I know: what a name. In an empty dancehall, Paré stands slouched tuning his guitar in bar light, a Lucky jammed in his ornate red lips like a toothpick in an oyster, while Berenger plucks a book from the sacred hip pocket of his fifties pegged jeans. Reads to him. "One evening I took Beauty in my arms— and thought her bitter—and I insulted her." He demonstrates reading it in different ways—pausing after one word, then another. It's his way of showing Michael Paré what a caesura is, though Paré knows one naturally. He doesn't need a book to show the best way to pause,

where to put the white space,

white smears that darkened his mane.

I understood Rimbaud as the wild young man from the provinces who, although stifled by his home life, was not precisely cut out for the big city. As a teen I had been brash myself and bitten off the hand that fed me. When he left little Charleville on the strength of some promises from a married man—the poet Paul Verlaine—Arthur Rimbaud must have been half mad with hope and excitement, and a sour undertone beat in his blood like absinthe; a tone that said: and if this doesn't work out, and it probably won't, I will destroy them.

I read Kathy Acker's novel about Rimbaud, *In Memoriam to Identity* (1990). I read Jack Spicer's 1960s-era *A Fake Novel About the Life of Arthur Rimbaud*. Patti Smith's first four LPs are drenched in Rimbaud as if in holy water. All of us who thought about him were deeply invested in two mysteries: what made Rimbaud tick, and what made him stop writing. Then, if we were older than Paul Verlaine (twenty-eight when Rimbaud intruded himself into his life), we had to think about what we would do if one such mad youngster came into our lives and offered up his ass to us.

You could see that boy anywhere, his shadow slithered under the sun. Anywhere the streets are hot the boy Rimbaud is skipping like a stone from one pavement to another. Maybe that was the point of the U.S. artist and writer David Wojnarowicz's project "Rimbaud in New York," in which he made a mask from the famous photo of Rimbaud, stuck it on the face of a friend, and then photographed him, tall and gangly, in unlikely purlieux. In a NYC subway car, he sits among festive passengers in a sleeveless vest, out on Coney Island he sulks, opposite a Times Square movie palace showing *Moonraker* he waves hi to the folks back home in my little town. There's a brand new Pléiade edition of Rimbaud, big and gorgeous, pristine and soft, whereas the *Season in Hell* book in Tom Berenger's back pocket is rolled and flattened by the continual caress of his buttocks. Open the pages of the Pléiade edition, feel the thin paper like rice, lay your head down on it, and let it be your pillow of dreams.

Brandon was a student at Naropa, the Buddhist seminary in Boulder, who enrolled in my "poet's theater" class. Seemed OK at first, maybe a tad thickheaded, and our week together passed without incident. Then, a year later, he *friended* me on Facebook and his case asserted itself. Right away he said that he had read my book *Argento Series*; it had changed his life. He declared himself my slave, my servant, and I was his inspiration, a god. Would I become his mentor? He was saying exactly the right things—right out of the Rimbaud playbook. In a way it's sort of like, when I was in school, I had a boyfriend of sorts who told me I looked like Neil Young—*exactly like Neil Young*—and he'd say it with such force I had no choice but to accept it as a compliment, but now I wonder. Brandon told me he had learned more about poetry from reading my one book one time than in his four years of college. I was flattered, but what he was saying made complete sense to me. Then another element crept in, his conviction that I had as much to gain from this partnership as he did. I would be watching him unfold and become the great poet he had known he could be since high school. Could I turn down the chance of such a spectacle?

In the meantime, he said, he was mine to command. I was to tell him the steps he should be taking. I could command him physically. If I wanted him to eat peanut butter, he would go to the store, find the peanut butter aisle, and buy a jar of the brand I recommended. At home he'd remove the lid, and if I liked he'd plunge his face into the stuff and swallow it. Anything physical that I wanted him to do. Till he gagged. Well, I thought of a few physical things, but somehow this aspect seemed equivocal. And yet wasn't that what total apprenticeship was all about, breaking the barriers that separated teacher from pupil?

"This. Here. Right now. Is all I need. Why hath we have been apart for so excruciatingly long? I long to finger you with my delicate vibrissae, peer into your eyes, feel your heat and screams as I writhe in ecstasy. Again. My compatriot. My friend. My captor. My captivity. My life. My mania. Thank you, kissing you is like iron, the delicacy of lips never kissed."

Still manic, he hissed at me, "I want you to finger me till I fall over." Brandon was free now, free of the antipsychotics that had limited his existence. The pills his mom and dad in Cleveland had baked him on, like a shish kebab. Once the skewer is withdrawn, the chunks of chicken and pineapple and onion and tomato are free to fall on their backs on the platter. Now he was in chunks and in communion with the angels. Go Brandon, go go go. "Once," he recalled, "I was told by a doctor to take medicine; it sucked the life from me like an unknowing hypnotic narcotic straitjacket." Now he would break the tablets carried down from the mountaintop. Just let them shatter. "Kevin, you are the sweet lexical nectar I yearn for. Finally a teacher who has tasted phlegm and blood, swilled upon death." What those drugs had done to his body— deadened his taste buds, closed his eyes, turned his balls to wood, made his ass a place for sitting instead of insufflating.

"And each discovery," Brandon predicted, "will be that of sweet classical music dripped upon the tongue and then ingested, until full, until understood." When he was manic he wrote with one hand wrapped around his cock, which was hard for the first time since forever. It looked like a candy stick, but glow-y, like the dick from the moon. What would happen to it as he moved it through time and space in his voyages out? He wanted nothing more than to lock down his rocket by sitting on my lap backwards and holding on tight while my jet fuel launched him.

OK, I thought. I had always been attracted to the wild, and in this case (in every case?), that meant the chemically unbalanced, the bipolar. What if Rimbaud was bipolar—was that possible? Did such a category exist? What did those who suffered from it do? How did they heal themselves? Absinthe? Poetry? A friend pointed out that they had opium then, laudanum, chloral, great clouds of drugs we know nothing of today, and they probably painted themselves with these clouds as artists do, to affect the correct temperature.

And when he came down from his manic phase, he wrote back contemptuously, "Did you think you could fuck me through the computer?" Instantly I experienced that furtive flash of shame, the kind that really hooks you on a guy. Verlaine must have felt: "I'm better than this," but knowing otherwise was what really got him high on the young boy from Charleville. Rimbaud seized Verlaine's hand, lifted it to the crown of his own skull, rubbed the protestant hand in that hair. "What is that in your hair, boy?" "Nothing but the best country butter." So saying his fluttering eyelids opening, to reveal pale blue holes beneath, and a narrow brain within. "In cities, the mud suddenly oozed red and black, like you in the mirror in the room next to mine when your window shade rolls itself up without warning.

Red and black, like the treasure you buried at the base of your perineum."

I didn't know much about Rimbaud in 1983, the year Avco Embassy released *Eddie and the Cruisers*. In its own day, the thriller had a sleeper cult following. Today's young readers won't even know its principal actors, but back then they were immense and everywhere and, as I say, represented the light and the dark, Berenger and Paré, so that seeing them interact was like watching an invisible authority flip a light switch back and forth to make the room light up, dim out, light up, dim out. You could tell the same story again today, though, for the plot itself has an uncanny, over-the-top richness. It's a wealth of signification. I guess all movies that investigate the past of a fabled, hard-luck rock band tell the same story—some sort of rewrite of the Camelot legend? Or the Theban warriors? (Avco Embassy was on a roll in this regard, for the studio's next picture was *This Is Spinal Tap*.) Anyway, in *Eddie and the Cruisers*, Ellen Barkin plays Maggie Foley, a tough-talking, sexy reporter pitching a story to a roomful of seasoned city desk pros. She plays a color clip of Eddie and the Cruisers in their heyday (1962–64), and then snaps off the projector and inquires: "Did you ever hear of a poet named Arthur Rimbaud?"

Her editor flashes her a dismissive glance. "French Lit 105—it was required. Get to the point, Maggie!"

Ellen Barkin lifts a brow and pulls the cigarette from her mouth. "OK, kiddies," she says like W. C. Fields (for some reason), "do you want to sit back in your seats and listen?"

Editor, now considering the possibility she's onto something, nods. "Sure."

Barkin gestures with a book and starts reading from its back cover, but really more out of her imagination, if you know what I mean. She says these words slowly; I suppose so that the movie-going public will be able to catch all the exposition: "*A Season in Hell*—a spiritual and confessional autobiography. Arthur Rimbaud was a genius. His writings were a quest, a search for perfection, an attempt to find total freedom."

The men around the table look blank, but they're quiet. That's the important thing, right?

"At the age of nineteen," Barkin continues, "Arthur Rimbaud committed suicide. Not of the flesh, but of the mind and soul."

A flunky speaks up, for the only time in the movie. "What's that supposed to mean?"

BARKIN: "It *means*, he never wrote another word, and disappeared off the face of the earth. He was not seen nor heard from again, for nearly twenty years, until he reappeared in a hospital, in Marseilles, on his deathbed." These last three phrases she delivers in a mounting rhythm, for each one is stranger and more important than the one before it. "IN a hospital . . . IN Marseilles . . . ON his *deathbed*."

EDITOR: "Maggie, it's a terrific story. I just don't see what this has to do with Eddie Wilson."

He's all reasonableness, even chivalry, but he comes off like a buffoon. Even I, ignorant of everything about Rimbaud, could see something coming.

BARKIN: "You know where Eddie was coming from the night of the accident?" [Tragic "accident," in which Eddie car's spun off a remote fishing pier and his body is never recovered from the depths of the river.] Roomful of reporters shrug at each other, as if to say: "Who knows, who cares?" Barkin's eyes grow steely. "He was coming from a recording studio, where he'd just finished taping an album. You know what the name of that album was? *A Season in Hell*."

EDITOR: "So what you're saying is that Wilson's pulling a Rimbaud?"

BARKIN (stubbing out cig): "I don't know. But if he is, we've got ourselves one hell of a story, don't we guys?"

To work through sorrow has been my religion. I have screwed my feet into the mud, and I dried myself off with your swine-flu-infected towel. I have played the fool like the Joker in *The Dark Knight Returns* book. It's spring, Joker, and your laugh is contagious, a ring round the moon, a dilly.

KEVIN KILLIAN has published two novels, *Shy* (1989) and *Arctic Summer* (1997), a book of memoirs, *Bedrooms Have Windows* (1990), three books of stories, *Little Men* (1996), *I Cry Like a Baby* (2001), and *Impossible Princess* (2009), as well as two collections of poems, *Argento Series* (2001) and *Action Kylie* (2008). With Lewis Ellingham, he has written a biography of the poet Jack Spicer, *Poet Be Like God: Jack Spicer and the San Francisco Renaissance* (1998). With Peter Gizzi, Killian edited *My Vocabulary Did This to Me: The Collected Poetry of Jack Spicer* (2008). Killian's next book is a novel, *Spreadeagle* (2010). The (untranslated) Pléiade edition mentioned is Arthur Rimbaud, *Oeuvres completes* (Paris: Gallimard, 2009); there are many English editions of his verse.

THE BOSTONIANS

(1886)

by Henry James

REGINA MARLER

I could have entitled this essay "Henry James: A Love Story," for I confess myself a shameless Jamesian, a devotee of the bald and bearded master of Anglo-American prose. Although canonical, James is not a universal taste. His stately, exacting sentences, famously qualified and elaborated—conscientious to the brink of neurosis—have broken better readers than me. But I must carry the James gene. I've found myself rooted in bookstore aisles, helplessly snared by the opening pages of *The Spoils of Poynton* (1897) or *The Wings of the Dove* (1902). The marginal notes in my old Penguin paperback of *What Maisie Knew* (1897) look like speech bubbles for Batman: "No!," "?!!," "*Wow!*"

James even played a crucial but characteristically subtle role in the direction of my professional life. I might have become a James scholar, rather than a Woolf scholar, if not for a wrong turn. At twenty-three, I was on my way to the James shrine—Lamb House, in Rye, East Sussex—when I ended up on the A26 instead of the A21. On the outskirts of Lewes, I spotted a sign for Monk's House, Virginia Woolf's country home. The arrow pointed away from Rye. I turned. As a result, my affinity for James remains at the level of a love affair, not a spiritual union. I took the veil—which comes with a crumpled straw hat, redolent of Bloomsbury summers—for Woolf.

So I approached *The Bostonians* with trembling hands, as another woman might approach a piece of *Sachertorte* and a double espresso. Rich hours were promised to me. After my immersion—my revelry in James's prose style: "sublime, nuanced, imbricated with a thousand distinctions and observations," as Cynthia Ozick, another James victim, describes it—I expected to surface storm-dazed but serene, my every thought illuminated, for days afterward, by the golden gaslight of *The Bostonians*.

For several pages, I clung to this dewy misapprehension. Gradually, the new light dawned. I did not like *The Bostonians*; *The Bostonians* did not like me. It went beyond dislike, in fact. I couldn't recall feeling such searing personal affront from a book until I remembered David Allen's *Getting Things Done* (2002). Kicking and groaning, I dragged myself through the remaining chapters, my ego battered, my eyes stinging with James's venom.

The Bostonians (1886) holds a strange, fluctuating position in American letters. James had high hopes for it as the first novel after his big success in *The Portrait of a Lady* (1881), and also the first in which he broke away from his characteristic international themes. Like his 1884 essay "The Art of Fiction," completed not long before he began work on *The Bostonians*, it was written partly to silence critics who had complained that he was repeating

himself and that, for all his stylistic virtuosity, his narrative limitations were showing. Set among the reform circles of Boston in
the 1870s, the novel hinges on a rivalry between two distant
cousins, a man and a woman, for the love of a beautiful, curiously
passive girl named Verena Tarrant, an inspirational speaker whose
parents are trying to launch her on the lecture and social circuit.
With the exception of their intelligence and their will to power,
Basil Ransom and Olive Chancellor are portrayed as opposites. A
handsome, reactionary Southerner, whose family lost its wealth
and plantation in the Civil War, Basil "takes things easy"—or
believes he does—while Olive, a socially awkward woman of
means and an ardent suffragist, patently does not. "There are
women who are unmarried by accident," Basil reflects on first
meeting Olive, "and others who are unmarried by option; but
Olive Chancellor was unmarried by every implication of her
being. She was a spinster as Shelley is a lyric poet, or as the
month of August is sultry."

Olive, who dislikes men "as a class," has always longed for an
intimate friendship with a working-class girl. Not five minutes
into her initial *tête-à-tête* with Verena, she begs her, "Will you be
my friend, my friend of friends, beyond every one, everything,
forever and forever?," demonstrating that the U-Haul joke has a
long provenance. The unflappable Verena lets Olive sweep her
into a world of tasteful manners, Bach concerts, and late-night
readings of Goethe, cheerfully consenting to almost all of her
new friend's schemes but sometimes pitying Olive for her emotional vulnerability and her intense, jealous nature: "Her whole
relation to Olive was a kind of tacit, tender assent to passionate
insistence." The older woman buys off Verena's impossible, vulgar
parents and educates her to be the voice of women's emancipation, while Basil launches a merciless campaign to win Verena for

himself. His victory would mean a completely cloistered existence for Verena: the little woman enclosed in the home, smiling and nodding for him alone.

From the novel's first installment in serial form in *Century Magazine* in February 1885, its reception disappointed James. Angry letters arrived from America accusing the author of lampooning Nathaniel Hawthorne's sister-in-law, the celebrated reformer Miss Peabody, in his elderly character, Miss Birdseye. The handsome sale of book and serial rights he had negotiated with his American publisher, James R. Osgood, evaporated when Osgood's business collapsed. Although he renegotiated the contract with Osgood's successor, the story sold dismally when it appeared in book form the next year. Reviews were mostly dispiriting. James's editor declared it the most unpopular book he had ever published, and James chose to omit *The Bostonians* from the 1907 New York edition of his novels. (This also means that it lacks the preface he affixed to these revised novels. We know that James was hurt at the time by the novel's failure, but not how he considered it in later years.)

The first entry on *The Bostonians* in James's journal describes Verena as the novel's heroine, and discusses his promising setting in the New England reform circles he knew so well from his childhood and his ongoing family connections. But the author's real interest, as any reader can see, was in the power struggle between Olive and Basil. He devoted the full force of his analytical gifts to each exchange between them, lavishing splendors on every glance and gesture. "He seemed almost hypnotized by his material," wrote James's biographer, Leon Edel. "The first evening of the novel is spread through nine chapters; the next day occupies three more." Such are the austere pleasures of *The Bostonians*. One result of James's microscopic focus is that he exaggerated

Olive and Basil's personalities to the point of caricature. They are giant insects. You want to force them to guzzle the "Drink Me" bottle from Lewis Carroll's *Alice in Wonderland* (1865) and shrink to human proportions. Olive's class distinctions and her sharp-taloned grip on Verena are reiterated to the point of nausea. Basil's racist and antidemocratic politics are so retrograde that an editor, in rejecting one of his essays, suggests he submit it to a journal of the 1600s. When Basil fully unveils his social views for Verena she can barely stagger home to Olive; she hopes that in his youth, "something really bad had happened to him—not by way of gratifying any resentment he aroused in her nature, but to help herself to forgive him for so much contempt and brutality."

Despite the cousins' shared unlikeability, many early readers regarded their tug-of-war as a classic struggle between good and evil—good, predictably, being represented by the Contemptuous Young Southerner in the white trunks, with the Tragically Shy Spinster, Olive, in the Jezebel red trunks, standing up for evil, depravity, and unnatural passions. As late as 1984, one critic, R. H. Hooder, remarked that "if we don't at first think of Basil Ransom as a threat to Verena's liberty no less dangerous than Olive, that is because we are so anxious for Ransom to win the struggle."

The gradual emergence of a public homosexual identity in the years following Oscar Wilde's trial in 1895 complicated critical response, and may have played a role in James's decision not to reprint the novel. Still, a surprising number of twentieth-century critics have overlooked the sexual underpinnings of Olive's will to possess Verena, while others have denied or downplayed it, as if to admit her lesbianism would drag the esteemed author into a roiling pit of lawless queer desire.

After a long period of neglect, as well as critical embarrass-ment at Olive's predilections, *The Bostonians* was rehabilitated by an unblushing group of readers, the pioneers of Gender Studies. Eve Kosofsky Sedgwick, in particular, made beautiful use of *The Bostonians* in *Epistemology of the Closet* (1992), and Terry Castle argued in *The Apparitional Lesbian* (1993) that it is "the first 'lesbian novel' written in English—that is, the first nonpornographic work in Anglo-American literature to engage fully and self-consciously with the love-between-women theme." There is nothing "apparitional," to use Castle's celebrated term, about the lesbian yearning at the novel's center, and James's audacity—his hiding in plain sight—now seems startling. *The Bostonians* can still be read as a battle between good and evil, if the reader enjoys such binaries, but the antagonists have changed corners: Olive is clearly the crowd favorite, and James himself is in hot water for what Sedgwick calls "a woman-hating and feminist-baiting violence of panic."

Although I'm on the Sedgwick bandwagon, my chief argument with *The Bostonians* isn't so much political as artistic. James's portrayals feel mean spirited; his cool observances spiteful rather than satiric. Although I don't require lovable characters, his are grotesques. The only character we are invited to admire is the vague and kindly Miss Birdseye, a moth-eaten old dear who has given her life and every penny that came to her to a miscellany of progressive causes. Her death provides the single soft touch in this novel of thorn bushes and acid pools. James told his brother he had wanted to describe "an old, weary, battered and simple-minded woman," so that no one could accuse him of treating the reformers with contempt. In fact, his contempt for the Boston reform establishment was near complete. You can still hear him grinding his axe, dreaming of vanquishing the enemies of his art: the small-minded, the conventional, and the so-called liberals. Even introducing Miss Birdseye, he can't restrain his urge to disparage: "Since the Civil War much of her occupation was gone; for before that her best hours had been spent in fancying that she was helping some Southern slave to escape. It would have been a nice question whether, in her heart of hearts, for the sake of this excitement, she did not sometimes wish the blacks back in bondage."

One more thing. When doling out the good looks, why give Basil the shiny black locks, towering height, and personal magnetism, when anxious, flat-chested Olive has to make do with being "distinguished?" What's wrong with a flat chest? I'm coming after you, James. This time, it's personal.

REGINA MARLER is the author of *Bloomsbury Pie: the Making of the Bloomsbury Boom* (1997) and has edited the *Selected Letters of Vanessa Bell* (1993) as well as *Queer Beats: How the Beats Turned America On to Sex* (2004). Quotations are taken from Henry James, *The Bostonians* (New York/London: Penguin, 2003), edited by Richard Lansdown, which is currently in print, alongside many other editions.

A SHROPSHIRE LAD
(1896)

by A. E. Housman

MARK MERLIS

Y ou will have read Housman in high school. "When I was one-and-twenty / I heard a wise man say . . ." Or per-haps, "Loveliest of trees, the cherry now / Is hung with bloom along the bough." Surely at least the one poem that for a century has stirred successive cohorts of bright, hormone-rattled sophomores, "To an Athlete Dying Young":

The time you won your town the race
We chaired you through the market-place;
Man and boy stood cheering by,
And home we brought you shoulder-high.

To-day, the road all runners come,
Shoulder-high we bring you home,

And set you at your threshold down,
Townsman of a stiller town.

Smart lad, to slip betimes away
From fields where glory does not stay
And early though the laurel grows
It withers quicker than the rose . . .

Through how many routes this verse threads its way into the
soul of an apprentice queer. It is about a hot jock carried, sweaty
and panting, on other lads' shoulders. It resounds, like so much of
Housman, with a lonesome kid's self-gratulatory stoicism: life is
fleeting, beauty is intensified by death, God's an indifferent wank,
vanitas, vanitas. (Much of his work seems like one long gloss on
"Dover Beach"; Matthew Arnold was perhaps his favorite poet.)
And the clincher: that hunk they elected prom king and who
doesn't even know you exist will be food for worms while you,
scrawny alienated bookworm, go on to grown-up glory. You can
imagine the Columbine boys reading Housman, as they cleaned
their weapons and plotted to help a bevy of lads slip more
speedily away.

A Shropshire Lad is replete, in between the tiresome mock-
pastorals, with an acid mix of calfish lad-love and doting reveries
about violence. The slaughter in Housman is so relentless that
even he had to acknowledge the aptness of Hugh Kingsmill's
famous parody: "What, still alive at twenty-two, / A clean,
upstanding chap like you? / Sure, if your throat 'tis hard to slit,
/ Slit your girl's and swing for it." The drive to rip the beloved
apart crops up in other crypto-gay verse of the period—sometimes in Hopkins, or in Wilfred Owen's bullets "[w]hich long to
nuzzle in the hearts of lads." But these poets also love living

flesh. For Housman, so precise in his depictions of flowers and hills and clouds, lads are mere abstractions, except when their bodies are made vitally present as the canvas for death to paint on: the bare neck stretched for the hangman's noose, the heels ready to dangle in air.

Alfred Edward Housman was born the year Darwin's *The Origin of Species* first appeared (1859) and died the year Edward VIII abdicated (1936). Though he lived nearly half his life in the twentieth century (long enough to read Joyce, correspond with Eliot, and tell all his friends to buy *Gentlemen Prefer Blondes*), he seems not Victorian, exactly, or even of the Mauve Decade, but out of time. He was one of the great classical scholars of his day, spending an entire career meticulously editing Manilius, a Roman poet who wrote doggerel about astrology. Housman himself wrote poetry only intermittently, mostly in two productive bursts that culminated in *A Shropshire Lad* in 1896 and, in 1922, *Last Poems*.

He was a sere man before his classes and in public, though playful and witty among friends. He was a High Church Tory, who even hinted once that perhaps slavery was a good foundation for a cultured society, but of course he also loved proles, soldiers, and farmboys, in the standard way. Sort of a Log Cabin Republican, then. He understood himself to be a homosexual, though of course he wouldn't have used that word, and chafed at the persecution of Wilde and at his own enforced discretion. (His brother, less closeted, was one of the ur-activists who surrounded Edward Carpenter.)

As an undergraduate at Oxford he fell very hard for Moses Jackson, an athlete and scientist who was just smart enough to appreciate Housman's wit and just stupid enough not to figure out why Housman was hanging out with him. Possibly Housman himself didn't fully understand; we didn't name our feelings as quickly back then. They were just good, good friends—even after college, lodging together in London: Alfred and Mo and Mo's brother Adelbert.

Until one night Alfred and Mo had a conversation, content unknown, after which Jackson remained friendly but more distant. I find this lost confrontation more tantalizing even than Melville's mysterious last meeting with Hawthorne. What could Housman have said that was merely off-putting and not disgusting? With what gesture or momentary aversion of the eyes did Jackson make it plain that, whatever unutterable further shore Housman hoped to reach, Mo would not be rowing with him? Soon enough Mo rowed away as far as he could get: off to India, he then married, settling at last in British Columbia. Housman, after perhaps briefly contemplating the end he recommended for so many other lads, settled into what British playwright Tom Stoppard has called his "unremitting, lopsided, lifelong, hopeless constancy to a decent chap who was in no need of it."

Constancy didn't mean celibacy. Though Housman is often spoken of as repressed, "reticent" is probably a better word. He had plenty of sex, usually during the summer recess and far from England: a years-long affair with a gay-for-pay gondolier, sojourns in the brothels of Paris, where one can imagine him crossing paths, if not swords, with Proust. There is a possibility that he even had some kind of weird surrogate affair with Mo's brother Adelbert, whose sudden death from typhoid in 1892 may have been one of the precipitants of *A Shropshire Lad*.

But he had just the one love, ever, leaving Housman numbed, stunted, locked in adolescence for a whole life. After the success of *Last Poems*, he wrote to Mo, then dying in Canada: "It is now 11 o'clock in the morning, and I hear that the Cambridge shops are sold out. Please to realize therefore, with fear and respect, that I am an eminent bloke; though I would much rather have followed you round the world and blacked your boots." This written forty years after he had, however obscurely, bared his love to this mild, weak-chinned nonentity who couldn't quite puzzle out what he was after. Forty years of knowing that he, so eminent, had shamed himself and couldn't stop shaming himself. God loved rubbing his face in it; how could he not have wanted sometimes to obliterate Moses Jackson and all the other happy mindless lads?

As, in Gore Vidal's 1948 novel *The City and the Pillar*, Jim Willard wants to obliterate Bob. Or, in Vidal's own life, the singular and unrepeatable boyhood love for Jimmy that may account for his Housman-like frigidity and the facile sterility of his writing. Once you start, you can find Housman's story in so many places. In John Rechy's *City of Night* (1963), the bitter professor whose Robbie stole everything from him. In Thomas Mann's story "Tonio Kröger" (1903). In Claggart, finally, in Melville's *Billy Budd* (1924). I would like to imagine that this particular style of desolation is obsolete, or will be. Not that unrequited love will ever go out of fashion, or even that gay boys will stop falling helplessly for straight ones. But that they won't despise themselves for having loved, that they will not feel that the only way to go on living is to turn into ice.

Oh, you didn't read him in high school? Maybe it's too late; maybe you're too grown up now. W. H. Auden thought he was best read by adolescents, partly because he never really developed as a poet or a man: you can't tell if a poem was written in 1895 or 1922. While the poets around him were stretching the limits of prosody, he straitjacketed himself in rhymed tetrameter, or even trimeter. De-*da*-de-*da*-de-*da*, he thumps, so relentlessly; you may coldly admire his virtuosity, but often a poem will offer just one small pleasure, an unexpected word, a clever twist. Or nothing: great lyrics and insipid drivel may be found on facing pages, even in the same poem. In his spitting-on-the-grave obituary, Cyril Connolly noted how much of Housman resembled barrack-room Rudyard Kipling, or boys'-school anthems or second-rate Hilaire Belloc: "The fate which Housman's poems deserve, of course, is to be set to music by English composers and sung by English singers . . ."

And yet. There are some poems that still hit me almost as hard as when I was sixteen. Like this stunning lyric to Mo:

Look not in my eyes, for fear
They mirror true the sight I see,
And there you find your face too clear
And love it and be lost like me.
One the long nights through must lie
Spent in star-defeated sighs,
But why should you as well as I
Perish? gaze not in my eyes.

A Grecian lad, as I hear tell,
One that many loved in vain,
Looked into a forest well
And never looked away again.
There, when the turf in springtime flowers,
With downward eye and gazes sad,

Stands amid the glancing showers
A jonquil, not a Grecian lad.

Of course it is Housman, not Mo, who was Narcissus. He saw
in Mo his perfected self, could not look away, and was sadly
rooted forever.

MARK MERLIS has published three novels: *American Studies* (1994), *An Arrow's Flight* (1998; published in Great Britain as *Pyrrhus*), and *Man About Town* (2003). Housman's *A Shropshire Lad* and *Last Poems* are available in numerous editions and online at www.gutenberg.org. Merlis adds: "After his death, his brother printed two more volumes of poems Housman hadn't chosen to publish, sometimes because they were a little too gay but usually because he could see they were tripe. *More Poems* and *Additional Poems* are included in several editions of the collected poems (New York: Holt, 1971; London: Wordsworth Poetry Library, 1999). There is a nice little selection from all the volumes, edited and with an introduction by Alan Hollinghurst: *A. E. Housman: Poems Selected by Alan Hollinghurst* (London/New York: Faber and Faber, 2005)."

DE PROFUNDIS

(1895–97; published 1905 and 1962)

by Oscar Wilde

FENTON JOHNSON

A mong our immortal dead perhaps only Jesus fell faster and farther. In May 1895 Oscar Wilde's comedy *The Importance of Being Earnest* opened to rave reviews and sold-out houses; by September, the play had been closed and he was in prison, after three humiliating trials which left him bankrupt and in debt to the vindictive father of his lover Lord Alfred Douglas ("Bosie"). Nearing the end of his two-year sentence for "acts of gross indecency," Wilde wrote *De Profundis* as a letter to Bosie, sending it shortly after his release, though Bosie claimed never to have received it. A bowdlerized edition was posthumously published in 1905; the full text did not see print until 1962.

Born to prosperity in Ireland in 1854, raised in the wake of the great potato famine, Wilde grew up amid a foment of rebellion and mysticism—the most reasonable responses to unreasonable suffering. His life and art are a movement from the former to the latter—from the elegant libertinism of the fiction, plays, and poetry to the mystic's search for meaning and redemption in *De Profundis*.

In part because of conditions of composition *De Profundis* is frankly a mess. Wilde was not allowed pen and paper until well into the second year of his sentence; once granted these privileges he was not allowed to retain or review each day's work, meaning that in his writing he had to rely on memory for organization and continuity. Those looking to read Wilde's most polished writings are better served by *The Picture of Dorian Gray* (1890), the plays, or the profound and touching *The Ballad of Reading Gaol* (1898).

The easy advice would be to read only the letter's eloquent later pages, skipping the finger-pointing and breast-beating of its first half. But that would be to miss the great pageant of the work—the pilgrim's progress from empiricist to mystic, the boulevardier of the cities of the plain to the prophet of the mountains, the lesser to the greater man. The lesser man must berate and blame; the greater man will be an artist in spite of his flaws—it is his vocation and his destiny. *De Profundis* charts the journey—in real time, so to speak, given the circumstances under which it was written.

The defining quality of genius—as distinguished from ambition, which is commonplace, and talent, which is unusual but insufficient—may lie in its holder's capacity to fashion a scrim onto which we can project and so perceive the secret, unacknowledged aspects of our characters. Wilde was an undisputed master of such fabrications, but the horrors of Reading Gaol tore away the scrim. Every lover of beauty must read these pages, because of their revelation of the desires and illusions that we project onto their author and for their portrayal of the conflicts of the soul of a man better known for his glittering surface.

Long before his imprisonment Wilde had spoken to French gay novelist André Gide of his intention to present the life of Jesus, including his Crucifixion, as the ultimate work of art and thus Jesus as the avatar of aestheticism, the philosophy (for which Wilde had become the world-famous proponent) that art need serve no moral or practical purpose. But he did not or could not undertake the task until after he had endured his own Crucifixion—until he became or made of himself a martyr.

As every artist knows or learns, art is about process more than product. The book or painting or performance is the fruit of what philosopher Jacques Maritain called "the habit of art," but—to extend the metaphor—the life itself is the tree: that which bears the fruit. In Wilde's Church of Beauty, the finished products are merely the fruits of a life that is in and of itself the greatest work of art. In *De Profundis* he offers Jesus' life as the most perfect example: "[Christ] is just like a work of art," he writes. "He does not really teach one anything but by being brought to his presence one becomes something."

"[W]hat the artist is looking for is the mode of existence in which soul and body are one and indivisible," Wilde adds. This achievement of *nonduality*, as Buddhism would have it, or *union with Beauty*, as Plato would have it, or *union with God* in Jewish, Christian, or Sufi terminology, is the heart of the mystic's enterprise, whatever the source tradition. For Wilde, art was the means to that end: "Truth in art is the unity of a thing with itself . . . the secret of life is suffering." The first half of the statement has its roots in Plato, the second in the Passion Play of Jesus' life and death.

As a vehicle for this mode of living Wilde imagines a new, apophatic church: "Religion does not help me," he writes. "The faith that others give to what is unseen, I give to what one can touch, and look at . . . I would like to found an order for those who *cannot* believe . . . agnosticism must have its ritual no less than faith. It has sown its martyrs, it should reap its saints, and praise God daily for having hidden himself from man."

In these eloquent later pages Wilde speaks with the voice of the prophet and mystic whom prison has taught to embrace suffering as wisdom's necessary condition—"the price of the ticket," in James Baldwin's apt rendering. "Clergymen and people who use phrases without wisdom sometimes talk of suffering as a mystery," Wilde writes. "It is really a revelation . . . whatever happens to oneself happens to another"—a simple inversion of Matthew 25:40: ". . . inasmuch as you did it to one of the least of these my brethren, you did it to me."

But a worm dwells at the heart of the prose. Biographer Richard Ellmann writes that in *De Profundis* Wilde "envisaged [an] essay to deal with . . . Christ as the supreme artist and Wilde as his prophet." But even in these later pages, Wilde is no one's prophet but his own. His intense self-awareness prevents him from attaining Jesus' characteristic simplicity except in glimpses. Wilde was born and raised in Catholic Ireland, yes, but of Protestant, Anglo-Irish parents, and though he romanticized the Roman church of "saints and sinners," in fact he owed his success to the institutions and society of Anglican England and was as committed as any good Protestant to the preeminence of individual achievement. In *De Profundis* he invokes Jesus' suffering while never touching upon his presumed Resurrection and its attendant promise of union with God—or, as Plato would have it, Beauty.

The omission provides insight into Wilde's divided sensibilities: As an Irish-born mystic, martyr, and megalomaniac, he embraces Jesus' story, with its many parallels with his own life (deserted by friends as Jesus was deserted by his disciples; rejecting opportunities to flee England as Jesus chose to remain in the Garden of Gethsemane). The "four prose poems" of the Gospels from which Wilde drew his inspiration inextricably couple the martyred and the risen Jesus. Their conflation is precisely the work of art Wilde invokes when he writes, "An idea is of no value until it is become incarnate and made an image." Jesus' Crucifixion and Resurrection incarnate, in a simple, unforgettable story and in indelible images, the ideas at the heart of Wilde's aestheticism and of the Platonic philosophy on which it drew.

But as a post-Enlightenment empiricist, Wilde cannot bring himself even to mention the risen Jesus, whose Resurrection is the logical, inevitable culmination of the story—the fruit of the tree, the work of art to which the life has pointed and led. The schizophrenic structure of *De Profundis* correlates this intellectual/spiritual divide: in the opening pages, Wilde the empiricist places Bosie on trial, seeking a logical sequence of events that might explain his fall from grace and in the process justify his own behavior. In the later pages Wilde the mystic arrives at the understanding of his fall as a combination of the ineluctable workings of destiny and what essayist Philip Lopate wryly calls "the catastrophe of character." At various points in the letter's opening pages, Wilde writes, "I blame myself," "I ceased to be lord over myself," and (to Bosie) "You were absolutely responsible." In the later pages, he makes an about-face to arrive at the place where he can observe, "The gods are strange. [T]hey bring us to ruin through what in us is good, gentle, human, loving."

The notion that we are always and everywhere in control of our destinies is a peculiarly Western affliction, given lie by the existence of people whose innate desires set us on unconventional paths. Together with the transcripts of Wilde's trials, *De Profundis* remains not just fascinating but necessary reading because it chronicles the education of a great artist out of that particular myth, in the process offering an unsettling exploration of the conflict between reason's absolute need to know and the necessarily unknowable recesses of the heart.

I take as self-evident that the horrors of prison broke Wilde's spirit and that as a result he turned to philosophy and religion, but I find this cause not for dismissal of the work but an imperative for its reading. When Nietzsche tells us that Christianity is Platonism for the masses, he points up not its weakness but the source of its enduring strength: religion—that peculiar, deeply flawed blend of passion and principle—is our most successful effort at making the comforts of philosophy available to the mass of people in a form that they can comprehend and at least aspire to live by.

Like art itself, the artist "is of his very essence quite useless," Wilde writes, but *De Profundis* offers *prima facie* refutation of its own logic. As Wilde repeatedly points out, art springs from the imagination, and any act of imagination requires that we rise above our particular circumstances to consider our sufferings as threads in the great tapestry of human sorrow. This is the noblest aspiration and function of philosophy—of religion—of art—of writing: the transformation of suffering into beauty. "To propose to be a better man is a piece of unscientific cant," Wilde writes. "To have become a deeper man is the privilege of those who have suffered. And such I think I have become." Considered in this light philosophy, religion, and art may be our most potent evolutionary tools.

Wilde argues that prison has been the ruin of his career, though with the hindsight of a century, the opposite seems true regarding his longer-term reputation. Had he never met Bosie, Wilde would surely have found a different, equally powerful catalyst for martyrdom; had he never endured prison we would still perform his plays and of his prose read at least *Dorian Gray*. But the notoriety of the trials and his imprisonment elevated his life from the merely brilliant to something closer to the immortality—in religious terms, sainthood—to which he aspired. Martyrdom is so much more interesting than ordinary mortality, and Wilde was a passionate devotee of all that is interesting. After conquering the pinnacle of success what remained to explore but the topography of descent? The very thesis of *De Profundis* is that his time in prison has been a great gift, without which he could never have learned the lessons he is setting forth.

Early in *De Profundis* Wilde writes that he must learn again "how to be cheerful and happy," a goal he can reach only by finding beauty in his terrible fate. But once freed, despite his eloquently argued principles he returned to his old ways in different streets. He lived, in fact, Jesus' Passion without its payoff. He seems to have found happiness only in glimpses, partly because life denied him the time—he died three and a half years later, of uncertain causes surely provoked or worsened in prison—but partly because, though he took Jesus as his model, his humility was imposed upon rather than organic to his character. He never embraced the ultimate humility—the submission of reason to the manifestly unreasonable story of the Resurrection. Like Milton's

Satan—whom many acknowledge as the most likeable character in *Paradise Lost* (1667/74)—Wilde preferred noble rebellion to humble submission, at least until his deathbed. There he completed the mystical journey by converting to Roman Catholicism, a transition that allowed him to live in the empiricist's celebration of individual genius but die in the embrace of Mother Church.

In life as in theater, timing is all.

These days Wilde is often identified as a "gay writer," but I wonder whether he would have welcomed the label. More than as a gay writer, I think of him as an outsider of the type elaborated by philosopher Colin Wilson, "a man who cannot live in the comfortable, insulated world of the bourgeois . . . it is not simply the need to cock a snook at respectability that provokes him; it is a distressing sense that *truth must be told at all Costs* . . ." Late in *De Profundis*, though writing of Hamlet, Wilde is clearly describing himself: "a dreamer . . . a poet . . . asked . . . to grapple with life in its practical realization, of which he knows nothing, not with life in its ideal essence, of which he knows so much." He was placed in the dock as much for his flamboyant effeminacy as for what he did in bed; for his refusal to hide as much as for what he was hiding. The "order" he proposes to found is not a great edifice of pomp and regulations but something humbler: an order of and for outcasts whose saint is a criminal; an order that Jesus ("counted among the lawless," Luke 22:37) might have founded; an order for me and—maybe—for you.

"You came to me to learn the pleasure of life and the pleasure of art," Wilde concludes *De Profundis*, addressing us, his future readers, more than Bosie. "Perhaps I am chosen to teach you something more wonderful—the meaning of sorrow and its beauty." If that strikes our postmodern, pleasure-principled ears as too self-consciously penitential, consider the following from Emily Dickinson, a near-contemporary and another student of suffering:

> I like a look of Agony,
> Because I know it's true—
> Men do not sham Convulsion,
> Nor simulate, a Throe—

"Sorrow is the ultimate type in both life and art," Wilde writes, a statement that evokes particular poignancy for its proximity to *The Importance of Being Earnest*, one of our most sparkling comedies, and his last work prior to *De Profundis*. "Behind joy and laughter there may be a temperament, coarse, hard, and callous. But behind sorrow there is always sorrow. Pain, unlike pleasure, wears no mask . . ." After the degradations of prison, having become as intimate with suffering as with any lover, Wilde can write of Jesus: "In a manner not yet understood of the world he regarded sin and suffering as being in themselves beautiful and holy things and modes of perfection."

Far from useless, this lesson may be the most important life can teach: the ripping away the veil of *maya*, as Hinduism would have it, to reveal the fundamental unity of all creation, including pleasure and pain, joy and suffering. It lies at the heart of all the great wisdom traditions, but Wilde—after Jesus, perhaps our greatest aphorist—sums it up most succinctly and eloquently: "The past, the present, and the future are but one moment in the sight of God . . . time and space, succession and extension are merely accidental conditions of thought."

"Love is fed by the imagination," Wilde writes, "by which we become wiser than we know, better than we feel, nobler than we are." Having lived in San Francisco in the first decades of the AIDS pandemic, I cannot help finding in Wilde's suffering and in *De Profundis* a prefiguring and a primer for that later, vaster trauma. In both tragedies—one particular, one general—one may find evidence of the cruel senselessness of life; or, not in the pandemic but in the gay community's response to it, the beauty which Wilde, taking his cue from Jesus, understood as the perfection toward which we must progress.

FENTON JOHNSON is working on his sixth book, a meditation on solitude based in the work of writers and artists who have lived and worked alone for most or all of their professional lives. Quotations are taken from Oscar Wilde, *De Profundis and Other Writings* (New York/London: Penguin, 1984), which is still in print, along with many other selected and collected editions of Wilde's writings in which *De Profundis* is included.

CLAUDINE AT SCHOOL

(CLAUDINE À L'ÉCOLE)

(1900)

by Colette

ALISON SMITH

In a recent rush of generosity, I gave away my copy of *Claudine at School* to a deserving and eager young reader. I've regretted it ever since. At the time I was trying to prove that I was not overly attached to material things; even my most beloved books I could do without. Well, I can't. I miss pulling *Claudine* off my bookshelf, opening to a random page, reading a line or two, and letting the audacious, too-clever-by-half, wise-beyond-her-years, and naughty-as-all-get-out Claudine leap off the page. Perhaps Judith Thurman said it best when she called Claudine "erotically reckless." I can't think of a nicer compliment.

Three weeks ago, I went to the Brooklyn Library and checked out a copy of *Claudine at School*. Opening the library's edition—published in 1956 by a London house called Secker and Warburg and translated by Antonia White—I've come full circle.

The first time I read *Claudine at School*, it was 1986 and I was holed up in the basement of Our Lady of Mercy School for Girls in Rochester, New York, reading another library copy. Not a school library copy (the nuns' collection did not include a single Sapphic French writer: go figure) but rather a copy procured from the city library. I'd been introduced to Colette, the author of *Claudine at School*, a few months prior when a classmate, a girl with more sophisticated taste (she was a junior; I was a sophomore) declared Jane Austen (my then-favorite author) prissy. She handed me Colette's collected short stories and I was immediately taken with the spare yet sensual, sophisticated yet earthy prose. Of course I was inclined to like anything this girl told me to like. A month later she and I would embark on a secret affair, culminating in the night we got caught in a nun's bed in the convent attached to the school; my own feeble attempt at erotic recklessness. That romance ended—not without copious tears on my part—but the attachment to Colette remains. *Claudine at School*, her first book, the book in which, many claim, she invented the modern teenager, is an excellent place to begin reading Colette.

Colette's story is almost as compelling as her work. Born in the Burgundy region of France in 1873, Colette didn't start out as Colette. She started out with a mouthful of a name: Sidonie-Gabrielle. When Gabri (as she was known to her family) was twenty and had a mane of hair so long it reached her ankles, she caught the eye of a family friend, Henri Gauthier-Villars, aka Willy, who was visiting from Paris. He was fifteen years her senior. They were soon married.

Willy, it turned out, was not the most upstanding of gentlemen. He was enterprising, I'll give him that. Mostly known as a music critic, he also produced sonnets, books of essays, and a number of mildly salacious potboilers. Few people believe he wrote much of what he signed his name to. Some people believe he didn't write the books at all. Legend has it that he had an arsenal of ghostwriters, conveniently stashed in the provinces. He played them off each other, sending a rough draft of a novel penned by the first ghostwriter to a second ghostwriter. Passing it off as his own, he'd ask the second ghostwriter to flesh out the story a little. Then he'd send it back to the first poor sod, passing the revisions off as his own, asking if ghostwriter number one could now tidy up his latest draft, and on and on until he had a satisfactory manuscript. He then brought it to his editor and passed off the resulting novel as his own work. Deplorable? Definitely. Kind of brilliant? Arguably.

Enter Colette—homesick, disconsolate, in over her head, and above all: bored stiff. Paris, it turns out, when you're young and surrounded by a bunch of old fogey friends of your not-so-attentive husband, is not all it's cracked up to be. Besides, Colette looked like a hick and she talked like a hick and everybody knows Parisians have always been terrible snobs. And that hair: floor-length locks were not exactly all the rage. She definitely did not take Paris by storm. Well, at least not right away.

Willy told Colette to jot down her memories of her school days. Since she had nothing better to do, she did as she was told; she wrote *Claudine at School*. Willy brought it to his editor. It was published. Over the next few months, *Claudine at School* slowly gained momentum with the reading public and soon it became one of the biggest best sellers in the history of France. There were sequels (*Claudine in Paris* [1901], *Claudine Married* [1902], *Claudine Takes Off* [1903]); there were plays based on Claudine, there were product spin-offs. There were even Claudine cigarettes. Claudine was huge. Willy, listed as the sole author of the books, claimed all the credit. He became a very rich, very famous man.

The next part of the story is the part I heard in high school. When I did, it raised Colette's stock even higher. After the success of the first *Claudine*, Willy locked Colette in a room all day every day and forced her to write. He stole everything she wrote and claimed it for himself. To a sixteen-year-old girl with an artistic bent and an overdeveloped sense of the tragic (it must have been reading and rereading the *Lives of the Virgin Martyrs*), this was the height of glamorous. Colette was a brilliant writer, imprisoned and exploited for her prodigious talent, unfairly used by an unscrupulous man, and she lived in Paris: she certainly won the heart of this Catholic schoolgirl.

Some have questioned the accuracy of the more scandalous details of this story. It certainly makes a good yarn. It definitely captures the imagination. This is what we know for sure: the books were solely authored by Colette and for years Willy took credit for them.

Eventually Colette left her husband, got a lawyer, and proved herself to be the true author of the *Claudine* books. She went on to be a prolific and celebrated author in her own right and a music hall star who appeared on stage, sometimes half-naked, sometimes in drag. She lived for a time with Natalie Barney. She took several lovers—of both sexes—and become a shrewd businesswoman. Oh, and she cut her hair. All of this—documented and proven without a doubt—is way more impressive than being locked in a room, don't you think?

When I first read *Claudine at School*, I was too young and too steeped in my own girls' school culture to see what a revelation the book really is. Claudine is one of the most intelligent, sharp-eyed, iconoclastic young women ever written. She could teach that Holden Caulfield a thing or two. Unlike Salinger's disconsolate teen, Claudine doesn't run away from school. Claudine does what she can to prolong her school days as much as possible. There were few prospects after school for a young woman at that time. And, frankly, she enjoyed the company of all those young, nubile, not-so-innocent schoolgirls.

To this day, Claudine makes me blush more than any other character in literature. Now I don't want to get your hopes up: I don't want to hear that you went rifling through the pages looking for the full-on sex scenes. There aren't any. Instead, it's Claudine's attitude that is so revelatory. She's knowing, sensual, wise beyond her years; nothing fazes this girl. And when she wants a girl, she gets her. She may not be able to keep her (competition is fierce in the provinces and these girls are not above stealing a classmate's love) but Claudine can make a girl weak in the knees. She is a very skilled seductress. Oh, and she is unapologetically queer—queer in a pre-identity politics kind of way.

Claudine and her contemporaries had no chance of designing their own destiny, of choosing a life independent from men, or deciding how to conduct their lives based on who they desired or loved. Because of these sad constraints, they are relieved of the anxiety of identity. What is the point of finding oneself, of declaring one's complex and nuanced identity, if there is nowhere to go with the information? Thus, they were free to act out their passions for each other until someone made them a wife and they were relegated to the endless grind of unpaid family laborer (usually on a farm). If there was no family money, a young woman's only other recourse was to enter the equally arduous, low-paying profession of school marm. To sum up, no one, least of all themselves, took French provincial schoolgirls' shenanigans seriously.

Of course, Colette's larger point is that the lives of women and girls were too conscripted. However, there's a small silver lining: you and I get to read about these girls' erotically reckless adventures. So please read *Claudine at School* because it's an important first book by an important woman writer; because Claudine— audacious, brilliant, fiercely independent—is a powerful character who broke new ground; because the book provides a sumptuously detailed portrait of the lives of women and girls in French provinces at the end of the nineteenth century. But most of all read *Claudine* because she is one of the all-time great seductresses, and she's got some things to teach you.

ALISON SMITH's memoir *Name All the Animals* (2004) won the Barnes & Noble Discover Award, the Judy Grahn Prize for Lesbian Nonfiction, and a Lambda Literary Award. It has been translated into seven languages. She lives in Brooklyn, New York.

DEATH IN VENICE

(TOD IN VENEDIG)

(1912)

by Thomas Mann

CHRISTOPHER BRAM

*D*eath in Venice (*Tod in Venedig*) must be one of the strangest books ever to become a classic. A middle-aged artist visits Venice, becomes fascinated with a beautiful boy at his hotel, lingers in the city too long, and dies of cholera while sitting in a beach chair and gazing at his beloved. When one remembers how uncomfortable the world is with both homosexuality and pedophilia, one is amazed this novella wasn't laughed to scorn when it appeared in 1912, or that people continue to take it seriously.

Let me say right off that I think everyone should read Thomas Mann's famous classic, but then question it, resist it, pull it apart. There are pages as true and real as the best of Chekhov. The setting is perfectly rendered: the world of strangers in hotels, the magic of travel, the beauty of Venice, the dream-like intensity of a look or gesture in a country where you don't speak the language. But mixed with the good stuff are the "meaningful" passages—the paens to Phaedrus, the musings on beauty and form, the fever dream of savages out of Joseph Conrad's *Heart of Darkness* (1900). For me this is all just intellectual liverwurst, an elaborate defense mechanism built around the subject of homosexual desire. But it worked! For decades now, critics have argued that the novella isn't really about a grown man falling in love with a fourteen-year-old boy, but about something more, well, philosophical.

> His honey-colored hair nestled in ringlets at his temples and at the back of his neck, the sun gleamed in the down on his upper spine, the subtle outlining of his ribs and the symmetry of his breast stood out through the scanty covering of his torso, his armpits were still as smooth as those of a statue, the hollows of his knees glistened and their bluish veins made his body seem composed of some more translucent material.

This is hardly the stuff of metaphysics, but is perfectly appropriate for a man who enjoys watching a boy. However, it is then followed by:

> His eyes embraced that noble figure at the blue water's edge, and in rising ecstasy he felt he was gazing on Beauty itself, on Form as a thought of God, on the one and pure perfection which dwells in the spirit and of which a human image and likeness had there been lightly and graciously set up to worship . . .

On and on it goes, three long, long paragraphs full of lyrical intoxication and philosophizing, until you want to cry out, "It's just a cute boy, dammit!"

These are Aschenbach's thoughts, of course, and Mann is aware of the comic discrepancy between cause and expression. Chickenhawks can get awfully longwinded describing their beloveds. But Mann goes on at length not only for psychological truth, but because he needs his gaudy metaphors—his Greek gods and Asian tigers of illness, his schticks of death and decadence—to justify the guilty desire to gaze at a pretty boy.

Because the future Nobel Prize winner was deeply conflicted. We have a better idea now of how deep his conflicts were after reading the diaries and letters published since his death. He was a gay man with a wife and six children. When he first published *Death in Venice*, he felt so guilty he confessed to a friend that a world that could produce such a decadent work needed a war. His wish was granted in the following year, 1914.

The tale of Aschenbach's love for Tadzio is overdetermined and overjustified. An extremely uptight, other-directed man cannot experience passion until he falls into the shadow of death. Death enables him to feel love even as it allows the reader to forgive his choice of beloved. After all, he will soon be dead. Aschenbach is the gay cousin of all those Victorian women who commit passionate adultery and then drown or throw themselves under trains. "Other-directed" is an old attitude, a belief that we should behave as the world wants us to. We are all more inner-directed nowadays (or so we're told), but the old social guilts still held full sway for most of the last century. I suspect this explains the book's enormous postwar popularity. Readers could be moved by Aschenbach's love of Tadzio without being closet pedophiles themselves. They felt trapped in their own other-directed prisons of marriage and family, and boy-love was only a metaphor.

The boy-love business is trickier now. It's not just a metaphor anymore, and is more forbidden than adult homosexuality. But *Knabenliebe* was the most common form of gay sexuality until the twentieth century. Mann protected himself by keeping the love pure and platonic. Aschenbach doesn't touch Tadzio. He doesn't even speak to him. But after pages and pages of looking and sighing, this high-minded regard begins to feel creepy.

There is good, clear matter in the story. As I said, the sense of place and travel are very fine. Mann can be dramatic and indirect in his storytelling. The fever dream is silly—the mob of savages carry "the obscene symbol, wooden and gigantic"—but it's deftly used to show that Aschenbach has fallen ill. The last two pages at the beach on the Lido are perfect: the sandbars and flat water, the boy strolling into the sea and looking back toward the sick man in a chair. I especially like the abandoned camera on its tripod as "the black cloth over it fluttered and flapped in the freshening breeze."

(I quote from the David Luke translation, which is famous for returning the missing death sentence to the next-to-the-last paragraph: "And as so often, he set out to follow him." The sentence was not in the H. T. Lowe-Porter translation, found in *Stories of Three Decades*, but is in the 1986 Vintage edition of her text. Did someone notice it was missing before Luke? Was it accidentally dropped after Lowe-Porter first translated the story in 1930? One cannot imagine her being so obtuse that she couldn't understand why it was there. It's in the Kenneth Burke translation, which appeared before hers.)

I admit I'd be much happier with a gay version of "Lady with a Lapdog," where this story was presented in a drier, more realistic manner, without judgment or allegory, and left a bit elusive. Such a piece, however, would've been attacked or ignored or soon forgotten. It would never have become a classic. But Mann found a safe way to package homosexual desire by wrapping it in Greek myth and melancholy sighs.

Does the story tell us anything useful now about love or death or homosexuality? Not for me. I don't understand why death has to be part of gay love. Oh, *Liebestod* and all that, I suppose, but we don't see this swoony love/death in heterosexual fiction anymore. *Lolita* (1955), that other twentieth-century pedophile classic, is full of death, but Nabokov does not eroticize it or use it to excuse forbidden desire. Love takes place in the face of death, in spite of death. (With *Lolita*, too, critics refused to admit this was the story of a grown man loving a child but insisted it was about other things, such as Nabokov's love of the English language.)

In short, Mann's fantasy is not my fantasy. After gay liberation, and especially after AIDS, I don't need death to romanticize gay love or offset homosexual guilt. For me it's just death kitsch, a sentimental lie. I was confused when people compared my novel *Father of Frankenstein* (1995) and the movie made from it, *Gods and Monsters* (1999), with *Death in Venice*. I know they found the literary comparison useful. But my protagonist, James Whale, does not feel guilty about being gay. He does not need death to free him. He hates death. He's been living in the shadow of death since the First World War. Death is now inevitable after his stroke. He wants a human death, a death with a human face, which is why he turns to his yard man. It's a mad desire and he knows it's mad. Maybe I only turned the old trope inside out—it is a potent trope—but I badly wanted to escape the old sentimental lie.

Death in Venice is a book one would love to rewrite, scraping away the death kitsch and keeping the good, sharp Chekhov story underneath. A movie adaptation could do this. Luchino Visconti had a chance in his 1971 film. Happily, the gay filmmaker had worked through the self-hating politics of *The Damned* (*La caduta degli dei*, 1969), where decadence and homosexuality somehow lead to Nazis. Because he was making a movie, Visconti dropped most of Mann's high culture nonsense—the fever dream and ancient Greeks and Asian tigers of illness—and focused on the simple spectacle of a solitary man visiting Venice in 1911. Unfortunately he made Aschenbach a Mahler-like composer and added flashbacks where he and a Schoenberg-like rival debate theories of music. The ideas seem to be drawn from Mann's later novel, *Doctor Faustus* (1947), but they add nothing to the story. The scenes come and go without logic or visual rhythm. God knows what ended up on the cutting room floor.

But these dialogues are minor distractions. What really hurts the movie is the casting of Dirk Bogarde as Aschenbach. At this point in his career, Bogarde had played so many conscience-stricken mopes and decadent aesthetes—*Victim* (1961), *The Damned*, *Accident* (1967), *Modesty Blaise* (1966)—that there was no surprise or pathos when the proud, puritanical artist started to fall. The rot is already present the first time we see this prissy man clutching a briefcase. But what if Visconti had cast an actor like Max von Sydow? The handsome, long-faced Swede would have been convincingly austere, coolly elegant, proper to the point of pain—as Mann describes Aschenbach. There would have been real drama in seeing his moral rigidity relax, soften, then dissolve. The high and mighty figure would have passed through real emotions on his way to death, like a snowman turning briefly human before he melts away.

I've been reading and rereading Thomas Mann since high school. I still love *Buddenbrooks* (1901). I love most of *The Magic*

Mountain (*Der Zauberberg*, 1924). I find *Doctor Faustus* clunky and exasperating with its loony juxtapositions of syphilis, Satan, twelve-tone music, and Hitler. Talk about intellectual liverwurst. But for me *Death in Venice* is the most troubling work by Mann, both because more people read it than anything else he ever wrote, and because I cannot entirely dismiss it.

CHRISTOPHER BRAM is the author of nine novels, including *The Notorious Dr. August* (2000), *Exiles in America* (2006), and *Gods and Monsters* (formerly *Father of Frankenstein*, 1995), which was made into the Oscar-winning movie starring Ian McKellen (1999). He grew up in Virginia and lives in New York City. His most recent book is a collection of essays, *Mapping the Territory* (2009). Quotations are taken from Thomas Mann, *Death in Venice and Other Stories*, translated by David Luke (London: Bantam Books, 1988), which is currently in print.

THE FLOWER BENEATH
THE FOOT
(1923)

by Ronald Firbank

BRIAN BOULDREY

About twenty years ago, I was standing on a stepladder in the home of my ex-boyfriend's new boyfriend's mother. Don't do the math; it's perverse. Her name was Esther. She was a Jewish widow raised on a Nebraska homestead, a nurse who sewed up members of the Abraham Lincoln Brigade in the Spanish Civil War and a good old-fashioned Red, who married a McCarthy-ruined member of the American Communist Party. She'd lived from the 1950s at the sidelines of life, watching and reading the signs. We were the best of friends. Each Tuesday after work, I would go to her house, and she would make us a simple supper, and afterward, we would sort her magnificent collection of books so vast they were three-deep in the shelves. Esther sat in her rocking chair with a legal pad and a ball point pen, while I, perched high, read to her the titles and authors of her collection. She had no idea what she had.

An edition of Alexander Pushkin's *Eugene Onegin* (1825–32) in the original Russian, inscribed to Queen Victoria. Two novels by Elizabeth Bowen with bookplates stating they were from her own library. Privately printed smut from Oscar Wilde. An entire edition of Darwin translated into Yiddish. Norman Douglas's *South Wind* (1917) printed on blue linen, bound in eel skin. And then this—this!—a novel by Frederick Rolfe (aka "Baron Corvo"), *Hadrian the Seventh* (1904), about an Englishman, George Arthur Rose, who becomes Pope.

Hadrian the Seventh was part of the Blue Jade Library, a series of books published by Knopf in the 1920s "designed to cover . . . the field of the semi-classic, semi-curious book." These included titles like *The Wooings of Jezebel Pettyfer*, *The Adventures of Hajji Baba of Ispahan*, and *Travels in Tartary*. Esther had one other Blue Jade volume, Ronald Firbank's *The Flower beneath the Foot*, published in 1923. Esther, my aged, sidelined friend, scribbled down these titles as I read them, and mildly cajoled me to keep up with my task, for she had fed me a decent meal earlier and I was to earn my keep up there on the ladder, compiling the list of books she'd eventually sell off in order to finance the handicap-accessible room she would need for the last five years of her life, this being the first of those five.

"What in the world is this?" I asked Esther from my perch, finally breaking down, having wasted valuable cataloguing time reading the first page of *The Flower Beneath the Foot* out loud to us both.

I can't help thinking, now, that this was a setup. She knew I would find this book there on the top shelf, two-deep, fifth from the end. Esther knew that she had found another who would watch from the margins, a kindred spirit. "Oh, that weirdo," she said. She told me some details of Firbank's life, a sort of Little Lord Fauntleroy who lived in the nicest suites of Europe's luxury hotels, survived for months on a diet of nothing but peaches and champagne, composed all of his novels on the backs of postcards, impressed his acquaintances (at least two Waughs, a Huxley or so, and a handful of Sitwells) as the most sickly timid pantywaist that Edwardian England could breed; and yet, for all of that, Firbank tirelessly traveled the world and, being neither fish nor fowl, as much in the margins as Esther or myself, manifested in his novels a vision of a world in which everybody was silly—not just him. "You should keep that one," said Esther. "Enjoy!"

That night, I climbed into the bathtub, lit a couple of candles, and became, accidentally, a character in the novel I was reading: "Lying amid the dissolving bath crystals while his manservant deftly bathed him, he fell into a sort of coma, sweet as a religious trance. Beneath the rhythmic sponge, perfumed with *Kiki*, he was St. Sebastian, and as the water became cloudier, and the crystals evaporated amid the steam, he was Teresa."

I read until dawn the story (in the case of Firbank, that word, "story," like "theme," "baroque" and "satire" confines his work to an irrelevant regularity) of the courtesan Mademoiselle de Nazianzi who loves, in vain, the handsome Prince Yousef ("He has such strength! One could niche an idol in his clear, dinted chin"), the dauphin and next-in-line to reign over some unnamed Balkan nation. She is inexorably led, by every despairingly comic scene, toward the nun's habit. I'm puzzled, wondering why nobody has composed music for a light opera version of *The Flower Beneath the Foot* with choruses of brides and grooms and nuns and priests, full of mistaken identities, disguises, overheard gossip, and mis-heard murmurings, recitative and pitched, congested emotional states, and—my favorite of all—unearned moments of forgiveness, of resolution, of merry naughtiness that somehow build from the ridiculous toward the sublime.

Now, I am not just a homosexual; I am an *American* homosexual. The first novel I wrote was a mandatory coming-of-age story, the *Bildungsroman* being not just part of the gay literary tradition, but the American literary tradition, which, I think in convenient hindsight, is merely or only focused on the building of character. The coming-of-age subject gives novelists an excuse for avoiding shape in their novels because it looks or seems "honest"; the meandering of a life toward some place, which is usually the end of the novel. Consider Twain's Huck Finn, Salinger's Holden Caulfield, and every roadie movie ever made. To stumble upon a novelist like Firbank made me, at first, suspicious; not because he describes characters who speak in nothing but punctuation marks (one courtier gossips, after mishearing His Weariness The King, that "Fleas have been found at the Ritz," and the second courtier eloquently replies, ". . . ! . . . ? . . . !!"), are born in The Land of Dates and have names like the Honorable Lionel Limpness, or Lady Something, or Madame Wetme (who worships the god "Chic," "a cruel God"). What stunned me was the mannerist approach to plot. I could only compare our shapeless, antistructured novels to this heavily structured funhouse made of cards. Postcards, to be precise.

Detachment is the genius of Firbank's fiction. His characters are all seen at once, and even all their interactions now and in the future are a solved puzzle in the end, which I mean in a gratifying and guileless way, rather than a predictable one. I think seeing Firbank use disastrous dinner parties, restoration comedy bedroom scenes with trapdoors and funhouse mirrors, creaky attics full of secrets, and cloisters full of disappointed nuns and priests may seem weird to serious American readers—myself included—who like our "honest" autobiographical shapelessness. I think we're so used to novels being *about* an education rather than being products *of* them. Firbank strikes me as the opposite of that; trying to get above all that human scene, in order to see.

And this, I learned from Firbank, is my own true task as a gay writer. I have been alarmed of late to hear from some colleagues that it is necessary for gay writers to put aside all these rococo chamber novels and write epic tales full of shameful tragedy and humorless chronologies of unremitting victimhood. Firbank is not interested in that stuff, and neither am I. His are comedies—in the truest, Aristotelian sense of that word. Aristotle's idea is that comedy is "an imitation of men worse than the average; worse, however, not as regards any and every sort of fault, but only as regards one particular kind, the Ridiculous . . ." Aristotle defines the Ridiculous as "a mistake or deformity not productive of pain or harm to others." Unlike tragedy, the comic mode proposes that such enslavements are more ridiculous than fatal, and comedy holds out the hope that a new arrangement of society may provide some relief. Yes, comic plots tend to be the most artificial, and arbitrary plot seems to win over consistency of character. But that's because the purpose of a comedy is to improve the culture, rather than improve an individual.

And, that, I think, would be the best thing we gay writers—we gay *gays*—can do to the larger culture: improve it by increasing its scope of manners. In fact, until the 1980s, that is the only thing gay writers *could* do. We showed the world from outside looking in, from our marginal corners, where we could see more. Early gay publishing was not about identity, but individuals swimming in a world that made us feel like monsters. And what fiction is woefully missing, these days, is monsters.

The tragedy of gay writing is that it has been commodified, placed front and center, rather than in the margins, where we have always had a better view. Now we are paid to view ourselves, rather than the world. And if you ask me, the difference between saying "I am interested" and "I am interesting" is the difference between being a hero (albeit a comic hero) and a villain. Firbank's was not a self-absorbed view (at least not on the page), but a view of the world that is so extremely queered that when an ordinary thing, an un-different thing, shows up in his novels—a telephone; a newspaper subscription—it shocks us readers, as if we've found a John Deere tractor in the hut of an Amazonian cannibal. "'With us there are no utensils,' murmured the Queen of the Land of Dates." There's a lot of murmuring in Firbank's novels, and therefore a lot that is misheard. "'I couldn't be more surprised,' responded the King, 'if you had told me that fleas had been found at the Ritz.'"

Oh, we would all like to burn with that hard gemlike flame of diamonds. But not everybody gets to be a diamond. Ronald Firbank is not a diamond; he is semiprecious Blue Jade. Blue Jade, as you can figure, is a gem, but not the usual sort—not as valuable, no, and not as common, either, because it's not as often mined. There are more diamond rings among us than there are netsuke carved from blue jade, for there is supply, and there is demand. This is not to say that blue jade is any less beautiful to the eye than a diamond. In fact, I find its hue much more enjoyable than colorless adamant. But I am in the margins, with my own baroque tastes. I have, in the twenty years since I sat at the top of that ladder, reading rarified titles to Esther (gone now, I'm sad to say, for more than fifteen years, but still a love of my life, if of the semi-precious sort), climbed up on other people's ladders and collected up the entire Blue Jade Library, and every now and then I'll draw a bath, ask my manservant to bathe me deftly, and then open up a copy of *The Diabolical Women* or the comte de Villiers de l'Isle Adam's *Cruel Tales* (*Contes cruels*, 1883), or something else by Ronald Firbank, like *Concerning the Eccentricities of Cardinal Pirelli* (1926) or *The Artificial Princess* (1915).

Did you know that a duck's quack cannot generate an echo? Scientists don't know why. There are certain writers that remind me of ducks: true, vital, amusing, oddly serene on the surface while chugging away with powerful webbed feet. But their voices will not resonate the way a moose or a wolf might spook us with their reverberant calls, as we ride our troika recklessly over the moonlit steppe of life. Still, ducks can make a difference to an ecosystem. Says Eliot Vereker, a Firbankian antihero in James Thurber's "Something to Say" (1932): "Proust has weight—he's a ton of feathers!" As a writer and reader in a life of ponderous responsibilities and grim experience, I can only bear to lift or foist this sort of weight. It seems immoral to force more tragedy on the world. I endeavor to live by those memorable, if not merely murmured, words of Mademoiselle de Nazianzi: "'O! help me, heaven,' she prayed, 'to be decorative and to do right!'"

Yes—and in that order.

BRIAN BOULDREY is the author of six books—most recently, *Honorable Bandit: a Walk Across Corsica* (2007)—and the editor of six anthologies, including the *Best American Gay Fiction* series. He lives in Chicago, and teaches literature and writing at Northwestern University and teaches at Lesley University's MFA in Creative Writing. Ronald Firbank's *The Flower Beneath the Foot* is out of print, but widely available in his *Five Novels* (New York: New Directions, 1950/61/81).

MRS. DALLOWAY
(1925)

by Virginia Woolf

JANE DELYNN

When I was young and naive, in the 1960s, I thought I was the only female in the world who wanted to have sex with a woman. When I say "the world," I mean that of middle-class, bourgeois people like my parents and their friends who lived on the Upper East Side of New York. A world that included my fellow (long have I yearned for a female counterpart of this word!) students at Barnard College, a Seven Sisters school across the street from the then all-male Columbia. No one like me at any other Seven Sister school either! No college at all for that matter! Nobody I could conceivably run into in New York City!—the United States!—the world!

Of course I knew lesbians existed. I had read Radclyffe Hall's *The Well of Loneliness* (1928), the only lesbian novel I'd heard of. (I would have read others had I known they existed.) The rather one-dimensional character of Stephen, an upper middle-class Englishwoman who cross-dresses, attends a lesbian salon in Paris, drives an ambulance during World War I, receives the *Croix de Guerre,* and even more heroically renounces her lover in order to let her live "a more complete and normal existence"—was no one I could relate to. I also eagerly devoured the (very few) nonfiction books I found in libraries or bookstores about "perversion" or "inversion." (Trade paperbacks were relatively new, so far fewer books were published then than now.) But these were texts written by medical professionals or sociologists, with an unquestioned assumption that such activities were a sign of moral depravity, mental illness, or both. "Invert" females in these books were either women who lived life as a man—"stone butches" who bound their breasts, wore suits and ties and oxford shoes, their hair cropped short so they could "pass" in their jobs— or femmes somehow conned into the lifestyle or too unattractive to appeal to men.

In that androgynous era, I could not identify with either of these types. I wore jeans, like everyone I knew; I wanted both to touch and be touched. High heels, heavy makeup, and role-playing seemed oh-so-fifties. There were class differences too— women in these books seemed only to have jobs as waitresses or bartenders or truck drivers. At night they hung out in bars where jealous fistfights frequently erupted; spurned by their families, they were subject to constant harassment and arrest. I knew I could never live in that world. I was not tough enough to reject everything and everyone I knew, nor did I want to. No one in these books resembled the kind of person I considered myself to be: ironic, intellectual, vaguely hip in a sixties sort of way; "normal," save for my desperate—I seemed to think about sex about 90 percent of the time—cravings.

I had had sex with one woman my senior year in high school—an English teacher twice my age. I was overwhelmed with guilt and isolation, for I couldn't be sure even my closest friends would keep my secret. My shrink was scarcely a help, declaring that sex with my teacher was "too disgusting to talk about." So apparently unspeakable were my actions that when my parents discovered a love letter from the teacher, they were unable to talk about it to me directly, but used the shrink as intermediary.

The traumatic reaction to the affair added shame to my guilt, and I considered it quite likely I'd pass the rest of my life without ever again having sex with a woman. Perhaps, if I were lucky, there'd be an occasional encounter with a stranger—most likely in a bathroom, for this was where the books said homosexuals hung out. I spent much of one summer wandering around Central Park, with an occasional stop in the ladies' room of the then usually empty Metropolitan Museum, giving "meaningful looks" to women who seemed *sympatique*, with no response save the occasional odd stare. On a really optimistic day, I'd fantasize about a woman I could have sex with in the afternoons while our husbands were off at work.

Through literature, I had heard of Gertrude Stein and Alice B. Toklas, of Natalie Barney and Romaine Brooks, Sylvia Beach and Adrienne Monier, Radclyffe Hall and Una Troubridge. But these were women wealthy enough to live where and how they pleased, proud rather than otherwise of their cross-dressing and other eccentricities. They belonged to another continent and time, for World War II seemed to have put an end to this aristocratic lesbianism. Even if that world still existed, there was no way I—middle-class and utterly without style—could have joined it.

My teacher was educated, middle-class, and Jewish like me. She was also overweight, unattractive, and badly dressed, her saving grace a charisma felt not only by me. (More than one classmate was jealous of what was assumed to be our "friend-ship.") Hardly a role model, this thirty-eight-year-old woman had had only three relationships before me: two with other high school students; one with someone in college. None of these had lasted as long as a year. Overcome with shame, she'd spent almost ten years (rather pointlessly) in psychoanalysis. At least the bull dykes had some fun.

Then, in my junior year in college, my addled brain was exposed to Virginia Woolf's *Mrs. Dalloway*. It's impossible to conceive of now, but in 1968 Woolf had yet to have a biography written about her. The first appeared in 1972, written by her nephew, Quentin Bell. (Similarly, Bloomsbury *qua* Bloomsbury only came into existence with the publication in 1967–68 of Michael Holroyd's biography of Lytton Strachey.) Virginia Woolf was so far off the charts that when I went to the Iowa Writer's Workshop in the fall of 1968, I discovered to my aston-ishment that almost none of my professors—let alone "fellow" students—had read her.

At Barnard, literature was taught from the fading perspective of New Criticism. One discussed the work and not the writer— let alone the social and political context of the writer's world. All I knew of Woolf was that her writing was considered man-nered and obscure, and that she had drowned herself in the River Ouse by putting stones in her pockets (an act inconceiv-able, once you have seen that tiny stream in person). And—oh, yes—to my mind she was the greatest novelist (hence writer) who had ever lived.

I thought this for many reasons: this book was compelling despite the absence of what is normally considered "plot"; metaphors that for once seem real, not forced; the way the trivial and profound, past and present, overwhelming joy and unspeakable sorrow were jumbled together in the mind (sometimes even within the same sentence) of a character who seemed—despite living in an era that no longer existed, in a world so different from mine—the first I could truly understand. And I don't mean just in fiction, but in "real life" too, where the brains of others seemed so alien and incomprehensible that even as a child I felt I had to hide my real self. I did this by creating a persona that attempted to mimic others' interests and concerns— not from the inside out, as a Method actor would have done (it was the insides I didn't understand), but from the outside in, like a classically trained actor. This persona became so ingrained I often forgot I was playing a role. But at times the edifice would collapse, and I'd be overcome with exhaustion and emptiness. Like a spy, I had to be in character 24/7, only presumably for a lifetime.

Mrs. Dalloway validated the world inside my head. Isolated I might be, but at least I was no longer alone.

What grabbed me most, though, was The Sentence. Clarissa is thinking about the long-ago summer when she got engaged. But it is not the engagement she recalls, but "the most exquisite moment of her whole life . . . [when] Sally stopped; picked a flower; kissed her on the lips." Despite her almost thirty-year marriage, with a beautiful daughter, a houseful of servants, and a social status sufficiently elevated that the prime minister bothers to make an appearance at her party, the memory of that time retains its power, when "if it were now to die 'twere now to be most happy' . . . all because she was coming down to dinner in a white frock to meet Sally Seton!"

I considered that the most important sentence I ever read. For I, too, had had my Kiss—from a teacher, as I stood in a doorway, marveling as a new world opened up. I had never met anyone as enchanting as Woolf's sylph-like Sally Seton, but that didn't prevent me from declaiming Romantic poetry by the hour as I dreamed of the more commonplace mortals who at various times filled my heart. And though I never had sex with any of these women save my teacher—no more than Clarissa Dalloway had with Sally—I, too, thought of these crushes as "love," utterly unrelated to the relationships I had with men.

Forget New Criticism. Clarissa Dalloway might have been married, might never have had intimate contact with a woman, but I knew that only a person who felt the way I did could have written those sentences about her. The greatest writer in the world was a lesbian too, if only in her soul.

Also, unlike the elegant Parisian cross-dressers I could never have imagined knowing, Clarissa Dalloway was in some sense an "ordinary" person—full of small vanities, petty snobberies, and silly fits of jealousy. Like my mother, her greatest happiness was in the company of others, with days spent in a manner not all that different from my mother's either—albeit in a sphere of much greater culture, wealth, and social connections.

And it was not just Clarissa's sexual feelings that were similar to mine, but the way those feelings manifested themselves in our lives. A bad heart gave Clarissa a welcome excuse to have a separate bedroom from her husband's—as well as a permanent respite from a sexual intimacy that could not penetrate her "cold spirit" or "dispel a virginity preserved through childbirth." I had sex with men and pretended I enjoyed it (and on rare occasions I did)—but it was mostly something I did to "prove" I was normal, and I usually tried to get it over with as quickly as possible. I understood Clarissa's choice of the dull but trustworthy Richard Dalloway over the more passionate and interesting (but emotionally volatile and relentlessly intrusive) Peter Walsh. I, too, had a boring, obtuse boyfriend attending college a convenient eight hundred miles away, while back home I dated far savvier and sensitive guys—until they sensed something hidden within me that I would not share, and frustration would tear the relationship apart.

The Sally Seton moments in *Mrs. Dalloway* are few and far between, and hardly the center of the story. One can argue that I read the book less as reader than detective. But Woolf's biography made it clear my intuitions were correct: she loved women, chose as husband a dependable (if more prosaic) man than her more scintillating but fickle friends, insisted on her own bedroom, and never lost that prudery; even with women, her relationships were more emotional than sexual.

Seen through the lens of today, *Mrs. Dalloway* is a very un-PC book, its central figure a "closet case" who represses her deepest feelings to conform to society. It represents everything the gay movement is against, even if its author led a life somewhat more liberated than that of her character. Its coded hints of lesbianism are reminiscent of the ways homosexuals used to signal their preferences to each other in a manner both public and invisible to all but themselves. (No doubt such signals are still used in societies where homosexuality is forbidden.)

Not surprisingly, it is *Orlando* (1928), Woolf's homage to Vita Sackville-West, which is generally considered Woolf's "lesbian" novel. But I have never been able to read more than a few pages of that fanciful book, finding it overwrought and uninteresting. That would have been even truer of the person I was in 1967, when, like most people, I tried to accommodate myself to the world as it was, rather than how I wished it might be. At a time when gay bars were routinely busted, faggots put in jail, or even (in seven states) legally castrated, the idea that homosexuality could be accepted by society—let alone sanctified by marriage—a mere forty years later would have seemed as contrived and implausible as *Orlando*. The most I hoped for then was to find someone I could relate to—if only in my head. *Mrs. Dalloway* gave me that, for which—amongst its many other gifts—I will always be grateful.

JANE DELYNN is author of the novels *Leash* (2002), *Don Juan in the Village* (1990), *Real Estate* (1988), *In Thrall* (1982), and *Some Do* (1978), and the collection *Bad Sex Is Good* (1998). Her work has been translated into German, French, Norwegian, Spanish, and Japanese. Virginia Woolf's *Mrs. Dalloway* is available in many editions.

TIME REGAINED

(LE TEMPS RETROUVÉ)

(1927)

by Marcel Proust

FELICE PICANO

I n a way, it comes back to those famous photos of the author: the deep-set eyes appearing bruised, as though from seeing far too much for his sensitivity; the complexion that even in black-and-white looks sallow, yellow, unhealthy to the touch. What nowadays is referred to by Fashionistas as "heroin chic." My first thought was "God, what a degenerate!" Then I read a bit about his life and realized he was increasingly ill, as he aged with worsening asthma that couldn't be controlled as anyone's can today with an over-the-counter inhaler. No, Proust had to lie in bed, unmoving, for hours, in a cork-lined room, as dust and noise and soot and allergy proofed as money could make it.

I first read *Swann's Way* (*Du côté de chez Swann*, 1913) in the summer of my seventeenth year. I would take that fat Modern Library edition of the Scott Moncrieff translation with me everywhere that Manhattan summer. I was attending Queens College, City University of New York, a free school not then under open admissions with a tight student body of forty-five hundred. We had to sustain a B-average and pass a "Comprehensive Examination" to move into sophomore year. Proust, Tolstoy's stories, and Melville's novellas were on my summer reading list.

It took me about ten tries to get into the "Overture," which I finally accomplished on a sizzling August afternoon, shaded by trees at the south end of the lake at Central Park. Only once I felt utterly debilitated did I give into Proust's endless sentences. But once inside the book, I didn't look back. *Swann's Way* was rejected by all publishers, and so printed by Grasset at the author's cost. Declining it, André Gide commented: "Too many Duchesses!" Yet if Proust had never written anything else, he would have made it into the pantheon of great writers.

Five years later, I came upon the two-volume Random House set of *Remembrance of Things Past* (as *A la recherche du temps perdu* was then known in translation; later, it would be more accurately rendered as *In Search of Lost Time*) in Strand Books. I read volume two—*A l'ombre des jeunes filles en fleurs*, or *In the Shadow of Young Girls in Flower* (to translate from the French directly; though Scott Moncrieff had called it *Within a Budding Grove*, 1919). It's a painterly book, impressionistic, almost purposely nondramatic, with characters—Marcel's grandmother, Bloch, Elstir, Vinteuil, Morel, Albertine—receiving a few new brushstrokes every time we meet them. Marcel's descriptions of his hotel room at sunset, while he's supposed to be napping at the seashore in Balbec, vary slightly daily, reminding me of all those Monet haystack paintings, one bluer, one more violet, one almost orange, etc.

Third is *The Guermantes Way* (*Le Côté de Guermantes*, 1920/21), with its hundred-page-long afternoon party, which, in effect, provides the historical and social background of the whole edifice. The Guermantes family comes to prominence here, as well as the opinionated Baron de Charlus. A new character, Robert de St. Loup, becomes Marcel's ideal young man. Well connected, regal, courteous: a white knight. I wanted him as I guessed Marcel did, and meant me to. The Proust scholar George Stambolian nearly threw me out of his car on the way to Amagansett when I casually remarked that as a writer I could see "all the lumber and nails" in that party scene. Critics are so touchy!

Sodome et Gomorrhe (coyly rendered by Scott Moncrieff as *Cities of the Plain*, 1921/22) is of course queer, and Baron de Charlus dominates this volume with his opposite (and pimp? boyfriend?), the femme tailor Jupien. Lots of lesbianism emerges too. I didn't read it until long after the Stonewall Riots, and then I had to take Proust's "theories of homosexuality" with many grains of salt.

La prisonnière (*The Captive*, 1923) and *La fugitive* (*The Fugitive*, 1925) follow. They concern jealousy, guilt, and sexual obsession, not one of which has ever interested me. But there were some good scenes between what Proust thought was the meat of those books, concerning the minor characters. Reading that Albertine was based on Proust's boyfriend, the dandy composer Reynaldo Hahn, and on a far more butch Italian chauffeur, Agostino, helped somewhat. But what did intrigue me is how suddenly in these novels we are in the twentieth century: with telephones and automobiles and airplanes, and, most memorably, zeppelins lighting the night skies of Paris during World War I, on the lookout for any invasive German Fokkers or Messerschmitt biplanes. Proust used several of these inventions in his plotting. Albertine gets into what may be the first auto accident in literature.

But it wasn't until last year, forty-four years after I first began reading Proust, that I read the last novel in the series, and now I really have to write it: God, what a degenerate he was!

The title, *Le temps retrouvé*, means what exactly? Scott Moncrieff's successors, Mayor and Kilmartin, used *Time Regained*; the newest translation has *Finding Time Again*. *The Past Recovered* is about the closest I've come, "retrouvé" being used for something that's lost and now found. Yet this last book is the only *contemporary* one in the series. It's set when? 1918–1921. The war is over. People are bobbing their hair and shortening their skirts. Proust would die in 1922, with five volumes unpublished but "in the pipeline." So that's weirdness number one: he's spent six volumes recapturing the past and it's now the present. Why name the book *Le temps retrouvé*? Was he boasting? "Look guys, I've recaptured the past," like no one else ever even tried?

Or was it, as I have begun to think, something else?

I once met a solid older author and admired a novel of his, then added, "It's elegant and so well-written, but am I the only one to find your book cruel and vengeful?" The author was elated. I *was* the only one, he said, and boy was I right, he added. He'd finally gotten back at his father, his mother, his brothers . . . The rest of our conversation was expletives. We never really know why anyone ever writes a book.

I've begun to think that Proust wrote—in his mind, if not all on paper—*Le temps retrouvé* first, and then was more or less forced to become a great novelist and to spend much of the last dozen years of his life writing those previous six volumes, in order to justify this book. Why? Because on the face of it, the last volume is really radical, really queer, and really—sick. And not in an asthmatic way, either.

Sure it's got those gorgeous moments: the moment in Venice when Marcel hits the two uneven paving stones, and remembers the past again—recapitulating the scene with the *Madeleine* dipped in a *tisane* in *Swann's Way*.

And this, the final sentence of the entire book, which no one else in history could have written: "So, if I were given long enough to accomplish my work, I should not fail, even if the effect were to make them resemble monsters, to describe men as occupying so considerable a place, compared with the restricted place which is reserved for them in space, a place on the contrary prolonged past measure for simultaneously, like giants plunged into the years, they touch the distant epochs through which they have lived, between which so many days have come to range themselves—in Time."

But it's actually a depressing book. The narrator, Marcel, is just out of a sanitarium, and only somewhat recovered. He returns to the seaside hotel of his youth and what does he see? Robert de Saint-Loup (Saint and Wolf), the supposed French epitome of heterosexuality, hitting on a male elevator operator. That imposing figure, the Baron de Charlus, needs two canes to walk he's so fat and sick, and he is being helped by Jupien's nephew. Everyone is old, fat, sick, or dead. The artist Elstir, hailed as a master, is now written off as a nobody. The dowdy music teacher Vinteuil is now a genius: his sonata conquers the recital halls. Morel, a former nobody, has bisexually social-climbed into being the violinist of the age. Gilberte, Swann's daughter by the arriviste Odette ("She wasn't even my type!", the intellectual moans) is now married to Saint-Loup, and so a half Jewess is the new Duchess de Guermantes, while the bourgeois Mme. Verdurin, always on the edge of caricature, is now a Guermantes princess! No one escapes the dissolution, the decay, the despair, the death's heads all about. And anyone not dead is revealed as a closeted homosexual.

Still, the section for me—and for the gay reader—that's most modern, and that I think may have been the reason for the entire 3,200 pages, comes when the narrator's car breaks down and his driver places his sick master out of the cold rain. Where? Into the kitchen of a house of male prostitutes, where working-class men nightlight: flogging the upper crust until they reach orgasm, and then laughing as they spill out the details around the table later. It's so shocking still, ninety years after it was written, that you just know Proust knew he'd never see it published in his lifetime. And it's so total a collapse of everything that preceded it. I believe that he really needed to "set it up" as he did, with six previous volumes; the way one explains in excessive detail a traumatic event, or the way one over-explicates a half-lie.

My recommendation if you've not read Proust (or only *Swann's Way*) is to begin (again) with *Le temps retrouvé* because immediately after reading it you will be impelled to go back to the beginning and read the whole novel (again). I was.

And so Proust's novel becomes for the reader what I'm increasingly certain it always was for the author: not a series of anything, but instead a looping back again and again to various scattered scenes as he lay in bed gasping for air. It's reminiscent of Borges's revelation concerning the six-hundred-and-something-th story of *The Arabian Nights*, where someone begins to tell the story of the King and Scheherazade that began it all, all over again. If followed through, that book would then go on forever, never ending.

Le temps retrouvé, then, is a great way to enter this infinite loop, this Proustian infinitely repeating universe.

FELICE PICANO is the author of many best-selling, prize-winning, mainstream, and gay-themed stories, poems, essays, novellas, memoirs, plays, and works of nonfiction. Along with Edmund White and Andrew Holleran, his colleagues in The Violet Quill, he received the 2009 Lambda Literary Foundation's Pioneer Award. Quotations are taken from the 1992 revised, updated edition of the Scott Moncrieff and Kilmartin translation: namely, Marcel Proust, *In Search of Lost Time, volume six: Time Regained* (New York: Random House Modern Library, 1999), translated by Andreas Mayor and Terence Kilmartin and revised and edited by D. J. Enright, which is currently in print.

MORE WOMEN THAN MEN
(1933)

by Ivy Compton-Burnett

LISA COHEN

"It must be a great thing in a life like this, such a friendship."

"Yes," said Miss Munday, stirring the cup and then raising her eyes. "It must."

"Are you interested in different human relationships?" said Mrs. Chattaway, on a more urgent note.

"Yes," said Miss Munday.

"You are interested in abstract theories, I am sure," said Mrs. Chattaway, with compliment. "But some human relationships, that arise out of certain conditions, are worthy of attention."

"Yes," said Miss Munday.

"Both Miss Luke and Miss Rosetti have great gifts for intimacy."

"Yes, they have," said Miss Munday.

There is the tradition of overheated, satisfying books about girls falling in love at school: girls making each other melt in the semiprivacy of a toilet stall; girls understanding literature and desire for the first time through the kind offices of a distant or proximate teacher. *More Women than Men* is not that. For one thing, it is all about the teachers. We hardly glimpse a student in this novel. For another—as in all Ivy Compton-Burnett's work— language is the main character. Compton-Burnett's novels are full of melodramatic plot twists, but the real drama is not in what happens but in how the characters converse; how the writer scrupulously uses the aggressive and analytical qualities of apparently polite speech to show off the unscrupulous behavior of intimates.

The idea is the emotional heat that emanates from the icy surfaces of talk. In the scene that follows that conversation over tea, Miss Rosetti and Miss Luke's "great gifts for intimacy" are on display, as the former handles the latter in a show of linguistic banality and erotic and institutional force:

> "The new young woman is along the corridor, is she not?" said Miss Luke.
>
> "I hope so, as that was the direction you gave her."
>
> "Is not her room the next but one to mine, next door to yours?"
>
> "I hope so again, as that is what you said," said Miss Rosetti, pushing the other against the wall, and looking into her face.

Push against any one of Compton-Burnett's sentences and you will find her already there, exerting her own pressure. No utterance is left alone: Her characters constantly reflect on and correct each other's choice of words. Cliché produces philological, philosophical, and psychological inquiry, as they argue about the meaning of idioms and the possibility of meaning itself.

For Compton-Burnett, the point of pushing language against the wall is also to push against those in power—in this novel, the headmistress of the school, the toxically benevolent Josephine Napier, whom one character calls "powerful for both good and bad." This pressure on the artifices of language is also related to Compton-Burnett's focus on the idea of "naturalness," a subject the characters in *More Women than Men* discuss nonstop. They wonder incessantly about the bounds of unconventional and conformist behavior—in language, work, and love—as well as about whom they wish to spend time with. More women, or men?

Critics of Compton-Burnett's early work, including this 1933 novel, "found her tone indefinably suspect," notes her biographer Hilary Spurling (*Ivy: the Life of Ivy Compton-Burnett* [1984]). There is what you might call an atmosphere of homosexuality in some of these books, and "tone" has something to do with it: a scrutiny of surfaces and flippant and serious play with paradox that recalls Wilde. Felix Bacon, the drawing instructor at Josephine Napier's school, speaks of his "whimsical side" and attitude of "limpness," and he is constantly interpreting his clothing to others. He says: "It is little, unnatural corners of the world that appeal to me. I am very over-civilised." If his language has some affinities with euphemism, the scenes in which he sits on the knee of the man he lives with eschew it. Some human relationships, that arise out of certain conditions, are worthy of attention.

Is a wedding a "natural" event? Compton-Burnett's pleasure is often to show how sibling or same-sex intimacy is sacrificed for the marriageable couple, and that plot is one strain of *More Women than Men*. But conventional couples are also in danger here; irritating partners of the opposite sex are repeatedly eliminated by sudden accident or fatal illness. Above all, nothing is settled; there is no such thing as "identity" in this fictional world. Felix Bacon, the character who seems most reliably "unnatural," turns out to be wedded to convention:

> "Ah, but the wedding-day is a great moment," said Miss Luke . . . "It must be the climax, the coping stone, the peak of youthful experience."
>
> "Oh, don't use the word 'climax,'" said Josephine. "It has such a suggestion of anti-climax. And we hope that things are not over for them yet."

Then there are the "quick, almost careless tones" of the words spoken by Miss Rosetti to Josephine at the end of the novel. Accepting the headmistress's offer of partnership in her school and life, Miss Rosetti says: "I have said that there is nothing to tell of my life, but there is one thing that I will tell . . . I have cared in my way for the women whom one by one I have tried to care for; and I have come without trying and almost without knowing to care the most for you." This is not euphemism, yet its circularity seems to make the avowal at once more emphatic and less direct. In response, Josephine makes a marriage vow of sorts: "'Then you are my partner,' she says, 'and I am yours; and we will live our partnership in our lives, observing it in thought and word and deed.'" (The narrator goes on: "Miss Rosetti knew that on some things there would be silence"—which may be, but there will probably be a lot of talking about that silence.) "We begin our new life from this moment," says Josephine. And Miss Rosetti replies: "It will easily cease to be new to me; it is my natural life; my happiness depends on women."

For over thirty years, Ivy Compton-Burnett's happiness depended on Margaret Jourdain, a furniture historian with whom she shared a long domestic and emotional arrangement, the probable, possible, or emphatically not sexual nature of which their friends argued about for decades. "Margaret and Ivy were both," notes Spurling, "unique, outside ordinary categories." Compton-Burnett might have agreed, but might also have said that there is nothing ordinary about any category, any assumption—linguistic, sexual, or otherwise. Jourdain could be disdainful of Compton-Burnett's "silly" books, and her coterie of young curators and historians of art and the decorative arts made up much of their social circle until Compton-Burnett's growing fame began to shift the balance, and more and more admiring young writers gathered around her, cherishing her toughness and support.

Compton-Burnett's own style in conversation did not always match the thorny obliquity of the dialogue in her novels. "He's getting married, like so many homos one knows," a friend once heard her say. "Come to tea," she said to her friend Madge Garland, the fashion writer, editor, and educator, "my lesbians are coming." This was in the 1950s and '60s, after Jourdain had died, and Garland had become one of her closest friends. She was referring to the writers Kay Dick and Kathleen Farrell. Madge Garland had lived with or been in love with women most of her life, and some of their mutual friends believed that Compton-Burnett fell in love with her. Compton-Burnett used these labels with a kind of thrill, but in her life as in this novel, the point was caring in one's way for the women whom, one by one, one tried to care for.

LISA COHEN's book on Madge Garland, Mercedes de Acosta, and Esther Murphy will be published by Farrar, Straus & Giroux. Her essays have appeared in *Ploughshares, The Boston Review, The Yale Review, Fashion Theory,* GLQ, and *Queer 13,* among other places. Ivy Compton-Burnett's *More Women than Men* is currently out of print, but was most recently published by London's Allison & Busby press in 1983.

POEMS

(1935 and later)

by Constantine Cavafy

DAVID PLANTE

I was made aware of the poetry of Constantine Cavafy by my Greek lover, Nikos Stangos, with whom I lived for forty years, and who died in 2004. Nikos translated poems by Cavafy, with some edits by the poet Stephen Spender, for a book of etchings by David Hockney, inspired by the poems. On our first meeting, he showed me the large book of etchings, some of naked young men, delineated in delicate lines, in bed together.

Nikos's translations of Cavafy's poetry are close to Cavafy's own originals: clear-minded and sensual, delicately clear-minded and delicately sensual, making of beautiful white flowers, of colored handkerchiefs, of a mirror hanging in the front hall reflecting the face of a beautiful youth, objects that subtly inspire the senses *and* the pensive too.

Nikos gave a lecture on Cavafy at the London Hellenic Society. The poet was born in Alexandria, Egypt, in 1863, to a well-off Constantinopolitan family. When, after his father's death, the family business went bankrupt, Cavafy's mother took him and his brothers to London and Liverpool. That failing, his adolescence was passed in Constantinople, and his adulthood back in Alexandria, which he thereafter hardly left and where he had a minor job in the Egyptian government's Irrigation Office. His first visit to Greece was in 1901 when he was thirty-eight years old, during which he kept an uneventful diary in English. Another two uneventful visits to Greece, and his last was when he was seventy, for medical reasons: a tracheotomy for cancer of the throat. He returned to Alexandria, where he died in 1933.

The educated Greeks of the diaspora of Asia Minor and Egypt were, Nikos said, not only cosmopolitan and, on the whole, well off. They also had a strong and justified sense of a national continuity with the past, and felt a direct link that went as far back as at least the Hellenistic period. Their attitude was imperial, not merely ethnic.

Through Stephen Spender, we knew W. H. Auden, who sometimes came to supper. He said to Nikos that, though he admired Cavafy's historical poems, he thought the erotic poems "kitsch." Though Nikos disagreed with Auden on a number of occasions—he became angry with him when Auden, after the dictatorship, said that, after all, Greece was a well-run and efficient country only under the Turks—he did not disagree with Auden's remark about the erotic poems.

Are they kitsch? Because inspired by fantasy?

The young male couples in his poems are fated to separate, to die, but never to grow old together, as if two men growing old together could not have been an inspiring fantasy for him. His young lovers *are* beautiful for him to be inspired, and to make sure they remained young, he made them separate while still young; he made them die young. This is fantasy.

There is no lasting love between Cavafy's lovers, but lust, as if he could not conceive of love lasting beyond lust, beyond the lustful impact of beauty. This is fantasy.

And outside his poem about the poor and debauched young man in a cinnamon-colored suit, almost in rags because of his debauchery, who, after a night of squalor, undresses at dawn to a body of Greek beauty to bathe in the sea—outside of that poem, what concern is it of Cavafy that this young man is morally and spiritually lost, and will die soon? There is almost a sense of Cavafy's manipulation of the sex of his beautiful young men as objects of sexual fantasy, a fantasy without responsibility, because the young men are, after all, of no consequence to life except as inspirations to poetry.

Cavafy relied, not on images, not on a pomegranate tree in blossom by a wall of stones and a view over the wall of the bright sea, but on language.

The Greek poet George Seferis wrote that his poetry was a plinth without a statue. The plinth was language, as if the gestures of the statue pointing to a picturesque olive tree, to a marble column fallen among chamomile, a poppy withered on a stone were what poetry *must* point to, to be poetry. There are few images in the poetry of Cavafy, and these rather generalized: a letter, a bed, a closed carriage, a portrait, a chandelier, and—perhaps the most particular—a Turkish rug, a wardrobe and mirror, and two yellow vases on a shelf, from "The Afternoon Sun."

At times his metaphors, so very rare, verge on the cliché: sapphire-blue eyes, eyes like grey opals.

And it happens often enough to be remarked that passages in his poems come across muddled in translation:

Ah, summer days of nineteen hundred and eight,
Aesthetically, the faded light brown suit
Is missing from your imagery.
("Days of 1908," translated by Evangelos Sachperoglou)

The Greek, here literally translated, is just as muddled:

Ah days of summer of nineteen hundred and eight,
From your imagery, aesthetically,
Is missing the much faded cinnamon-(colored) suit.

Is this clearer—my version, with liberties?:

Those summer mornings
Of nineteen hundred and eight,
Strip him, for beauty, of his faded brown suit.

But these muddled passages do not detract from the overall clarity, from the beauty of the Greek language he was so aware of as "elegant and musical" ("For Ammones, Who Died Aged 19, in 610"). Far beyond Cavafy's bringing together of the formal language—*katherevousa*—and the idiomatic language—*demotiki*—in his work, what gives his poetry its imperial timelessness, as timeless as an epigram from the Greek Anthology, is Cavafy's seeming to depersonalize his poetry—as unmistakably his as it is—and in depersonalizing it, raise it above personal fantasy.

This epigram from the Greek Anthology is not remote from the depersonalized sensibility of Cavafy:

Mindlessly as you go on your way,
When you see Thrason's tomb, stranger, stop and have pity.

The wonder is that his almost generalized style, his almost depersonalized style, should have such a specific effect, as in:

τ'ην λε πτ'η 'εμοπφιά
his delicate beauty

As if to keep attention on the writing itself, Cavafy did not want sex to be overt in his poetry, and in his poem "Whenever They Are Aroused," he admonishes poets to "stop . . . visions of the erotic" from entering their poems; and if that can't be done, to "infer the visions" into their poetry "whenever they're aroused—at night or in the brightness of the day."

By my count, there are only one or two poems set in Classical Greece (more in Homeric, Hellenic, Ptolemaic, Roman, Byzantine Greece, and in contemporary Alexandria), and perhaps it is an exaggeration of mine to make too much of, say, Plato in Cavafy's poetry. But I like to think that Cavafy's inferring sex was inspired by more than his being constrained by the "common morality" of his time from being overt; by, say, Plato's *Symposium*, in which Socrates seems to accept that Pausanias and Agathon are sexual lovers, though we have no idea in what way. Sex is left vague.

Unlike Cavafy, Socrates believes there must be something more lasting between lovers than sex, when, having been attracted to each other for sex, they, over time—and living together, sleeping together, with sex: oral?; anal?—rise in their love for each other above sex and earn their wings, the wings to take them to the highest level, the level from which they will look down at other lovers and inspire them to rise, too, from sex into pure love.

No, there is no lasting love in Cavafy, no rising through sexual love to pure love—except, in a way, there is: for if sex between Cavafy's lovers is left vague, it is as if the act of sex were evocative of something more, of a halo of sexual desire that, in its brightness, obscures the lovers in their sexual act, and remains after the sex, suspended over the bed even after they have left and gone their separate ways. There is, yes, sublimity in the recollection of the halo, however "debauched" the actual act—if the actual act is ever even referred to.

It takes a careful reading of the poetry to bring out the inferences that Cavafy admonished poets to limit the erotic vision to. What else can be meant, in the poem "Portrait of a 23-Year-Old, Painted by a Friend of the Same Age, an Amateur Artist," but oral sex in the last lines "His mouth and his lips, made for consummations of choice eroticism"? The lines are heavy and dull in translation, and only a little light and lilting in the Greek. In fact, Cavafy finds it awkward even to infer acts of sex that are too specific to be generalized. He wanted to keep sex vague.

In "A Young Man of Letters in His 24th Year," Cavafy invites the reader to understand what is inferred in the poem by a first line that is cumbersome both in Greek and any translation into English I know of. Evangelos Sachperoglou has: "Mind, henceforth work as best you can—" I infer that the reader is meant to see that of two lovers, one is obsessed with having anal sex with the other, who, allowing kisses and fondling, refuses; which refusal causes the one obsessed, his love unconsummated, to have a breakdown. I suggest as a first line: "Let me try to figure this out," which is not, after all, difficult. The surprise is that Cavafy *does* refer to specific acts of sex. But the overall effect is of sex made hauntingly vague.

I offer this version of the poem:

Let me try to figure this out—
His pleasure in love is only half
And he longs for love to be whole,
Is desperate for love to be whole.
Yes, his would-be lover gives into his kisses day after day,
Yes, at night his would-be lover gives him the pleasure of
his body in his arms,
But though he has never before desired so passionately,
His lover denies him consummate love, aberrant to him,
But not to his lover.
His obsession unnerves him.
He's lost his job, borrows money, at times almost begs.
All he has is: kisses, the body of his would-be lover—
This lover only consenting to be kissed, to be held,
For whatever pleasure his lover allows him in kisses, in
holding his body.
His pleasure unfulfilled, he drinks and smokes, smokes
and drinks,
All day in and out of coffee houses,
Feeling his beauty is wasted—
Try to figure this out.

Yes, Cavafy's most often-used expressions of sex are generalized: "sensual pleasure," "sensual bliss," "lustful passion," "fateful
pleasure"—which in a lesser writer would come across as banal.
But in Cavafy these have a curious tension to them, as if the tension were between the general and an elusive particular; between
the impersonal and the personal.

What gives the tension of particularity to these generalizations? Is it caused by the irony Cavafy is known for, irony that always undercuts the general for some particular but, yes, elusive revision of the received idea? Cavafy's poetry is so often too close to the received idea, as in his early "philosophical" poem about Time repeating itself monotonously. In later poems, the irony is more and more evident—at least among Cavafy's historical poems, in which the irony often seems a separate comment about vanity, vain hopes, vain desires, and vain power. But—and I'd like to stress this—in his erotic poems, irony seems to be one with the twang of longing his poetry arouses. Ah, the longing! Ah, to drink a herbal concoction made by Greco-Syrian magicians that would bring back the room one made love in with one's long-lost lover! This *is* fantasy. But fantasy is belied. The reader knows that all the most passionate memories of sensual pleasure, sensual bliss, lustful passion, fateful pleasure—and how many of the erotic poems have to do with memory!—are fantastic memories. The irony is that Cavafy allows the reader to indulge in sexual fantasy, and at the same time, by his undercutting, he lets the reader know that this *is* fantasy. (It occurs to me that there is in the reverberant twang aroused by Cavafy's poetry a vibration of longing for consummation of love in death, or at least in love fated to end tragically; to make sexual love no longer a reality, but a memory to be contemplated with the longing for high drama; for grand nostalgia. Cavafy at times just about escapes this danger.) Oh, but yet, the fantasy does cause that twang!

What about fantastical "Beauty," beauty capitalized? Doesn't this cry out for irony to excuse it? What irony? I try to think of the bodies of Cavafy's beautiful young men—young men renowned for their beauty, remembered above all for their beauty, loved passionately for their beauty—as ideas, the concept of Beauty arousing the bodily senses for factual physical fulfillment, as much as the bodily senses arouse the concept of Beauty for Beauty's mysterious fulfillment. In the slow evolution of Greek, back further than Homeric Greek, ἰδέα meant not "idea" so much as "form." So, back then, "the idea of the body" was "the form of the body." Pindar describes a beautiful athlete ἰδέα τε καλόν, rendered into English "beautiful of form," making idea form, making form beautiful. "Idea" beams about the bodies of the beautiful young men in the erotic poetry of Cavafy, and the "idea" is Beauty; is Cavafy's sublime appreciation of the beautiful body at Beauty. (Yes, yes, Cavafy should be seen in terms of his age—an age when such concepts as Beauty and Time had their artistic and moral validity. But something in his work impels one to read him as if not in any way limited to his age, and to validate once again, with longing, such grand concepts as Beauty and Time.) *Is* there irony here?

And his appreciation of Art? Is there irony in creating poetry, beautiful poetry, out of what could never have been, but is fantasy? Is there irony intrinsic to poetry about poetry? The best erotic poems have to do with the making of the past—often a debauched past—into Art, as in "To Stay" (my version):

One o'clock in the morning, perhaps one thirty,
And we, in the dark club, the almost empty club,
Lit vaguely,
The bouncer asleep by the entrance,

Knew that no one would see us—We,
So hot with passion,
Not caring,

Our clothes half open—
Clothing light because of the July heat, the heavenly July
heat—

Delighting in exposed skin—

This image of us surviving twenty-six years,
Surviving now in this poetry.

The transformation of raw sex into the refinement of poetry, and, at the same time, the very subject of refined poetry raw sex! Transitory sex made eternal in poetry! Homosexual sex seen as the truest inspiration of poetry, which sex exists in and for itself, as does poetry! There must be irony here.

But, oh, I want now to give up trying to justify the fantasy—the kitsch—in Cavafy's poems with irony, which has been a labor. I want the sublime, and I want Cavafy to bring me up to the level of the haloed, *un-ironical* sublime. Cavafy was right to see his beautiful young man, stripped of his cinnamon-colored suit and standing naked on a beach, as inspiring poetry, inspiring the beauty of the language, inspiring the sublime.

Cavafy knew, of course, that fantasy has no fulfillment, but perpetuates more fantasy than the last attempt at fulfillment. And he knew, too, that not to try to fulfill the fantasy is to regret what was not done, not risked, was recognized as mere fantasy and let go—for fantasy, however it is known that fantasy cannot be fulfilled, demands fulfillment.

But now I admit: I *want* the fantastic in Cavafy's poetry! Cavafy's poems thrill me for the fantasy of sex, sex even in a fantasy *maison de passe*, on the sheets the intimate hairs of previous lovers.

Well, let the spirit of sex inspire sex! Let the fantasy of Cavafy's erotic poetry thrill, and give to sex what sex in sex's self—rank sweat, pubic hairs in the mouth, literal pain in the ass—doesn't have: the sublime!

Let the youth in some small town, the youth who in Cavafy's poem "The Dull Town" wastes his life away—let him believe that in his sex he is special, that he participates in Cavafy's erotic poems, that his sex is glorified in that marvelous poetry.

DAVID PLANTE is author of numerous novels, most notably *The Francoeur Trilogy* (*The Family* [1978]; *The Country* [1981]; *The Woods* [1982]), which was nominated for The National Book Award in America. *The Catholic* (1986) attempts to reconcile sex and the spirit, and has been an inspiration to many gays struggling for that reconciliation. His latest book is a memoir about Nikos Stangos, *The Pure Lover* (2009). Plante is a fellow of the Royal Society of Literature and of the New York Institute of Humanities at NYU. He is currently a professor at Columbia University in New York, and makes his home in London. Many editions of Cavafy's verse are currently available in translation, including C. P. Cavafy, *Collected Poems* (New York: Knopf, 2009), translated, with introduction and commentary by Daniel Mendelsohn and C. P. Cavafy, *Collected Poems: with parallel Greek text* (Oxford: Oxford University Press, 2007), translated by Evangelos Sachperoglou, from which one quotation is taken. The edition of Hockney's etchings mentioned is C. P. Cavafy, *Fourteen Poems by C.P. Kavafy, Chosen and Illustrated with Twelve Etchings by David Hockney* (London: Editions Alecto, 1967), translated by Nikos Stangos and Stephen Spender.

NIGHTWOOD
(1936)

by Djuna Barnes

ERIC KARL ANDERSON

ightwood has never been a popular novel, although it is notorious and its influence within the literary community is far reaching. Its author Djuna Barnes was familiar to many of the great authors in the Parisian expat scene of the 1920s, including Ezra Pound, James Joyce, and Gertrude Stein (who Barnes disliked intensely). Since its publication in 1936, *Nightwood*, her most celebrated novel, has exerted a strong influence over authors as varied as Dylan Thomas, Jeanette Winterson, William Burroughs, and Siri Hustvedt. The novel focuses on a love triangle between three women, but to call it a lesbian novel would be too simple. In fact, nothing about this book is simple, nor was there anything easy about its famously witty, intelligent, beautiful, and, in her later years, highly reclusive author.

Nightwood's plot is equally hard to summarize, given its highly poetic, sinuous, and experimental structure. It begins with a description of the character Guido Volkbein's origins. Lineage and blood are important themes in much of Barnes's writing, including her first novel *Ryder* and the short story "Smoke." Volkbein marries a bewitching figure named Robin Vote who bears him a son. Robin begins wandering at night and, utterly discontent in her domestic role, soon abandons her little family. She meets Nora Flood at a circus. There is an immediate passion between the two, who move in together. But soon Robin begins her nocturnal wanderings again, leaving Nora for a woman named Jenny Petherbridge. Nora is left pining for her lost love and seeks advice from one of the most peculiar and vivid characters in all fiction: Dr. Matthew-Mighty-Grain-of-Salt-Dante-O'Connor, a transvestite and ostensible gynecologist/abortionist. It's no wonder that T. S. Eliot, who wrote an introduction for *Nightwood* and assisted in its publication, commented that he initially felt that Dr. O'Connor "gave the book its vitality" because the last three-quarters of the novel are primarily taken up with this character's rambunctious, bizarre oration.

The offbeat ideas and startling thoughts expressed in dialogue that compose the bulk of *Nightwood* make it difficult to situate in any particular genre, lesbian or otherwise. The women portrayed have sexual relationships with each other, but the characters are firstly individuals struggling with issues of an existential nature. Rather than reading *Nightwood* as a story that speaks specifically about lesbian experience, it might be more useful to understand the flailing relationship of Robin and Nora as a more universal doomed love story. After all, we have a real example of a long-term lesbian relationship from the period of Parisian Bohemia in Gertrude Stein and Alice B. Toklas. As Jeanette Winterson noted about *Nightwood*, "its power makes a nonsense of any categorisation, especially of gender or sexuality" ("Creatures of the Dark," *The Guardian*, March 31st, 2007). The main thrust of the novel records the coupling of two temperamental individuals with divergent needs who cannot find happiness together. But Barnes achieves this by using a highly experimental structure which captures the flavour and energy of Paris at this time.

None of Barnes's writing is conventional, although it is heavily informed by a diverse range of writing styles. No doubt this is partly due to her informal education. She grew up under an eccentric, polygamous father, who raised Djuna in a kind of commune. In her late teens she moved to New York City, determined to make her own way. She was only able to afford six months of art school before beginning full-time work as a journalist and writer. She published a number of stories while living amongst the New York City bohemian scene, as well as her first book of poetry and drawings called *The Book of Repulsive Women* (1915) in which the women depicted are skewered in the author's fascinatingly oblique satirical style. If readers worry that women get a bad rap in much of Barnes's writing, they should be assured: men don't get it much easier. The author is famously quoted as saying: "Women are no good, but men are much worse."

However, in the case of this particular text, it"s also important to be aware that, as Mary E. Galvin points out, "'repulsive' may refer not to our reaction to the women, but to the women's active stance of repelling some of us" (*Queer Poetics* [London: Greenwood Press, 1999], p. 87). Indeed, some of the women depicted harbor desires and pleasures that we are not invited to participate in. Reading some of the poems, it's startling to think that the censors at the time allowed writing so heavily scented with female sexuality to be published at all:

See you sagging down with bulging
Hair to sip,
The dappled damp from some vague
Under lip.
Your soft saliva, loosed
With orgy, drip.

Barnes moved to Paris in 1921 on a journalist's assignment, but remained for many years. The years she spent mingling with other expatriates and artists were the most active and fruitful of her long life. Barnes became familiar to a famous lesbian social circle here centered round the American heiress Natalie Barney. She satirized the inner workings, relationships, and personalities of this circle in a book named *Ladies Almanack* (1928). Written in mock-Elizabethan style, it pokes fun at the women it portrays. Barnes claimed to have primarily written it for money—which worked, as she earned the longstanding patronage of the wealthy Barney, who enjoyed being immortalized in writing. But this book also raises a number of compelling issues specific to lesbians, which were being debated within Barney's female salon. For this reason, perhaps more than *Nightwood*, *Ladies Almanack* should be marked as a valuable testament concerning female homosexuality.

In Paris, meanwhile, Barnes also began a love affair with the silverpoint artist Thelma Wood, who would become the model upon whom the character of Robin is based. Djuna longed for a monogamous relationship, but Thelma, like her fictional counterpart Robin, often wandered. The disappointment and longing she felt from the dissolution of this relationship would stay with Barnes for many years, during which she obsessed over the long arduous task of *Nightwood*'s composition. After grappling with several false starts, she wrote the majority of the book while staying in an English country retreat named Hayford Hall and rented by Peggy Guggenheim. Here she found a valuable critic and supporter in the fascinatingly intense writer Emily Coleman.

It was Coleman who encouraged Barnes in the process of writing *Nightwood* and who championed the novel, convincing T. S. Eliot and Faber & Faber of its importance after the manuscript had been rejected by several publishers. Some editors objected not only to the novel's lack of cohesive structure or storyline, but more justifiably to some unsettling statements it makes about racial issues. An editor for Simon & Schuster rejected the manuscript of *Nightwood*, not only for being too "written" for mainstream publishing, but also because he thought it rather anti-Semitic.

Coleman suggested to Barnes that the novel should focus more on the relationship between Nora and Robin, which is at the heart of *Nightwood*. However, Barnes was disinclined to do so for fear of offending Thelma Wood. As it turned out, Wood physically attacked Barnes after the novel's publication anyway because of the way she was portrayed—as did Dan Mahoney, upon whom Barnes based the character of Dr. O'Connor. In *Nightwood* we aren't given the full story of the love affair between the two women, but the meaning rings through clearly enough. It's the truthfulness, rather than the truth, of Barnes's prose that rouses us. We divine a rare honesty out of this impatient narrative and its series of convoluted metaphors and elusive characters. As with the best poetry, meaning remains just out of reach, and the impact of it uncoils at the back of the mind slowly over a long period of time.

If Barnes didn't portray the relationship as voluptuously as she might have if she weren't inhibited by these worries, the book still conveys the violent passion of the affair—perhaps recreating it in the process. As Carolyn Allen observed: "As she recasts for

Matthew her past life with Robin, Nora experiences more intensely her longing for her lover, so that her retrospective narrating is both about her desire and itself an act of desiring" (*Following Djuna* [Bloomington: Indiana University Press, 1996], p. 25). In writing *Nightwood*, Barnes created one of the great modernist texts of the period, which speaks deeply about thwarted desire and the solipsistic nature of the individual.

With Barnes's soured view of humanity, her approach to some characters is confined to a short, single, brilliant flash that manages to reveal their whole being before they are relegated to the forgotten annals of history. Thus characters who initially assert an important place in the narrative can die unobtrusively, the reporting of their deaths sometimes summed up in a few words within a subclause: "Hedvig Volkbein—a Viennese woman of great strength and military beauty, lying upon a canopied bed of a rich spectacular crimson . . . gave birth, at the age of forty-five, to an only child, a son . . . she named him Felix, thrust him from her, and died." As with Mrs. Ramsay's passing in Virginia Woolf's *To the Lighthouse* (1927), Barnes's modernist vision often doesn't carry characters through a journey to arrive transformed and enlightened at a satisfying conclusion. Instead, they are abruptly snuffed out, and the "story"—which is merely the marching forward of time—carries on regardless. It's revealing that in a profile Barnes wrote on James Joyce, she admired his ability to "arrange, in necessary silence, the abundant inadequacies of life, as a layout of jewels—jewels with a will to decay" (*I Could Never Be Lonely Without a Husband* [London: Virago, 1987], p. 290). Barnes's sober understanding of life's limitations is marked in her distinctive voice throughout *Nightwood*.

Barnes is not a modernist who stands behind the work quietly, paring her fingernails. Her personality is bluntly obvious on the page. The narrative voice is so unique, so wilfully difficult, so perplexing, that Barnes the writer feels alarmingly ever present; so much so that when I read *Nightwood* I'm often unsure if I'm being told sacred truths or being laughed at. With her emphasis on impersonation and performance, the reader is left guessing who the author is, and what her opinions might be, while puzzling over the non-naturalistic dialogue and fantastical descriptions. Yet this is also a writer who maintains a magisterial control over her language. In a single extended sentence, Barnes has the ability to drain words like "alter" and "flower" of their meaning, fix them in a metaphor, and reuse them for her own purposes. We see through Barnes's prismatic lens a bohemian Paris populated by characters created through veiled memories and obscured by artistic rendering.

Yet never have characters on a page felt so real and wilful. Their viewpoint is uninhibitedly sincere precisely because they are dislocated and entirely self-created. As Lorna Sage observed, "this was the stuff of *Nightwood*, the Paris of abject carnival, a kind of human menagerie. Those who wander this city want, impossibly, to be what they desire" (*Moments of Truth* [London: Fourth Estate, 2001], p. 116). *Nightwood* indelibly captures the atmosphere of a particular age when a disparate group of individuals congregated to propagate new attitudes and new methods of artistic expression.

Still, if Barnes herself was so thoroughly immersed in the progressive movements of her time, why did she not become a cavalier for lesbian identity politics? There is still the niggling problem of inserting *Nightwood* into a canon of lesbian literature which the author herself was so resistant to. For example, with its complex exploration of identity and longing, *Nightwood* would rest uneasily alongside J. D. Glass's more straightforward coming-of-age novel *Punk Like Me* (2006). The marked difference between the two lies not in happy endings, but in the ease or uneasiness with which the characters inhabit the self.

After what became an almost permanent move back to New York City in 1940, Barnes produced little writing, had numerous affairs with men, and lived a fairly solitary existence. Women who came to express their admiration for her literary work and/or their love for the woman herself received a cold shoulder (in some cases with good cause). Barnes claimed: "I was never a lesbian; I only loved Thelma." One suspects, given the author's ornery nature, that what she meant was that she wouldn't be a member of any club that would have her. Nor was Barnes inclined to be known for her literature, as she actively blocked republications, translations, and adaptations of her work during her later years. Nevertheless, *Nightwood* has managed to survive. It is filled with perversity and offensive points of view, but for all this, it should be celebrated. Djuna Barnes lived to be ninety, having left her distinctive fingerprint on the pages of literature, but the author herself remains something of a chimera. As the great Dr. O'Connor muses: "One's life is peculiarly one's own when one has invented it."

ERIC KARL ANDERSON is author of the novel *Enough* (2004). His writing has been published in *The Ontario Review*, *Blithe House Quarterly*, *Harrington Gay Men's Fiction Quarterly*, *BiMagazine*, as well as in the anthologies *From Boys to Men: Gay Men Write About Growing Up* (edited by Ted Gideonse and Robert Williams, 2006) and *Between Men 2* (edited by Richard Canning, 2009). Quotations are taken from Djuna Barnes, *Nightwood* (London: Faber & Faber, 2007). The American edition currently in print is Djuna Barnes, *Nightwood* (New York: New Directions, 2006), preface by Jeanette Winterson, introduction by T. S. Eliot.

THE LETTERS OF
VITA SACKVILLE-WEST
TO VIRGINIA WOOLF
(1922–41; 1985)

by Vita Sackville-West

CAROL ANSHAW

omewhere in the early part of my coming out, I read these letters and mistook them for a field guide. They gave me the ridiculous notion of a future populated by slouchy, casually elegant, literary women. I conjured up settings of city apartments and country houses. Gardens and dogs. Delicious, stolen evenings in bed. Muted, civilized partings.

This was before real life came barreling at me. Before the teary arguments on street corners. The malicious mischief of this or that "other woman." The hours-long phone calls, the packs and packs of Camels. Before those moments, as Amy Winehouse puts it, when "I cried for you on the kitchen floor." Before the day when the beautiful, married woman took my bag and books and papers and tossed all of it onto a busy Chicago street and peeled off in the car. Only it was *my* car.

The letters addressed none of this. What I hadn't factored in—beyond the fact that Chicago in the last part of the twentieth century was quite different from England in the first part—was that letters provide a shaped rhetoric of any romance, but especially the letters of writers.

Virginia Woolf met Vita Sackville-West at a London dinner party in 1922. Both were married; Vita had two sons. The women were immediately and mutually attracted. Virginia, at forty, was ten years' Vita's senior, and already a respected writer. Which made her a catch—a "big silver fish." For her part, Virginia wrote to a friend that she had met a "high aristocrat called Vita Sackville-West, daughter of Lord Sackville, daughter of Knole [the largest country house in England], wife of Harold Nicolson, and novelist, but her real claim to consideration, is, if I may be so coarse, her legs."

Their salutations slowly evolve from "Dear Mrs Woolf" and "Dear Mrs Nicolson" through "My Dear Virginia" and "My Dear Vita" to "My Darling Virginia" and "Dearest Creature." They became lovers in December 1925, at Vita's house, Long Barn in Kent. Once back in London, Virginia wrote with coy modesty, as though her hands now required clothing, "I am dashing off to buy a pair of gloves." Vita, soon to leave for Persia—where her husband, a diplomat, had just been posted—wrote from Milan, "I am reduced to a thing that wants Virginia."

According to Vita, for Virginia, "the excitement of life lies in the *béguins* [fancies, infatuations], and the 'little moves' nearer to people." Still, whatever happened between them was enough to provoke Virginia to write, in 1927:

Should you say, if I rang you up to ask, that you were fond of me?

If I saw you would you kiss me?
If I were in bed would you—

For a time, their letters (sometimes letters folded within other letters) carried plans for assignations. "So you're going to Rodmell on Tuesday," Vita wrote in January 1927. "Very well: that involves the natural consequence that I'll come up tomorrow (Monday) and come to the basement. Now never say again that I don't love you. I want dreadfully to see you. That is all there is to it." Even quite a ways on, in 1933, Vita starts a letter written from her castle at Sissinghurst:

Dear Mrs Woolf
(That appears to be the suitable formula.)
I regret that you have been in bed, though not with me—
(a less suitable formula.)

From here, it is difficult to pin down the exact nature of their relationship. Vita was fearful of Virginia's fragility, and a little put off by her age. At some point, it seems likely that whatever the sexual aspect of their relationship, it got tamped down by time and by Vita's distraction. She was romantically vampiric; she required a constant feed of grand passions. So while her letters to Virginia imply devotion, she was in reality off to conquer her next married lady, and then the one after that. Vita's specialty was home-wrecking. Over the couple of decades that comprised her prime—often by implying she was prepared to leave her own marriage—she did terrible damage to those of others: several by sleeping with the wife; one by sleeping with the husband; another by sleeping with both women in a partnership. "With the years," writes Victoria Glendinning in her excellent biography, *Vita*,

"Vita's list of emotional pensioners grew, and with it her correspondence and the demands on her time." ([London: Phoenix Orion, 2005], p. 194).

It would be easy to count Virginia Woolf among these pensioned-off lovers, but the letters indicate that the two of them maintained an engaged relationship. They had meaning to each other outside of that basement (although it's hard to resist imagining them down there). They read each other's work. Virginia and Leonard Woolf's Hogarth Press published much of Vita's fiction and poetry. They continued to write and see each other for all the rest of Virginia's years. Vita was aware of and concerned for Virginia's illnesses, both physical and mental; these brought out the maternal in her. In return, Vita brought excitement to Virginia's life, and even spurred her take a very interesting turn in her work. Just as their affair was settling down and Virginia was expressing in her letters petulance and jealousy of new objects of Vita's affection, she nonetheless had an ace up her sleeve. In 1927, Virginia began writing a new novel—one Vita's son Nigel would later call "the longest and most charming love letter in history." *Orlando* (1928) re-imagines Vita as a young nobleman in the sixteenth century, racing through history, until he arrives in the 1920s as a woman writer. Other women may have gotten Vita into bed, but Virginia got her onto pages. What could be more seductive, or binding?

It would be hard to overstate the effects of the Second World War on the two women. Virginia and Leonard Woolf were bombed out of two houses in London. At both their country home in Rodmell and at Vita's castle at Sissinghurst, more bombs fell. The two women didn't know which time they spoke or saw each other would be the last. At the end of 1940, Virginia wrote to Vita, "You have given me such happiness." Vita wrote: "You mean more to me than you will ever know." Valedictions.

And then in March 1941, Virginia—fearing another bout of madness—broke the connection, and her life, by walking into the river Ouse with stones in her pockets. Vita lived on until 1962. Visiting Sissinghurst a couple of years ago, I climbed up into the tower to see her writing desk. There, still tilted against the wall by her writing blotter, is a framed photo of Virginia.

It's impossible to know the whole story of a love affair. Letters give a hint, but in reality just fill in the interstices of a liaison, capture the moments of reflection *about* a relationship. Who knows what went on between them—and within themselves about their great affection? Perhaps they had their own, unrecorded, terrible scenes. Maybe they cried on *their* kitchen floors.

Carol Anshaw is author of the novels *Lucky in the Corner* (2002), *Seven Moves* (1996), and *Aquamarine* (1992). Quotations are taken from Vita Sackville-West, *The Letters of Vita Sackville-West to Virginia Woolf, 2nd Edition* (San Francisco: Cleis Press, 2001), edited by Louise DeSalvo and Mitchell A. Leaska, which is currently in print.

BRIDESHEAD REVISITED
(1945)

by Evelyn Waugh

BOB SMITH

Over thirty years ago, I read *Brideshead Revisited* for the first time and discovered Evelyn Waugh's best-known and most popular novel wasn't my favorite. While I enjoyed the first half of the novel because of the love story between Charles Ryder and Sebastian Flyte, I was put off by the second half where the author's hand was heavier than God's in proselytizing for the Roman Catholic Church. I'd grown up Catholic, knew I was gay, was aware that the church was homophobic, and felt—then and now—about crucifixes as vampires did; I didn't want to see or read about them. I was also a virgin then, and had serious reservations about a story in which a character chooses the love of God over the love of Sebastian, whose beauty is described as "arresting" and "magical."

Although something about it didn't ring true, I accepted Charles Ryder's loss of interest in Sebastian and his falling in love in with Sebastian's sister, Julia. The problem was that, at twenty, my lack of life experience made me regard every fictional life as believable. If I could accept a hobbit finding a magic ring, then I could imagine that Charles Ryder's homosexuality was a phase, improbable as that seemed. But rereading *Brideshead Revisited*, I found Charles Ryder's declarations of heterosexuality more fantastic than the existence of Humpty Dumpty or the Houyhnhnms.

Brideshead Revisited didn't put me off Waugh though. I read the rest of his novels, his travel books, diaries, and letters, and his collected journalism. In college I was a romantic reader. I'd fall in love with a writer and felt compelled to read every word he or she wrote. Waugh was part of my plan to read all the comic gay writers. Joe Orton's complete plays led me to Ronald Firbank's complete novels, then to all of Oscar Wilde, progenitor of both of their epigrammatic styles. I'd spent the previous summer devouring E. M. Forster and Christopher Isherwood, and would soon commence upon Denton Welch, Saki, and Noel Coward. In addition to my queer crushes, I went through ardent phases with straight, lesbian, and spinster writers: Jane Austen, Willa Cather, Barbara Pym, Flannery O'Connor, Mark Twain, Charles Dickens, and Wallace Stegner. (I still swing both ways: a recent crush was Dawn Powell; currently I'm moon-eyed over Richard Yates.)

I counted Waugh as one of the funny gays, because I'd read he'd had a "homosexual phase" at Oxford, and I recognized in his second novel *Vile Bodies* (1930) that he'd cribbed a bit from Firbank. A character going through customs is asked what she has to declare and her answer is: "Wings." In Firbank, the answer was "Butterflies," but I knew the joke's lineage began with Wilde who said, on arriving in New York: "I have nothing to declare but my genius."

The first Evelyn Waugh novel I read was *Scoop* (1938), a comic masterpiece. I decided Waugh was a genius, as he hilariously eviscerated the know-nothingness of journalists, starting with the press baron Lord Copper, publisher of the *Daily Beast*:

> . . . Mr. Salter's side of the conversation was limited to expressions of assent. When Lord Copper was right he said, "Definitely Lord Copper"; when he was wrong, "Up to a point."
>
> "Let me see, what's the name of the place I mean? Capital of Japan? Yokohama, isn't it?"
>
> "Up to a point, Lord Copper."

Each subsequent book of Waugh's revealed his brilliance, but my besotted admiration was tempered by the racist descriptions of some characters, and by sentences that I'd have to read twice in an attempt to figure out whether or not they were anti-Semitic. Normally professions of bigotry would be enough to make me stop reading an author, but I continued reading Waugh because I wanted to learn how to be funny and Waugh, for all his faults, is definitely funny.

I still love the first half of *Brideshead Revisited*. The prologue is set at the start of World War II, when Captain Charles Ryder arrives with his soldiers at Brideshead, the Marchmain family's historic home, which functions as an architectural Madeleine, triggering Ryder's memories, sacred and profane. The next section of the book is entitled "Et In Arcadia Ego," and the Arcadian paradise it recalls is Oxford during Ryder's student days. Waugh creates a seductive midsummer term, where the fairies smoke Turkish cigarettes, wear Charvet ties, and drink champagne from Lalique glasses. Ryder first meets Sebastian Flyte when the handsome young lord sticks his head through the window of Ryder's ground-floor rooms and "makes sick." The next day the apologetic Sebastian fills Ryder's room with flowers and invites him to luncheon. Charles tells us that he senses he is about to enter the low door that opens on an enchanted garden. At the luncheon party, Ryder meets Sebastian's friends, among them his teddy bear Aloysius and the last guest to arrive, the stammering Anthony Blanche: "'My dear,' he said, 'I couldn't get away before. I was lunching with my p-p-preposterous tutor. He thought it very odd my leaving when I did. I told him I had to change for F-f-footer.'"

Anthony Blanche is described by Charles as "the 'aesthete' *par excellence*, a byword of iniquity from Cherwell Edge to Somerville, a young man who seemed to me, then, fresh from the somber company of the College Essay society, ageless as a lizard, as foreign as a Martian . . . I found myself enjoying him voraciously, like the fine piece of cookery he was." Waugh's portrait of an epicene young queen is the greatest comic character in the book, and in a ten-page tour de force of a monologue, Blanche tutors Ryder in the history of Sebastian's family, the Marchmains, and also reminds his dinner guest: "You see, my dear Charles, you are that very rare thing, An Artist."

Charles and Sebastian embark on a romantic summer of wine, strawberries, and nude sunbathing. A day trip to Brideshead is followed by a month-long stay at the palatial country house, and then a subsequent trip to Venice (Ryder's first). Charles's exploration of Brideshead's baroque marvels dovetails with the discovery of what will become his life's work: painting architectural portraits. Waugh's lush, almost florid prose evokes falling in love for the first time, and the flowering of a life.

Charles's life has been constrained up to this point. His father is a reclusive, antiquities-collecting widower whose dry humor is always used to contain any unseemly emotions between father and son. While at Oxford, Charles's cousin Jasper, a pompous pipe-smoking young fogey advises him, "Don't treat dons like schoolmasters; treat them as you would the vicar at home." To Waugh's credit, even these dull characters are amusingly drawn.

But the reader soon suspects that the first half of the novel is prelapserian, before the fall of our Oxonian Adam and Steve. Anthony Blanche foreshadows Sebastian's fate early on by telling him: "My dear, I should like to stick you full of barbed arrows like a p-p-pin-cushion." Unfortunately this blond Saint Sebastian will instead become an alcoholic, pierced by swizzle sticks and cocktail umbrellas. On their trip to Venice, Lord Marchmain's mistress Cara warns Charles: "These romantic friendships of the English and Germans . . . they are very good if they do not go on too long." There's no explanation as to why long romantic friend-ships between two men are detrimental, but it's clear from the context of the story that Cara is supposed to be worldly. Her homophobia almost sounds like a snobbish question of etiquette; it's rude for a gentleman to talk with a mouthful of cock.

Sebastian and Anthony Blanche also warn Charles against meeting Sebastian's family: his mother Lady Marchmain, a pious control freak whose withering stare would have made Jesus feel guilty for using the wrong fork at the Last Supper; Bridey, the older brother, a matchbox-collecting dullard; Cordelia, the plain younger sister destined to lead a spinster's life of "thwarted pas-sion"; and Julia, Sebastian's other sister, who will eventually replace Sebastian in Ryder's affections.

Ryder first becomes aware of his attraction to Julia early in the story: "As I took the cigarette from my lips and put it in hers, I caught a thin bat's squeak of sexuality, inaudible to any but me."

It's a sound the reader strains to hear because the wham-bam of heterosexual attraction is entirely missing between Charles and Julia. On rereading *Brideshead*, I found its most peculiar element was the way Julia is repeatedly, almost obsessively, described throughout the book as a secondary Sebastian:

> Her voice was Sebastian's and his her way of speaking.

> She so much resembled Sebastian that, sitting beside her in the gathering dusk, I was confused by the double illusion of familiarity and strangeness.

> Her dark hair was scarcely longer than Sebastian's, but blew back from her forehead as his did; her eyes on the darkling road were his.

> On my side the interest was keener, for there was always the physical likeness between brother and sister, which caught repeatedly in different poses, under different lights each time pierced me anew.

> I had not forgotten Sebastian. He was with me daily in Julia . . .

> Even Sebastian says: "I love her. She's so like me . . . in looks I mean and the way she talks."

Charles's love for She-bastian—the only way I can think of Julia now—should be disturbing for readers of any sexual orientation, as it manages to seem misogynistic as well as homophobic. Ryder loves a woman who resembles the man he loves because it's more socially acceptable than loving the man. Sebastian eventually moves to Morocco to drink full-time, while Ryder marries another woman, whose beauty is praised as the "curiously hygienic quality of her prettiness," which is a curiously tepid description of heterosexual desire. Charles becomes a successful painter, but is admittedly unhappy, lamenting, "For nearly ten years I was borne along a road outwardly full of change and incident, but never during that time, except sometimes in my painting—and that at longer and longer intervals—did I come alive as I had been during the time of my friendship with Sebastian."

If anyone in *Brideshead Revisited* reveals a thwarted passion, it's Charles—and possibly also his author. Conflating the lives of character and author is risky, but I've read several biographies of Waugh and evidently his homosexual phase at Oxford was the happiest time of his life. In Waugh's diaries and letters, he often gives the impression that heterosexuality is more a painful duty than a passion. There's no telling whether Charles Ryder or Evelyn Waugh would have been happier living as gay men rather than as half-hearted heterosexuals. But reading *Brideshead Revisited* today makes one wish someone had introduced Waugh to Isherwood, who proved that the "romantic friendships" of the English and Germans can actually be quite a bit of fun.

Near the novel's close is the deathbed scene of Sebastian's father, Lord Marchmain. Charles, the professed agnostic, prays for the first time, and Lord Marchmain shows contrition for his sins by making the sign of the cross. Waugh's early novels *Decline and Fall* (1928) and *Vile Bodies* seem less dated than *Brideshead Revisited*, and what makes the novel feel antediluvian is its old-school Roman Catholicism, where Sin is always capitalized, divorce and remarriage are unthinkable, and the soul is regarded as a slop jar that we carry with us for our entire lives.

In *Brideshead Revisited,* Waugh's snobbish Roman Catholicism posits that one's social status in the afterlife, where the high look down on the low, is more important than joy in this life. But the Church guarantees that no matter how hellish it makes our temporal lives, it holds out the promise of a heavenly happy ending. Unfortunately, any close reader of Waugh will question that assumption, because in his other novels he's repeatedly shown that happy endings can be comically disastrous. In *Black Mischief* (1932), the main character ends up dining on his mistress at a cannibal banquet, while *A Handful of Dust* (1934) concludes with Tony Last being held prisoner in the Amazon, forced to read Dickens aloud to the insane Mr. Todd. In Waugh's universe, it's more plausible to believe that heaven won't be a piece of cake and will have its hellish aspects. God could turn out to be another mad recluse who forces the trapped prisoners of Paradise to read aloud his favorite book—the one he authored—for eternity.

Brideshead Revisited ends with Ryder entering the arts-and-crafts chapel at Brideshead, where he finds a beaten-copper lamp burning—symbol of his new-found faith. It takes chutzpah to question the ending of a comic master's novel, but in this instance I think Waugh faltered. Since Ryder is still beset by his thwarted homosexual desires, a more satisfying and apt conclusion would have had him entering the priesthood, the apotheosis of being Roman Catholic and frustrated.

BOB SMITH, a comedian and writer, is author of two collections of essays, *Openly Bob* (1997) and *Way to Go, Smith!* (1999), and, most recently, a novel, *Selfish and Perverse* (2007). Quotations are taken from Evelyn Waugh, *Brideshead Revisited* (London/New York: Penguin Modern Classics, 2000), which is currently in print.

Memoirs of Hadrian

(Mémoires d'Hadrien)

(1951)

by Marguerite Yourcenar

Edmund White

Marguerite Yourcenar (who was born in 1903 and died in 1987) was the last echo of a heroic chorus of European writers that included Thomas Mann and André Gide, older men whom she particularly admired and whose work influenced hers. Like them she was a philosophical writer with a deep and wide culture, a moralist with a taste for historical perspectives, and a virtuoso equally at home in crafting novels, stories, and essays (she also wrote rather bad plays and poems).

Like them, she joined a dignified, not to say marmoreal, manner to a penchant for shocking subject matter, for she was as fascinated as they were by sexual ambiguity. Mann explored incest in "Blood of the Volsungs" (1906), and an exalted if over-ripe Platonic homosexuality in *Death in Venice*. Gide touched on bisexuality and reveled in hedonism in *The Immoralist* (*L'immoraliste*, 1902) and avowed his own homosexuality in *If It Die* (*Si le grain ne meurt*, 1926). In a daring if over-the-top essay, *Corydon* (1924), Gide defended homosexuality as natural and even useful to society.

Yourcenar in her very Gidean first novel, *Alexis* (1929), showed how a young husband's homosexuality could compromise his marriage while in her masterpiece, *Memoirs of Hadrian*, she invented one of the great same-sex love stories of all time: the Roman emperor's passion for his Greek lover. In her splendid essays on the Alexandrian poet Constantine Cavafy and the prolific Japanese novelist Yukio Mishima she honored two of the remarkable talents of our epoch, each so different from the other but both homosexual. Indeed her critical introduction to Cavafy is a particularly acute evaluation; for instance, she remarks: "We are so used to seeing in wisdom a residue of dead passions that it's difficult to recognize in it the hardest and most condensed form of ardor, the gold nugget pulled out of the fire, not the ashes." This Nietzschean celebration of passion would mark her own fiction. In her essay she also contrasts Cavafy's "exquisite freedom from posturing" about his homosexuality with Proust's dishonesty (which led him to give "a grotesque or false image of his own tendencies") and with Gide's need "to put his personal experience immediately in the service of rational reform or social progress." In her own writing and conduct Yourcenar would avoid the Proustian and Gidean extremes and cultivate Cavafy's emphatic self-acceptance.

Cavafy's honesty is also similar to that of the Emperor Hadrian in Yourcenar's brilliant recreation. As she explained, in giving the background to her most famous book and how she came to write it, she had been struck as early as 1927 by one of

Flaubert's letters in which he observed, "There was a unique moment between Cicero and Marcus Aurelius when the gods no longer existed and Christ had not yet emerged and humanity was all alone." This was the supremely humanist moment that Yourcenar captured with such success.

Marguerite Yourcenar was born in Brussels to a Belgian mother and French father, whose name was Michel de Crayencour (Yourcenar, a pen name, is a nearly perfect anagram). Her mother, Fernande, died ten days after Marguerite's birth, and the child was watched over from afar by a woman whom Marguerite later imagined must have been her mother's lover. She was raised, however, by her father, a compulsive gambler (already fifty years old when Marguerite was born), who destroyed the family fortune but conferred on his brilliant daughter a love of travel and learning. She was not sent to school nor did she embroider or play with dolls. She had few toys and preferred reciting poetry to playing, which must have made her seem unbearably priggish to her friends. At a precocious age she developed a sense that she was "important, even very important," as she later recalled.

She and her father spent the beginning of the First World War in England, where they studied Latin and Greek together but made little headway with English. They returned to Paris in 1915, where she was tutored at home. Her father passed on to the child his favorite books by Goethe, Tolstoy, Huysmans, and the controversial (because pacifist) Romain Rolland. She and her father read out loud Virgil in Latin and Homer in Greek. At age sixteen Marguerite wrote a poetic drama, *Icarus*.

The young writer developed a deep complicity with her father, who paid to have her first two books published, who wrote and signed letters for her in her absence—but who expressed no warmth to her. Yet when he was dying he was pleased to have lived long enough to read her first genuine literary achievement, *Alexis*. In the same year, 1929, she began to work on a first (and soon abandoned) version of the life of the Emperor Hadrian. She was twenty-four years old. The *Memoirs of Hadrian* would not be published until 1951.

Yourcenar had in fact already discovered in her twenties almost all the literary themes she would develop over the next sixty years. She belonged to that small tribe of artists (Dante is another) who don't evolve but simply explore their chosen subjects with ever greater intensity.

She quickly forgot about her father after his death and thought about him only several decades later. Passionate and cerebral, Yourcenar spent the ten years after her father's death and before the outbreak of war in 1939 traveling, living in small hotels, reading, writing, and seducing both men and women. She had an unhappy experience pursuing a man, a French writer who was homosexual; the suffering was indirectly expressed in *Coup de grâce* (1939), the short novel that is perhaps her strongest piece of fiction.

Its title also alludes to her meeting with Grace Frick, an American with whom she would live until Frick's death forty years later. Frick would help Yourcenar with her research, organize her social life, translate her books, and sustain her financially over the decades. Because Frick was American, Yourcenar—the most thoroughly French of all modern French writers—would spend the majority of her life in the United States and, from 1950 on, in Maine on the remote island of Mount Desert. Yourcenar was the first woman ever to be admitted to the French Academy and one of the first living French writers to have her complete works published in the prestigious Pléiade series, usually consecrated to classic authors of the past; how strange that this monument of French letters should have lived as a virtual recluse on an American island, where many of her neighbors assumed "Madame" could not even speak English. Her American years, moreover, affected her only in minor ways. She translated African-American spirituals into French as well as a collection of Blues and a play by James Baldwin and she became a committed ecologist; otherwise her adopted homeland scarcely left a trace on her work.

Meanwhile, Frick was forced into playing the bad cop in order to scare off reporters, graduate students, editors, and other time-wasters long enough for Yourcenar to get on with her work, but most of her victims never forgave her and wrote about her as a neurotic shrew. Yourcenar herself dismissed the relationship after Grace's death: "Essentially it's very simple: first it was a passion, then it was a habit, then just one woman looking after another who was ill."

Marguerite Yourcenar was entering her glory years of international fame in the 1970s at the same time that Frick was becoming terminally ill. This disparity produced considerable bitterness in both women. After Frick's death in 1979 Yourcenar was taken up by Jerry Wilson, a thirty-year-old American gay man. They enjoyed a stormy relationship, during which Wilson often reproached Yourcenar for being tired all the time (she was in her eighties). Despite their fights and her weakness, Wilson enabled Yourcenar to return to her greatest passion—travel. She and he were in constant motion—Kenya, Japan, India, Europe—until 1986 when Wilson died of AIDS. Despite her continuing travels and honors, she lost the will to live and died on December 17th, 1987.

Like several other lesbian writers (Mary Renault is the most obvious parallel), Yourcenar wrote best when she projected herself into the mind of a male homosexual character. In a note appended to *Memoirs of Hadrian* she said that it was impossible to make a woman her main character since "the life of women is too limited or too secret." Yourcenar's was far from limited, however—though she did her best to keep it secret.

EDMUND WHITE has written more than twenty books, including biographies of Genet (1993), Proust (1998), and Rimbaud (2008), seven novels (among them *A Boy's Own Story* [1983] and *Hotel de Dream* [2007]), and two collections of essays. He teaches at Princeton and lives in New York City. He has published two memoirs, *My Lives* (2005) and—most recently—*City Boy* (2009). Marguerite Yourcenar's *Memoirs of Hadrian* (New York: Farrar, Straus & Giroux, 2005), translated by Grace Frick, is currently in print.

CAROL

(THE PRICE OF SALT)

(1952)

by Patricia Highsmith

STELLA DUFFY

There was not a moment when she did not see Carol in her mind, and all she saw, she seemed to see through Carol.

Patricia Highsmith's *Carol* is, to me, an ideal "lesbian novel"—that is to say, it is a novel about a lesbian relationship, rather than a novel about the angst involved in being a gay woman, or a novel about what it is to be lesbian, or a novel about how the world doesn't understand us. While there are the occasional touches of that in this book, what it is mostly is a love story. And that's why it's such a successful novel. It is not about being lesbian; it is about two women. One young, new to the world, new to love, and hopeful; the other wiser, older, impossibly glamorous, and already aware of how simultaneously rash and careful one needs to be not merely to survive a gay relationship, but to survive any relationship. It is stylish, elegant, spare, and cleanly written—as are all of Highsmith's works. It also has a humanity and compassion which readers who only know her as the creator of the Ripley novels might find surprising. And, perhaps most importantly given the time it was written, it has a happy ending. Even today, the lesbian happy ending is an all-too-uncommon occurrence in fiction about women as lovers. In the late forties and early fifties, it was practically nonexistent.

It is particularly surprising to realize that *Carol* was published almost sixty years ago. Of course, there is Highsmith's prose to account in part for its longevity. But I also think the core relationship is so real in both the good and bad of love and lust—the pleasures and the false starts; the discomforting presence of ex-lovers and difficult friends and confused family—that it becomes possible for us to read the novel as a thing in itself, not a historical account of "how it was for them."

Highsmith published *Carol* under the pseudonym Claire Morgan in 1952. She wrote it after she finished *Strangers on a Train* (1950), which was then bought by Hitchcock to make into a film (1951). In her "Afterword" to the Bloomsbury (UK) revised edition of *Carol* (1989), Highsmith recounts that her agent and publisher were keen for her to write a second novel similar to *Strangers on a Train*. Publishing is a business like any other; it thrives on the slightly different packaging of more of the same. *Carol* was definitely not more of the same. After *Carol*, Highsmith went on to produce the Ripley novels, with her trademark blend of darkness and cool style—noticeable in *Carol*, though not so prominent as to undermine the love story. Eventually *Carol* was published by a different publisher, with the title *The Price of Salt*, selling respectably in hardback and then spectacularly in paperback. The publishers might have been frightened of selling a Patricia Highsmith novel about a lesbian relationship; the public were happy to buy it written by "Claire Morgan."

The reaction of Highsmith's publisher is certainly understandable, if regrettably staid. The reading public, ever keen to conflate writer with protagonist, might not have been quite so hungry for an amoral antihero written by a writer they also assumed was lesbian. In McCarthy-ite America, falling in love with a Europhile character as devious and deliciously transgressive as Ripley was permissible—at least in the context of a genre where the good reads are not always about the good guys. Falling in love with that character, if written by an author presumed to be lesbian, at a time when homosexuality equated with communism (which in its turn was hysterically equated with all things evil) would no doubt have been an honesty too far. When we think of the number of public figures we may privately know to be LGBT but who are still lying about their sexuality, even now, it is to Highsmith's enormous credit to consider that she pushed to have it published in the first place, and then again later under her own name, outing her work and herself.

As a writer of lesbian fiction myself (and crime fiction, and literary fiction . . . ah, the stultifying and narrow cult of labels!), I believe *Carol* is also praiseworthy for what it is not. Even when I first started writing fiction in the early 1990s, all too many of the books you would have found on a putative lesbian reading list were rehashing the same basic ideas: all men are bad; all women are good; lesbians are better. And that was about it. Unlike so much of the lesbian fiction that came out of second-wave feminism in the seventies and eighties, Highsmith in *Carol* was not overly concerned with coming out. She does not give us a study in agonized (and usually unrequited) passion; she does not give us characters cut off from nongay family or friends, living in a lesbian ghetto. What we have instead are rounded characters with friends and relationships and lives outside of the central story relationship between Therese and Carol, a beautifully evoked New York, and a passionate love story that slowly, and realistically, takes flight. (And for my money, this is a far better way to change the world: to make a difference through writing, rather than offering up thinly disguised political analysis masquerading as plot.)

All of Highsmith's work thrives on what is not said, what remains hidden; a holding back that allows the reader to engage with both the characters and the storytelling, giving us enough to pull us in, but not so much that we are spoon-fed with plot and need make no effort ourselves. This is not to say that reading Highsmith requires hard work; simply that, even here, writing as a fairly young woman (she was in her late twenties when she wrote *Carol*), Highsmith accords the reader the respect of assuming an engaged intelligence, and offers us material of a standard to match. As all too many of us know, this has not always been the case with lesbian fiction, where our invisibility in the mainstream has meant that we were, as readers and consumers of fiction, so hungry to see any glimpse of ourselves that we would take what we were given, no matter how inelegantly written. Even today, when so many things about being gay are far better than they were a generation or two ago (for those of us in the privileged West, at least), we still find that "gay" very often means "gay men" in actuality. While the acronym would have us all joined up as "LGBT," the truth is that most of the heterosexual world, and all too many in our own community, think that adding a gay male character, bringing in a kiss between men, mentioning the protagonist's gay best friend, covers the "gay brief," and the L, B, and T of us are nowhere to be found. Women, yet again, are relegated to "minority" status. What a joy, then, to read a beautifully-written novel with a passionate relationship between women at its core.

A grey-eyed blonde in a fur coat wearing memorable perfume; a vibrant young woman trying to find her way as a theater designer; a trickster best friend; a confused and angry boyfriend; Manhattan in the early fifties; sad-comedy neighbors; and a private detective recording conversations in a dingy hotel room . . . all this, and a road trip. What more could you ask for?

STELLA DUFFY has published eleven novels, over thirty short stories and eight plays, and coedited the anthology *Tart Noir* (2002). She was winner of the 2002 CWA Short Story Dagger Award for "Martha Grace," and the Stonewall Writer of the Year for her novel *The Room of Lost Things* (2008). Two of her novels have also been longlisted for the Orange Prize. She was born in the UK, grew up in New Zealand, and has lived in London since 1986. She is married to the writer Shelley Silas. Quotations are taken from Patricia Highsmith, *Carol* (London: Bloomsbury, 2005); the American edition currently in print is Patricia Highsmith, *The Price of Salt* (New York: Norton, 2004).

In the Making

(1952)

by G. F. Green

Peter Parker

S ome books arrive seemingly out of nowhere to lodge at once
and forever in one's consciousness. I cannot now recall how I
first came across *In the Making*, but it immediately secured a
place among what I think of as My Books, a virtual library of fiction to which I feel a special connection and which I find myself
rereading at regular intervals with increased pleasure and admiration. It is not so much that I dig deeper into these books at every
reading; it is more that they dig deeper into me. *In the Making*,
which is subtitled "The Story of a Childhood," describes the experiences undergone between the ages of six and fourteen by a boy
called Randal Thane and evokes with astonishing empathy the
pleasures, pains, and perplexities of first love. Much of the novel
takes place at Randal's preparatory school, and the book is one of
the most sophisticated and powerfully felt school stories you are

ever likely to read, as well as being a fine work of literature in its own right. It is easy enough to say that everyone should read it, but it has never been reprinted since its original publication over half a century ago. Indeed, nothing by G. F. Green (1911–1977) is currently in print, and his name is either forgotten or confused with those of his fellow novelists F. L. Green and Henry Green. His output was small but absolutely individual, and in its time highly regarded by E. M. Forster, Christopher Isherwood, Stephen Spender, J. R. Ackerley, John Lehmann, Elizabeth Bowen, and Alan Sillitoe. This is, by any standards, a formidable jury of literary reputation, but Green has since sunk almost without trace to lie in the deep silt of "lost" authors.

Green's career falls into three main phases. The first took place during the 1930s when he drew upon his own background as the son of a prosperous Derbyshire iron founder to write stories of working-class life in the industrial north of England. These appeared in most of the leading publications of the day (*New Writing*, *The Listener*, the *London Mercury*, the *Spectator*, *Horizon*, *Argosy*), were frequently anthologized, and finally collected in *Land Without Heroes* (1948). Called up in 1940, Green was posted to colonial Ceylon, where his war service came to an abrupt end after he was caught *in flagrante* with a Sinhalese rickshaw puller. He was court-martialled, cashiered, and sentenced to two years' imprisonment, publishing an account of his ordeal in *Penguin New Writing 31* (1947) under the pseudonym "Lieut. Z." As a result of his experiences Green suffered a breakdown after his release, but recovered his sense of identity and his ability to write after being treated by the celebrated psychiatrist Dr. Charlotte Wolff, who had been recommended to him by his close friend Michael Redgrave. *In the Making* (1952) belongs to the second, postwar phase of his career. Though ostensibly relocated to the

Quantocks, the novel draws upon Green's own experiences at a prep school in the Malvern Hills and is closely related to *Tales of Innocence*, the anthology of short stories about childhood he edited in 1950 and dedicated to the memory of Denton Welch. The third phase of Green's career is represented by *The Power of Sergeant Streater*, a triptych of interrelated novellas which appeared in 1972 after a long silence, and is based upon his early years in Derbyshire and later experiences in Ceylon. He subsequently worked on a further volume of stories "on the theme of the failure of Love," set in Ceylon and Morocco, but he died before he could finish it. The five stories he completed were published in a posthumous volume titled *A Skilled Hand* (1980), edited by his sister-in-law Chloë Green and the publisher A. D. Maclean. The book also contains extracts from Green's other books, interspersed with "memoirs and criticism" by those who knew and admired him.

One of the principal reasons for admiring Green is his prose, the distinctiveness of which was apparent from the outset of his career. His writing could be absolutely simple and direct, but he was also unafraid of elision, compression, and exhilarating syntactical complexity, even when describing the outwardly ordinary lives of miners and foundrymen. For obvious reasons his early stories are reminiscent of Henry Green, whose second novel *Living* (1929) is a challengingly impressionistic account of life in a Birmingham factory; but the other writer with whom he has clear affinities is Elizabeth Bowen, and it is no surprise she should have so admired his work. A comparison between this little-known writer and two of the twentieth-century's greatest stylists may seem extravagant, but at his best Green can easily bear it. In "The Proud Friend," for example, the laconic dialogue of the characters is set in counterpoint with prose as dense, as elaborate, and as gorgeous as anything by Green or Bowen:

They made as couples do the changeable summer's tale, part of the turned hay, the lad biking to the pit, the tock of glasses at the pub's open window. Together with her he was kind, but alone the burgeoned season angered him by fondness for her to seek Jack, where he forced his glass to its bright spilt circle on the dark bar, and frowning drew his hand across his mouth.

"Money's for use," he said.

Although the style of *In the Making* is not quite so oblique and highly wrought, Green remained a writer who shows rather than tells. The novel is full of verbal echoes and reflective images, and while its plot is conventionally linear, its narrative method is brilliantly suggestive of the inchoate nature of Randal's apprehensions of life and love. As Green wrote about the stories he selected for *Tales of Innocence*: "It is through the peculiarities of the child's mind that the story is told. He has for instance a clarity of associations which is not yet stunned by verbal labels nor blinded by self-regarding calculations. Intuition takes the place of reason. A sense of timelessness makes his present eternal and space is so fluid that a dark cloud may be Africa or a flower-bed a continent."

The exact period of *In the Making* is left vague, but references to the First World War and the fact that the book is partly autobiographical place it in the early 1920s. The novel opens with Randal in his dressing gown and pyjamas kneeling beside the fender in his nursery, "an Indian Prince watching his caged and fiery tiger." Green immediately plunges the reader into the boy's intensely imagined world, and signals Randal's acute awareness of physical sensation. The close companion of Randal's early childhood is his older sister, Kit, but a distance opens up between them when she is sent away to boarding school. Randal nevertheless

decides that his love for her can exist independent of reciproca-
tion, and he submits willingly to his fate: "Randal knew no more
of the magic securities of childhood, learning his sentence of per-
petual dependence on another, to whom his renunciation would
mean nothing, and he entered gladly the prison of another's life."

A similar pattern obtains when Randal is sent to prep school,
where he falls unwillingly but hopelessly under the spell of a
charismatic older boy called Felton. The course of their relationship unfolds in a series of richly imagined set pieces, to which
Randal's heightened senses lend a near-hallucinatory quality: a
snowbound half-holiday on which the two boys go tobogganing;
drives through the countryside on summer evenings with a
doting master nicknamed Little Willie; the school's Halloween
fancy-dress party, at which Randal and Felton are dressed respec-
tively as Pierrot and Harlequin. The atmosphere of these scenes
is not explicitly sexual, but is deeply sensual. There is an almost
hyperaesthetic attention to the contrasting textures of clothes and
bare skin—something that is a hallmark of Green's writing
throughout his career, whether he is describing the hand-me-
down suits, frayed at wrist and ankle, of impoverished north-
erners or the colorful sarongs casually draping the slender limbs
of Sri Lankans. Much is made throughout the novel of the boys'
striking (but surely rather impractical?) uniform, which consists
of a white shirt and pullover, white shorts held up by a red snake-
clasp belt, and a red blazer. This near-fetishism of clothes recalls
the most unsettling of all Green's stories, "A Skilled Hand," in
which a fourteen-year-old calmly plots and carries out the
murder of another boy simply because he covets the smart uniform his victim wears when playing with the local Works Band.

Randal's intense responsiveness to the physical world is an outward manifestation of his passionate feelings about Felton. For

example, when the boys go tobogganing, "the warm firm sweater covering Felton's body" is minutely described. When the toboggan comes to a standstill at the end of the run, Randal wants to hold the moment, "to die there": "His hand closed over Felton's fingers crooked round the cord on the boards, and he pressed his face into the thick collar of the sweater. His breath made the wool damp. He raised his head and gazed into Felton's face, beautiful and firm in the strange reflection of the snow. It was terribly close to him under the short bright hair. The snow was chill in his shoes. Time was endless where he gazed at Felton and was held by him in his arms. He need never move. The darkening and glistening snow lay round them for a still instant in the silent combe." This sense of the two boys existing in a kind of bubble that isolates them from their clamoring schoolfellows and in which time is suspended, the metaphysical notion of lovers creating and inhabiting their own private world, is echoed at the ravishingly described Halloween party. Amid the noisy and colorful throng, Felton stands alone beside the fire, seen entirely through Randal's eyes and with a lover's attention to physical detail: his body "pressed into the skin-tight diamonds of red and green and yellow . . . his ruffled flaxen hair and his mouth and chin gold as if sunlit."

Unfortunately for Randal, he never quite grasps the fact "that this new world which he shared with Felton did not exist for Felton, that the moments from which it was created were for him as easily dispelled as a few friendly or angry words. He never discovered that this happiness, keener perhaps than any he would experience again, was derived from his own imagination." That love can be like this, and is sometimes squandered on an unworthy or finally unresponsive person, is a lesson we all must learn; it does not make the love any less real. Green's school friend John Marshall recalled that the model for Felton was "a well-knit athletic boy with no spiritual interests. He was generally considered to be 'topping' because of his athleticism and bravura. It was the bravura that got [Green], and Randal's emotions were certainly real. [Green] himself had very few dealings with Felton—his anguish only bore fruit in an unusual school story thirty years later. A happy ending, really."

There is, of course, no traditional happy ending for Randal, the more loving one in this tale of unequal affections—though the novel's conclusion is rather more optimistic and redemptive than in many of Green's stories, which often end in death or disaster. Haunted by Felton in his dreams, torn between love and hatred, Randal is driven to rash action which results in him having to leave school early. A coda finds him waiting on a railway platform for a train to take him to his public school. As he moves forward into his new life, still possessed by and now possessing Felton, he begins translating his experience into literature by sketching out a poem. This ending suggests that what makes Randal as a person may also make him as a writer. Imagination may mislead the heart, but can also be creative and transformative, as love can be.

PETER PARKER is author of *The Old Lie* (1986) and biographies of J. R. Ackerley (1989) and Christopher Isherwood (2004). He edited *A Reader's Guide to the Twentieth-Century Novel* (1994) and *A Reader's Guide to Twentieth-Century Writers* (1995), and was an associate editor of the *Oxford Dictionary of National Biography* (2004). Quotations are taken from G. F. Green, *In the Making* (London: Peter Davies, 1952).

FORBIDDEN COLORS
(1953)

by Yukio Mishima

RANDALL KENAN

For those who admire his fiction, the obvious choice, when it comes to the best "gay" novel by Yukio Mishima, would probably be 1949's *Confessions of a Mask*. Among his best known works in the West, it was his first major success in his homeland, Japan. The story of adolescent awakening to same-sex attraction—sometimes among the falling bombs of World War II—the novel is a weird, wonderful, at times macabre, erotic adventure into sexual self-discovery. There are passages that are still among my all time favorites: the fixation and masturbatory fantasies over the famous portrait of the nearly nude and arrow-pierced St. Sebastian; watching a young sailor dance; the obsession with a classmate's underarm fuzz; the fantasy of literally feasting on young male bodies.

But aside from the bald and soaring poetics of homoeroticism in which the book exults, I believe the book has some significant flaws, most having to do with it being such an early work; an apprentice work in many ways (this, from a twenty-three-year-old who would go on to write over twenty-three novels, over ninety short stories, forty plays, and abundant nonfiction). *Confessions of a Mask* is a very young man's book, perhaps rife with more hormones than art.

Mishima's 1953 novel *Forbidden Colors* is a much more ambitious and much darker work. Its main character Yuichi is no one's gay role model. In fact, he is perhaps one of the world's greatest realizations, on paper, of a beautiful simpleton. But the intellectual center of the novel is the sixty-five-year-old Shunsuke Hinoki. He is a prolific novelist of great acclaim whose long life has been bedeviled by a lack of success with women. Now his beautiful young mistress—his tenth—Yasuko, is to wed an even more electrifyingly handsome young man, Yuichi. Upon meeting this God-like airhead, the aging and self-proclaimed "ugly" writer devises a diabolical plan: Shunsuke Hinoki will use the witless yet sly Yuichi, so easily manipulated, to wreak havoc on all the women who have—in his eyes—wronged him. His thieving ex-wife. His crazy ex-wife. His sex-starved ex-wife. And a few others, including a few men. Thus Shunsuke spins a vast web of deceit, with himself as the spider and Yuichi as the lure.

The long and complicated plot that ensues is reminiscent of Balzac (*Cousin Bette* [*La Cousine Bette*, 1846]; *Lost Illusions* [*Illusions perdues*, 1843]); and even Moliere; Mishima was absorbed with French literature from an early age. The book revels in farce and narrative intricacies, in the dissection and sending up of the status quo and of society-at-large (in this case that of post-World War II Japan). Parallel to this whirligig of a story is Yuichi's bemused yet highly sensitive introduction to the underground world of homosexual men—which seems to include every male in Tokyo! Yuichi's Boswell-like journey through this forbidden world makes for some piquant observations about gay life, almost microscopic in terms of its attention to detail. In fact, the only moments of genuine affection and tenderness in the book are those overseen by Yuichi between men. Perhaps the most moving incident in the entire novel is a "wedding" scene, the ritual being a gathering of men watching two lovers plant a tree together.

Mishima's fascination with classical European (read: Greek and Roman) aesthetics, and his growing obsession with the way of the samurai and their ancient vision of the purest love existing only between two warriors, fighters who would protect themselves in battle until death: all this combines to make a compelling cosmology about male-male love, a homoerotic aesthetic; almost, even, a philosophy of gay love. In one scene, after pining after a particularly rambunctious youth, Yuichi thinks:

They had turned away from society and dreamed of a youth of daring deeds, exploration, heroic evil, of the brotherly love of comrades-in-arms who face death on the morrow, of sentimental exploits they knew would end in disaster, and of all manner of youthful tragedy. They knew that they had been cut out for nothing but tragedy . . .

This is followed by a litany of boyhood fantasy scenarios straight out of pirate tales and heroic legends of battle and exciting derring-do, ending with the statement:

Indeed, these were the only catastrophes meant for youth. If such opportunities for catastrophe are allowed to pass, youth must die. What is the death of the body, after all, compared with the unbearable death of youth?

This is the stuff of boyish romance, and in many ways the very heart of homoerotic bonding: not so much in the illicit nature of same-sex attraction, but in the dream of a pure love, one to which only the innocent can abandon themselves, but about which old people often dream.

To be fair, Yuichi is not exactly dumb. The novel would not work if the young man couldn't observe, register, and on some level understand what is going on around him. This aspect makes him seem all the more sinister in hindsight. He is, after all, a college student:

> It was not yet time for exams. All he had to do was look over his notes. Economic history, public finance, statistics—all his notes were arranged there, transcribed meticulously in tiny notes, though it was a mechanical precision. Mornings in the sunlit autumn classroom, amid the rustling agitation of hundreds of pens, the machine-like character was what particularly marked Yuichi's pen. What made his passionless jottings look almost like shorthand was his habit of treating thought as nothing more than an exercise in mechanical self-discipline.

Yet something seems to be missing in his make-up. Call it a soul, call it empathy, call it a moral compass: "Yuichi earnestly believed in his own innocence; perhaps it would be more appropriate to say that he prayed for it." While watching his wife go through a harrowing childbirth, Yuichi has an epiphany:

At this time, however, Yuichi's heart, pondering his wife's face at the pinnacle of suffering, and the burning coloration in that part of her that had been the source of his loathing, went through a process of transformation. Yuichi's beauty, that had been given over for the admiration of man and woman alike, that had seemed to have existence only to be seen, for the first time had its faculties restored and seemed now to exist only to see. Narcissus had forgotten his own face. His eyes had another object than the mirror. Looking at this awful ugliness had become the same as looking at himself.

Yuichi is a right complicated fellow. In the end, he seems quite incapable of truly understanding his own mind, only his desire, which comes down foursquarely on the masculine sex. His marriage, his fatherhood are all pro forma, as it was for the vast majority of same-sex-loving men, not only in Japan but throughout the world in 1953, making Yuichi a much more resonant figure even as he remains singularly a rogue. Perhaps that ubiquitous and closeted recognition is what undergirds this often hilarious book with such a sense of doom, dread, and unrequited romance, just as much of Mishima's own life was so ruled.

(Of course, Mishima would become famous not only for his alarmingly spectacular suicide, after taking hostage the commandant of a military base in his own office, but also for forming a private army, the Tatenokai, sanctioned by the government. In this latter-day version of the loyal samurai was his lover, who died with Mishima that infamous day. Indeed, just before he left to commit this bizarre series of acts, the author finished the last page of *The Decay of the Angel* [1970], last in his magnum opus, the four-novel series *The Sea of Fertility*. Curiouser and curiouser.)

So why recommend a book featuring a beautiful, narcissistic gay idiot (married to a woman) and an evil, misogynist old man with little love left in him? Because the novel is delicious good fun. *Forbidden Colors* is powerfully complex, and, like our greatest novels, it represents life as it is and not life the way we might want it to be. Sometimes the wicked prosper; sometimes the bad guys win; and all of the time it's fun to read about their misguided exploits in this amusement park ride of a novel.

And yet I also feel a great tenderness for all these flawed and sin-filled characters, who are trying, at least, to figure stuff out. Mishima achieves a quality of honesty in portraying their groping towards truth that is at times breathtaking and always compelling.

Who knows but that, on some of the lower frequencies, you might see your own reflection in their diabolical mischief.

RANDALL KENAN is author of a novel, *A Visitation of Spirits* (1989) and a story collection, *Let the Dead Bury Their Dead* (1992), as well as a biography of *James Baldwin* (1994), the nonfictional *Walking on Water: Black American Lives at the Turn of the Twenty-First Century* (1999), and, most recently, *The Fire This Time* (2007). Quotations are taken from Yukio Mishima, *Forbidden Colors* (New York: Vintage, 1999), translated by Alfred H. Marks, which is currently in print.

HOWL AND OTHER POEMS
(1956)

by Allen Ginsberg

DAVID BERGMAN

Nearly everyone who writes about Allen Ginsberg begins with a personal reminiscence. I have my own trivial if telling account. He had come to read at Kenyon College, where I was a student, and the professor with whom he was staying invited me and other student poets to join them for breakfast. I was not yet out, but as soon as we entered the room, Ginsberg seemed to look into my heart. He patted the seat beside him. "You sit here," he said, and then out of kindness, paid me no more attention.

Everyone seems to have a Ginsberg story. What is important is that I can think of no other poet for whom the entry into their work is so commonly a personal encounter. Of course, during his life Ginsberg was ubiquitous. He always seemed to be giving a reading, attending a conference, teaching a seminar—and not just in New York and San Francisco but in Boston and Baltimore, Biloxi and Boulder. And in those personal encounters he was remarkably available. Lines might be long to meet him, but in the short interval while he signed a book he gave you his complete attention. He generated kindness particularly if you were a young male, and especially if you were blond and lithe. Yet there is another reason people start with their personal encounter with Ginsberg before they discuss his poetry, and that is, like Walt Whitman, he invites the equation of holding the book and holding the man, that flesh and the page are one.

There are poets whose work is more autobiographical—Frank O'Hara, for example, whom I was also reading as an undergraduate. But his I-do-this-I-do-that poems are often about him alone, and although he often evokes his friends, I felt somehow that their charm relied on my exclusion. Yet when Ginsberg and Whitman stroll together in "A Supermarket in California," "dreaming of the lost America of love past blue automobiles in driveways, home to [their] silent cottage," I felt then—as I do now—that I might join them, that Ginsberg might pat the seat and ask me to accompany them for pancakes and coffee. And when Ginsberg evokes the best minds of his generation, he seems to be talking not about his friends from Harvard, but for all the bright young disaffected men driven mad by America. You could look at the photograph of Carl Solomon, skinny, bespectacled, sitting in his underwear on his hospital bed, a mad, silly-looking, Jewish version of Gandhi, and know no matter how odd you were, Ginsberg wouldn't cast you out. Some of the best moments in a documentary devoted to Ginsberg are clips of a *Firing Line* television interview with the arch-conservative William F. Buckley. At the start of the program, with his knives sharpened and at the ready, Buckley is clearly out to get Ginsberg. But by the end of the evening, Buckley is disarmed, almost ready to join Ginsberg. Ginsberg's success as a poet was his readiness to embrace everyone. Anyone could join his merry band.

Mark Doty in a wonderful essay—"Form, Eros, and the Unspeakable" (*The Virginia Quarterly Review* [Spring 2005])—discusses why despite its sexual explicitness, Ginsberg's work has become so acceptable, for even after more than fifty years, "Howl" is still strikingly explicit. The best minds of his generation are men

> who let themselves be fucked in the ass by saintly motor-
> cyclists, and screamed with joy,
> who blew and were blown by those human seraphim, the
> sailors, caresses of Atlantic and Caribbean love . . .
> who hiccupped endlessly trying to giggle but wound up
> with a sob behind a partition in a Turkish Bath when the
> blond & naked angel came to pierce them with a sword.

For Doty, Ginsberg could get away with such talk because "everybody understood that on some level it wasn't really his ass he was talking about anyway. It was an attitude toward the world and toward the body, a sweet-natured, laughing acceptance of earthliness." I don't entirely agree. I would rather say that Ginsberg learned to allow his audience to believe that he wasn't really talking about his ass, that a kind old man like Ginsberg couldn't possibly be having anal sex. But Ginsberg's achievement is that he was both talking about his ass and talking about spiritual transcendence at the same time, and he got away with it in just the way queers have always been getting away with it, by a sweet campy zaniness that gains pathos from boyish vulnerability.

Ginsberg's strategy in reading "Howl" changed over the years. In an early recording, Ginsberg declaimed "Howl," emphasizing its indictment of an evil, insane, and unremitting social structure, but when I heard Ginsberg read "Howl"—at no less august occasion as the annual meeting of Modern Language Association—he performed it as a sort of sacred fool, wiggling his head and arms, raising his voice up and down, stressing words with a joyous italics. He turned the poem into the kind of divine comedy Doty discusses in which sex is "just as capable of offering the ridiculous as it is the transcendent." It was exactly the sort of road show to delight the convention of college professors who had read their Herbert and Donne, and recognized the allusion to Plotinus.

Such a comic presentation makes you forget that these sexually explicit lines must have cost Ginsberg a great deal. I don't know of another poem before "Howl" that spoke so straightforwardly and rapturously about anal sex, and this declaration is all the more astonishing since Ginsberg only months before had been trying to go straight. The fact is that Ginsberg was expressing a comfort with himself and his body he either had not quite achieved or had achieved only recently. One can see this lack of assurance in his changes to the manuscript. In the earliest typescript that has been preserved, he fiddled with the line "who blew and were blown by those human angels, the sailors," altering *human* to *inhuman* and cancelled out the word *blew*. The alterations turn the incident into a less mutual, more bestial encounter. Thankfully he later returned the line to his original wording.

Still, machismo haunts the entire poem. The best minds of his generation are strictly male; women are reduced to "snatches" that need to be "sweetened." Steven Taylor argues that "Beneath 'Howl' is the protracted process of losing his mother," and indeed, the moment of incest is a climax to the poem, the last strophe before he turns to Carl Solomon, who is "the shade of my mother." Yet even as Ginsberg raises the specter of incest (he replaces the word *fucked* with a series of asterisks) he almost immediately turns away from it. He is not ready to address his mother, and the poem's misogyny is a strategy of distancing himself from all women.

The first part of "Howl" gets most of the attention, but it seems to me in their less startling ways that the second and third parts of the poem are just as queer in content. Part II is the more Blakean as it raises before us the great furnace of Moloch, the Canaanite fire god. Moloch is heterosexuality turned against itself—the god that demands parents to destroy their own children. Ginsberg's relationship to Moloch is complex, for although he sometimes stands outside of Moloch, he also sits in Moloch ("Crazy in Moloch! Cocksucker in Moloch! Lacklove and manless in Moloch!"), and has assimilated Moloch ("Moloch who entered my soul early!"). It is Moloch finally who has destroyed the best minds of Ginsberg's generation, and the escape from madness requires cleaning by both fire and water.

If Blake dominates the middle section of the poem, then Whitman returns to preside over the concluding movement, the lyric expression of solidarity with Carl Solomon. Solomon later noted that Ginsberg never visited him in Rockland State Hospital nor was he a patient there at the time Ginsberg wrote "Howl." Yet Rockland seems more allegorically suitable, more metonymic for the condition of America. I find something particularly Jewish in this psalm-like section. Ginsberg must have read during Passover the traditional passage of the four sons—the evil son, the wise son, the simple son, and the one who cannot speak. The evil son excludes himself from the story of the Jews' enslavement in Egypt and therefore cannot participate in their liberation. Ginsberg is the wise son who sees other people's suffering as his own. He is spiritually connected to Solomon who remains exiled and oppressed, subjected to ping-pong and electric shock. Ginsberg extends to Solomon what Ginsberg's own mother cannot extend to her son, a home where he is safe and loved. "Howl" closes in the way that "A Supermarket in California" closes—with Ginsberg retiring with a man he loves into his "cottage in the Western night." Ultimately "Howl" brings us to a queer home, where children are not dispensed to Moloch or driven mad in Rocklands, but loved and protected and appreciated, where they can forget their underwear because of the "starry-spangled shock of mercy" that will set them free.

DAVID BERGMAN is the author of *Gaiety Transfigured* (1991) and *The Violet Hour: the Violet Quill and the Making of Gay Culture* (2004). His books of poetry include *Heroic Measures* (1998) and *Cracking the Code* (1986), which won the George Elliston Poetry Prize. He won a Lambda Book Award for editing *Men on Men 2000* (2000), and his newest book is the anthology *Gay American Autobiography: Writings from Whitman to Sedaris* (2009). He teaches at Towson University. Quotations are taken from Allen Ginsberg, *Howl: Original Draft Facsimile, Transcript and Variant Versions* (New York: HarperPerennial, 2006), which is currently in print, as is a version of the original collection—Allen Ginsberg, *Howl and Other Poems* (San Francisco: City Lights, 2001).

GIOVANNI'S ROOM
(1956)

by James Baldwin

DOUGLAS A. MARTIN

The Picture of a Boy Not Black

LOOKING

I took photos of the copies of *Giovanni's Room*, stacked atop the title card telling students "required," for the class I'd offer as Visiting Assistant Professor, two-hundred level, "Queer Literature and Studies." The author, James Baldwin, in *Conversations with James Baldwin* (1989): "those terms, homosexual, bisexual, heterosexual are twentieth-century terms which, for me, really have very little meaning." Still, a crisis of identity, or meaning if you will, arises in our book, for the David character, just one of many in Baldwin; his stepfather David (adopted, Baldwin knew not his real father), a brother David, the biblical even, in addition to other fictional ones.

The edition of the book we'd be reading from was the widely available Delta Trade, a division of that giant, Random House conglomerate, and you might miss it, if not given to scanning a book's colophon, otherwise directed there: a dedication reduced to space left available, left-facing side pushed above matters of publication history. The dedicatee does here arguably figure, to a lesser or greater degree. Certainly he does in the completion of Baldwin's first novel, *Go Tell It on the Mountain* (1953).

His friend: they would each see it differently, meeting up in Paris (first in a shady bar I translate as The White Queen), pooling money to eat—like a younger brother, then lover—takes him to family's tiny Swiss Village chalet in the Alps, Baldwin in one particularly bad way, holding onto his dream of settling down, does want them to share a life together. For three months, Winter 1951–52: they will be there together, Baldwin in longed for harmony ("dream of a domestic life with a lover," David Leeming writes in his 1994 biography), finishing up finally the novel to be *Mountain*—while mostly Lucien is just helping his friend; for him, having someone with whom he could just be himself.

Giovanni's Room, first edition 1956, Dial Press (the once-independent publisher Michael Joseph does the book in London); Knopf decides to pass—they'd wanted another novel, like they tended to, after publishing Baldwin's first to great acclaim, but not this one. Baldwin had completed a play, *The Amen Corner* (1955), and was working as well on essays, a volume to be published between his first two novels. "For LUCIEN" rests upon one page unto itself in the Dial edition. On a second page following, the Whitman epigraph, from *Leaves of Grass* (1855): "I am the man, I suffered, I was there." (Remember, it's England, overseas, where Whitman's work is first better received; Baldwin sets the heart of his second novel in Paris, France.) *Giovanni's Room* goes into a second printing within six weeks of initial publication.

Eponymous Giovanni speaks of the "fearful energy" of Americans. David, who has become his lover, notices: "When Giovanni wanted me to know that he was displeased with me, he said I was a '*vrai américain*'; conversely, when delighted, he said that I was not an American at all; and on both occasions he was striking, deep in me, a nerve which did not throb in him. And I resented this: resented being called an American (and resented resenting it) because it seemed to make me nothing more than that, whatever that was; and I resented being called *not* an American because it seemed to make me nothing." Baldwin had been darling writing the condition his home wanted him to know, the Black one: throwing his particular, lyrical slant upon, illuminating it for them, powers that were. But two men shacking up . . . one blond and one Italian, to boot . . .

Novels tend to swell in his country. Norman Mailer, who followed Baldwin's work for a time with just as much passion as Baldwin would in turn Mailer's (e.g., "I was black and knew more about that periphery [Mailer] so helplessly maligns in 'The White Negro' [1957] than he could ever hope to know," "The Black Boy Looks at the White Boy" [1961]) faults Baldwin, feeling generally "even the best of [Baldwin's] paragraphs are sprayed with perfume"—effectively diminishing/feminizing the stylist, relegated to "minor" status, as in "doomed to be" until he "really tells it" (stops with his "noble"—I prefer the French flavor—*eau de toilette*—to Mailer's "toilet water") and confesses along with assessment of *Giovanni's Room* as "a bad book" ("but mostly a brave one") how "[he—'one' Mailer writes in a universalizing, generalizing? attempt]—itches at times to take a hammer to [Baldwin's] detachment, smash the perfumed dome of his ego, and reduce him to what must be one of the most tortured and magical nerves of our time." Not unlike my cut-through redistribution of this one capsule in Mailer's "Evaluations—Quick and Expensive Comments on the Talent in the Room." (Capote, "tart as a grand aunt, but in his way . . . a ballsy little guy," Mailer decides, though "his short stories are too often saccharine"— reminding me of that phrase the black boys in my elementary school would say—you look like you might have some sugar in you. Gore Vidal, "in need of a wound which would turn the prides of his detachment into new perception.") To all this, compare Giovanni's claim he "is not afraid of the stink of love."

JAMES

When I screen Isaac Julien's film *Looking for Langston* (1989)— not only the Hughes of the title appears, but Baldwin: in sequences of photos enlarged, overlapping textual excerpts—in a blush of inspiration, one of three students more regularly in attendance (in the end only five enroll, Tuesday evenings, discussion, three hours) says, "We don't have the language to speak about this." An English major at UGA, we didn't even read Baldwin in my African-American Literature class. When a writing student in the city, with the first two novels, we read just the opening of his *Another Country* (1962)—you see, he's trying to put the two halves together, Europe and America, sexuality and race. A mentor at one point more insistent about desire to be with me is effusive: imitating style or subject matter or some combination thereof, move the texts before us somewhere else. I was researching La Reine Blanche, the bar providing the model for the one where David and Giovanni meet, where Baldwin and Lucien do. Paris: the writer also begins to "explore"—as the Chronology in the Library of America's *Collected Essays* has it— Henry James, author of "The Beast in the Jungle" (1903), one story to hold up to David's prescience: "The beast which Giovanni had awakened in me would never go to sleep again; but one day I would not be with Giovanni anymore."

Lucien, seventeen when he and Baldwin first meet: "living on his good looks and charm," "kept," and in the words of one Baldwin biographer had "a healthy appetite for pleasure" (James Campbell, *Talking at the Gates* [1991]); Baldwin rooming in hotels, one more expensive than the next, more accommodating space sought, clerks in Paris for an American lawyer, lands in jail for days once, a mix-up.

Lucien: "not an intellectual," "tall, slim, and good-looking," "had a gentleness to him," "a runaway" (parents don't want him in Paris). Baldwin is in a sense running, too, from America ("I left because I was driven out, because my homeland would not allow me to grow in the only direction in which I could grow" ["Notes for *The Amen Corner*," 1968]). Lucien marries within three years of meeting Baldwin, who thinks he should do the right thing, pregnant girl involved ("nasty little beasts," Jacques in *Giovanni's Room* jokes of boys who sleep with girls—chides, "Confusion is a luxury which only the very, very young can possibly afford and you are not that young anymore," David still claiming himself "queer for girls"). Baldwin is named godfather of the boy called after the two men, Luc-James.

"What kind of life can two men have together anyway?" in "this miserable closet of a room," site of a "regurgitated life," David wonders. He seems to be particularly concerned in metaphors Baldwin has him think and feel in, in psychology created for him, with in any way "blackening" himself—that place gone when mining for the poetry of the worried man's mind. As to what his son might be up to in Paris all this time, David's father is "living, obviously, in a pit of suspicions which daily became blacker and vaguer"—"he would not have known how to put them into words, even if he had dared."

Through the character of David, Baldwin routes to understand any perceived ambivalences projecting from apparently much more clear-cut Lucien, to shut them down. ("And my private life had failed—had failed, had failed" ["The Black Boy Looks at the White Boy"].)

AN OFFICE

At times I'm no more happy playing teacher than David wifey to Giovanni, one problem felt within the couple. A mentor I have now that I've gone back to school again, trying to be some kind of academic, believes my student David probably would remember, more so than me, if we slept together, if my experience up by this point has undoubtedly been more varied, vast: over a summer when all there felt to be was lower level of library, where stalls swing open, another like you could come in, I might have. He's from where I am, just up for school, too.

Another Visiting, this one "Instructor"—distinctions, (but he must have been here for some time to know) tells me my office once was a Men's room, converted, why a gender neutral one has been instated since across the way; the thing about the lock is you really have to play around with it or it just won't click, slide so easily into place. (The potential oddness in naming a bookstore—once Mecca for like-minded—after the place David before long begins to obsess upon escaping, not being swallowed alive by, I wanted to point out to the class; outside, though, through future projections, desire is imagined to be located in "God knows what dark avenues," followed into "what dark places.") David looks like one of the ones I kept looking out for, because, like I'd tell him I've said of him even to another Professor, he seemed smart—he catches my *seemed*, that's how much so he is. Having pulled a knee muscle, he hasn't been in class. He wanted to go through the book, pointing out particular places he's connected to what's written.

In the vicinity of the campus (in the parking lot of the movies I translate Destination), the man in his Cherokee, dark windows he's telling me to look out for, proud of, says, "What a freak, man," when I change my mind, from one side to the other of the car, when I don't want to just get in, just let him suck, decide to run off. Discernibly he's no other way for me but "white," "athletic," about all I can see: old sweatshirt, older man.

Baldwin, 1985, "Freaks and the American Ideal of Manhood," first published in *Playboy*: "The human being does not, in general, enjoy being intimidated by what he/she finds in the mirror." (I should teach this next time along with the novel.)

Baldwin, 1971: "People invent categories in order to feel safe. White people invented black people to give white people identity . . . Straight cats invent faggots so they can sleep with them without becoming faggots themselves" (quoted in Jonathan Ned Katz, *The Invention of Heterosexuality* [2007]).

David: "it had not occurred to me until that instant that, in fleeing his body, I confirmed and perpetuated his body's power over me."

DOUGLAS A. MARTIN is author of the novels *Outline of My Lover* (2002) and *Branwell* (2006), as well as a short-story collection, *They Change the Subject* (2005) and a volume of poetry, *In the Time of Assignments* (2008). His latest book is a lyric narrative, *Your Body Figured* (2008). Forthcoming is a new novel, *Once You Go Back* (2009). Quotations are taken from James Baldwin, *Giovanni's Room* (New York: Delta, 2000), which is currently in print.

FIRST LOVE AND
OTHER SORROWS: STORIES
(1958)

by Harold Brodkey

NOEL ALUMIT

Picture this: 1986. A Filipino boy. Eighteen. A terribly self-conscious college freshman. He's a life-long public school kid attending a private Southern California University. He knows his Difference. He's aware of the fact that he's darker than most of his classmates. Dark in skin color. And mood. He studies Drama. He can count on one hand how many other Asians there are in his department. (Even then, he doesn't have to use all of his fingers.)

He is not wealthy. The University of Southern California was known for its wealth. USC was also known as the University of Spoiled Children. The Freshmen still wears used clothes—Vintage, they're now called. Buying used clothes was something his mother taught him as a child. They went from Goodwill to Goodwill looking for clothes for themselves and for relatives back in the Philippines.

In his English class, he is assigned to read *First Love and Other Sorrows* by Harold Brodkey. It is a collection of stories written by an author of ambiguous sexuality. By the time he had reached college, the Freshmen had read many books: mostly classics, with a smattering of Stephen King and Ray Bradbury. With its lyrical language and youthful voice, *First Love* was the Freshman's first love for a book.

The collection offers stories of collegiate life, mostly of the Ivy League variety. Harvard, Princeton, Yale are names that are bandied about. However, it's the first-person coming-of-age narratives, guided by a nameless protagonist, that most intrigues the Freshman. They somehow spoke to the young man during his first semester at college, almost mirroring feelings he experienced at school.

In the first tale, "State of Grace," the protagonist is a "queer duck," a teenage boy painfully aware of his social economic status:

I knew many people in the apartments but none in the houses, and this was the ultimate proof, of course, to me of how miserably degraded I was and how far sunken beneath the surface of the sea. I was on the bottom, looking up through the waters, through the shifting bands of light— through, oh, innumerably more complexities that I could stand—at a sailboat driven by the wind, some boy who had a family and a home like other people.

The pain of his social class was augmented by his ethnicity:

Being Jewish also disturbed me, because it meant I could never be one of the golden people—the blond athletes, with their easy charm. If my family had been well off, I might have felt otherwise, but I doubt it.

The Filipino Freshmen understands these sentences well. Not the Jewish part. (He was raised Catholic.) He understands that other people get things. They're born into privilege sometimes. He saw how students went to the school cafeteria, using their parent's money to buy meals. The Freshman was on the other side of the counter, serving hamburger and fries to well-heeled kids from the suburbs. His classmates saw right through him, ignoring his face, seeing only the silly uniform and stupid cap. He resents this, believes it is unfair. He works at the cafeteria, hoping that it won't always be this way.

I was irrevocably deprived, and it was irrevocableness that hurt, that finally drove me away from any sensible adjustment with life to the position that dreams had to come true or there was no point in living at all.

The Freshman feels ugly and alone, walking the halls of the university. It seems most of his classmates dormed. He did not. He lives at home to save money and takes the bus to school. He does not have the luxury of returning to his dorm room between classes. Instead he walks through the various buildings of the campus, sitting in Doheny library or reads postings on bulletin boards at the Von Kleinsmid Center.

To rise above his feelings of inferiority, he decides to join a fraternity. Not one of those ridiculous fraternities with beer-drinking guys who threw toga parties. He rushes the Gammas, an Asian-American fraternity, concerned with community building and brotherhood. In this fraternity, he encounters Asians who turned out to be beer-drinking guys who threw toga parties.

His acceptance into the fraternity means the world to the Freshman. With the fraternity came a built-in social life, a posse of guys who stood behind him. It meant no more loneliness. He goes to school feeling a little more secure. In his English class, he reads the titular story in the collection, "First Love and Other Sorrows." Class is a continuing theme. The protagonist observes how his mother hopes their social status might change if the beautiful sister could only marry the right man, the right rich man. In this particular story, the Freshman notices something obscure. Harold Brodkey has a keen eye for describing the young men in the story. In this story, Brodkey describes the track star, Joel Bush:

> Joel was so incredibly good-looking that none of the boys could quite bear the fact of his existence; his looks weren't particularly masculine or clean-cut, and he wasn't a fine figure of a boy—he was merely beautiful. He looked like a statue that had been rubbed with honey and warm wax, to get a golden tone, and he carried at all times, in the neatness of his features and the secret proportions of his face and body that made him so handsome in that particular way, the threat of seduction. Displease me, he seemed to say, and I'll get you. I'll make you fall in love with me and I'll turn you into a donkey. Everyone either avoided him or gave in to him; teachers refused to catch him cheating, boys never teased him, and one never told him off.

The Freshman feels flattered that these frat men of various hues of gold and copper would accept him. In addition, the Freshman notices that the men of this fraternity are gorgeous. There's Jonathon, a tall, slender Chinese youth from New York. His long, angular face hinted at something regal. Mac, from San Francisco, a robust, athletic Japanese guy whose picture was often found in the university catalogue modeling sweat clothing. Luke, an incoming pledge, from Orange County. Luke's a cute Vietnamese dude with a surfer boy charm. The Freshman feels attractive by association.

He meets his "brothers" by a bench in front of the bookstore. He sits and chews the shit with them. The Freshman is the only one of them pursuing a career in the arts. The others major in business, economics, engineering. He finds solace in their encouragement of his involvement in Theater.

"There aren't a lot of Asian men there," Jonathan said. "That's why you should do it."

In this fraternity, the Freshman witnesses the bonding of males. The goofy way men act. Drinking and more drinking; the high-fiving; the strut of fellows who enjoy the feeling of balls between their legs. The Freshman becomes enamored. He loves their arrogance, their vanity.

It took him half an hour to get dressed. He'd stand in front of the mirror and flex his muscles endlessly and admire the line his pectorals made across his broad rib cage, and he always left his shirt until the last, even until after he had combed his hair . . . he loved his reflection and he'd turn and gaze at himself in the mirror from all sorts of angles while he buttoned his shirt.

In "The Quarrel," Brodkey illustrates the protagonist admiring a fellow student named Duncan—in the same way the Freshman wishes to emulate his fraternity brothers. In the story, the main character goes on a life-changing journey to Europe with Duncan.

The journey the Freshman takes with his frat brothers is joyous. He does not feel the alienating distance that he feels with other students. Indeed, they have a lot in common. His frat brothers also know Difference. Most of them are first- or second-generation Americans. They understand the word Minority. Some are considered upper middle-class, but no one exudes wealth. The Freshman feels almost identical to his "brothers." Almost.

> What did dismay me was the way he had of being rendered speechless by a color, or a pretty woman's gesture of welcome, or an automobile, or the way a girl's hair blew. He would stand, quite tense and excited, held by a kind of surprised rapture. When he had these quiet transports, I was embarrassed—for myself, because I was unable to share a friend's emotion.

The Freshman listens to other men talk excitedly about girls. They talk about the young women in the sister sorority, the Sigmas. He watches his fellow pledges get drunk to build up the nerve to talk to a "sister."

He listens to Luke, the cute Vietnamese surfer from Orange County, complain about a girl he's seeing. He wants to get closer to her, but can't.

"She's just using me for sex," Luke says, shaking his head. He appears disgusted at himself and his relationship.

"Then why are you seeing her?" the Freshman asks, genuinely concerned.

Luke doesn't answer, just continues to shake his head. They part to attend class.

The Freshman respects and admires the other men in the fraternity, but knows he's not as similar to them as he'd hoped. There is a matter of difference that his Asian brothers did not know. (One the Freshman himself is barely comprehending.)

Late in the semester, the fraternity hosts an event for alumni. Men who belonged to the Gammas years before show up to a picnic with their wives and children. The Freshman looks at his fellow pledges, then at the middle-aged men on the lawn trying to keep their children in check. The Freshman knows that his life will not be this. There will be no wife, no family like these on the lawn.

The Freshman has no words to explain to his fraternity brothers why he is leaving. He excuses himself, claiming that the rigor of his major prevents him from doing anything else. He feels guilty. In his sophomore, junior, and senior years, he bonds with other creative types in his department. When he encounters his old fraternity brothers on campus, he shakes their hands and laughs. And laughs.

The shadows, blue, liquid, were gathering across the beach. There we were, the two of us, with all of our fears and flaws, and our hopes that we didn't really believe in, and our failures; there we were nineteen and twenty. From one of the houses along the beach came the strains of a phonograph playing "La Vie en Rose." Duncan began to hum the song. The kindness of France spread around us like the incoming night. I listened to Duncan and the distant phonograph and the dreamlike rush of the waves, and I knew I would survive my youth and be forgiven.

POSTSCRIPT, 1993: Years after college, he would be in a bookstore, and picks up *People* magazine. He sees a picture of Harold Brodkey with his wife. The bisexual author is dying of AIDS and documents it for the *New Yorker*.

POSTSCRIPT, 2006: He walks in downtown and runs into a "brother" he hadn't seen in over twenty years. He gives a hearty handshake. They talk and exchange cards. The Brother owns a hip restaurant in Koreatown. Sometimes, he drops by for Bar-b-que.

NOEL ALUMIT is author of *Letter to Montgomery Clift* (2003) and *Talking to the Moon* (2007). He blogs at www.thelastnoel.blogspot.com and can be reached at noelalumit@hotmail.com. Quotations are taken from the most recent edition of Harold Brodkey, *First Love and Other Sorrows: Stories* (New York: Henry Holt, 1998).

A Taste of Honey
(1958)

by Shelagh Delaney

John Weir

My parents ran a community theater group in Clinton, New Jersey, in the 1960s and '70s. It was in an old stone mill on the South Branch of the Raritan River, fifty miles from New York. The tiny stage was on the ground floor, set against stone walls and a window overlooking a waterfall. Upstairs was a gallery hung with bad art, farm scenes done by local Sunday painters, and on the third floor, which was bowed with age, there was a storage space for sets and costumes, a great place to play dress-up while my parents and their friends drank six packs of Rheingold and rehearsed downstairs. In 1970, my mother directed *Man of La Mancha*, and my dad played drums, and you could hear the crash of water going over the falls between verses of "The Impossible Dream."

The next year, a man came out from New York with a teacher from the Sanford Meisner Acting School, and my parents and their pals did improvisational scenes and repetition exercises: "You're wearing a blue shirt!" "Yes, I'm wearing a blue shirt!" "I said you were wearing a blue shirt!" "That's right, goddammit, I'm wearing a blue shirt!"—which resulted in their putting on Shelagh Delaney's 1958 British working-class drama *A Taste of Honey*. Was that a likely choice? *A Taste of Honey* is a kitchen-sink melodrama about hard times in the northwest of England, where a white girl with a whore of a mom hooks up with a black sailor, gets pregnant, and moves in with a gay guy who cooks.

My parents and their friends were middle-class suburbanites in their thirties and forties. Married with children, they were working dads and stay-at-home moms, transfixed by their memories of World War II. They were opposed to the Vietnam War, though they were not the kind of people who joined in marches. If you asked them, they might have said that homosexuals made them nervous, but on the other hand, what the hell. "Que sera, sera," they'd sing, reaching for a gin and tonic. They were tolerant, not especially religious, more liberal than anyone else in the country but, like all the rest of them, white. I don't know where they found a black guy to play the sailor Jimmy in *A Taste of Honey*. Maybe he was a student at Princeton, which was an hour away. (A year later, they were not so lucky: Doing Anthony Newley's allegorical musical *The Roar of the Greasepaint—The Smell of the Crowd*, they had to convince a local dad with a lovely tenor voice and distinctly Irish coloring to smear his face with black pancake and sing "Feelin' Good," a song given to a character called The Negro.)

How they got someone to play a homosexual is not as surprising to me in retrospect as the fact that the guy they found was actually gay. His name was Steve, and he must have been about twenty-two years old. I was thirteen, finishing the eighth grade. I guess he was my first homosexual. Well, second, counting me. From the time I turned eleven, my grade school classmates had been hassling me and calling me a faggot. What made them so sure? As far as I could tell, I was the only faggot in rural northwestern New Jersey. What was their point of comparison? Surely their parents hadn't taken them to the film version of *The Boys in the Band* (1970)? So, when I saw Steve playing Geoffrey, the sweet, nurturing, ultimately rejected gay best friend of pregnant Jo, the heroine of *A Taste of Honey*, I thought, "Oh, that's what they mean. I'm him."

It was the most thrilling play I had ever seen. Of course, I didn't know anything about it. I had no idea that Delaney had written it when she was seventeen years old, and that it had been first performed in London in 1958, a year before I was born. Nor did I know about Delaney's subsequent career, her short stories and screenplays and radio plays. Clearly, I could not have known in 1971 that she would inspire the Smiths to write a song called "Girlfriend in a Coma." I had heard of the Angry Young Men playwrights, because my parents had a paperback copy of John Osborne's *Look Back in Anger* (1957). But I wouldn't have been able to place Delaney in the context of that theatrical moment and movement. I'm not sure I entirely grasped that the characters were British, though I must have noticed their dialogue about putting a shilling in the slot to turn on the heat in their fleabag apartment, which had a view of the gasworks and a communal latrine and wash house.

But I recognized Steve. He was amazing, flamboyant, silly, a wonderful actor with crack comic timing and, in addition to everything else, a beautiful voice. He wandered around backstage singing Barbra Streisand's arrangement of "A Taste of Honey"—a song that had also been recorded both by Herb Alpert and the Beatles—and if there was anything about him that was a cliché, I didn't care. I can't believe the local audiences didn't want to lynch him, because I went to school with their children, and I knew how aggressively the boys policed each other in order to ensure that none of the eighth-grade guys were acting like girls. Yet there was Steve as the best gay boyfriend of a single mom-to-be who clearly loved him more than she loved her mother or the sailor who stuck around for a month.

Of course, this was long before *Will and Grace*. Straight girls in love with their gay guy roommates and vice versa: by now it's a sitcom cliché. But it was news to me in Clinton, New Jersey in 1971, and it must have been a big surprise to London theatergoers in the late fifties. There was a ten-year British craze for grim dramas about working-class folks, but the main characters in plays by John Osborne, John Arden, and Edward Bond were men, and women were bystanders to the trauma of class consciousness and masculinity in crisis. *A Taste of Honey* was unique to the canon of working-class drama not just in its focus on women, but its audacity in including black and white characters, interracial love, and a homosexual man who was not put onstage specifically to represent "homosexuality."

A Taste of Honey is more lowkey and matter-of-fact about gay men than either Ang Lee's *Brokeback Mountain* (2005) or Gus Van Sant's *Milk* (2008). Its nervousness and curiosity about "what gay men do" is limited to a couple lines at the beginning of the scene where Jo first gets to know Geof. "I've always wanted to know about people like you," she tells him, but he doesn't reveal much: "I don't go in for sensational confessions," he says—and the matter is pretty much dropped. OK, Geof kisses Jo, and he proposes to her. He wonders what it would be like to be the father of her child. He makes a half-hearted effort to prove he could be a straight dad. And when Jo's mom, abandoned by her latest boyfriend, comes back on the scene at the end of the play, Geof disappears like a martyr from the family scene and makes a last-minute bitchy comment about women: "Yes, the one thing civilization couldn't do anything about—women."

Is he a nasty woman-hating, self-sacrificing queen who wishes he were straight, with no purpose in life except to help hetero-sexuals have babies? Not really. Most of the time, he and Jo hang around the apartment trying to deal with their poverty and boredom. And Geof is the only character in the play who it is possible to like. Jo is selfish and self-absorbed and a bit of a simp. Her mother Helen is a monster. Jo's sailor and Helen's boyfriend Pete both run away. Geof shows up and sticks around and cares about somebody other than himself. Of course, Steve played him with a feather boa. It was a campy performance, and it was wrong for the part. I was shocked years later when I saw the film ver-sion, in which Murray Melvin plays Geof as if he were nothing special, no more queeny or campy than a teen schlub in a film about the nerdy kid down the block. Melvin was right for the play, but I missed Steve. I have always been terrified of acting like a girl—those punishing eighth-grade boys had their effect!—but, oh, what Steve could do with a feather boa!

I saw every performance. I was on the Light Crew. Our family dentist ran the lights, and because the theater had no real back-stage—there was no fly space and the wings consisted of about ten square feet off left—our dentist couldn't see the stage, and I had to stand and signal him whenever one of the characters turned a light on or off. The play had been directed experimen-tally, influenced by the acting teacher from New York, and none of the action was blocked. The actors were supposed to move around the stage only when they "felt it." "Feel it, feel it," the director had yelled at them during rehearsals. They could do whatever they wanted, sit or stand or jump in place, cross or not cross, leave the scene if they liked and wander into the wings, as long as they were feeling it. It's a play where Helen breaks curtain at one point and turns to the audience to ask what they would do with such a daughter, and so it didn't seem odd for Steve to whirl and whirl his feather boa nearly in the face of the married suburban dad sitting in the front row of the sixty-seat theater.

Steven. What was he doing in the Jersey woods in 1971, with his pretty voice and his swinging hips and his taste for theatrics? He was not ironic; he was completely in earnest, and his performance never ended. He was as flirtatious and fabulous and funny offstage as on. The Stonewall Riots had happened only two years earlier in the West Village, and surely he belonged in Manhattan, throwing bricks at police officers and chanting, "Out of the closets and into the streets." "I used to be a patrol leader in the Boy Scouts," Geof says, joking with Jo, and I still remember how Steve played that line, how he seemed to dare the audience not to adore him, and how I wished I had been able to handle a roomful of homophobes—my eighth-grade home room—with as much genius, and foolishness, and reckless self-control.

JOHN WEIR is author of the novels *The Irreversible Decline of Eddie Socket* (1989) and *What I Did Wrong* (2006). Most recently, his stories have appeared in *Between Men* (edited by Richard Canning, 2007), *Vital Signs: Essential AIDS Fiction* (edited by Richard Canning, 2007), and *Between Men 2* (edited by Richard Canning, 2009). Quotations are taken from Shelagh Delaney, *A Taste of Honey* (London: Methuen, 1959), which is still in print.

A SINGLE MAN
(1964)

by Christopher Isherwood

PATRICK RYAN

"Don't you see," asks Christopher Isherwood's protagonist in *A Single Man*, "what I know is what I am? And I can't tell you that. You have to find it out for yourself. I'm like a book you have to read. A book can't read itself to you. It doesn't even know what it's about. I don't know what I'm about."

The unintended irony is that *A Single Man* is so brilliantly written, it practically reads itself. The speaker, a fifty-eight-year-old gay English professor named George, is talking to Kenny, a student who is admiring, attractive, and (for all we know) heterosexual. The scene comes near the end of this highly economic and compulsively readable novel which, like Joyce's *Ulysses* (1922), Woolf's *Mrs. Dalloway* (1925), and, more recently, Ian McEwan's *Saturday* (2005), paints an entire life—and the various worlds that life has known—in a solitary day. In addition to being as good as or (depending on your taste and loyalties) better than those books, *A Single Man* is loaded with compassion and charm, devoid of sentimentality, and rivals the achievements of all four of Updike's Rabbit Angstrom novels in just over one-hundred-eighty pages.

George claims not to know what he's about because he dismisses experience as useless. And yet, like the rest of us, experience is all he has. Each morning he's made anew; each day he goes through the motions of living; each evening he's broken down and shelved away. Or so the narrator would have it seem. Isherwood's camera, in this case, is aimed very intently at the inside of George's brain for *almost* the entire novel, and starts off literally constructing its main character as if from scratch, John Locke be damned:

> Waking up begins with saying *am* and *now*. That which has awoken then lies for a while staring up at the ceiling and down into itself until it has recognized *I*, and therefrom deduced *I am*, *I am now*. *Here* comes next, and is at least negatively reassuring; because *here*, this morning, is where it has expected to find itself: what's called *at home*.

The third-person, present-tense point of view feels just as intimate as if it were written in the first person, and it allows the reader to both observe and *be* George as he comes into consciousness. Never mind, for the moment, that this mild-mannered college teacher, both boyish and curmudgeonly, would in all likelihood be unfamiliar with how his fears are affecting his "vagus nerve," or how of his cortex is "at the central controls" of his own rising movements. These slips in the narrator's otherwise direct attachment to George's consciousness are deliberate and, by the novel's close, brilliant.

Staring and staring into the *mirror*, it sees many faces within its face—the face of the child, the boy, the young man, the not-so-young man—all present still, preserved like fossils on superimposed layers, and, like fossils, dead.

Before long, familiarity sets in—a familiarity that can only be attached to experience:

It knows its name. It is called George.

So begins the day. George lives in Los Angeles, in the house he once occupied with his long-time companion Jim. Jim has died in a car accident in Ohio, and, this being 1962, almost no one in George's life knows about the tragedy because almost no one officially knew they were a couple. George doesn't lock himself in the closet so much as keep himself boxed away—for the sake of convenience—from those stupid enough to be afraid of him. And just as there's no apology in the novel for its gay subject matter, there's no apology for George's occasional reactions to homophobia (he sounds, at times, like an ACT UP veteran, his thoughts blossoming into anarchy).

As the day unfolds, we learn both the current and past worlds of a man on the cusp of old age, a man so familiar with the texture of his landscape that every moment seems to have a chain of echoes trailing behind it. At the same time, every moment is private, significant, crucial.

George may only be fifty-eight, but his life-clock is ticking.

On campus, the air is abuzz with Cold War panic. George runs into the aforementioned Kenny, teaches a course on Aldous Huxley, and lingers a bit longer than he'd like in the faculty dining room with colleagues, where he suffers a conversation about the building of bomb shelters and the future need for personal submachine guns because, post-nuclear fallout, there'll be plenty of people still alive but not enough food: a "Rubble Age," as George imagines it—only he doesn't seem scared. He's still interested in observing humanity but knows all too well what there is to be observed. He's still capable of stimulation—both mental and physical—but is tired of the mop-up. Ultimately life is about loss, and he embraces that bleak notion without a trace of self-pity, but with a nagging fear that he's soon going to lose himself.

His loneliness irks him. During a visit to a dying hospital patient—a woman he loathes because she once tried to steal Jim away from him—he sees how decrepit she's become and is finally able to let go of his hate for her. And yet even though George's existence has morphed into a series of seemingly isolated moments—the day parceled out particle by particle—everything is connected. In losing his hatred for this woman, he's lost the anger for Jim's having an affair with her, and in losing that, he realizes, he's lost yet another aspect of Jim.

Again, this isn't sentimentality. It's cool monitoring—that of a scientist marking down an anticipated observation; you can almost hear the acknowledging *hmm* in George's head.

Earlier, he's declined an invitation to dine with his old friend, Charlotte, and as he navigates the grocery store aisles, having second thoughts and attempting to cobble together a meal, he wonders:

Should we ever feel truly lonely if we never ate alone?

But to say, I won't eat alone tonight—isn't that deadly dangerous? Isn't it the start of a long landslide—from eating at counters and drinking at bars to drinking at home without eating, to despair and sleeping pills and the inevitable final overdose? But who says I have to be brave? George asks. Who depends on me now? Who cares?

The question goes unanswered. But George abandons his shopping, rings Charlotte, and winds up at her house, where a flow of alcohol begins that won't stop until the end of the novel. The good news is that Charlotte is in low spirits, allowing George's own mood to improve (*Schadenfreude!*). However, as the drinking continues and Charlotte bemoans the loss of her husband to another woman, George's thoughts can't help but return once again to Jim:

> If I'd been the one the truck hit, he says to himself, as he enters the kitchen, Jim would be right here, this very evening, walking through this doorway, carrying these two glasses. Things are as simple as that.

Life is only as frightening—and only as comforting—as the random collision of molecules that make it possible.

They reminisce about England, where Charlotte longs to return. George doesn't, much to her chagrin, and he goes on to tell her:

> The past is over. People make believe that it isn't, and they show you things in museums. But that's not the past. You won't find the past in England. Or anywhere else, for that matter.

She informs him that he's tiresome. Then, in an awkward (and comic) moment of good-bye, she shoves her tongue into his mouth. He makes his exit, turning groggily away "with a punching heart," and talking himself down the precarious front steps of her bungalow.

He's both wound up and tired. He feels both dour and silly. He is dignifiedly drunk. He's pushed himself twice as hard as normal in the gym that afternoon—and it should be highlighted that, at least to my knowledge, Isherwood is the first author to explore the various dynamics that occur at an overtly gay gym. His observations are as relevant now as they were then. He allows us to laugh and wince at ourselves as he maneuvers George around the weight machines, the other exercisers, and the cruel plethora of mirrors.

Isherwood may also be the first author to openly explore the phenomenon of the *bromance*. He writes with startling clarity about the fuzziness of inebriation, and it's in such a state that George wanders into a local bar and spots, once again, his handsome and affable student Kenny. Of course, it's something of an exaggeration to say that what occurs between teacher and student in the closing hours of the novel is *bromantic*, but Kenny—currently embroiled in a fight with his girlfriend—is at least "brocurious." The two men down one drink after another and engage in some spirited arguing. George once again eschews experience as having nothing to do with the present moment. (Isherwood himself, it should be observed, "formed" fairly early in life into the person he would forevermore be. He was an emotional prodigy, and to a prodigy, experience is indeed nothing.) Impulsively, George and Kenny strip off their clothes and throw themselves into the rolling Pacific surf. The flirtation underway here is mutual, to say the least. And it's one of the most charming and erotic flirtations in contemporary fiction. They end up back at George's house, where George dons nothing more than a bathrobe and Kenny huddles naked, wrapped in a blanket that seems to have trouble staying around his shoulders.

And then the worm turns. Fueled by booze and sexual desire, George-the-lonely-widow becomes irritated and accusatory. His target is Kenny, but his anger is displaced. In reality he's berating himself, and at the height of his tirade, he passes out:

> For a moment, Kenny's face is quite distinct. It grins, dazzlingly. Then his grin breaks up, is refracted, or whatever you call it, into rainbows of light. The rainbows blaze. George is blinded by them. He shuts his eyes. And now the buzzing in his ears is the roar of Niagara.

Sometime later, George awakens to find that Kenny has carried him to bed and dressed him in his pajamas; a jovial note thanks him for "a great evening."

Unsure of whether or not he's made a fool of himself, he drifts in and out of sleep, and in and out of interweaving thoughts. He's worried that he'll forget Jim, but then concludes that Jim is synonymous with death. Jim is experience. He wants "another Jim," worries that he's too old to find one, and then redefines *now*—his present moment—as the quest for a new Jim. If there's a contradiction in denying the usefulness of experience while craving more of it, George doesn't care. He's tired.

Grief, hypocrisy, homophobia, the miracle of birth, the cruelty of aging, and the mystery of death: this short novel takes them all on with stunning grace. And just as the narrator has made George at the beginning—piece by piece, pulse by pulse—so he unmakes him at the end. And let us suppose George *does* know what a "vagus nerve" is. Let us suppose he *is* aware of his cortex controlling his motor movements. He might be imagining his own demise in the closing paragraphs, but he can't describe the corporeal breakdown we experience now. Isherwood's camera, having remained focused so sharply on George that there's almost been no lens between photographer and subject, dollies out and "can no longer associate with what lies here, unsnoring, on the bed." The same narrative entity that brought the *it* that was George to life has brought it to death. And the intervening frames—word for word, a masterpiece—shoot the lights out.

PATRICK RYAN is author of the short-story collection *Send Me* (2006), as well as two young adult novels, *Saints of Augustine* (2007) and *In Mike We Trust* (2009). He is a recipient of a 2006 National Endowment for the Arts grant, and his work was included in *The Best American Short Stories 2006* and *Between Men* (edited by Richard Canning, 2007). His third young adult novel, *Gemini Bites*, will appear in 2010. Ryan lives in New York City and is at work on a new short-story collection. Quotations are taken from Christopher Isherwood, *A Single Man* (Minneapolis: University of Minnesota Press, 2001), which is currently in print.

PARADISO

(1966)

by José Lezama Lima

RICHARD REITSMA

José Lezama Lima—renowned poet and essayist; founder and editor of such influential literary magazines as *Orígenes* (1944–56)—was also patron saint of Cuban literary inventiveness. While some readers may find his writing overly oneric or hallucinatory, verging on soporific enchantment, others will revel in his linguistic mastery. Admittedly, the text of *Paradiso* can be challenging. However, Lezama Lima's own philosophy on this, repeated as a mantra of the main protagonist Cemí, is that one must "always try what is most difficult."

The novel was first published in Cuba in 1966 in a limited edition of four-thousand. It was republished in 1968 outside Cuba with a larger print run. The first English translation by the inimitable Gregory Rabassa was published in 1974, and subsequently reedited and republished in 2000.

Paradiso was initially censored by the Cuban revolutionary authorities for its lack of revolutionary commitment and its depiction of homosexuality. The fact that it was published at all is owing to Lezama Lima's stature and reputation, as it would have been more costly to censor than to limit the publication. It is part autobiography, part literary criticism, with large doses of polymath inferences, reflecting Lezama Lima's notion of Cuban, Caribbean, and American identities as hodge-podge and hybrid. It has been called the quintessential Latin American novel of the neo-baroque; a modern reinvention of Góngora. However, the effusiveness of its language, the elaborate intertextuality, the allusions to traditions not merely Judeo-Christian and Greco-Roman, but also those of ancient Egypt, India, China, and the various Aboriginal Nations of the Americas; these are all combined into a cornucopia of loquacious bounty, dripping with an extravagance of language that is more rococo than baroque in its curlicues of excess and exuberance.

The novel is a *Kuenstlerroman*; an artistic *Bildungsroman*, or an exploration of the makings of the young artist. It is also a polemic on education and a lampoon of nationalistic literary criticism. At its core, it is effusive poetry. In Lezama Lima, "sex [is] like poetry," and poetry, like homosexuality, is rebellion. Therefore the more linguistically rebellious the narrative, the more Rabelaisian the sexual exploits of his characters, the more dangerous the writer is.

As family drama, the first half of *Paradiso* is reminiscent of Faulkner's more complex novels (*The Sound and the Fury* [1929] and *Absalom, Absalom!* [1936]): there's the creation of a world unto itself, the characters living out their lives against the backdrop of history. It is the story of a family and of a nation living through the wars of independence, the arrival of Americans (1898 until 1959) and the anguished transformation of the island's agriculture from tobacco to sugarcane, the effects of the Spanish flu outbreak of 1918, and the student rebellions against the dictator Machado. This history of the Cuban nation, told through the family history of the asthmatic adolescent Cemí and his two closest friends, Foción and Fronesis, is, in many ways, reminiscent of that of Quentin in Faulkner's novels. It should also be noted that Cemí carries in his blood the history of the island nation, in the throes of discovering its identity as the descendant of revolutionaries and Spanish immigrants, whose very name refers to the aboriginal deities of the Caribbean peoples.

The middle chapters of *Paradiso*, which focus on the main character's education at university, are structured very much like the dialogues of Plato's *Phaedrus*, dealing with love, art, sexuality, madness, and the divine. In these Cuban dialogues, Lezama Lima assimilates André Gide's discourse on the justification of homosexuality in *Corydon* (1924), as well as Jean Cocteau's *The White Book* (1924), with its sprinkled references to Freud and Havelock Ellis, one of the founding fathers of homosexual identity discourse.

Some critics have argued that the book is ultimately an indictment of homosexuality, since the main practitioner of homosexual behavior, Foción, goes mad. I would argue, however, that for its time and place, *Paradiso* represents a very frank discussion of homosexuality, leaving it up to the reader and Cemí to accept or reject it as a viable path towards selfhood.

Lezama Lima's work is also obsessively infused with instances of the word made flesh. The voluptuousness of his prose—poetic, abundant, fecund, Faulknerian in its excess;

beyond Baroque in its linguistic arabesques is part of the search for the "poetic logos." It is a verbal game, and as much a part of the narrative as the plot of Cemí and his friends. *Paradiso* is an expedition into the power of the word, of the verb as body. Lezama Lima explores the nature of art, of literature and homosexuality, and the efficacy of poetic, sexual rebellion.

For Lezama Lima, the body is a lesson in island geography. The text explores the geography of sex and of death, equating this island nation to an androgynous body. One makes love to this body through "poets of verbal rebellion" or heals its cancer-ridden body through "verbal exorcism." To Lezama Lima, sexual excess is akin to verbal excess. We are treated to the intricacies of both. When, however, sexual and textual repression are present, and there is a lack of sexual fulfillment, or a lack of linguistic fulfillment, the result is madness. This indictment of censorship of both the sexual body and the textual corpus is a direct attack on the Revolution's stated goals—of reforming society; of controlling the body politic as well as the body erotic, through the control of its literary production. Lezama Lima's rebellion is the poetic word.

An often overlooked aspect of *Paradiso* is most appealing to me. There are several mentions of the appearance of a comet, and specific references to 1910. This reference to the comet is an important metaphor in Latin American literature, as the comet is seen as the harbinger of revolutionary change. References to 1910, of course, draw a link to the birth of Lezama Lima, and to the first twentieth-century appearance of Halley's Comet. In addition to the intertextuality here, given the comet's apparition in many other Latin American texts, there is the connection to Faulkner. In *The Sound and the Fury*, Quentin kills himself in 1910, during the return of Halley's

Comet. Reinaldo Arenas also takes advantage of Halley's Comet in his short story of the same name ("El Cometa Halley" [1986; published 1991; translated into English, 2000]).

There is, however, a further connection to Faulkner that draws me in. In *The Sound and the Fury*, Quentin is homoerotically enchanted with a rower, to the point that he drowns himself in the Charles River to become one with the river and thus implicitly be penetrated by the rower. As a scholar of Faulkner, and a devoted rower, I was entranced by the presence of the rower in *Paradiso*. Cemí's friend Fronesis is also a rower. There's a scene involving the epitome of athleticism, the rower Baena Albornoz, whose virility, rowing prowess, and homophobia each have no peer. Of course, this prime example of masculinity, this paragon of machismo's virtues is caught *in coitus interruptus* by being penetrated by a novice. He is discovered in the ecstasy of his humiliation and attempts to burn down the boathouse. He and his sexual accomplice are expelled, their memories erased, "uprooted from the gardens, fortresses, pools, gymnasiums, colonnaded porticoes, from all spaces real and symbolic where naked bodies might be displayed in the purified ascendancy of day." The homosexual but homophobic rower's expulsion from school and from all geographic spaces reflects a particular anxiety on the part of the school (a metonym of the nation here) about manliness and Cuban identity. This anxiety concerning Cuban national identity was paramount after the 1959 triumph of the Revolution, in Fidel Castro's attempt to create the "new man", someone who is ideologically committed to the "revolution nation." In the construction of the revolution's new man, there is no space for the homosexual, who is seen as nothing more than a (sexual) traitor. One can read the text as a sort of rebellion on Lezama Lima's part, a rebellion as much sexual as textual. The rower's expulsion and erasure can be read as a commentary on the whole revolutionary agenda of exorcising the (sexually, artistically, or philosophically) different in order to create the new man for the new nation.

Many gay cinephiles will already have encountered José Lezama Lima, even though they probably didn't know it or have never read his work. Their first encounter would have been in the 1993 film *Strawberry and Chocolate* (*Fresa y Chocolate*, directed by Tomás Gutierrez Alea and Juan Carlos Tabío), based on Senel Paz's short story "The Wolf, The Woods and the New Man" (1990). This narrative recounts the cultural education of a young, naïve communist (David) by the artistic, homosexual Diego, who has lived through both the Cuban Revolution and the reeducation camps. While Diego's initial goal is to bed the naïf David, his role transforms into that of teacher, enlightening David as to the decaying architectural glories of the city of Havana, its illustrious literary and cultural past, and all the while educating David in the ways of becoming a true Cuban writer. Diego's function is to transform the ideological commitment of David into a more nuanced portrait of the artist as a young man.

A great deal of this artistic reeducation is mediated through books and writing. At the culmination of David's development as an artist under the tutelage of Diego, they celebrate a "Lezamian dinner." This dinner is an identical replication of the family dinner at the center of *Paradiso*. The only differences in the cultural summation of sumptuous culinary practices are the need to substitute certain ingredients no longer available in the Cuba of 1990s austerity. The details of the dinner in Paz's story repeat, right down to the beet stains on the table cloth. For most, this homage to Lezama Lima is likely to be overlooked.

And yet it is of extreme importance, in linking contemporary Cuban letters to the originator of modern Cuban literature.

Lezama Lima follows a well-established trope of adolescent sexual exploration through literature, via libraries and book stores. This literary seduction, which also seduces the reader with the author's extreme erudition, is the scene for the second encounter gay cinephiles may have had with Lezama Lima. This would have been in the film *Before Night Falls* (directed by Julian Schnabel; 2000), based on the autobiography of Reinaldo Arenas (*Antes que anochezca*, 1992; English translation 1993). In the film, Arenas is awarded his one and only literary prize in Cuba, which is overseen by Lezama Lima. Arenas is then invited into Lezama Lima's library. The scene is reminiscent of a blessing; a laying-on of hands of the patriarch of Cuban letters to the next generation. Arenas leaves the library, loaded down with a hodgepodge collection of books and an eclectic reading list. As in *Strawberry and Chocolate*, Lezama Lima is the pivotal figure in the literary and cultural education of the artists as young men.

Arenas, like the ill-fated rower in *Paradiso*, suffers censorship and eventual exile for his sexual and textual rebellions. While gay readers may be familiar with Senel Paz or Reinaldo Arenas, it is imperative that we not forget their engendering father. Lezama Lima himself became, essentially, an internal exile, estranged from the Cuban literary world he was so influential in guiding, deemed a counterrevolutionary, whose work did not support the ideological commitments required of the new regime. After *Paradiso*, he was essentially prohibited from publishing, and was not "rehabilitated" to the Cuban literary canon until the last decades of the twentieth century. The danger of his art—seemingly superficial; often deemed escapist—is the rebellion of poetry in the face of oppression (exemplified by Machado, Batista, or Castro). Difficult and challenging as it may be to read *Paradiso*, one must remember that the path to heaven is fraught with danger, but the rewards of entering the enchanted spheres of paradise are worth the rebellion.

RICHARD REITSMA received his B.A. from Grand Valley State University, his M.A. from Purdue University, and has studied abroad in Mexico, Cuba, and France. His Ph.D. studies in comparative literature from Washington University–St. Louis focused on issues of sexuality and race in plantation fiction from the American South and the Caribbean. He previously taught world literature at the College of William and Mary, and has served on the Spanish and Latin American Studies faculties at several universities, most recently Gettysburg College. He has also developed courses on sexuality as political discourse in Europe and Latin America. In addition, he has regularly served as a judge for the Lambda Literary Awards. His research has recently branched out to examine gay themes in children's cartoons. Quotations are taken from José Lezama Lima, *Paradiso* (New York: Dalkey Archive Press, 2000), translated by Gregory Rabassa, which is currently in print.

EUSTACE CHISHOLM AND THE WORKS
(1967)

by James Purdy

JONATHAN FRANZEN

I don't know if anyone remembers a 2004 college football game between Stanford and the University of California. Just to remind you: Stanford had a much smaller and weaker team with a 2–7 record. But the first half of the game, it looked as if Stanford might actually beat Cal, because its defense was so pumped up that its players had entirely lost their fear of injury. There were young men running at absolutely full speed, as hard as they could, with their arms open wide, flinging themselves against stronger young men who were running just hard in the opposite direction. There were these spectacular, gruesome collisions. It was like seeing people run full tilt into telephone poles. Sickening numbers of Stanford players were getting seriously hurt and carted off the field, and still they just kept flinging themselves at Cal. The experience of watching their doomed effort, these repeated joyous, self-destroying collisions of young people who desperately wanted something, all of this chaos in the context of a larger suspenseful, formally gorgeous game whose outcome was nonetheless pretty well foreordained . . . I haven't been able to find a better analogue for the experience of reading James Purdy's *Eustace Chisholm and the Works.*

Purdy's novel is so good that almost any novel you read immediately after it will seem at least a little bit posturing, or dishonest, or self-admiring in comparison. Certainly, for example, J. D. Salinger's *The Catcher in the Rye* (1951), which Purdy once described as "one of the worst books ever written," will betray its sentimentality and rhetorical manipulations as it never has before. Richard Yates, whose ferocity sometimes approaches Purdy's, might do a little better. But you'd have to wipe away every vestige of Yates's self-pity and replace it with headlong love; you'd have to ramp Yates's depression up into a fatalism of such bleakness that it became ecstatic. Even Saul Bellow, whose love of language and love of the world can be so infectious, is likely to seem wordy and academic and show-off if you read him directly after *Eustace Chisholm.* One of the darker chapters in Saul Bellow's *The Adventures of Augie March* (1953) ends with Augie's accompanying his friend Mimi to the office of a South Side abortionist. While Bellow draws a curtain over what happens inside this doctor's office, Purdy in *Eustace Chisholm* delivers—famously, unforgettably—on the horror, in an unbelievable scene. The extreme margins of the stable, familiar world of Bellow (and of most novelists, including me) are at the extreme normal end of Purdy's world. He takes up where the rest of us leave off. He follows his queer boys and struggling artists and dissolute millionaires to places like:

This out-of-the-way ice-cream parlor near the state line, a favorite stop for truck drivers hauling smuggled merchandise, ladies committing adultery with local building and loan directors, where a preacher was shot to death by a widow who was losing his love, where the local fairies used to come late afternoons . . .

He instills these locales with a weird kind of *Gemüetlichkeit*. You miss having been there yourself, the way you miss having ridden on a sleigh with Tolstoy's Natasha Rostov in *War and Peace* (1869). Near the end of *Eustace Chisholm*, two characters walk out onto the rocks piled up alongside Lake Michigan:

They sat down there, remembering how less desperate and much happier, after all, they had used to feel when they sat here the year before, and yet how desperate they had been then too. A few gulls hovered near some refuse floating on the oil-stained water.

What constitutes *in extremis* for most of us is the daily bread of Purdy's world. He lets you try on desperation, and you find that it fits you better than you expected. His most bizarre freaks don't feel freakish. They feel, peculiarly, like me. I read about the humiliation and incest and self-loathing and self-destruction in *Eustace Chisholm* with the same lively, sympathetic, and morally clear-eyed interest with which I follow the broken engagements and bruised feelings in Jane Austen. You can be sure, when you begin a Purdy novel, that all will most certainly not end well. It's his great gift to narrate the inexorable progress toward disaster in such a way that it's as satisfying and somehow life-affirming as progress toward a happy ending. When Purdy finally does—as in the last three pages of *Eustace Chisholm*—toss you a tiny scrap of ordinary hope and happiness, you may very well begin to weep, as I did on both my first and second readings, out of sheer gratitude. It's as if the book is set up, almost in spite of itself, to make you feel what a miracle it is that love is ever requited, that two compatible people ever find their way to each other. You've so reconciled yourself to the disaster; you've been so thoroughly sold on his fatalistic vision that a moment of ordinary peace and kindness feels like an act of divine grace.

Purdy shouldn't be confused with his late contemporary, William Burroughs, or with Burroughs's many transgressive successors. Transgressive literature is always—secretly or not so secretly—addressing itself to the bourgeois world that it depends on. As a reader of transgressive fiction, you have two choices: either you can be shocked, or you can shock other people with your failure to be shocked. Although Purdy, in his public utterances, is implacably hostile to American society, in his fiction he directs his attention inward. There isn't one sentence in *Eustace Chisholm* that could care less about whether some reader is shocked by it. The book's eponymous nonhero—a cruel, arrogant, freeloading, bisexual poet who is writing an epic poem of modern America with a charcoal pencil on sheets of old newspapers—is an obsessive reader of the letters and diaries of other people:

> Unlike small towns, cities contain transient persons . . . who carry their letters about with them carelessly, either losing them or throwing them away. Most passers-by would not bother to stoop down and pick up such a letter because they would assume there would be nothing in the contents to interest or detain them. This was not true of Eustace. He pored over found letters whose messages were not meant for him. To him they were like treasures that spoke fully. Paradise to Eustace might have been reading the love-letters of every writer, no matter how inconsequential or even

illiterate, who had written a real one. What made the pursuit exciting was to come on that rare thing: the authentic, naked, unconcealed voice of love.

Chisholm eventually becomes so addicted to other people's real-life stories that he abandons his own work and devotes his attention entirely to the book's central love: a crazy, unconsummated relationship between a young former coal miner, Daniel Haws, and a beautiful blond country boy named Amos Ratcliffe. Purdy was a vastly bigger and tougher and more protean figure than his creation, Chisholm—he was, after all, author of forty-six books of fiction, poetry, and drama—but, as an author, he was palpably driven by the same kind of helpless fascination and identification with human suffering. However high Purdy's authorial opinion of himself may have been, however much of a son of a bitch he may have appeared in public pronouncements, when he sat down to tell a story, he somehow checked all of that ego at the door and became entirely absorbed in his characters. He was and continues to be one of the most undervalued and under-read writers in America. Among his many excellent works, *Eustace Chisholm* is the fullest bodied, best-written, the most tautly narrated and the most beautifully constructed. There are very few better postwar American novels, and I don't know of any other novel of similar quality that is less like anybody else's work, more uniquely and defiantly itself.

JONATHAN FRANZEN is author of the novels *The Twenty-Seventh City* (1988), *Strong Motion* (1992), and *The Corrections* (2001), as well as *How to Be Alone: Essays* (2002) and *The Discomfort Zone: a Personal History* (2006). Quotations are taken from James Purdy, *Eustace Chisholm and the Works* (New York: Carroll & Graf, 2004), which is currently in print.

MY FATHER AND MYSELF
(1968)

by J. R. Ackerley

ANDREW HOLLERAN

Recently a friend asked me for an example of a great prose style, and without thinking very long I said: *My Father and Myself.* Its author, J. R. Ackerley, who died before this book was published, insisted *My Father and Myself* "is *not* an autobiography." But of course it is—one of the greats—and what is interesting is how it manages to be one, despite the author's claim that it's only about relations between him and his father. Indeed, at times the self-analysis even threatens to take over, never more brilliantly than in the chapter describing his difficulties with homosexuality. *My Father and Myself,* you might say, is the great book on homosexual alienation.

My Father and Myself is also a memoir about the gulf between a father and a son, the horrors of World War I, the misery of searching for a vocation when one is young, the search for love, the search for sex, the pathos of old age, and the record of a quest to unravel certain family secrets. Ackerley says he wrote the book to figure out why he and his father did not communicate more with each other when both were alive. But it is also a wonderful comic portrait of people with an almost Dickensian cast. If, indeed, it accomplishes what Ackerley's father requested in a letter to his son—leave a "kind memory" of him—by the time we get to its last line, the delicious acid in which this book is written leaves everyone else pretty much eaten away. This includes the author. ("I was always one of life's natural vassals, a voluntary subordinate to minds or personalities stronger than my own.") There is a wonderful misanthropy in this book. Ackerley's father seems to have been nice enough: a garrulous, tolerant, loving, and prosperous businessman (a banana importer). His mother a beautiful erstwhile actress whom Ackerley says he adored. But their second son (Ackerley) describes himself as "a chaste, puritanical, priggish, rather narcissistic little boy, more repelled by than attracted to sex, which seemed to me a furtive, sordid thing." And that's just the beginning.

In a brief list of his mother's idiosyncrasies, Ackerley recalls that when she encountered a bad smell, while taking a walk with her children, she would spit and tell them to do the same. That, in a way, is what *My Father and Myself* is: a spit over a bad smell—only in this case, the bad smell is Life itself: Ackerley's brother's death in the war, the guilt he felt ever after for having survived him, the unwelcome advances of his classmates at boarding school, the hopelessness of finding love through sex or sex through love as an adult, the very physicality of existence.

A certain distaste for the latter pervades every sentence in this book. Take, for instance, this catalogue of his brother's body:

. . . his straight dark brows that almost met, his narrow palate and weak over-crowded teeth, the brownish stain round his loins from the leather of his truss when he took it off to go to the baths at school, the yellow mark just above the cleft of his thin white buttocks where the wash-leather pad rested, and his abnormally long dark cock, longer than my own or any other I had seen. I remember feeling rather ashamed of it when we went to the baths together, and wondered how he could expose it as he did with such seeming indifference and what the other boys must think. Unspectacular though my own was I always shielded it modestly from view with my towel, like a Japanese. I recollect that I had a feeling of distaste for his thin sallow body, and believe that he had no such unfriendly thoughts about mine, which was always erupting in cysts and boils.

The stain from the truss, the long dark cock, the cysts and boils: these are the essence of Ackerley's prose. Even a description of the boyfriend he thinks may have been "the best and most understanding friend I had ever made: a Welsh boy, gentle, kind, cheerful, understanding, self-effacing, always helpful, always happy to return to me in spite of neglect, and in control (a rare thing) of his jealous wife" climaxes with: "His feet smelt, poor boy, some glandular trouble, and out of politeness he preferred not to take off his boots." (The final pathetic fact: "He was killed in the war . . .") The stain from the truss, the cysts and boils, the smelly feet, make it no surprise when Ackerley tells us that he always carried peppermints or chocolate for fear of having bad breath when it came time to kiss someone.

That's because the "chaste, puritanical, priggish, rather narcissistic little boy" in this astringent memoir finally grows up—into "a young, upper-middle-class, intellectual homosexual . . . lonely, frustrated, and sick of his family, especially the women, his feckless chatterbox of a mother, his vain, quarrelsome and extravagant sister, and the general emptiness and futility of their richly upholstered life" and then "becomes emotionally involved with a handsome young workman."

This workman was what Ackerley came to call—when he moved to London after the war—The Ideal Friend. One of the most famous passages in *My Father and Myself* is the list of requirements that individual had to meet. Yet Ackerley found this paragon early on, in the guise of a Navy boxer, whom he eventually lost, for a reason that is as astonishing as everything else in this peculiar book. After that the search for love seems to have been very hard work—because there was a problem: "in my case, the feelings of the heart and the desires of the flesh have lain in different compartments." And so: "Unable, it seemed, to reach sex through love, I started upon a long quest in pursuit of love through sex."

What was arduous in real life makes for very entertaining reading on the page; when Ackerley came upon, years later, a record he'd kept of these cruising days in London (here, even London is "that vast, puritanical, and joyless city"), he destroyed it, "as though it were an evil thing. The evil was in the misery. It contained no single gleam of pleasure or happiness, no philosophy, not even a joke; it was a story of unrelieved gloom and despondency, of deadly monotony, of frustration, loneliness, self-pity, of boring 'finds,' of wonderful chances muffed through fear, of the latchkey turned night after night into the cold, dark, empty flat, of railings against fate for the emptiness and wretchedness of my life."

But here is the paradox: *My Father and Myself* is none of these things—it's never boring or monotonous. In fact it's extremely funny—because Ackerley, whatever else he was, was an artist. Indeed, never has remorse—the remorse Ackerley apparently felt about everything (read Peter Parker's excellent biography for that)—been so regenerative. Remorse in all its permutations soaks *My Father and Myself*, which "germinated, as I have said, out of a sense of failure, of personal inadequacy, of waste and loss; I saw it as a *stupid* story, shamefully stupid that two intelligent people, even though parent and son, between whom special difficulties of communication are said to lie, should have gone along together, perfectly friendly for so many years, without ever reaching the closeness of an intimate conversation, almost totally ignorant of each other's hearts and minds." At the same time, Ackerley knew he had a great story: "That I had also been handed ready-made an unusual and startling tale did not escape my journalist's eye."

Truman Capote blurbed *My Father and Myself* as "the most original autobiography I have ever read." One reason for this may be that Ackerley worked on the book for over thirty years, and was still working on it when he died. Another may be that Ackerley was the editor of a BBC magazine called *The Listener* for many years (and said of his own sentences, "I love a thing to be as perfect as I can make it"). So though we cannot know what he would have done with the final revision of this memoir, one can scarcely imagine how it could be better. The book dismayed, however, his friend E. M. Forster: "It seems so ill-tempered, and such a reproach to all his friends . . . I wish I could give him a good smack!" I suppose Forster was offended by the dyspepsia that runs throughout it. But if Proust is right—that every writer has two selves, the social being and the one that writes the book—it's no surprise that Forster and others were fooled by Ackerley's charm; even if in *My Father and Myself* he quotes stinging criticism from friends fed up with his behavior. That's why *My Father and Myself* is one of the great autobiographies. It is full of contradictions. It is a monument to self-loathing and self-love.

In the end one wonders: Why is this book so unflinching, acerbic, and enjoyable? What made this man so angry, so fastidious, so outraged by life? Toward the end of his cruising days, Ackerley recalls, "I wanted nothing now but (the sad little wish) someone to love me." But, thinking about his mother, he says: "I do not know . . . how deeply she was capable of caring for anyone; it is a question that applies as unanswerably to myself." Perhaps the answer lies somewhere between those two lines. The full answer requires reading his other famous book—*My Dog Tulip* (1956)—which describes the portion of Ackerley's life left out of the main text of this one; except for the following line: "It is, for me, the interesting part of this personal history, that peace and contentment reached me in the shape of an animal, an Alsatian bitch." (Could he not have said a dog? Of course not! How he must have relished those words: their precision, their vinegar sound!) In short, Ackerley was freed from cruising only when his last boyfriend (the subject of the novel *We Think the World of You* [1960]), going to prison, left his dog with Ackerley. To talk about his true love, Tulip, Ackerley had to add this appendix to *My Father and Myself*, which binds up the various strains of what has gone before.

Looking at Tulip, he writes: "I used to think that the Ideal Friend, whom I no longer wanted, perhaps never had wanted, should have been an animal-man, the mind of my bitch, for instance, in the body of my sailor, the perfect human male body always at one's service through the devotion of a faithful and uncritical beast." It doesn't get more acerbic than this; or more honest. What Ackerley called "the cold clear light of objective self-criticism" is what makes *My Father and Myself* so brilliant; as for his finding the affection he craved in a dog, it could have been worse. His mother, he tells us, "ending up, as I am, with animals and alcohol, one of her last friends, when she was losing her faculties, was a fly . . ."

My Father and Myself is like no other book you'll ever read.

ANDREW HOLLERAN is author of the novels *Dancer from the Dance* (1978), *Nights in Aruba* (1983), *The Beauty of Men* (1996), and *Grief* (2006). He has also published a short-story collection, *In September, the Light Changes* (1999) and a book of essays, *Ground Zero* (1988), which was revised and republished as *Chronicle of a Plague, Revisited: AIDS and Its Aftermath* (2008). Quotations are taken from J. R. Ackerley, *My Father and Myself* (New York: Harvest, 1975). The American edition currently in print is J. R. Ackerley, *My Father and Myself* (New York: NYRB Classics, 1999).

Betrayed by
Rita Hayworth
(La traicion de Rita Hayworth)
(1968)

by Mañuel Puig

R. Zamora Linmark

Betrayed by Mañuel Puig (for Lisa Asagi)

December, 1990. Honolulu. Nightfall. You are in the living room of your one-bedroom apartment in Waikiki. You're bored, broke, and more restless than a nineteenth-century French housewife. You already maxed out your credit cards, thanks to your trans-Pacific trans-Atlantic relationship with a bisexual-identified British ESL teacher. In fact, just the other day, American Express commemorated the bombing of Pearl Harbor by phoning you and ordering you to grab the nearest pair of scissors and cut, yes, cut the green card in half, yes, now. Above all, your midnight meditations on life after eighteen months of hopping from Honolulu to London then Madrid then back to Honolulu are becoming as redundant as a Phillip Glass CD playing on repeat mode. You tell yourself that this is what happens when you fall for a guy with a Merchant & Ivory accent imported from Bromsgrove, that this is what you get when you stretch a one-night stand in Gilligan's Island to a year-and-a-half. Drama, bills, regret, ennui. Though not necessarily in this order.

You snap out of Flaubert. Convince yourself you are not, and will never be, Madame Bovary. You consult your personal library, hoping you'll run into another you, a better memory. You browse through all five shelves, all used books, arranged alphabetically by author's last name but not by genre because, as your Detroit-blooded creative writing professor told you, there is no such thing as fact, fiction, or creative nonfiction, that one's imagination is another's reality. And if you don't believe me, she said, go ask any blank page.

You park your gaze on Borges. You're tempted, but the night is too humid for tigers and labyrinths. Cortazar? No, thanks, remembering the last time you read his collection of stories you ended up in the belly of a salamander. You skip over Garcia Marquez, creator of the Arcadio-Buendia name game. You pass on Hagedorn, Kundera, Lorca, Lorrie Moore, and Fernando Pessoa, the grandfather of the *Find Waldo* series. Your eyes go on ADHD mode until they land on a catchy title. *Betrayed by Rita Hayworth* by Mañuel Puig.

You pull it off the shelf. The hardbound edition, published by E. P. Dutton, was a gift from your dear friend Lisa, who bought it for a buck at the annual library book sale last July. Lisa, who is also an aspiring writer, meaning a masochist in-progress, gave it to you as a welcome-back present in August. You look at the book jacket with its cover design of filmstrips, then at the author's handsome, Romanesque face that takes up the entire back cover; at his expressive eyes seducing the camera. You've never read Puig before, though you've seen, countless times, the film adaptation (1985) of one of his novels, *Kiss of the Spider Woman* (*El beso de la mujer araña*, 1976), starring William Hurt, who won an Oscar for his portrayal of Molina, a gay window dresser who ends up in prison for corrupting a minor.

You turn to the opening chapter—"Mita's Parents' Place, La Plata, 1933." Immediately, you are thrown smack in the midst of gossip, as if you've just walked into a movie—or a play—and you have to catch up with the plot. The incognito dialogue format disorients you. You feel lost as a Japanese without a manual. Who's talking? What happened to the "she says/he says"? Where did the quotation marks go? What kind of novel have I stepped into?

Despite these nagging questions, you continue reading, frustrated eavesdropper that you are. You tell yourself: if you can survive a workshop session with your mentor/tormentor, you can overcome Puig's unconventional style. Next thing you know, your mind is racing to the next page. You know these women. You've met them before. They are your grandmother, her fourteen sisters, and their army of girlfriends who got together in the living room of your paternal great-grandfather's house to swap stories, ranging from the mundane to the vulgar, from the rising cost of fabric to the mayor's latest mistress. Over coffee and rolls coated with sugar and butter, these women—who sported towering dos, penciled their eyebrows, and fanned themselves with fancy fans imported from Manila—updated each other on the latest gossip, deemed true until replaced by another version. Together, they exhausted the remains of the afternoon with laughter and sighs, dug up the past, corrected each other's memories, embellished them to their own design.

You know these women, you tell yourself again. You've eavesdropped on them before: as a child living with your paternal grandparents in the provincial town of San Mañuel, Pangasinan, four hours by car north of Manila. You stop. You marvel at the coincidence between the names of the author and the town that housed your first memories. A place so small and remote it does not even merit a dot on the regional map; nor an asphalt road. You remember the "Welcome to San Mañuel" arch, and right after it, the cemetery.

After ten pages, you not only figured out the identities of the three women—Mita's mother, Mita's sister Clara, and Mita's friend Violeta—but you also got a sneak peek of the main and secondary characters: Mita lives in drought-stricken Vallejos with her husband Berto and their baby, Toto, and works as a pharmacist in a hospital. You close the chapter, knowing a thing or two about embroidery.

Chapter two—"At Berto's, Vallejos, 1933"—is also a dialogue between a maid and a nanny, with a surprise cameo by Berto. But this time, the OC in you is not obsessed over the absence of quotation marks. In fact, you're beginning to get used to Puig's unconventional approach to storytelling. You're beginning to love the disorientation.

Two chapters into the novel and already the book has affected you in more complex and engaging ways than your British ex—or any of your exes, for that matter. It has magnified your desire to become a writer. It has inspired you to start working on your dream novel the moment you graduate from college. It has opened that can of worms called childhood. And it has managed to keep you lemur-eyed past midnight. The last time you held such vigil was in elementary school, in the late seventies: Judy Blume's *Forever: a Moving Story of the End of Innocence* (1975).

You scan the rest of the book. Sixteen chapters, all titled with the name of the speaker followed by the season and year, e.g.,

"Paquita, Winter, 1945." More dialogues in play format minus stage directions. More monologues, more monsoon-of-consciousness from the principal character, Toto, and the supporting cast: his mother, his cousin Hector, his cousin Tete, his friend Alicita, and his enemies, including his classmate Cobito, the poor, tough teenage Jewish boy who tries to rape him.

Puig, however, does not confine the narrative structure to monologues and dialogues. One chapter is in the form of a diary entry—Esther's, Toto's classmate and the daughter of a Peron loyalist. Another is an essay entitled "The Movie I Liked Best," written for the annual literary competition by Jose Casals, aka Toto. Others include an "Anonymous Note Sent to the Dean of Students of George Washington High School, 1947," a journal by a spinster piano teacher, and, the concluding chapter, a letter by Berto, Toto's father, dated 1933, the year of Toto's birth.

Sure, you've read novels with alternating narrators before. You've read William Faulkner and Toni Morrison, and, most recently, Terry MacMillan's *Waiting to Exhale* (1992). You know the difference between multiple points of view and multiple levels of reality, between postmodernism and pretense. You are, after all, an English lit major, fifteen credits shy of a B.A. degree. But *Betrayed by Rita Hayworth* is different. In terms of originality and eclecticism, it belongs on a shelf of its own. It defies literary convention. It forces you to rethink your definition of a novel—the novel as collage or a work of embroidery. More importantly, it is hitting you on several levels, in several Yous: as a child, as an artist, and as a lover of movies.

You feel overwhelmed. You can't breathe. You dog-ear the page and go to the lanai. You light a cigarette because it is the only thing in this world that reminds you to breathe before you die from emphysema. You can't stop thinking about the book and the memories it has unleashed. You compose a list of notes in your head. *Betrayed by Rita Hayworth* is Puig's homage to the movies. To enter its world is to be thrown right into the midst of gossip and kitsch, glamour and nostalgia, sadness and sigh.

An Italian movie you saw months ago at Varsity Twin theaters—the only art house in Hawaii—enters your mind: *Cinema Paradiso* (1988). You "oh" and "ah" at another coincidence: the lead character in that movie, a child who's in love with the movies and grows up to be a famous director, is also named Toto. You ask the night: are all the film buffs in the world named Toto?

Your mind returns to the book. You zero in on Toto. And you. How you saw the remains of your childhood scattered across the pages of his story. For you, too, grew up in a small town, loving the movies, which only played at night because the cinema was open air. You, too, had a scrapbook of your idols; cutouts from magazines and newspapers. You, too, manipulated tragic endings in exchange for happy ones. You, too, were picked on, teased at by classmates and bullies because you were hypnotized by the Rita Hayworths and seduced by the Tyrone Powers.

Toto.

You.

Parallel childhood with matching passions for men and movies.

But the similarities end there. Unlike Toto, whose only wish was for his father to love the movies as much as he did, you had your grandfather to accompany you to the cinema located at the end of your street.

You think of your grandfather who, at seventy, is still going strong in San Mañuel, still smoking a pack of Marlboro Reds a day, still giving your grandmother her daily dose of migraine. It is he who introduced you to the world of movies (and reading). It is he you hold responsible for ushering you into a non-paying profession where the only benefit is that you get to lie as much as you want and, if you're good, get away with it.

Exhausted from reading and remembering, you go and lie down on your bed. You stare at the book on the nightstand. The betrayal can wait, you tell yourself. You pick up the phone and call the hospital where you work as a part-time ward clerk. In your A-for-Acting-101 voice, you tell the nursing supervisor the truth: you caught a bad bug.

The following morning, you phone Lisa. You tell her how Puig's book has inspired your night, how it has given you all sorts of resurrections. In fifty words or fewer, you give her a brief synopsis of the book. It's about a small town that can't live without the movies but more than that, it is about longing. Then you share with her your growing desire to return to the motherland. It's been fourteen years, you say, fourteen years and counting. And, last night, the book brought you one step closer to the past—a past that, in five months, you will finally come face to face with. Marked by a volcano waking up after six centuries of dormancy, Imelda Marcos's homecoming after five years of exile, and, in San Mañuel, a betrayal long overdue.

R. ZAMORA LINMARK is the author of *Rolling the R's* (1995), the novel and stage adaptation, and two collections of poetry, *Prime Time Apparitions* (2005) and *The Evolution of a Sigh* (2008). He has completed his second novel, *Leche*. Linmark divides his time between Honolulu and Manila, where he is currently working on a new full-length play, a novel, and a one-man show entitled "You: A Curse In Progress," which includes this essay. Quotations are taken from Mañuel Puig, *Betrayed by Rita Hayworth* (New York: Dalkey Archive Press, 2009), translated by Suzanne Jill Levine, which is currently in print.

The Wild Boys: A Book of the Dead

(1971)

by William Burroughs

Kathy Acker

A Girl Is Reading William Burroughs (1996)

There aren't many women in *The Wild Boys* and most are found in the first chapter:

Tía Dolores . . . "Her evil eyes rotate in a complex calendar . . . she can pop one eye

out onto her cheek laced with angry red veins while the other sinks back into an enigmatic grey slit . . . Tía Dolores waddles out onto the balcony like a fat old bird."

Lola La Chata . . . ". . . a solid 300 pounds . . . She sells heroin to pimps and thieves

and whores and keeps the papers between her massive dugs."

"And now Tía Maria, retired fat lady from a traveling carnival, comes out onto the lower balcony supporting her vast weight on two canes."

After this first chapter, "Tío Mate Smiles," the Green Nun who runs a junky lunatic asylum Margaret Thatcher–style makes her appearance and that's pretty much the end of women in this book or world whose initials are WB. WB for either *The Wild Boys* or for William Burroughs.

A GIRL IS READING WILLIAM BURROUGHS

Read, a little, along with me . . .

We're in the slums of Mexico City. These slums are just a camera shot; reality is a film scene; there's *really* nothing else, just film scene after film scene. Reality is virtual, only in the late sixties when Burroughs penned *The Wild Boys*, there was no VR.

Burroughs might be a traditional fiction writer and he's definitely a prophet.

Prior to the days of Microsoft there were prophets. There might have been VR, but it was called something else back then. Dreams, writing. Burroughs works by means of dreams.

Enter in VR Mexico City slum reality a whole bunch of characters, including Graham Greene's "ugly American," and they're all doing their usual acts. Enter Tío Pepe whose "magic consists in whispering potent phrases from newspapers . . ." That is what Burroughs, in his writing, is doing, mumbling even breathing what you've heard, what you've read elsewhere, into your ear. Tío Pepe is one of the author's many clones. Or vice versa. Where, among all of the Burroughs clones including the author, is the real Burroughs?

Answer: nowhere. In VR there are only icons and aliases and all icons and aliases are real.

Second answer: In VR Mexico City slums, as in Burroughs's film scene after film scene, the fat ladies and the con boys and other agents get killed off or kill each other off. Tío Mate is left. Who is Tío Mate? ". . . the Mayan Death God . . . DEATH DEATH DEATH." Question: Where is the real Burroughs? Answer: Every doctor needs death.

Worried about your pet neurosis or psychosis? Got a reality problem? You don't believe in yourself? Come to the identity doctor. Mr. WB is the doctor who doesn't exist and everything is real.

Here, in VR Mexico City, we might have gone beyond *human* and we've certainly journeyed beyond identity as a singular close construct, beyond and into the world of fiction. Truth is situated here, in fiction, because here everything is obviously false and simultaneously true.

One explanation of all I've just said: Burroughs seems to have little interest in what goes on in his film sets; a good riff is simply a good riff, except, perhaps, when he waxes romantic about young boys. But every human, excuse me, every clone slips up now and then. Throw what the literati call *fiction*, all the rules about story-telling, character, and action, all the paraphernalia of *good writing* and *proper speech*, out the window, for what matters, the only question that matters, is why there are rules that govern writing and speech. Who is trying to control writing and speech, how and why? This question is what Burroughs calls *fiction*. These questions about social and political control in regard to identity and language.

Who or what is WB? As William Burroughs rather than *The Wild Boys*, he's the alias "sexist pig," he's also "the quickest trigger in the west," no nonsense allowed when this guy is in town, and the alias "Zen monk disguised as junky." Remember: Zen monks aren't what you think they are.

This is only background, one film set.

I AM READING WB, *THE WILD BOYS*

April 3, Marrakech . . . Wild girls in the street whole packs of them vicious as famished dogs. Almost all the men have gone. Which means there is almost no police force in operation . . .

I am reading *The Wild Boys* my style.

At dawn two girls got up and walked out naked into the ruined garden. Coming to a thick tangle of rosebushes, Farfa leaped through and emerged untouched by the thorns on the other side and then I jumped a sweat tearing pain landed on hands and knees . . . I turn the page feeling the rose twist alive in my flesh.

When and where I grew up, there were no boys, only mother's mother, my mother, me, and my sister. I've never met my father. My sister and I, especially me for I was the older, weren't allowed anything. I wasn't allowed to be sexual and to perceive my body with my own eyes.

I read *The Wild Boys*, my favorite Burroughs novel, and I see girls everywhere, girls being sexual, girls doing all and more than the boys I saw did when I used to snake in my twenties down to the New York City wharves and hide there, in those shadows, when curling into one of the back corners of CBGBs, I would watch the endlessly skinny and black-clad legs of boys stride across a stage that was separated from me far more by gender than by space. Maybe I'm being perverse, but above all, I'm romantic and reading *The Wild Boys* makes me sing louder than Marianne Faithfull, "Give me more more more more . . ."

KATHY ACKER, who died in 1997, was author of many works of fiction, including *Blood and Guts in High School* (1984), *Don Quixote* (1986), *Great Expectations* (1983), and *Empire of the Senseless* (1988). An anthology of her writings, *Essential Acker*, edited by Amy Scholder and Dennis Cooper, was published in 2002. Quotations are taken from William Burroughs, *The Wild Boys: a Book of the Dead* (New York: Grove Press, 1994), which is currently in print.

THE PERSIAN BOY
(1972)

by Mary Renault

JIM GRIMSLEY

I can remember vividly the day I first understood the meaning that Mary Renault would have in my life—a hot Sunday afternoon in 1971 when I picked up a novel called *Fire from Heaven* (1970). I had reached the halfway point of the story, drawn to it out of fascination with the life of Alexander the Great, yet having no notion what the final pages contained.

I was an unsophisticated reader at the time, more excited by the science-fiction dramas of Robert Heinlein than by more literary works. I was in high school, with the resources of weak rural libraries at my disposal. Coming from a family in which reading was a bit of an oddity, the activity for a bookworm and not for a regular lad, I had learned to read for pleasure but not for much more than that. Escape was the point. Renault's sense of language, sophisticated and precise, at times puzzled my fifteen-year-old intellect.

In the middle of *Fire from Heaven*, Renault introduces the character of Hephaistion, Alexander's best friend and first love. On this particular Sunday I reached that part of the book and found myself in a state of shock, drawn into the novel so completely, with such devastating totality, that I could no longer face my family. I was gay and in hiding, knowing little of what it meant to be drawn to my own sex. Retreating to my bedroom, I devoured the remainder of the novel, the love story of the two boys both enthralling and reassuring.

As a queer in the early seventies, I had been terrified by the fact of my difference from everyone around me into silence and paralysis. In that era of our history it was possible to reach my age and never hear anything about the lives of gay people; nothing, that is, beyond the various playground slurs that I had learned to endure. I read Renault's novel with shock, feeling the charge of it, and most of all feeling the passion of these two young men for each other rendered with her clear sense of drama.

Three years later, headed home on a visit during my first year of college, I had learned only a little more about queerdom, and had begun tentatively to come out to friends. I had bought the paperback of Renault's second novel of Alexander's life, *The Persian Boy*, to read on the trip. As it happened, I might as well not have made the visit, since I spent the weekend reading the book from cover to cover and then reading it again, hardly speaking to my family out of my romantic fog.

Much as the first novel had changed me, the effect of the second was greater by whole orders of magnitude. The story of Alexander and Hephaistion was not at the center of *Fire from Heaven*, but the love story between Alexander and Bagoas, his Persian courtesan, occupied the whole territory of *The Persian Boy*. Renault's Bagoas is in love with Alexander and travels with him over the whole of his epic journey of conquest. His voice, transmitted to us with her extraordinary skill, is both wise and wizened; authentic in a way that felt uncanny.

Renault's ability to channel ancient Greece drew to her a whole legion of readers, and spawned interest in history among many who would never have heard of the Peloponnesian War or the Delphic oracle without her teaching. I can still recall searching out Arrian, Alexander's closest contemporary biographer, to find the actual references to the historical figure Bagoas, a real eunuch who was given to Alexander by one of the defeated Persian generals after the downfall of Darius II. Renault's portrait of the Persian beauty is surely one of her finest, and her novel remains, to my mind, the highest example of the art of the historical novelist. She recreates history with such living, breathing totality that, even today, rereading the novel for perhaps the twentieth time, I can still feel the heat of the Macedonian army camp, the ecstasy of the mountain heights, the tenderness of Bagoas toward his king-lover. Never has such a slightly remembered figure in the historical record taken on such a life in a book. I ached to believe that every page was true.

Few books existed in the late fifties, sixties, and early seventies in which men loved men at all, other than porn novels. Renault, in making the history of ancient Greece the territory of her best fiction, shed a light on a vital part of history mostly neglected in high school and college history classes. Love relations between men were not always proscribed as they were in my day. Classical Greece had been a friendly place for such love, to the degree that it could be described as a friendly place for anything at all. For this revelation, Renault has been chastised by historians who would prefer to downplay the truth of classical sexuality.

Renault herself, a lesbian from England who settled with her life partner in South Africa, was no stranger to literary daring, having written novels in contemporary settings about platonic love between women. In writing about love between men, however, she found her strongest material, beginning with *The Charioteer* (1953), a novel set during World War II. Her writing about ancient Greece provided her with the great works of her life—*The Last of the Wine* (1965), *The King Must Die* (1958), *The Bull from the Sea* (1962), *The Mask of Apollo* (1966), *Fire from Heaven*, *The Persian Boy*, *The Praise Singer* (1978), and *Funeral Games* (1981). Some chord of her inner life was struck by the idea of love between men; perhaps because it borrowed from her own isolation as a lesbian, while at the same time giving her the distance and detachment required of a novelist. One senses from her writing an immense core of privacy.

In my life, she was my teacher in terms of love, since she was the first writer whose love story I could feel with my whole heart. She gave me this gift in an era before Edmund White or Andrew Holleran had begun to publish, and it was probably no accident that her choice of illuminating historical truth allowed her books to circulate more widely than other gay texts of the era. She wrote impeccable prose and stories of immense integrity, and the truth she illuminated saved many a life, including my own.

JIM GRIMSLEY is author of the novels *Winter Birds* (1994), *Dream Boy* (1995; made into a film in 2008), *My Drowning* (1997), *Comfort & Joy* (1999), and *Boulevard* (2002). He has written eleven full-length and four one-act plays; a collection of them, *Mr. Universe and Other Plays*, was published in 1998. Grimsley's fantasy novel *Kirith Kirin* (2000) has been followed by two further volumes set in the same universe, *The Ordinary* (2005) and *The Last Green Tree* (2006). His story collection *Jesus Is Sending You This Message* appeared in 2008. Mary Renault's *The Persian Boy* (New York: Vintage, 1988) is currently in print.

TOO MUCH FLESH
AND JABEZ
(1977)

by Coleman Dowell

BRADLEY CRAFT

I t's quite impossible to write about *Too Much Flesh and Jabez*, or its author Coleman Dowell, without discussing failure first. Both the novel and its author were failures, and even then perhaps not really of the first rank. Never managing much more than a minor *succès d'estime* now and again, poor Coleman Dowell's failure was not for want of trying: first as a composer and lyricist, then as a writer of fiction, and finally, as a jumper-suicide, wherein he might have achieved at least something of *succès de scandale*, had he landed, say, on Truman Capote. Alas, he did not. He could cook, too, on top of the rest, as the old song (not his) says. And as a host, he was memorable enough to be memorialized as such by the likes of Edmund White. Had he lived long enough, Dowell might have been celebrated for the length of his marriage to his husband, though theirs was far from the now increasingly acceptable, unthreatening standard. Many a dangerous trick was turned up from the streets of New York to fill the empty afternoons while Dowell's somewhat anonymous husband was off at the office. So, Coleman Dowell rather failed at everything, even conventional fidelity, but always in an admirable way, and never more so than in my favorite of his novels.

His ambition was enormous and therefore distinctly American. We like even our failures to be BIG—think George W. Bush. Failures, gay or straight, if American, must be considered competitively and understood in that context. It is not enough to not succeed here, or even that one's friends must fail. In the first place, one must succeed publicly, at least a little, to fail in the proper, spectacular American manner. The true measure of one's failure cannot be judged by just the man or the body of work alone. Promise or talent, dreams deferred or unfulfilled, artistic achievements, even on a rather grandiose scale, are not enough. Notice must be paid, else what's a failure good for? It is not enough to drink, and be wittily bitchy at parties, as Coleman Dowell did, to excess. It is not enough to have one's plays unproduced or if produced, flop, as Dowell's all did. It is not enough to write clever, even accomplished songs and have them sung only in cafes, by clever, accomplished cabaret artistes, as Dowell's were. Finally, it is not enough to write good, even great books and have them badly reviewed or ignored, as Dowell's more often than not were. No. The fall must be from a not inconsiderable height to be noticed. Coleman Dowell, long before he stepped out onto the air and into the dark, understood this, and the failure of even his failures to make him famous, broke his heart.

In the long and inglorious history of American nonachievement, one's reputation must be slotted, like denominations in a drawer; from the highest dramatic value to the lowest, from the height of the fall to the depth of the failure, and Coleman Dowell, again, never having gained the heights, falls somewhere nearer the middle than the bottom of the gay bone-pile. At the top, among the truly popular flops, rest the remains of Gore Vidal's "Glorious Bird," Tennessee Williams, fallen from the stratospheric success of *A Streetcar Named Desire* (1947) onto very hard times indeed by the time he choked on the pill-bottle-cap. Truman Capote, descending rapidly from his masterpiece, *In Cold Blood* (1966), to drunken chat-show promotions of his never-quite-begun Proustian *Bildungsroman, Answered Prayers* (1987), rests just a little further down. Then the truly queer corpses, the coterie queers, must be turned to get at Dowell. Dowell's own mentor and collaborator, rather unpleasantly memorialized by Dowell in his unfinished memoir *A Star Bright Lie* (1993), forgotten novelist and inevitably rediscovered photographer Carl Van Vechten, is interred perhaps just under Capote. And topping the list, and therefore claiming the true bottom of the pile, would have to be the recently late James Purdy, a writer who might be said to have written the book on perverse and bitter, long-lived and lifelong avoidance of real fame.

Like the last mentioned, Dowell wrote in such a way as to ensure mainstream neglect; setting sensibility bombs of queer content and empurpled fine writing in even his simplest stories, waxing too blatantly lyrical about cock-sucking, for instance, particularly the sucking of big black cock, sucking thus as Purdy sucked, and thus queering the works, time and again, for selection by the *Book of the Month Club* and good reviews in the then required and prudishly unsophisticated *New York Times*. Of roughly the same generation as Purdy, and like Purdy, a provincial boy come to the Big City in search of fame, Dowell's American dream was rooted in rural repression and the hardship of the Great Depression, his imagination liberated and strangely limited by the then popular revolutionary—and as yet undiscredited—Freudian theories of sexual compulsion. Again, like Purdy, Dowell both wrote and lived in defiance of the hetero-normative and yet never quite overcame the delicious shame of being a dirty queer.

Too Much Flesh and Jabez was, I've always suspected, Dowell's last real attempt at a popular success. Gay Liberation (remember that?) had made queers, if not yet fashionable, *news*. Before this, Dowell's novels had always been queer, but never gay. In his previous, metafictional assumption of many masks and voices, Dowell's own resonant faggotry had been impossible to hide, even if he'd really wanted to do so. But his queerness had always been checked by a certain and sly, almost Jamesian reserve, a refusal of the declarative, an aesthetically modern and yet touchingly old-fashioned insistence on never quite coming right out, without ever being other than obviously "so." Dowell did this brilliantly—in *Island People* (1976) in particular, perhaps his best novel. Here he comes parlously close to what I hear as direct address, narrating in the first person, as a comfortably off, if failed playwright. The tone is traditionally predatory, even a little fey, what with the beloved wiener dogs, the sniffy misogyny, and the desired straight boy. But Dowell mixes and twists the narrative, as only he could, to undermine any assumption of responsibility for the unpleasantness. In *Too Much Flesh and Jabez*, Dowell again reverts to Southern type and speaks through a spinster lady, though he can't be much bothered with her after the first chapter, when the story she is meant to be inventing goes careening from a weird, if still familiar Redneck Gothic, into something entirely new, and all but unique in the literature: the Camp Pastoral. It is this unexpected and if not wholly successful, then certainly fascinating invention that makes *Too Much Flesh and Jabez* the most interesting of Dowell's novels, and the most worthy of his books for elevation to the "Gay Canon." In trying to write a gay novel for the new gay times of 1977, Coleman Dowell failed. But he succeeded in writing a true camp classic, the only such entirely sympathetic treatment of the tragedy of the well-hung, ever.

Miss Ethel, Dowell's antic and antique drag persona and teller of this tale (lest we forget, lest we forget), as described in the charming jacket copy, endows the hero—Kentucky farm boy and her former student, Jim Cummins—with "unnaturally large genitals." Frustrated by the failure of his nice little farmwife, Effie, to accommodate his gift, even by means of some truly creepy, if never quite described "device" designed to ease her onto it, poor, noble Jim is left howlingly blue-balled, jerking off in the barn, even, in perhaps the most hilariously tongue-in-cheek scene in the whole book, fucking the dirt in the front yard as he wakes, all hot and bothered, from a restless midday nap. Enter Jabez, the "musical" neighbor boy; voyeur, private cross-dresser, and scamp. Guess who rises, and descends, to meet the challenge of "all that flesh"?

There is, in this short novel, much that is merely good. There is a detailed and true understanding of rural American life in the midst of drought and Depression. This is perhaps most vividly represented in a disturbing scene wherein the starving mother of a starving child tries to force the precious food Jim gives the boy back down his throat even as it comes back up. But even the smallest and less grotesque observations—of hitchhiking to work for want of a car, of gardening just to eat, of the heat, and the bugs, and the isolation—are beautifully and movingly made. Dowell was a genuinely gifted writer; his prose carefully disciplined, occasionally, deliberately lyrical, his scenes dramatically, professionally accomplished. Had he not been so talented, his departures from realism and traditional narrative structure here would be no more interesting than the average porn story in a skin mag. But because he was a serious artist, his self-conscious departures from the bucolic to the hilariously, even mythically heated fantasy of a man cursed with a huge cock, and the magical faerie who, alone, can take him in, rise, if not straight to archetypal permanence, then amazingly enough to constitute something just shy of real tragedy. If this novel failed—and it most resoundingly did in its day—the failure was of a majestically, fiercely unique character. This failure, of all his many failures, tragically, belatedly, should earn Coleman Dowell all the respect he never felt in life. *Too Much Flesh and Jabez* is a triumph of sensibility over sense, of queer mischief done to the great gay novel, of the newly minted gay self-assertion brilliantly undermined by an irresistible self-loathing and an irrepressible, old school bitchiness. It is the glorious antithesis of the "good" gay book.

Coleman Dowell did not live to see Camp triumphant, the conquest of the wider American culture by irony, dirty-mindedness, and pornographic, laissez-faire postmodernism. Yet he was, if not among the fathers of this new day, certainly among its gay uncles. It's a pity he didn't stick around long enough to see himself celebrated as, at least, one of the great American gay failures. He might not have cottoned to that accolade, but he might have relished the irony of being elevated, at last, into the company of Forster, et al. How one wishes one might be at the table when he served up his opinion of "the greatest gay books" with his justly famous fried chicken, prepared, according to Edmund White, "according to the elaborate dehydration and deep-lard frying method of yesteryear."

BRADLEY CRAFT is a bibliophile and bookseller of more than twenty years' experience. He lives and works in Seattle and writes almost daily for his blog, www.used buyer.blogspot.com. Quotations are taken from Coleman Dowell, *Too Much Flesh and Jabez* (New York: Dalkey Archive Press, 1995), which is currently in print.

DANCER FROM THE DANCE
(1978)

by Andrew Holleran

MATIAS VIEGENER

*D*ancer from the Dance is as much an American literary classic as a gay classic, with its American roots in F. Scott Fitzgerald's *The Great Gatsby* (1925) and Mark Twain's *Adventures of Huckleberry Finn* (1884), and its queer roots perhaps further afield—in Proust and Thomas Mann. Framed by a series of letters between the narrator and a friend who has fled gay New York for the deep South, its literary quality fairly leaps off the page. The correspondents address each other as "Ecstasy", "Vision," "Madness," "Delirium," "Life Itself," and "Existence," and sign their florid letters with the names of aristocratic French women, Victor Hugo, the Duc de Saint-Simon, and ("Yours in Christ") Marie de Maintenon. Through them, we learn that the narrator—like the main character, Malone—is working as a prostitute, and that his refugee friend is tending old women dying of cancer in an unnamed town in Georgia, elated to feel the pulse of the dying and to smell the azaleas, rather than the living death of shallow glamour in New York.

Discussing the agonies and ecstasies of the gay party life, the letters reveal the genesis of the book itself: "A gay novel, darling. About all of us." The refugee cautions the narrator that gay life fascinates him only because it is the life he was condemned to live, yet coaxes him to record "the madness, the despair, of the old-time queens . . . the true loonies of this society, refusing to camouflage themselves for society's sake." Though campy, the "reality effect" of the opening and closing letters forms a frame for the intense artifice of the hot-house world of the novel.

The novel itself opens with the narrator coming to collect a dead man's clothes; those of Malone, "the emblem of so many demented hearts," "the central beautiful symbol" on which everything in that world rests. Gifted with a handsome face, a hot body, and a big cock, he embodies all the material values of the gay world, but he is also "the most romantic creature of a community whose citizens are more romantic, perhaps, than any other on earth." The first paragraph echoes *The Great Gatsby* in the narrator's recalling his father's observations on the great sadness of collecting a dead friend's clothes. Yet Malone is less a friend than "just a face I saw in a discotheque"; an emblem of an era, no less than Gatsby was of the Jazz Age. The era here is the disco years, and *Dancer from the Dance* is the greatest and perhaps the only real Disco Novel. (The Roaring Twenties, with their hedonism, speed, and glamour, foreshadow the years of Gay Liberation). As if to underline the relationship between Malone and Gatsby, the narrator's description of Malone, with radiant blue eyes and blond hair, echoes no one more than Robert Redford himself, the handsome but also sensitive star who played Gatsby in the 1974 film.

I first read *Dancer from the Dance* in college, not five years after it was published, but already I sensed that the world it depicted had been washed away. I longed for its melancholy and melodrama, the mixture of unknowable sexual freedom with sleaze and glamour. AIDS was already on the horizon, the great bathhouses and underground discos already closed, disco itself had become an object of scorn, and the cynicism and sobriety of punk had swept New York. Yet for all its vitality and excess, death is everywhere in Holleran's novel, from old women dying of cancer to fags jumping off buildings from broken hearts. The fabulous men in the discotheque disappear from their families into New York as into a grave; they lie to their parents "because it's like having cancer but you can't tell them." When, near the age of thirty, Malone stops suppressing his homosexuality, it's "as if he finally admitted to himself that he had cancer." Few books so well illustrate conservatives' convictions that gay men's excesses had brought the scourge of AIDS upon themselves. And yet the spirit of the book is entirely the opposite. Suffused with love and compassion, *Dancer from the Dance* has the liberal temperament of the great memoirists of revolutionary France, such as Madame de Staël, famous for her adage *"tout comprendre, c'est tout pardoner"*: "to understand everything is to forgive everything."

At the core of the novel is "The Twelfth Floor," a disco hidden on the twelfth floor of a factory building in the as-yet-ungentrified West Thirties. Bound together by a certain type of music, physical beauty, and a love of style, the coterie of the disco resembles "the ecstasy of saints receiving the stigmata." A mix of busboys and doctors, Wall Street lawyers, and bicycle messengers, this world is a "strange democracy" such as the world never permits, "because its central principle was the most anarchic of all: erotic love." Living only to dance, "everyone was a god, and no one grew old in a single night." Their beauty is "a vocation," a career, and they rush out each night to simply exhibit themselves "much as a priest on Holy Saturday throws open the doors of the Tabernacle to expose the chalice within." At every moment the deep pull of the sensual and the erotic duels with the power of style and spectacle. Published a year after the film *Saturday Night Fever*, Holleran's novel similarly captures the frenzy of disco, but is sited at its anarchic source, the euphoric fire of the newly liberated gay man.

Malone mesmerizes the reader, much as he himself is mesmerized by his new life. Similar to Gatsby, he is a blank screen onto which others project their fantasies. After being born in the American Midwest, he was raised in Ceylon while his father worked overseas, and his first memories are of being enchanted by warm tropical breezes. In a theme borrowed from Thomas Mann's story "Tonio Kröger" (1903)—that of the pollination of the Northern temperament by Southern passions—Malone comes to long for dark Latin and Italian men, for hot nights and exotic passion. Infected by the somatic zones, Malone is, like his tribe, a "prisoner of love," living to fuck and dance, incapable of resisting the ecstatic gloom of the disco inferno.

In the manner of Proust's *In Search of Lost Time*, *Dancer from the Dance* is a novel of social observation, of the contrast between what appears to be and what is, or the disjuncture between what we desire and what we finally find. Malone, like Gatsby, is unknowable and desired by all, yet nearly oblivious to everything but his own desires. The novel is a *Bildungsroman*, a novel of development or coming-of-age story, but also a novel of passionate friendship—like that of Tom Sawyer and Huckleberry Finn. The primary relationship throughout the book is between Malone and Sutherland, a mad queen. Perhaps as attractive as

Malone fifteen years ago, Sutherland is doomed by his small penis, "the leprosy of homosexuals." He is also Malone's guide to the underworld—like Tiresias, blind prophet of Thebes, famous for being transformed into a woman for seven years. Encouraging yet another timid young initiate to take a red pill of speed, Sutherland reminds him not to believe everything he reads. "You mustn't for instance read the newspapers; that will destroy your mind faster than speed. The *New York Times* has been responsible for more deaths in this city than Angel Dust, *croyez-moi*."

A decadent aesthete in the mold of Joris-Karl Huysmans's character Des Esseintes in *Against Nature* (*A Rebours*, 1884), Sutherland chooses to live his life among the men he desires, rather than retreat into a phantasmic world of his own creation. He had been a "candidate for the Episcopalian priesthood, an artist, a socialite, a dealer, a kept boy, a publisher, a film-maker, and was now simply—Sutherland." He shares Malone's class background, and was raised not just to marry and procreate, but to rise to a position of importance among the professional elite. And like Malone, he walks away from his class preemptively, to forestall their abandoning him. Sutherland is Malone's queen and also his mother, plotting to marry him to the wealthy heir of a fertilizer fortune. Moving down the ladder of social mobility, we come to understand that Sutherland survives as a drug dealer and kind of pimp, and Malone—like the unnamed narrator—as a call boy.

Sutherland's flamboyance is the candy of the novel, a foil to Malone's somewhat blank sincerity. He is the embodiment of camp, wildly mixing high culture and low, butch and femme, saint and slut. And yet as time passes interesting shifts occur: Malone meets a "dark-eyed and grave and beautiful" bank teller, follows him home for sex in the tub by the light of a dozen candles. He falls deeply in love by their second meeting, but the third time he simply sits beside him in the bathtub, and finally it's enough for him to just look up at his window as he passes on the street. Rather than having fallen out of love, Malone's love feels purer than ever to him. Like Sutherland he is an aesthete, and his love more an abstraction than an embodied thing. Holleran's novel is less about sex than desire, but really more about the idea of desire than its actuality. Even the sex, frequent though it is, falls away from view.

There are many forms of death in *Dancer from the Dance*: the gay men dead to their straight families; the heterosexuals locked away in their anodyne worlds; the living dead, gay men trapped in their compulsive, glittering lives; and the real dead at the end. Malone and Sutherland die either by their own design or by accident on the same day, after a grand party intended to finally seduce the young fertilizer heir. After speaking as frankly as he can to the young millionaire in hopes of disabusing him of his Sutherland-induced romantic illusions, Malone walks into the ocean off Fire Island and tells the narrator he is going away to a simpler life. When he fails to reappear, rumors fly that he was among the fourteen men who died that same night in the fire at the Everard Baths in the East Village. Sutherland overdoses on sleeping pills at almost the same time, but the note beside his bed reads more like an apology for leaving the party too early. His funeral is a great spectacle held at Campbell's, like Judy Garland's a decade before, while Malone's body is never found. Malone haunts the novel in his death as in his life.

Behind this haunting lies a doubling, not just of the two characters or even lover and beloved, but of the duality of Malone's desire for both domestic happiness and "some adventurous ideal of homosexuality." Digging deeper into the doubling between the novel and the letters that frame it, we detect a collision between an old (if internalized) homophobia and the horror of a new radical freedom, when all barriers appear to fall. Total freedom seems entirely within the grasp of countless gay men, but the moral lesson appears to be that no one is as yet capable to rise to it. It's false to argue that gay men were freer in the 1970s than they are now, but they certainly wore their freedom differently. What is remarkable here is Holleran's consciousness of the bittersweet nature of the sexual revolution. "We're completely free," says Malone halfway through the story, "and that's the horror."

The theme of value versus waste hovers over the novel. Asking if one can waste a life is a restatement of an older question: is the homosexual life a waste? In the first chapter, Malone says he'd rather do anything than waste another summer on Fire Island. "Who can waste a summer on the Island?" Sutherland snorts in response, "Why, it's the only antidote to death we have." As the discourse on waste develops, it becomes apparent that only one who possesses something can squander it, and if one doesn't already hold a thing, one holds its promise. While the politics of gay liberation warrant nary a mention from the characters, its effects are everywhere. Is the life of a queen tragic or ridiculous or something else altogether? *Dancer from the Dance* unfolds on a fulcrum between moral tale and seductive reverie. While Malone moves from faith in God to faith (often tinged with despair) in his homosexuality, what he argues for is a choice beyond sexuality: to live for pleasure not productivity, to live for romance, ideals, and beauty. It's an argument with the bourgeoisie that dates back to the Romantics, but probably much further back than that—to the stoics and the epicureans. Yet despite its ambiguities of good and bad or illusions and reality, *Dancer from the Dance* is ultimately a joyful novel.

In the letters we are offered a new figure, that of the gay author. He is writing a new gay literature, without evil homophobes or punished, noble, or victimized homosexuals. He's a writer of a new gender: the fag, not a woman but certainly not a heterosexual man. In Holleran's novel, we find the riotous flowering of Gay Liberation, one of the great social experiments of the twentieth century. We might critique it as being less about democracy of course than privilege: all the men are handsome, white, and able to do what it takes, but of course no democracy arises everywhere equally. And with the figure of the gay author, less than a decade after Stonewall, we are presented with the assumption of a gay reader. Older gay books were for the most part apologias, aimed mostly at the heterosexuals whose judgments held far more power than any collective of homosexual readers. Books by later gay writers such as Dale Peck or Dennis Cooper are arguably written to neither gay nor straight readers. But here, at last, is a novel for us and to us: "A gay novel, darling. About all of us." It is a wild and unexpected fulfillment of Walt Whitman's utopian call for the "love of comrades" to "sing the body electric."

MATIAS VIEGENER is a writer and artist living in Los Angeles and teaching at CalArts. Quotations are taken from Andrew Holleran, *Dancer from the Dance* (New York: Harper Perennial, 2001), which is currently in print.

The Cancer Journals
(1980)

by Audre Lorde

Tania Katan

In 1993 I was angry, really angry. Angry because one year earlier, at twenty-one years old I had lost a breast to breast cancer; angry that none of my peers understood what I was going through; angry that I had to choose between saving my breast or saving my life; angry that all of my doctors urged me to get reconstructive surgery; angry at losing my hair; angry at chemotherapy; angry at psychotherapy; angry at anything that ended in therapy; just plain angry! And then I found Audre Lorde. And she was pretty angry too. I remember feeling like I had found my pissed-off cancer sister and together we would throw our silly prostheses into the wind, wearing nothing but our collective scars and huge smiles; changing the face of breast cancer forever! But in 1993 I was still pissed off, working on developing my own writing voice beyond one-note anger. Audre Lorde's writing voice was well developed, nuanced, she knew that anger plus action equaled power. I was just finding my voice, so action and power would have to wait.

The Cancer Journals was a gift from Debbie, a grad-student director who had chosen to direct a play that I was writing called *Stages*, which detailed my story of being a snarky lesbian breast cancer survivor. Debbie looked like she could have costarred in *Little House on the Prairie*, like Laura Ingalls Wilder's long-lost cousin, Debbie. She had pale white skin, an earnest smile, and was always nodding in agreement with whatever you were saying, causing her freshly washed honey-brown bangs to bounce with optimism and affirmation. Before our first rehearsal for *Stages* she handed me Audre Lorde's book and said, "I love this book. I think you'll love it too. You and Audre have a lot in common."

"Thank you," I said. But what I really wanted to say was: "What the hell do you know about lesbians? About breast cancer? About loss? About surviving? About being black?" OK, I'm not black, but at the time I felt like Jews were the new blacks.

After rehearsal, I went home and cracked open *The Cancer Journals*. I began reading Audre Lorde's journal entries and quickly found affirmation of my anger, of the choice I was making to give voice to my story of survival. Audre was like this radical lesbian cheerleader choosing voice in the face of adversity, turning anger into power, and when faced with her own mortality she chose to live. And all of this was in the first three pages!

Each page of *The Cancer Journals* felt like Audre was writing to me, like we were sitting around having coffee, chatting about scars and women we've loved and what it means to be a warrior. Her descriptions of post-mastectomy pain, her foggy brain filled with anesthesia, the delight she took in not wearing a prosthesis, in feeling empowered by her new physique, all of these descriptions were so clear and visceral that they shook me awake, made my writing more fierce and urgent. The only thing I didn't understand at the time was how she knew exactly what I was feeling; how she was able to address all women but made it sound like she was talking to directly to me; how she acquired my journals.

It's 2009, the first time I'm rereading my worn copy of *The Cancer Journals* since 1993. The pages are a warm ecru now, due to years of living in boxes, moving, and waiting patiently to be found again. On the title page, written in pencil, are notes I wrote about my play *Stages*, about the main character not having the energy to fight cancer anymore. Flipping through the book, dog-eared pages stop me, demanding that I read specific journal entries to find out why I bent the corner in 1993. I couldn't imagine what relevance *The Cancer Journals* held now—twenty-nine years after their publication—until I started reading. But this time I am reading as a thirty-seven-year-old, two-time breast cancer survivor, lesbian, writer, and activist. This time I am reading *The Cancer Journals* with much less anger in my body and infinitely more power in my voice.

On one of the dog-eared pages there is a sentence circled in pencil: "I realized that the attitude towards prosthesis after breast cancer is an index of this society's attitude toward women in general as decoration and externally defined sex object." I'm blown away by the relevance of this statement today. This is still a radical notion in 2009. But Audre was exploring it in 1979. Today, in 2009, I hear her loud and clear as she writes about prosthesis, about the ridiculous idea of covering up one's scars of survival thus relegating them to those of victim rather than survivor; about the "travesty of prosthesis." She talks about the prime minister of Israel at the time, Moshe Dayan, who wore a patch over his empty eye socket because he was a warrior, had something to be proud of. She argued that all women with breast cancer were also warriors; that we are amputees who have fought for our lives and our scars are our badges of honor.

I read further. Ten days after her mastectomy, Audre Lorde is feeling strong, even confident in her new body without a breast, so instead of wearing the lambswool prosthesis to visit her breast surgeon, she struts her stuff into the office, sans prosthetic, proud that she is surviving, and the doctor's nurse greets her: "You're not wearing a prosthesis." And Audre proudly replies: "No." The nurse makes her point more clear. "You will feel much better with it on, and besides, we really like you to wear something, at least when you come in. Otherwise it's bad for the morale of the office." Lorde writes in response to this odd comment: "Nobody tells him (Moshe Dayan) to go get a glass eye, or that he is bad for the morale of the office. The world sees him as a warrior with an honorable wound, and a loss of a piece of himself which he has marked, and mourned and moved beyond. And if you have trouble dealing with Moshe Dayan's empty eye socket, everyone recognizes that it is your problem to solve, not his."

In my rereading *The Cancer Journals*, Lorde's mantras become overwhelmingly significant: *I am a post-mastectomy woman. I am a poet. I am a black woman. I am a lesbian. I am a warrior. I am here.* Like friends, these declarations seem to carry her through the highs and lows of illness and wellness. By Lorde stating who she is and why she is here, over and over again, we get a sense of her living through her words, beyond her words, being alive and vibrant through voice rather than form.

I only put down her book long enough to research the exact date of Audre Lorde's death: November 17, 1992. It turns out that Debbie was right; Audre Lorde and I have a lot in common. Both of us are lesbians. Both writers. Both refused to wear prosthesis. In November 1992, Audre Lorde passed away after battling breast cancer for fourteen years; in November 1992 I was diagnosed with my first primary breast cancer.

I'd like to think that perhaps when Audre Lorde passed away, she threw the breast cancer baton to me. I caught it, and have been running ever since. Every time I take off my shirt, two mastectomy scars proudly displayed, and run a race to raise money for breast cancer research, I am running with all of the women who have come before, who have survived cancer through their words, their stories, their voices. I am running with Audre Lorde. She is smiling, her eyes are tired, but her spirit is fierce. We hold hands as we cross the finish line. We look at each other, feeling grateful for this unusual journey. Audre says, "I would never have chosen this path, but I am very glad to be who I am, here."

TANIA KATAN is an author, playwright, and performer. Her memoir *My One-Night Stand with Cancer* was winner of the 2006 Judy Grahn Award in Nonfiction, an honoree of the 2006 American Library Association's Stonewall Book Award in Non-Fiction, and a finalist for the 2006 Lambda Literary Award. Since the success of her first book, Tania has been performing her one-woman show *Saving Tania's Privates* (adapted from *My One Night Stand with Cancer*), across Europe and the United States. For more information, please visit www.taniakatan.com. Quotations are taken from Audre Lorde, *The Cancer Journals* (San Francisco: Aunt Lute Books, 2006), which is currently in print.

THE COLOR PURPLE
(1982)

by Alice Walker

MARK BEHR

THE READER DISCOVERS COLOR

The Reader is a student. This one has an attractive girl-friend. He is a Christian who believes in God with a capital G. He is certain of many things. He enjoys taking hikes through landscapes with mountains, rivers, and wild flowers. He is proud of having been a soldier in a foreign war at the age of eighteen, epaulettes signalling to the world that he had indisputably, visibly, and forever passed the test of manhood. He would like to travel one day; perhaps write books about heroism in war, valor, love, desire, and glory. While sympathetic to those who are hungry or live in poverty, he believes in strong government that both controls and disciplines the revolutionary aspirations of the poor. If he does think self-consciously of politics, questions of order, security, and responding to the demands of his time are foremost in his mind. Not even his girlfriend knows that he is a secret agent and that he is having his university tuition paid by the state. She also doesn't know of his sexual desire for men. Both these things he keeps from her and anyone else close to him. He is profoundly ashamed of this aberrant yearning and chastises himself whenever he feels it—which is almost always. A disturbing and recurrent memory from boyhood is of being caned till his buttocks bled for a playful sexual romp with other boys. For years he has barely been able to look at his own penis and scrotum; his anus he can scarcely think of. He slips his penis into his girlfriend as rapidly as he can, almost as if he wishes to hide from view this root of shame, pleasure, and anguish. He plans to marry this lovely blonde girl and have two children and a house in the suburbs. No one will ever know. Part of his job as a secret agent is to infiltrate a small band of leftist students who are in favor of the violent overthrow of the state. During a weekend in the country with this group, he sees his name with the names of other men scribbled alongside the names of women on a roster for kitchen duties. Only half-joking he says that he is not in favor of men doing women's work. The leftist, feminist women look at him askance: from which cave did you crawl? Giving him the benefit of the doubt, they lend him a copy of a book. It is the first book he has read written by a black person. From the very first sentence he is entranced: "Dear God . . . I have always been a good girl." The story consists mostly of letters from a girl named Celie. Celie has always done what has been expected of her. She confides in no one but God that she has been raped by the man she knows as her father and all but sold into a loveless marriage with Mr., another nameless man who beats and abuses her. When Celie and other black characters venture into town for shopping, they constantly monitor their every word and censure every gesture while they're amongst white people. Their very lives seem to depend on the appeasement of whites. When one of Celie's circle, Sophia, resists the way things work in the white world, she ends up beaten, imprisoned, and scarred for life. Celie does not even have the words to question or to say that she hates her existence. This is merely the way life is. One day, a blues singer named Shug Avery comes into Celie's life. Shug, who is Mr.'s lover, develops a thing for Celie. Celie tells Shug that Mr. having sex with her is akin to him "going to the toilet" on her. Shug introduces Celie to her own body: she lets Celie look at her "private parts" in a mirror. She touches Celie's clitoris. They become lovers. Celie falls in love with Shug. The earth moves for Celie: her life will never be the same. It is the first time The Reader reads—in words, from a book—of two women making love. It is not their lovemaking alone that moves him. It is also that Celie has grasped that she is wounded and is set on a path of healing. That she can and is learning to take back something of her body and her enjoyment of it. More than in any of the hundreds of books by white men and the few white women he has read, The Reader sees something of himself in Celie *and* in Mr. He looks at himself in the mirror: at his face and his anus and his penis and his navel. He notices not only his own body, but also his body beside his girlfriend and the bodies of women in general. It is not only that he starts to look differently at his own desire, it is that he sees the rest of himself in relationship also to black women: that as a privileged white man, as a soldier, as a spy, his agency and the way he now uses it in the world may be partly responsible for the way any woman of color—anyone poor or less privileged—is compelled to live a life of subjugation, repression, appeasement, and resistance. He rereads the book a number of times and gives it to others to read. He now notices people of color on the roadside, waiting for a lift, where mere months before he would at most have been aware of them. He dares, still almost silently, to think of loving a man. He reads other books, and rereads some previously read that at the time made only so much sense to him but now suddenly open up to offer extraordinary, hitherto *unimagined* meaning. In meetings for which he is meant to write reports to the state, he begins to listen to every word of the enemies of the state and he finds that he has begun to agree with much of what is said. He begins to filter the information he gives to the state. His mind is a tumble of contradictions and he no longer believes he understands or believes anything he once did. How, he wonders, is it that man can go all the way to the moon but not the short distance to his own rectum? He falls in love with more than one of the revolutionaries. With women and with men. He will leave the girlfriend of his youth who no longer understands his language and he will go to the revolutionaries and tell them that he is an agent of their enemy and that he would like to join their ranks. They too will swear him to discipline, secrecy, and loyalty. For a while, convinced and led by the revolution's moral authority, he will do what the revolutionaries say, but when he sees and feels that there is still too much of the old in what the revolutionaries claim is new, he will strike out on his own, fumbling, casting about to make his own newer paths alongside others who believe in solidarity, but only in a relentlessly critical solidarity. He will see that weighty autobiographies and often profound contingencies accompany us into the pages of each book we read. Some stories seem to keep us in their thrall from our first encounter for the rest of our days. Others, like people we once loved, that changed our lives irrevocably at one point may be revisited, only to leave us bemused or even perplexed at why and how they managed to affect us so deeply, with such passion or with such indifference in another time. Still, if The Reader allows memory to speak and himself to hear its voice, he cannot deny that certain texts like certain lovers helped lay the foundation for so much of his subsequent reading, writing, and life. And so, in his reading and writing life, as in the years when he himself stands in front of classes—at times he wonders fleetingly which student might carry a professor's name to the state—he rejoices in the tyranny of his gratitude and sometimes reteaches those books that helped unmake and remake him. The Reader no longer believes in orders of secrecy, discipline, and conforming to the demands of his times. He thinks and behaves and loves differently, sometimes changing his mind and revising what he thinks and does and believes. The Reader doubts, often. From book to book, his doubts multiply. The Reader believes that if more people were less certain more often and tasted the emancipation that comes with doubt, there would be fewer wars and fewer hungry and unhappy and angry people in whose eyes he sees himself reflected. He can pass down streets or through malls or he can page through a new book; he could be hiking through forests or his fingers may be tracing a lover's collarbone, lips, or the flower of an anus, when The Reader suddenly smiles to himself, again remembering to never pass by the color purple without noticing it and nodding in thanks, to any and all of the gods everywhere, in everything, always.

MARK BEHR is author of the novels *The Smell of Apples* (1995), *Embrace* (2000), and *Kings of the Water* (2009). He divides his time between South Africa and the United States, where he is Associate Professor of World Literature and Fiction Writing at the College of Santa Fe, New Mexico. Quotations are taken from Alice Walker, *The Color Purple* (New York: Harvest, 2006), which is currently in print.

A BOY'S OWN STORY
(1983)

by Edmund White

ROBERT GLÜCK

W hen I retrieved my copy of *A Boy's Own Story* for this essay, I was surprised by how short the book is—a little over two-hundred pages. By the time I finished it I had come to think of it again as a big novel. Why is that? The story is not grand; its events are poised between tableau and anecdote. Except for the narrator, characters don't emerge very far past the proscenium arch of the prose. Of course, it's the prose and the corresponding isolation of the narrator/hero that give the novel grandeur.

One is always guided back to the surface. For example, White abandons the conventional time line of story about a boy's education. We don't travel with this boy into his future. He is fifteen when the book begins. He spends the summer with dad at a beach resort and has an affair with twelve-year-old Kevin. In the second section, during the previous summer, the boy is fourteen and working for his father. In an impressive display of *Realpolitik* he negotiates his failed plan to run away into the purchase of a hustler.

He's seven in the third section; we learn about his parent's divorce, his life with mother. Then we go forward to his eleventh year, and the family drama extends to include eccentrics at home and at camp, where the boy has sex with a dysfunctional camper. In the fifth section, the boy, now thirteen years old, rises to the call of popularity and falls in love with a girl. In the last section he's fourteen: he encounters more eccentrics at a pseudo-Anglo prep school, and he stages the betrayal of a teacher that heralds the onset of adulthood.

This manipulation of forward momentum sends us into the thematics of the story; it provides the leisure for these thematics to develop associatively and through figurative language. For example, the father's sexual life is described as follows: "This hint of mystery about a man so cold and methodical fascinated me— as though he, the rounded brown geode, if only cracked open, would nip at the sky with interlocking crystal teeth, the quartz teeth of passion." Two pages later the simile is revamped to include the son, a manipulation of imagery at once subtle and outlandish: "What if I could write about my life exactly as it was? What if I could show it in all its density and tedium and its concealed passion, never divined or expressed, the dull brown geode that eats at itself with quartz teeth?"

The problem set up at the start of *A Boy's Own Story* is: How can I put myself in relation to my dad, who is all powerful? This problem is elaborated throughout the novel by means of a governing trope, the king or sovereign. The novel, you could say, magnifies the education of a boy through images of sovereignty. That a novel of sexual maturation addresses forms and relations power is one reason *A Boy's Own Story* is so un-American, so French.

These images comprise a system or fundamental structure (like Hegel's Master-Slave dialectic) because they are made to address such a broad spectrum of social relations. Sometimes they are mock epic (home is a fake Norman castle), but mostly they illustrate a continental wisdom: that desire and power are linked, that they are based on a kind of betrayal, a crime against love. These lofty images comprise a "theme and variations" that lend grandeur to the large movements and to the details. Images of sovereignty are brought to the isolation in the nuclear family, racism, male privilege, class privilege, issues which lift the book out of the box of psychology and the overheated nuclear closet. They remind me of Georges Bataille, certainly Friedrich Nietzsche, who might have written: "I even envied his sovereignty, though the price of freedom—total solitude—seemed more than I could possibly pay."

Many of these images center on the father, a Zeus, a deity, a king, and then they devolve onto the son as he matures. When he was alone he was "not a boy at all but a principle of power, of absolute power." In a nice twist, in the last of these images our young fag attains full royal stature—as a queen. "Or I felt like someone in history, a queen on her way to the scaffold determined to suppress her usual quips, to give the spectators the high deeds they wanted to see."

A Boy's Own Story appeared in 1982, and I encountered it, as I encountered everything in those years, as a gay man. Its publication was greeted by me and others both as a literary and cultural event. We were grateful to find incontestable literature that applied to us—an expressive possibility had arrived. In the early eighties, few books offered a reading of our experience, and we approached them with the emphatic interest of looking into mirrors, testing new reflections against expectations. We were alert to every nuance of sexuality and always searching for possibilities of identification.

A Boy's Own Story was published by a trade press and we needed to see our new identities in the national forum. We wondered how this book, which treated our sex in such an offhand manner, got past the guards. It's not enough to say that its ticket was quality because other literary books—those of Jean Genet; Irving Rosenthal's *Sheeper* (1967); John Rechy's *City of Night* (1963), for example—were published by wicked Grove, rather than august E. P. Dutton. New Directions published Isherwood's *Berlin Stories* (1945).

The answer, I think, is partly the times and partly the prose. A gay market had been created by small presses, and suddenly editors working at large houses, like Bill Whitehead, could act on their interest in gay fiction. And in *A Boy's Own Story* every sentence tells a story—and that story is, "Look, this is literature." Sentences go to it like trumpets at Jericho: "I say all this by way of hoping that the lies I've made up to get from one poor truth to another may mean something—may even mean something most particular to you, my eccentric, patient, scrupulous reader, willing to make so much of so little, more patient and more respectful of life, of a life, than the author you're allowing for a moment to exist yet again." That is, this writing already comes to you from beyond the grave, a location more grandly French than English or American.

Perhaps this beauty "underwrote" the content, the recognizable (to us) push toward truth in sexuality. Two tykes are on an outing to buy Vaseline in order to ease the way: "He pulled it off without a trace of guilt, even asked to see the medium-size jar before settling for the small one. Outside, a film of oil opalesced on the water under a great axle of red light rolling across the sky from azimuth to zenith." So their sex is splayed across sea and sky (before the days of water solubility). You could say the prose safeguards the experience of being gay.

Still, the book was a bit confusing in 1982. Unapologetic homosexuality was not the only unusual matter it brought to the larger realm of American letters. There's its portrayal of aggressive child sexuality, its savaging of the nuclear family, its unapologetic love of surface and preoccupation with artifice. *A Boy's Own Story* didn't jibe completely with the smaller realm of gay community self-description—healthy, moral, natural—or nature that had been victimized. On the cover, a boy in a tank top gazes outward, to the sea, to the future—his promise of health and offer of physical beauty were certainly on the movement's agenda. But the boy between the covers is entirely corrupted by self-consciousness and the knowledge of gender roles.

A Boy's Own Story's claim to the largest forum was not only based on its lyrical prose, a feather in our cap, but on its negative vision, its grand homosexual theme of betrayal. Love is not something you give to others, but something you do to them. Sex and friendship are taken from people. It's a description of extreme isolation.

A Boy's Own Story is so amoral. The blurbs promised a cross between J. D. Salinger and Oscar Wilde. I'd keep Wilde for prose that generates at once feelings of precisian and incredulity, the great queen's aggression and assertion of surface that foregrounds the relation between writer and reader. But the moral anguish and problems of belief in Salinger are not even close. *A Boy's Own Story* may be a *Bildungsroman* with a Dickensian enthusiasm for eccentric guides, but at heart it has more in common with Machiavelli's *The Prince* (1513) than with Salinger's *Catcher in the Rye* (1951).

If *A Boy's Own Story* does resemble *Catcher in the Rye*, it's because both books ask: What constitutes maturity? Certainly every adult is an unacceptable model, and that is the joke of *A Boy's Own Story*. So, why not take revenge and betray one of these adults into revealing his false relation to life? That is, if your sex is viewed as a weakness, why not weaken an adult with it?

The hero has a lack of naiveté which he loathes in himself; in fact, he is the manipulator that many of us felt ourselves to be. I am reminded of another wonderfully chilling child portrait, that of baby Sartre in *The Words* (*Les mots*, 1964). The hero of *A Boy's Own Story* is made unlovely because he is frozen on the grid of natural/not natural. He wonders, as we had, whether he is estranged by his sexuality, or whether his sexuality is just another symptom of deeper isolation. He can't take people for granted because his secret poisons every attempt to belong with them.

After reading *The Beautiful Room Is Empty* (1988), I think I see an overall thematics in these fictionalized memoirs. *The Beautiful Room Is Empty* ends with the Stonewall Riots, the beginning of the present gay movement. White seems to be saying, you can't have love or moral life in a void; in a void you are just trying to survive. Moral life can't exist outside the context of a community.

A Boy's Own Story could be taken both as a model for the crossover novels of its period and as the novel that subverts the genre. Crossover novels tended to be family novels, tales of growing up and coming out, like Robert Ferro's *The Family of Max Desir* (1984). The family remains the national forum, so it's no surprise that the family romance would fall to us just as we were claiming space on the national stage. Entrance into the mainstream would have to be a battle for public existence in the family.

But the family value White describes is lust for power: the indifference and brutality of those who have it, the craven self-loathing of those who don't, and the internecine battle to acquire some. And sex destroys families rather than binding them together. Hatred of the family and the assertion of child sexuality seem to go hand in hand. Dad is a philanderer; our hero mimes his father's sexual exploitation of Alice, the class evil made explicit: "I'd used and discarded him—just as my dad had mistreated Alice, the Addressograph operator."

As earlier forms are swallowed by later ones, I wonder if the theme of betrayal is domesticated here, its existential consequence replaced by a social one. The gay self (whatever it is) is extremely aware of itself as the product of historical and familial tensions. In *A Boy's Own Story*, the existential terror remains, along with the sense of isolation. Why should they be eliminated? But they are framed and "flattened" by an awareness of the self as a construct as they undergo series of middle-class remedies: prep school, camp, therapy, imported religion.

This awareness of the self-as-construct is mirrored in *A Boy's Own Story* by an attention to surface and an obsession with manners and mores, the nuances and ins and outs of communication. The message is always membership and status rather than specific content. Any society thus examined becomes every society. The outsider puts everything on a single plane, that of artifice. That is the wisdom of the closet: the anthropologist or imposter sees the extent to which everyone is playing a role with degrees of self-awareness based inversely on degrees of success.

Examining nuances that signal status and affiliation has been a practice of White's since *Forgetting Elena* (1973). That this examination is first the study and imitation of heterosexuality by a little fag will be immediately recognizable to all gay people. So here we have the poles of *A Boy's Own Story*. On the one hand, conversance is perfected. The outsider's imitations gain meaning through his struggle for self-preservation and his risk of being unmasked. Conversance—even when it's expressed as a highly ornamented surface—becomes a strategy for safety: "Somehow— but at what precise moment?—I had shown I was a sissy; I replayed a moment here, a moment there of the past days, in an attempt to locate the exact instant when I'd betrayed myself." On the other hand, this passage leads into an historical awareness: identification with black people who were "exiled, dispersed into the alien population," and a wish for their community life: "I really believed I, too, was exuberant and merry by nature, had I the chance to show it."

But White does not conclude by giving the boy's suffering a pious moral value, because it is also linked to the will to dominate, to seize power. In the next paragraph White writes, "I was desolate . . . I wanted power so badly that I had convinced myself I already had too much of it . . . I was appalled by my own majesty. I wanted someone to betray."

───────────

ROBERT GLÜCK has written nine books of poetry and fiction. His latest—a book of stories—is entitled *Denny Smith* (2004). Other publications include the novels *Jack the Modernist* (1985) and *Margery Kempe* (1994), another book of stories, *Elements of a Coffee Service* (1983), and *Reader* (1989), a book of poems and short prose. Along with Camille Roy, Mary Burger, and Gail Scott, Gluck has also edited *Biting the Error: Writers on Narrative* (2005). His forthcoming novel is entitled *About Ed.* Quotations are taken from Edmund White, *A Boy's Own Story* (New York: Penguin, 2009), which is currently in print.

ORANGES ARE NOT THE ONLY FRUIT
(1985)

by Jeanette Winterson

V. G. LEE

ORANGES AND EASTER EGGS

As a child I was nurtured on a diet of corned beef sandwiches and the words and pictures of an illustrated copy of John Bunyan's *The Pilgrim's Progress* (1678). Life for me, it seemed, was to be spent like the pilgrim Christian, on a hard and stony path—which for some reason wasn't going to be the same path as my mother's. Hers was strewn with new clothes and matching accessories, Consulate cigarettes, Campari and Dry Sac sherry. "I only wish I could afford to live like Christian," Mum said, "but with two kids to look after, I need to earn a living."

It wasn't till much later when I was in my thirties that I first read Jeanette Winterson's *Oranges Are Not the Only Fruit*, and realized that at least one other woman had worked her way through a similarly constricted childhood.

Winterson has been quoted as saying, "Regarding whether the book is autobiographical, *Oranges* is the document, both true and false, which will have to serve for my life until I went to Oxford." I like to imagine that Jess the child is really the young Jeanette. I'm immediately fond of this child, whereas I was unable to like myself as a child. She has a sense of humor and a sharply observant eye. She has odd friends, talks to demons, accepts the extraordinary as matter-of-fact.

In the book, one night a woman sets off walking.

"She would get a child, train it, build it, dedicate it to the Lord:

a missionary child,
a servant of God,
a blessing."

The child is Jess. She is brought up within the strict Old Testament constraints of her mother's church, which makes her different, out of step with other children. When in early adolescence Jess falls in love with a young girl called Melanie, she mistakenly trusts her mother enough to confide in her. The mother and the church elders all unite behind their pastor, to drive out what they see as a demon in Jess.

"It was 10 p.m. that same night before the elders went home. They had spent the day praying over me, laying hands on me, urging me to repent my sins before the Lord. 'Renounce her, renounce her,' the pastor kept saying. 'It's only a demon.'"

For two days Jess is locked in the parlor until she repents. She and Melanie are separated.

Jess says, "Families, real ones, are chairs and tables and the right number of cups, but I had no means of joining one, and no means of dismissing my own; she (her mother) had a thread round my button, to tug when she pleased."

It was Easter time. I was five years old. Mum, I, and my brother lived with my grandparents in a terraced house in Birmingham. The front room was never used, except to store Christmas and birthday presents, and Easter eggs. That Easter, when Mum went into the front room to fetch the eggs, they were gone. All that was left was the colored foil wrapping. There was no amazed discussion. No, "could it possibly have been mice/rats?" Not even, "perhaps one of the children . . ." Mum roared back into the kitchen, where I sat drawing at the table. I don't remember where my brother was.

She said, "You greedy little devil—you've eaten the Easter eggs."

When she was angry, her whole face shook.

I looked up. I understood her words but not quite what she meant.

"I haven't."

She put her hands flat on the table, one each side of my picture. "Don't lie to me."

I said, "Mummy, I didn't eat the eggs."

"You knew they were in there?"

"Yes."

And that was enough. Instances were recalled of previous dishonesties: a scarf I'd borrowed from her dressing table drawer and never returned; pretending to read the *Encyclopedia of the Natural World*, just to get attention from the adults; my tendency to exaggerate. Mum convinced my grandparents immediately. I remember Gran, whom I loved and admired, saying: "Tops, (her pet name for me) if you'd just admit that you ate the eggs, we could forgive you."

"She's as hard as nails," Mum said, lighting a cigarette and tossing the spent match into the fireplace.

They went on at me for hours. I remember their hard faces, the disappointed face of my grandfather. I remember mum trying to light the fire by holding a newspaper against it and the newspaper kept catching alight. "See what she's made me do," Mum said looking at her sooty hands.

I remember my bewilderment, how I felt I had nothing and no one to help me.

To prove Mum wrong about me being hard, so Gran would forgive me, so Grandfather would be able to say in his cheery way, "Well, all done and dusted." I finally blurted out, "Yes, I did eat the eggs."

But that was just the start. Gran did not forgive. Mum was proved right. Grandpa looked shocked. I cried.

"Crocodile tears," Mum said. "She turns them on like a tap."

"But I didn't really eat the eggs. I didn't. I only said I did."

Even at five I knew it was too late to accuse my brother, so I became the liar of the family. Nothing I did for years and years was ever accepted immediately as the truth. I only ever talked about it once to my brother, a few years ago. He was annoyed that I'd chosen to bring the subject up. As adults we get on very well so I let it drop. He'd only been six years old at the time of the Easter egg incident. He would have been frightened, and each child wants to be the love object not the disappointment.

But my mother? As an adult, I've wondered why she did that to me, yet I never asked her. I'm sure she knew I hadn't eaten the eggs. Eventually she officially forgave me, but, as Jeanette Winterson writes after the mother has burnt all Jess's letters and cards from Melanie, "in her head she was still queen, but not my queen any more, not the White Queen anymore."

When I was ten my brother went to boarding school and I began life in earnest. Like Christian, I would carry on my back a weight of sin. As I grew up, the vivid Biblical imagery and lessons faded into the background tapestry of my mind, but they never went away entirely. They were like someone hiding behind a curtain, listening in to my innermost thoughts and then moving the curtain ever so slightly to make their presence known.

My mother went her own way. I was her scapegoat which I now see was to ease the discomfort of her own life-long dissatisfaction. In the end, like Jess, I made an escape of sorts.

One of our worst arguments was over whether I'd put half a spoon of sugar in her tea rather than a quarter of a spoon. I was fourteen. In the past I'd always cried or got upset and asked her forgiveness. This was the first time I did nothing. I went to bed and read my book. I remember her popping her head around my door. She said, "Are you OK?"

"Fine, Mum."

For some days after, there was awkwardness between us. I'd behaved differently toward her and she felt my withdrawal. From then on I protected myself. She retained the power to hurt me but I never let her know it.

Oranges is also a very funny book, which I think is part of its great success. It portrays tragic circumstances but makes them bearable because humor and affection does creep in. I completely understand the child's bewilderment; how on the one hand she admired, even loved the mother, yet the mother breaks her trust, determinedly, without thought to her daughter's welfare.

My and Jess's childhoods may not be everyone else's stories, but at some time, most of us will experience that sense of losing our way within the normality of our ongoing lives, becoming isolated and at odds, even with members of our own family. Or we recall that odd child at school—the one who got it wrong, or whose parents made it wrong for them, so they were out of step. Avoided, maybe bullied, maybe bullying.

This is what *Oranges* did for me: it reworked *The Pilgrim's Progress*, adding passion, realism, understanding, and some incredibly funny lines.

V. G. LEE was born in Birmingham, England. Since then she's spent her life travelling slowly toward the south coast, where she now lives and writes. She has published three novels, one collection of short stories, *As You Step Outside* (2008), plus poetry and essays. For her sixtieth year she has embarked on a new career in stand-up comedy. Her Web site is www.vglee.co.uk. Quotations are taken from Jeanette Winterson, *Oranges Are Not the Only Fruit* (London: Vintage, 1991). A 1997 U.S. edition from Grove Press is currently in print.

To the Friend Who Did Not Save My Life

(A l'ami qui ne m'a pas sauvé la vie)

(1990)

by Hervé Guibert

Alistair McCartney

The Inscription

I teach at a small, private university in Los Angeles, and for the past five years I've lectured on Hervé Guibert's autobiographical novel *To the Friend Who Did Not Save My Life*. Set in Paris in the first decade of the AIDS epidemic, this sublime novel recounts the experience of a young Parisian writer dealing with his friends' AIDS-related deaths and then upon seroconverting, facing his own death. Published in France in 1990, the first English translation appeared in 1991, shortly before Guibert's death at the age of 36.

Naturally, as I began to think about writing this essay, I turned to my lecture notes. As I was leafing through them, my eyes began to blur. I began to doubt whether these ideas could do justice to the severe beauty of this book. Instead, I got up and took my own copy off the shelf.

My copy is actually the one I gave to my beloved, Tim, when we first met in London in 1994, just as I was falling in love, and I opened it to the inscription. What I wrote is far too long and more importantly far too sentimental to reprint here, but one sentence leaps out: 'Perhaps someday we'll learn to read this book.'

Like all great books, *To the Friend* does not immediately offer itself up. Although accessible, and eminently readable—it's the kind of book the reader can devour. It also evades easy comprehension, just as death, or the meaning of death, evades us.

As I held the worn copy in my hands, I was struck by a certain correspondence: I was entering an overwhelming and abiding passion when I first encountered this book, which relays a passion of a vastly different though not irreconcilable kind, one more in keeping with the Latin root and theological connotation of the word, a narrative of suffering.

But enough of this autobiography. Let's return to the notes.

THE DOCUMENT

The primary plot of this book is relatively simple, yet terrible in its simplicity. On the first page, the narrator announces he has AIDS, which of course in the 1980s was still regarded as a death sentence: "I had AIDS for three months. More precisely, for three months I believed I was condemned to die of that mortal illness called AIDS." But along comes a reprieve: "after three months something completely unexpected happened that convinced me I could and almost certainly would escape this disease . . . I would become, by an extraordinary stroke of luck, one of the first people on earth to survive this deadly malady." His friend Bill, who manages a pharmaceutical company, promises to get the narrator into a trial for a new vaccine that he claims stops the onset of the virus. The narrative is driven by the question of whether or not this friend will come through with his promise to save the narrator's life: "I don't know if this salvation is a decoy intended to soothe me, dangled before my eyes like a trap about to be sprung, or a genuine science fiction adventure in which I shall play the role of a hero . . ."

However, in another sense, the plot is historical—the narrative of AIDS that occurred outside the book. For this book is not only an intensely personal account of Guibert's own dealings with his predicament, but also a public document. The depictions of the various bureaucracies the narrator and his friends find themselves at the mercy of, whether it's the bureaucracy of the medical establishment, the pharmaceutical companies, or the syndrome itself, renders this book as a historical account of that frightening time. The book offers a timeline, a window into the intense vertigo of that moment, where gay men were confronted with a virus that seemingly came out of nowhere.

THE PHOTOGRAPH

Actually, as I think of it, my relationship with this book begins before that inscription. It begins with the image of Guibert himself. Long before I read *To the Friend*, I was aware of Guibert's physical presence. *Aware* is the wrong word; I was besotted with his image, and had his photo pinned to my bedroom wall. Perhaps *presence* is also the wrong word, for I don't believe I saw the photo until after Guibert's death.

In this image, which served as his author photo, Guibert looks directly into the camera, his eyes wide open. He wears a black shirt. His hands with their long, elegant fingers are placed one on top of the other and he wears a wristwatch with a black band, marking time. But it's his gaze we return to; it's fierce yet serene. He's impossibly handsome, yet it's the same face the narrator describes unflatteringly, the face that appears after his lover Jules cuts off all his curls: "a long angular face, a bit thin, with a high forehead and a hint of bitterness around the mouth, a face unfamiliar to me and to others. . . ." It's the face he sees as forecasting his own death.

I fell deeply in love with this image.

Essentially, I fell in love with Guibert's ghost.

THE QUESTION AND DESTRUCTION OF GENRE

The "characters" in this "novel" respond to the epidemic in various ways. Their reactions range from the incredulous—when first informed of the "mysterious illness," the philosopher Muzil responds: "A cancer that would hit only homosexuals, no, that's too good to be true, I could just die laughing!"—to passive acceptance: "We're all going to die of this disease, me, you, Jules, everyone we love," announces the narrator to his friend Gustave as they sunbathe.

The words "character" and "novel" must be placed in quotation marks, for the narrator goes by the name of Hervé Guibert, and all the other characters are thinly concealed versions of people from the writer's life (most famously Muzil "is" Michel Foucault; the first third of this book recounts Muzil/Foucault's death from AIDS in 1984).

All of Guibert's oeuvre blurred the line between fiction and nonfiction, but it is in this book that this aesthetic practice comes fully into being. It not only reflects the stark unreality of that moment, but the interstitial space Guibert finds himself in, somewhere between fiction and nonfiction, somewhere between life and death, crossing back and forth between these poles: "I felt as though Jules and I had gotten lost between our lives and our deaths, that this no-man's land, ordinarily and necessarily rather nebulous, had suddenly become atrociously clear . . ."

Death destroys the question of genre, reveals the instability of all categories.

GHOSTS

Guibert died on December 27th, 1991, which happens to be my birthday. In my narcissism, which is so strong perhaps even death won't be able to eradicate it, I've often attributed significance to this fact, entertained the notion that some mystical transaction took place.

Most likely this is pure fantasy. I've never seen Guibert's ghost, or any ghost for that matter. Though sometimes as I write, particularly as I write this essay, which is something between a lecture and a confession, I do feel inhabited by Guibert's authorial voice, just as he writes of being possessed, virtually infected by the prose style of the great Austrian writer Thomas Bernhard, who haunts *To the Friend*. And what is all writing if not an exorcism of ghosts, an incantation intended to free us from evil spirits? Though as is so often the case, the ghosts don't flee us but are pushed deeper into us, where they can't be touched; where they're safe.

The book's narrator often describes his own state as ghost-like, particularly in terms of the negative effect the virus has on his libido. Drained of desire, all he feels is "an incorporeal attraction, the helpless longing of a ghost, and never speaking of desire ever again . . ." He finds himself caught in the dreadful dialectic of death and desire that was played out in the epidemic: desire leads to death, death inhibits desire and ultimately replaces, abolishes desire. In a world abandoned by desire, the gay self is no longer a self but the ghost of a self.

CONSOLATION / NO CONSOLATION

Throughout *To the Friend*, Guibert refers to the process of writing this book as his only source of consolation. He likens it to "a companion, someone with whom I can talk, eat, sleep, at whose side I can dream and have nightmares, the only friend whose company I can bear at present." Yet it is also a "dreadful book," for its story is the story of his illness, his unjust fate.

Although we could identify a number of literary influences upon Guibert and locate points of affinity between this novel and other novels written during the frenzy of literary production that occurred in the first decade of the epidemic, its most striking predecessor is Boethius's *Consolation of Philosophy*. Written in AD 524 in Pavia while Boethius was in prison awaiting trial for treason, *Consolation* contemplates how one should live when faced with misfortune and how one should approach death.

It is generally acknowledged that Boethius was the victim of political maneuvering; he would eventually be executed. Like the philosopher, Guibert writes not from a prison cell per se, but from the prison cell that his body has become by virtue of the disease. Even the book's form, divided into one-hundred numbered sections—each section a paragraph of varying lengths—recalls those notches prisoners inscribe on the walls of their cells, to count the days. Guibert faces this "calamity [that] had hit us . . . [this] period of rampant misfortune from which there would be no escape" with stoicism worthy of Boethius, but also with virtues wholly his own, with passion, irony, ferocity, and a perverse intelligence.

The Immunologist

Years ago, I met a young, French North African man, who was at UCLA studying immunology, the science of the disorder of the immune system. He was passionate about his field and wanted to develop an HIV vaccine. What's more, he'd done a Masters in Literature in Paris, writing his thesis on *To the Friend*. I should also mention that this boy was beautiful and I was captivated, not only by his beauty, but by the uncanny parallel between his endeavors and the concerns of this book; it was one of those rare moments where art and life meet, correspond exactly. For a few hours we drank and talked about Guibert and Gide and Flaubert. The passion between us was palpable, but I had a boyfriend and he disappeared. "I know myself," he said. "I couldn't bear it. I'd want you all to myself."

It's interesting how everything disappears. I'd forgotten about him. I wonder where he is today. I wonder how his vaccine is developing. Perhaps he'll read this and remember me.

THE UNTIMELY MEDITATIONS

Like many other AIDS narratives, *To the Friend* is a race against disappearance. It is a book in which Hervé Guibert—the author, the character, and the man who lived on earth for all of thirty-six years—confronts the dreadful predicament of an untimely death. In this sense, its other philosophical precedent is Friedrich Nietzsche's *The Untimely Meditations* (1876), for surely the first wave of the epidemic's chief characteristic was untimeliness, a speeding up of time, turning young men into old men overnight.

By the novel's end, writing refuses to console Guibert. Rather, it turns against him: "My book is closing in on me. I'm in deep shit." Abandoned by his friend Bill, the offer of a vaccine withdrawn, Guibert offers the most pure and devastating final images of any book: "My muscles have melted away. At last my arms and legs are once again as slender as they were when I was a child."

What's astonishing is that there is not a moment of self-pity in this novel. Guibert faces his own tragedy with honesty and an exuberant, wicked wit, and I must stress the latter, for I fear I have offered a far too sober account of *To the Friend*. I fear I haven't done justice to this book which reveals there is no justice in this world, this miraculous book in which no miracles are performed, a world profoundly void of miracles, and if I really wanted to do it justice I would need to put these notes to the side, to abandon them, perhaps even destroy them. (Ah, yes, there is Guibert's ghost.)

Guibert learns from this tragedy, uses it as an education of a kind: "And it's true that I was discovering something sleek and dazzling in its hideousness . . . it was an illness in stages . . . whose every step represented a unique apprenticeship." Later on he states that: "AIDS will have been my paradigm in my project of self-revelation and the expression of the inexpressible . . ."

I say this cautiously, for to suggest that AIDS was an education for gay men is highly problematic. But what I can say without caution, with Guibert's own fearlessness, is that we need to recall what happened. Gay culture has repressed this period, the tragedy that we were given one brief decade, one golden epoch, before we were plunged into the epidemic. Regardless of whether we learnt anything, it is essential to who we are. This experience needs to be recuperated.

We need to listen to our ghosts. Our history is a haunted one, full of spectral presences. Perhaps like me you've never seen a ghost, but we need to go looking for them. One need look no further than this book. Guibert's beautiful ghost, the one that I am faithful to, is on every page, his presence simultaneously invisible and indelible.

ALISTAIR MCCARTNEY is the author of *The End of the World Book: a Novel* (2008). Originally from Australia, he is based in Los Angeles, where he teaches in the MFA Creative Writing Program at Antioch University. He is currently at work on *The Death Book*, the second novel in a five-book cycle. Quotations are taken from Hervé Guibert, *To the Friend Who Did Not Save My Life* (New York/London: High Risk/Serpent's Tail, 1993), translated by Linda Coverdale, which is currently in print.

THE TERRIBLE GIRLS
(1990)

by Rebecca Brown

CAROL GUESS

S ome time ago, in response to a lecture on Rebecca Brown's novel *The Dogs* (2001), a student posed a puzzling question. *The Dogs* describes a female protagonist whose studio apartment is occupied by a pack of unruly, violent dogs.

"Why didn't the narrator just send the dogs to the Humane Society?"

At first I thought my student was joking, but no. Her dogs were real; they had to be. As a reader, she was a Fundamentalist. The author wrote *dogs*, and dogs came to be.

This misrecognition of metaphor is the place I begin when I teach Brown's work. I use her texts regularly in "Introduction to GLBT Literature," a course that enrolls seventy-five college fresh-man and sophomores each year. We start with imagination and cre-ativity, with the difference between creative writing and criticism. We talk about how frightening it can be to read a text with multiple meanings, and how to decide which meanings read best. We talk about pleasure: how curiosity and mystery coexist, and how gaps and erasures contribute to meaning. Brown's dogs switch codes, shapes, and genres. My students understand this as serious play, particularly in "The Big Queer Class" my colleagues refer to as "Literature of Historically Marginalized Groups."

I teach Brown's *The Terrible Girls* less frequently than *The Dogs, The Gifts of the Body* (1994), or *Excerpts from a Family Medical Dictionary* (2003). Sometimes I have to protect myself from my students, from their uglier misreadings and casual dismissals. I am protective of *The Terrible Girls*. Brown's approach to familiar lesbian literary tropes feels wholly original here. Certainly the book startled me when I first read it. Here was the image of the closeted lesbian lover; here self-sacrifice; here invisibility; here conflicts between politics and passion. Yet none of these things existed strictly on a realist level. They were coded, not in the subtle language used by pre-Stonewall writers, but in vivid metaphors and magical realism. The code wasn't written to protect the writer, but to engage the reader. The code was a device meant to outlast whatever conditions might alter later literary approaches to same-sex desire.

Take away the closet in Radclyffe Hall's *The Well of Loneliness* (1928) and there's no story. Take away the closet in *The Terrible Girls*, and you still have the pain of a lover's betrayal, the misuse of power that comes with privilege. When I read *The Terrible Girls* I see my lesbian history, but it's possible to read the book without engaging its queerness. While such a reading isn't preferable or honest, it speaks to the significance of the book's themes, and their applicability to any human relationship. The book endures misreadings in generous fashion.

In the opening chapter, "The Dark House," the protagonist serves her lover coffee at a conference. Disguised as a maid, she sacrifices visibility, allowing her lover to dismiss not only their relationship, but all similar relationships. As the protagonist states, "You had made me the coffee-cart girl." I gasped when I first read that line, both because it's a great and memorable line, and because it broke a tacit rule that had long burdened my writing. As Sarah Schulman notes, "in what appears to me to be an attempt to manufacture, rather than reflect lesbian culture, like the Stalinists we have developed a sort of lesbian Socialist Realism which has come to dominate lesbian fiction" ("Is Lesbian Culture Only for Beginners?" in her *My American History: Lesbian and Gay Life During the Reagan/Bush Years* [New York/ London: Routledge, 1994]). How liberating to come across Brown's work, where poetic language takes priority over crippling political correctness, and where gothic imagery elevates metaphor to the level of spiritual iconography.

Years after first reading *The Terrible Girls*, I came across Richard Siken's poetry collection *Crush* (2005). Again I felt the thrill of gratitude for a queer writer who dared turn a critical eye on himself and his lovers. The best queer writing does this, I think. There's *Cool for You* (2000), Eileen Myles's brilliant non-fiction novel; there's *Notice* (2004), Heather Lewis's masterpiece of self-deception. Something in me longs for queer voices that dare admit our own guilt and responsibility; not because I don't see how the world damages us (and *how* the world damages us!) but because I am easily bored. Yes, homophobia nearly killed me; yes, it has damaged or even killed many of my friends and lovers. Yet as an artist, I can only say that so many times. At some point what's between us is between us, and if we ruin it, we must bear witness.

The Terrible Girls doesn't answer the questions it asks, but it asks the right questions. Like the speaker in Adrienne Rich's *Twenty-One Love Poems* (1977), Brown's protagonist wonders whether lesbians are partly responsible if we allow the outside world to distort our relationships. The self-sacrificing protagonist in *The Terrible Girls* was damaged before she met her lover, but that isn't Brown's focus. Her focus lies in the present of the protagonist's life, in the sacrifice of her right arm:

We kept my arm in the bathtub, bleeding like a fish. When I went to bed, the water was the color of rose water, with thick red lines like strings. And when I woke up the first time to change my bandages, it was colored like salmon. Then it was carnation red, and then maroon, then burgundy, then purple, thick, and almost black by morning.

Here and elsewhere, Brown substitutes sound and imagery for narrative logic, evoking Gertrude Stein's pleasure in word play and musical repetition. Yet Brown's obsession with lying and truth-telling also links linguistic pleasure to betrayal: "language is the only thing that lies." What a burden for a writer; what a gift. If language lies, we are all creative writers. Our stories are never true, our metaphors always fabulous. Our dogs are dogs, then ghosts, then cities, then lovers who fail to fall back into bed.

When I challenge students to imitate a writer we've studied, Brown is often their first choice. Their narrators unburden themselves of gravity, falling into crooked arms. What stays with me is the voice of a protagonist addressing her lover without concern for what the world thinks. Direct address, rage coupled with passion, violent imagery that may or may not be literal: I see these things in contemporary writers, and think of a lineage that includes Stein, Woolf, Plath, and Brown.

I don't remember what I told my student about *The Dogs* and the Humane Society, but I remember her puzzlement turning to relief. It's a relief to free oneself of narrow-mindedness. It's the burden of the queer female writer to escape both the straitjacket of political correctness and the spangled bodice of Romance. Reading Brown's work did this for me.

CAROL GUESS is the author of two novels, *Seeing Dell* (1995) and *Switch* (1998); a memoir, *Gaslight* (2001); and the poetry collections *Femme's Dictionary* (2009) and *Tinderbox Lawn* (2008). She is Associate Professor of English at Western Washington University. Quotations are taken from Rebecca Brown, *The Terrible Girls* (San Francisco: City Lights Books, 2001), which is currently in print.

THE MAN WHO FELL IN LOVE WITH THE MOON

(1991)

by Tom Spanbauer

LARRY DUPLECHAN

I first read Tom Spanbauer's *The Man Who Fell in Love with the Moon* (hereinafter *Moon*—I tried *TMWFILWTM*, but really, just *look* at it!) shortly after its initial publication in 1991. I bought it in hard cover, probably after reading one of the many (appropriately) glowing reviews of the novel. I was nearing the tail end of a six-year creative frenzy—I was at that time writing *Captain Swing*, my fourth gay-themed novel since 1985—and I was buying a lot of hardcover books (I could write it off on my taxes) and reading a good deal of gay fiction; both because one wants to keep up with one's "competition," and because gay publishing was still a boom town then (as opposed to the tent city it is today), and there was quite a selection of easily accessible (in big cities, anyway) really good gay fiction to choose from. Among the fine gay-themed novels published around this time were Michael Cunningham's *A Home at the End of the World* (1990), Melvin Dixon's *Vanishing Rooms* (1991), Lev Raphael's *Dancing at the Tisha B'av* (1990), and Michael Nava's *How Town* (1990). And while it was reviewed and advertised in the gay media, and it features as much man-on-man action as an old Jeff Stryker video, it seemed to me back in 1991 that *Moon* wasn't a gay novel at all. Upon recent rereading, it still doesn't strike me as gay fiction. A dust jacket blurb calls *Moon* "something like a cross between William Burroughs and *Little Big Man*." And while I'd also factor in Marquez's *One Hundred Years of Solitude* (1967) and just a bit of Sophocles's *Oedipus at Colonus* (before 406 BC), *Moon* utterly defies categorization, certainly as a gay novel.

So when is a gay novel not gay? For one thing, when the era in which the novel's story takes place predates the notion of a gay identity, and the concept of same-sex-loving and same-sex-fucking people being an oppressed minority, being a political force, being a "people." Not including an epilogue, *Moon* takes place in the last several years of the nineteenth century and the first few years of the twentieth, in a tiny town ironically named Excellent, in rural Idaho—part of the territory we now refer to as "The Old West." If the story is to be believed, in that place, in that time, there was no "gay"; only "fucking," to those characters in the novel who engage in same-sex couplings; and "sodomy" and "perversion," to those characters who disapproved of such goings-on (even when, as with several characters, the disapprovers also occasionally came to the engagers for sex). Even the term "homosexual," though it had been coined, would have been considered a medical term—and a European medical term at that; about as likely to be used by the average Old West shit-kicker as "*Weltschmerz*" might be bandied about by your auto mechanic today.

One term that *was* used in the 1890s to describe a group of people in terms of their alternative sexual/gender identity was "Berdache," a French-pedigreed word for what some Native American tribes (we used to call them "Indians") called "two-spirits": people who smeared gender demarcations—females who became warriors, and more commonly, males who wore women's clothes, nurtured children, tended the cook fires, and were (usually) passive sex partners with other men. The Berdaches were often credited with spiritual powers beyond the ordinary, and worked as healers, conjurers, and medicine men/women. (The near-genocide of the Native American peoples, the dilution of Native American cultures, the reservation and later the gay liberation movement all spelled the end of the Berdache.) Again, it's up for discussion whether the kind of folk depicted in *Moon* would actually use the rather specialized anthropological term "Berdache" in everyday conversation (as a couple of them do), even if one of them happened to *be* a Berdache.

Moon is narrated in the first-person singular voice of a big, strapping buck of a Berdache named Duivichi-un-Dua; better known as Out-In-The-Shed—Shed for short. It is, in Shed's own words, "a crazy story told by a crazy old drag queen"; it is a rambling, overstuffed, near-mythic tale repeatedly overlapping upon itself and playing a constant game of "gotcha" with what you've been led to believe is going on and who you've been led to believe the characters (and what their relationships) are. Mostly, it's the story of Shed's life; but as with every other "human being story" (Shed's term), his story is also the story of the people he loves and who love him, and those he hates and who hate him. It's the story of how Shed loses his parents and later finds his father; of how he forms a surrogate family and how that family is ultimately destroyed. There are no gay rites of passage in Shed's story—no inner realization of differentness; no "How do I break this to the folks?"; no cruising, dating, or courting. But there is plenty of sex in Shed's human being story; and a good bit of it is homosexual.

Shed, a half-breed (father white, mother Bannock, or maybe Shoshone, or maybe not), turns tricks for Ida Richilieu, the owner of Excellent's barroom/bawdy house, who adopts him at the age of twelve, upon the murder of his mother (or maybe not) by one Billy Blizzard—Mr. Blizzard having recently dealt the young boy a brutal gun point anal raping. Out in the shed behind Ida's saloon (hence the name), Shed takes care of those of Ida's clients whom she surmises is looking for "something different." If Shed can be said to have a love of his life, it would be Dellwood Barker, the man who seems by all circumstantial evidence to be Shed's long-lost father, with whom Shed shares transcendent (if somewhat guilt-burdened for being incestuous, or maybe not) lovemaking, and from whom Shed learns the healing art of "Moves Moves," that is, male orgasm without ejaculation. Shed and Dellwood first cross paths in Excellent's jailhouse, where Dellwood facilitates their escape by treating the sheriff to some unsolicited fellatio. Plenty of homosexual activity here (occasionally forced, but mostly quite voluntary); but the word "homosexual" is never used, and nobody's talking about gay marriage, or even the notion two adult people of the same gender setting up housekeeping.

Further, no one in the novel appears to be exclusively, or even overwhelmingly homosexual in orientation or practice. Just about everyone—male and female, hero and villain, white and otherwise—seems to be (to use another term anachronistic to the setting of the novel) bisexual. *Moon*'s ensemble of protagonists (the Berdache, the cowboy, the madam, and a couple of her whores) create among themselves an odd little family, rather like a group of protohippies. They drink a good deal of alcohol, smoke both "loco-weed" and opium (which they call "stardust"), and fuck in every conceivable combination—for pleasure, for commerce, even as a form of faith-healing. And for these people, and for those outside their circle who are allowed in to visit, the thought of dividing themselves by who enjoys lovemaking with which gender, would seem to be anathema. Indeed, in an (arguably anachronistic) gesture of utopianism, Shed and his cohort share their food, their bath, and their beds with a group of black ex-slaves working as traveling minstrel performers. It's as if the Age of Aquarius dawned seventy-odd years early, and life is one big love-in.

And because its story is both chronologically pre-gay and sexually extra-gay, for the twenty-first century reader nearly two decades after its debut, *Moon* might well be seen as presciently "post-gay." Shed, Dellwood, Ida, and the girls are the nineteenth-century prototypes of today's young people who insist that they're "not into labeling" themselves gay, straight, or bi (and I know several such people personally); the kids who go in groups to gay bars or straight bars, wherever the music is better and the drinks cheaper; who sleep with people of either gender (and often care not whether gender is all that clear-cut); and who, when asked about preference, tend to respond as Dellwood Barker does, when asked if he prefers fucking men or women (and please note, no one asks about loving, dating, or marrying, only fucking): "It depends on the person."

Indeed, Shed's little family ("better than any Mormon family," Ida insists, often and loudly) represents, in its own rather drug-addled manner, a sort of Paradise. And while Ida's neighbors would no doubt vigorously disagree, and alcohol- and drug-use notwithstanding, there is something inescapably first-century

Christian at work here: communal living, shared goods, love the only rule. But American society is often an inhospitable place for attempting to create one's own Paradise—now, and even more so in Idaho in the 1890s. So it comes as no great surprise when Ida's upstanding, flag-waving (though sometimes lasciviously curious) Mormon neighbors see to it that Ida's little Paradise is destroyed; not only her house, but her friends, and very nearly herself (I won't spoil it for you if you haven't yet read *Moon*—I will only warn that it isn't pretty). As supporters of same-sex marriage in the U.S. will attest, nothing makes some people more vengeful than the attempted redefinition of "family,"

And this odd sort of timeless timeliness is at least part of what makes *The Man Who Fell in Love with the Moon* should-be-required reading for queer folk. In the year 2008, some one hundred years after Out-in-the-Shed and his friends/lovers/family are set upon by gun-wielding religious fundamentalists for choosing the wrong people to love and/or fuck, the California Supreme Court legalized same-sex marriage, only to have that decision struck down by a popular vote later that same year. As I write this, the Supreme Court of the State of Iowa has recently legalized same-sex marriage; and in a "guest editorial" in the April 28th, 2009 edition of the Des Moines *Register*, one Karl Schowengerdt of West Des Moines, whose unhappy gay son died of AIDS, wrote: "[f]or the Iowa Supreme Court to sanction homosexual 'marriage' is to encourage and underwrite the negative results that naturally come from the homosexual 'lifestyle.'" LGBT people can easily recognize themselves in the inhabitants of Ida Richilieu's brothel, defiantly asserting that their family is better than any Mormon family; yet ever aware that the majority is very much in control, and capable of opening fire at any moment.

Read *The Man Who Fell in Love with the Moon*, and find yourself transported to a time and place unlike any you have known, a time and place that may or may not have truly existed at all; and yet, a time and place remarkably—often disturbingly—similar to our own. And as if gazing into an antique mirror, you will likely see yourself reflected.

Or maybe not.

LARRY DUPLECHAN is author of five acclaimed gay-themed novels, including *Blackbird* (1986) and *Got 'til It's Gone* (2008). He lives in Los Angeles with his husband of thirty-three years and a large Chartreux cat named Mr. Blue. Quotations are taken from Tom Spanbauer, *The Man Who Fell in Love with the Moon* (New York: Grove Press, 2000), which is currently in print.

Take Me to Paris, Johnny
(1993)

by John Foster

Rob Beeston

Juan Gualberto Céspides was born in July 1953, the son of a baker in the city of Guantánamo, Cuba, just across the border from the U.S. naval base. A sickly child, when he balked at milk, his grandmother gave him guava juice, and when he didn't eat for fear of diarrhea, she fried him sweet white fish for breakfast. As a teenager he was taunted over his effeminacy by a neighbor and childhood friend, whom he subsequently refused to forgive. He soon became a regular along the secluded banks of the Guantánamo River, adopting a new name—Michel(le) D'Ambreville—to let it be known that, although he was a faggot, he certainly wasn't common. Eventually he went to Havana where he enrolled in the National Ballet, where he danced like an angel in display of an obvious talent, and where they kicked him out for conduct unbecoming a man: masculinity, not deviancy, is the engine of the Revolution. It was less the injustice of this that dogged him ever after than a basic, boyish incomprehension. As he protested to the love of his life for the rest of his life, "Johnny, I didn't do *nothing*!" At fourteen he was still too young for correction in the Military Unit to Aid Production. But as the Revolution neared its tenth year, the effeminacy had obviously begun to affect Juan's brain: whisperers report the onset of counter-revolutionary tendencies. And so at fifteen, he followed the lead of a friend and fellow noncombatant, and, without saying good-bye to his mother, escaped Castro's Cuba forever. On U.S. soil at last, he asked excitedly to be sent to Paris. Second best: they managed New York. Either way, he would never see his family again.

Take Me to Paris, Johnny is Juan Céspides's story from this point on until his death from AIDS at thirty-three, in Melbourne, Australia. By virtue of its prose, and despite a certain authorial reserve, it is his lover's—Australian academic John Foster's—story too.

Foster's book begins at the end: with a pilgrimage to Juan's mother, who had once written that she could barely remember her first-born's face. En route, Foster muses on the Cuban landscape through the bouncing bus window. In mind of his destination— Guantánamo: "First Trench of the Revolution"—it takes less than a page for political history to intrude upon Foster's thoughts. And barely another to see for himself the pain it caused. Juan's mother opens the door, and, through a combination of her son's sporadic letters and Foster's flushed white face, knows immediately who he is, and, more importantly, why he has come. With the kind of restraint that marks *Take Me to Paris, Johnny* to the end, Foster devotes barely five pages to this momentous, kaleidoscopic meeting. This is just enough to clarify, first, that Juan's mother's last letter—"I must tell you that on Mother's Day I received no word from you which gave me great pain"—was opened not by

Juan but by John because her son was already dead. Second, that, along with a pair of Juan's ballet shoes, he had brought as a gift a copy of a recently published book, not relevant to her because of its content, but because the dedication—"to Juan and John"—was the only place their names had ever appeared together; "the next best thing to a marriage notice."

Ensconced in the Céspedes's house, Foster's narrative once again diverts. In a tone that leaves anything other than even-handedness entirely to the reader, he sets about bringing political history home. Year Zero: 1953, Juan's birth at the beginning of Carnival, at the very moment Fidel's guerrillas were planning their attack on the Moncada Barracks, not far away to the west. Woven into this poignant opening, Foster's critique of the later Revolution is shot through—evenly but bitingly—with its effects on a young boy, and their reverberations for the rest of his life. Given the angle of this attack, one of Cuba's own counter-revolutionaries inevitably comes to mind: poet and novelist Reinaldo Arenas. Perhaps because he was witness-and-confidante, not subject-and-dissident, Foster preserves the raw emotion that rarely makes it through in Arenas's harder, wilder, and more satirical psychic histories. He writes, though, in such a calm, almost placid, even soporific manner that, in condemning an entire regime from the perspective of one small boy, he remains as far from sentimentality and unchannelled rage as Arenas at his triumphally incisive best. Arenas's is the relentlessly inventive, self-devouring and—vexing world of the magic realist; Foster's is the assured and strategically primed critique of the thinking-feeling academic. They have important things in common. Love, mainly.

The story begins properly in New York in 1969: Juan's arrival as drag queens at the Stonewall Inn retaliate against police brutality. Foster, though, rather than make some auspicious connection to the supposed birth of gay liberation, remains true to the boyish-ness of his subject. Working from Juan's notebooks, Foster has him arrive in New York not with sexual liberation, but "with the man on the moon." This choice of image—Juan staring open-mouthed at astronauts and spaceships—is an early indication of Foster's sensibility as a writer; less that of the academic, or even the memoirist, than the novelist inhabiting his protagonist.

It's not too far along in Foster's narrative before Juan and Johnny first meet and straightforward memoir can assume control. Until then, however, a degree of writerly assurance is required to develop what Australian literary critic Peter Craven calls "this life of Juan before the life he shared with him." Foster has no tricks or devices in this, only words. There's a brief aside some way in, indicating that, just as his account of Juan's life in Cuba was born of their life together, so too the time more immediately before they met "has my memory's shape." Foster sharpens this recall on the events that befell Juan in his first years in New York. Auditions and rejections, priests and lovers, accidents and injuries, friends new and old . . . and an horrific homophobic murder. They might not be Foster's own memories, but they are written with a writerly omniscience; one he perhaps liked to think was true in reverse: Juan, long dead, watching him write their life.

Their first years together are spent flitting between New York, London, and Berlin, largely at the behest of Foster's academic work on the German-Jewish Holocaust. Juan's statelessness would prove a bureaucratic headache to the very end. But in these early years too, the crisscrossing of borders is apt to push all the wrong buttons. Without glossing Juan's tendency to melodrama, Foster captures a fierce and unrelenting pride amidst moments of impoverishment and disempowerment. True, Juan is rarely too proud to ask for money, but Foster paints this as mere practical necessity. When, through no fault of his own, Juan loses his job, he writes in broken English of his welfare accommodation: "I who had an apartment for more than 11 years with all my things to nothing is very very depressing."

1981. The new and nameless scourge lands on Foster's page with the same abruptness it had in the *New York Times*. Had it led to nothing, Larry Altman's notorious article—brief as it was—would have disappeared in the same breath with which Johnny passes it off, like so many others, at breakfast on July 3rd.

The Melbourne years are typified by interminable wrangles with the Department for Immigration and what Foster calls his "Dear Johnny letters" from Juan, still stuck in New York. Given their broken English and abrupt switches in register, the inclusion of so many letters appears whimsical, even cutesy at first, before turning pithy in the swiftness with which they cover the period 1983–85. Their true purpose, however, is the introduction of illness within the complex web of Juan's continued statelessness. If what Australian novelist and critic Robert Dessaix says is true about the art of AIDS memoir being more than the virus alone, then *Take Me to Paris, Johnny* is very much art in the geopolitics it traverses all the while AIDS is setting to work; in the same way that fellow antipodean Douglas Wright's more recent memoirs *Ghost Dance* (2004) and *Terra Incognita* (2006) are expansive along different lines. Though both writers, coincidentally, know a thing or two about dancers.

There are prosaic ways of portending AIDS and there are richly inventive ones too. Foster's is neither. Had he been as inventive as, say, Arenas or Severo Sarduy, he wouldn't have written a book as straight down the line as he did. Had he been prosaic, I probably wouldn't have read him cover to cover with barely a pause for breath. His introduction of the *New York Times* article is perhaps less "literary" than it might have been. But that's only relative to epicenter habitués, like the American short-story writer Allen Barnett: "The *Times* as it knows us," indeed. Foster's epistolary introduction of Juan's first symptoms, however, is little concerned with any of this. He lets the symptoms portend themselves: "How are you? I mess you very much. My impretion with Australia are really very marvellous. Beside been sick for so long, I am still bother by this terrible 'itch'."

Two things happen from here on in. One is the realization that *Take Me to Paris, Johnny* was written before the major tropes of AIDS narrative were fully formed. The other is that, all the while this portentousness is at work (being one of the first of those tropes to emerge), so too is the statelessness of a dissident Cuban national. Of course, it might just be that Foster is a naturally restrained writer. Certainly it's easy to infer from his prose that he was an even-handed character more generally. But there's a real sense that, even when AIDS is in full effect, the world remains at work, and the more wrenching aspects avoid becoming overloaded; that is, overly reliant on the emoted reader. The counterpoint is fellow Australian Timothy Conigrave's *Holding the Man* (1995). In reference to Dessaix's question, and glib though it sounds: can this truly be art when you can barely read for tears? *Holding the Man* is many things, many vital and virtuous things (and popular too). But does it stand when stripped to the words? *Take Me to Paris, Johnny* definitely does.

Barring a last trip to New York, the last two years are spent with Juan—in need of stable medical attention by this point—in immigration limbo in Melbourne. And so begins the final phase. There are lots of memoirs where vivid description (shitting, wasting, hacking, suffocating, dementing, purpling) and heavy emotion (heavier than all the shelves stacked of all the memoirs in all world) characterize the final days of AIDS. Dialogue, though, is rarer. A return to boyishness, true, is not uncommon. But the boyishness Foster recoups comes more often than not through the dialogue of these final weeks and days. Juan's boyishness never went away, of course; never stopped staring at the moon since Armstrong stepped off his ladder. In that respect Foster-the-writer has it easy. But careful sampling pronounces it to full effect, capturing the confusion (what is god?), the rage (how dare they?), the pain (take it away), and the political history come home: sugar cane, mother, Cuba.

After four years of bureaucracy, and subject still, cruelly and ironically, to an immigration-department medical, Juan finally receives leave to stay in Australia less than a month before he dies. Between hospital visits, Johnny, dignified as ever, cancels the medical and decides to keep his own counsel: "While, unbeknown to Juan, the fate of his soul had been determined, the fate of his body was still under active consideration."

Juan Gualberto Céspides died on Good Friday, 1987.

Foster died himself of AIDS-related toxoplasmosis seven years later, less than a year after the publication of *Take Me to Paris, Johnny*. His friend John Rickard—whose book dedication Foster took to Cuba—wrote an insightful afterword, in partial answer at least to the not uncommon question: Foster wrote Juan's story; who'll write Johnny's?

ROB BEESTON, thirty-six, lives in Sheffield, England. He is currently pitching his first two novels. One is about love, loss, risk, blood-borne memory, and San Francisco. The other—about working-class English boys, Korean martial arts, and K-Horror cinema—mentions AIDS just the once. Quotations are taken from John Foster, *Take Me to Paris, Johnny* (Melbourne: Black, 2004), which is currently in print.

PALIMPSEST
(1995)

by Gore Vidal

PAUL REIDINGER

When Gore Vidal published his memoir *Palimpsest* in the United States, on October 3rd, 1995—his seventieth birthday—I was deeply enmeshed in an almost-not-platonic affair with a high school baseball star, a pitcher no less, and so the memoir's news that there had been such a figure (a pitcher no less!) in Vidal's past brought me a certain amount of comfort, mostly of the cold sort. He had loved a pitcher long ago, and now I had a pitcher of my own, and this seemed right. It confirmed we were kin. I read the book in the course of a long journey—by planes, trains, and (hired) automobiles—to Italy, where Vidal was then living as a baronial expatriate.

Just as gay people tend to choose their families, writers choose their ancestry, or discover it, and I had come to see Vidal (whether he liked it or not, cared or not, or even knew or not—most likely not) as important literary forebear of mine. Although, in interviews, he often insisted on calling himself a novelist, I saw him as a writer in the term's broadest sense, a master of fiction, essays, history, and criticism, a true example of that rarest of birds, the literary intellectual. He was rather on the acid side of the human pH scale, seemed to suffer from a congenital instinct to be honest—telling the truth is one of life's unpardonable sins; another is being right—and was robed in the cool manners of the U.S.'s venerable Protestant culture, but he also had, as the memoir revealed, a molten heart. And a very American thing for baseball players.

My own baseball player entanglement that autumn was an exciting morass of awkwardnesses and potential embarrassments. My star, at seventeen, was slightly less than half my age and, by most of the signs, heterosexual. He lived practically around the corner from me with his parents, whom I knew and, to some untested degree, felt accountable to. Vidal and *his* star, on the other hand, had been the same age during their idyll in the 1930s and 1940s, and when I read in the pages of *Palimpsest* a description of "dangerous older men" (thirty-six-year-olds?) who sometimes accosted comely teenage males at movie theaters, I felt a stab of alarm.

My star and I managed to avoid sitting next to each other in movie theaters—a straightforward accomplishment for two people who did not go to the movies together; I hated movies—and I would have kept my hands to myself in any case, even if it killed me. I accepted, as Justice Oliver Wendell Holmes once put it, that "man is a dangerous animal—or ought to be," and I was a man and therefore I must somehow be dangerous, but I did not want to be a dirty old man who gave renewed life to vile stereotypes. And yet, and yet, and yet . . . "All life is an experiment," Holmes had written in dissent in *Abrams v. New York* (1919), but surely he'd meant to add: "and a temptation."

Palimpsest is a memoir whose core, as Vidal himself puts it at the very end of the book, is a love story—a gay love story, the story of a love between two young men—and since Vidal often insisted he would never write a memoir and equally often went out of his way to express his distaste for the word "gay" and his scorn for love, at least in its middle-class, Marvin-and-Madge American guise, the book's air is thick with irony. It is, perhaps, the greatest achievement in irony by one of modern literature's great ironists. It is also deeply moving, and is that yet another level or layer of irony.

Literature is a layered confection, after all; a tiramisù of words. A literary narrative must move on several levels simultaneously, like a well-trained troupe dancing a ballet; it must make some kind of cognitive, moment-to-moment sense, be aesthetically pleasing and—perhaps most important and most difficult—carry an emotional charge, all at the same time. A story, to live, must have a beating heart, and to give that gift, the writer must risk his own heart. He pours his own feelings—his sympathies, vulnerabilities, quirks, fears, and obsessions—into a fragile sac of words and sends the sac into the public domain, where it might be held up as an object of veneration or beaten to a pulpy mess.

The literary fates are not dependably rational and frequently not kind, and the rational writer—Gore Vidal is such a writer—might be forgiven for hesitating to commit this reckless act of personal investiture. Over and over across the decades, Vidal has reminded us of the brutal literary smackdown he endured in his late twenties—in the wake of the 1948 publication of *The City and the Pillar*, a gay novel before the category existed—but the fact that the tale has been rehearsed with numbing frequency does not make it less sobering and revealing, or less important.

For years I felt a certain emotional energy had gone missing from Vidal's fiction. The novels were brilliant, learned, stylish, and funny—*Myra Breckinridge* (1968) spectacularly so—but they were also cold and left no emotional memory. One learned a good deal without much caring about the characters, and one suspected the author didn't much care about them either. They were chess pieces being cunningly moved about a board to make various intellectual or historical points, or jokes. This was a good game and often an absorbing one, even a worthy one, but when the game ended—the last page read, the book closed, checkmate achieved—these narratives evaporated without a trace, like damp spots on a patch of pavement under a warm spring sun. The real Vidal, the emotionally invested author, was elusive: a kind of literary Houdini. He was elsewhere, but where?

Then, quite late in the day, came *Palimpsest* and its unguarded language of love and shipwreck—of inconsolable loss, for Vidal's pitcher, his other half, Jimmie Trimble, had died as a nineteen-year-old Marine at the tip of a Japanese bayonet on Iwo Jima in March 1945.

"Was there ever so furious and restless a ghost?" Vidal writes of Jimmie, a half-century later. "Or is it that we, the survivors, are so traumatized to this day by his abrupt absence from our lives that we are still trying to summon his ghost? For years, whenever I was in a numinous place like Delphi or Delos, I would address the night: Jimmie, are you anywhere? and almost always the wind would rise. But I am neither a believer in an afterlife nor a mystic, and unlike Santayana, I cannot begin to imagine what it must be like. Yet I still want Jimmie to *be*, somewhere, if only on this page."

How odd, I thought, that that page, and the others like it, should be part of a memoir—a memoir, moreover, Vidal had assured us again and again he would never write. (Here I must note that his 1970 book *Two Sisters* carries the subtitle "a novel in the form of a memoir," but seems to be the other way around; it is, in effect, a memoir in slight disguise.) How odd, too, that such a powerful emotional charge should have been displaced into a memoir from its natural home in fiction. *Palimpsest* would have compelled even without the affecting story of Jimmie; it was a rich trove of personality, incident, and tragicomedy, often in high places among the well-born. It did not need its love story to engage, amuse, or elucidate.

At the same time, the love story didn't need the rest of the memoir. It explained much about the arc of its author's life but itself needed no explanation; it was an irreducible tale of the sort the pearls of fiction often form themselves around. Yet just as Jimmie was "the half of me that never lived to grow up," as Vidal puts it at the end of *Palimpsest*, so the love story between Jimmie and Gore was the emotional heart of a novel that never got written.

Of course, there are hints of Jimmie throughout Vidal's work: He lurks in Bob Ford, the object of obsession in *The City and the Pillar*—the material of lost love obviously attracting the young writer but too hot for him to handle easily. He recurs by implication in *The Judgment of Paris* (1952), in an opium addict's dream of "one green day long ago in June." He is even mentioned by (misspelled first) name in *Two Sisters*, whose middle-aged narrator "still mourns the past, particularly in darkened movie houses, weeping at bad films, or getting drunk alone while watching the Late Show on television as our summer's war is again refought and one sees sometimes what looks to be a familiar face in the battle scenes—is it Jimmy?" But he is never more than a shadow, or ghost, until *Palimpsest*.

I would sometimes wonder, in laboring at my own imaginative scribbles, whether it was bad form to take these sorts of defining and intimate emotional experiences and turn them into fiction. But there was no other way for me to write fiction—nor, for that matter, was there any other way for me to reckon with my own catalogue of such experiences than by writing about them—and so I went ahead and did it. If I were to write with anything like meaning, I had to *care*, and what could I care more about than certain wounds and injuries, misunderstandings and losses, unrealized or mismanaged possibilities, episodes of emotional adhesion that had somehow failed the great stress test of time by ripping or crumbling?

Love wasn't the same as loss, but the two were inseparable, like body and soul. You couldn't have one without the other, and if you had neither, you hadn't really lived. If you chose to live, if love came to you and you accepted it, you would suffer sooner or later. But if you chose not to live, you would suffer anyway, so you might as well choose to live, to take the bitter with the sweet— the bittersweet—instead of settling for the purely bitter. If you were a writer, at least you'd have something to write about, and if you described and explored those experiences through fiction, you were giving yourself a freedom to invent that, paradoxically, would be an enhancement to truth-telling.

In our confessional, exhibitionistic culture, "true stories" like memoirs excite people's prurient interest, while fiction, because made up, somehow can't be true and must be of lesser value. Yet the (paradoxical) truth is that the greatest truths are to be found in fiction. And often they are sad. Perhaps we clothe such truths in the made-up to shield ourselves from the often unbearable rawness of reality.

"The heart of the wise is in the house of mourning," says the prophet Ecclesiastes (7:4), "but the heart of fools is in the house of mirth."

Vidal's house at the time, La Rondinaia, was in Ravello, on the Amalfi Coast near Naples. But *Palimpsest* wisely gave no directions, and I wasn't going that far south anyway, not on some fool's errand. I would content myself instead with a short week in Florence, where in the mild autumn twilight I would sometimes watch an Italian soccer team practice in a grassy park on the banks of the Arno. They were a little older than seventeen, early twenties probably, and wore gear quite different from baseball uniforms—more revealing, even in the failing light. It was the legs I noticed, like pitchers' legs, curvaceous with muscle. Pitchers draw much of their throwing strength from their legs. All of the faces were young and handsome, none familiar. Yet the wind rose, gently.

PAUL REIDINGER is the author of several novels, including *The City Kid* (2001), *Good Boys* (1993), and *The Best Man* (1986), and has written widely on literature, law, politics, culture, and food. He grew up in Wisconsin and was educated at Stanford and the University of Wisconsin-Madison. He lives in San Francisco and is a longtime contributor to the *San Francisco Bay Guardian*. Quotations are taken from Gore Vidal, *Palimpsest* (New York: Penguin, 1996), which is currently in print.

ALLAN STEIN
(1999)

by Matthew Stadler

BLAIR MASTBAUM

Fellow Portlander Matthew Stadler once lived in Seattle. There, he wrote the 1999 novel, *Allan Stein*, a book of such beauty, wry humor, and honest sexuality that it feels much more substantial than the small-format hardback copy of the book I have. During my first reading, and since, I stared at the photo of Matthew on the back of the book. It's black and white and he looks somehow classical (the piano doesn't hurt), but in a good way—like classic literature, not the boring ones, but the ones that are revolutionary, the ones that tell of lives more exciting than 99.9 percent of humanity. He looks fiercely smart, and a little mysterious, and after reading his novels, I know he is both. Matthew and I have probably more than five friends in common, but I've never met him. I don't mind. I sort of don't want his real personality to interfere with the personality I'd like to think he has, which is that of *Allan Stein*'s protagonist (unnamed through most of the novel) sitting with his friend Herbert (old, lecherous, funny, awesome) in a medieval-themed bar in downtown Seattle, where both men talk and drink and stare at their hot blond server boy, a college student who seems to know what's up and plays Herbert like an expert (at least as well as straight male strippers play dudes at a gay bar). The scene is thrilling to me. You are simply *there* when you read it. There's no disconnect between the symbols, the words, the paragraphs, the eyes, the brain processing—you're *there*. I'm sure of it. I can taste the rye whiskey.

Honesty, in my opinion, makes great art, rather than creating a new world (although there are thousands of exceptions). *Allan Stein* is all honesty. It's desire, and searching for drawings by Pablo Picasso of Allan Stein, a nephew of Gertrude who was allegedly sort of hot.

As a future teacher, I realize that it's dangerous territory to even say you like this novel, yet alone love it. Matthew (the main character whose name we don't find out until much later in the novel) has been accused of a sexual affair with a sophomore boy while teaching in a Seattle school. He didn't do it, but the accusation is enough to make him act on his fantasy and then basically take off, as if he were being pursued by the morality police.

In terms of visuals, the light in the book is remarkable. Every scene seems dimmed. There is just enough light to make Stéphane's—the fifteen-year-old object of Matthew's affection—skin glow. His power, which is his light, seems to come from within, from his age and his delicate nature, but like most teenage boys, he doesn't know how to successfully wrangle his power and light. It seems to me that this is why in a relationship between someone younger and older, particularly when one of them is a boy, the power always remains with the older person. It may seem that the man is being drawn to the boy, so the boy is in control, but this seeming draw is an obsession that doesn't exist outside of the man's mind. This feels different. Stéphane is in control I think, and it's cool.

As I've said, the main character is called Matthew. It's not Stadler, but it's a version of him, a version that gets to do something much more directly.

I'm in love with Stéphane because the image of him is perfect. He's perfectly shaped, at an ideal place between childhood and adulthood, and he's accessible. He wants it. With reservations, but he wants to have an exciting life. He tries out different personas and poses, but because he's a European boy, we know where he'll likely end up. History in Europe is much too heavy to escape for all but the weirdest, the most exceptional of its citizens. This history weighing on them is part of what makes them desirable. For we Americans are sure they have a classical education, extensive knowledge of all Shakespeare and Greek plays and myths. We're sure they know how to cook, well, and find their way to beaches on the Mediterranean where no one wears clothes and all the young men are lean and mysterious and smart. Stéphane is an image more than a person, just as Allan Stein is an image. We know nothing about him other than the fact that Picasso painted a portrait of him at the age of eleven. It's this falling in love with an image that drives much of our lives, at least it does if you're led by passion, as I am, and Matthew, both Stadler and *Allan Stein*'s protagonist, are. A rocky bluff on Puget Sound, a mountainside of Douglas firs, a certain bicycle (fixed gear, black, no labels), even a pickup truck (Toyota, the smaller ones) can drive sexual desire. The image of Allan Stein is enough to make Matthew take on his friend Herbert's name and fly across ten time zones to look for sketches that Picasso may or may not have drawn in preparation for his portrait of the boy.

Sex with Stéphane is transcendent and artful—passionate but more aesthetic than anything else. You can imagine Matthew's heartbeat as their skin touches for the first time. Stadler writes about sex with teenagers better than any other writer, I think. He knows them so well (in the way he wishes to see them) that it's sometimes alarming that an artist can nail something so perfectly, so unhindered by words and visions.

In a way, it seems that sex with someone like Stéphane is more an artistic experience than a sexual one, more like jumping into a painting than having an actual relationship with someone—talking and deciding things, and making choices and arrangements—to have sex with someone your own age. Seducing him—although it's not a one-way street—runs parallel with searching for these drawings. We know that Matthew wants these drawings to depict a striking, beautiful boy, a boy of mystery and unrealized intellect, and the certainty that he'll grow up to be brilliant and handsome and witty and then he'll probably take in some amazing looking eighteen-year-old, letting the boy live at his stylish loft in the fifth district of Paris and helping him through school just down the rue de Seine at *L'académie française*, the school with the authoritarian dome and the bust of Voltaire nearby. Stéphane's one fault that we see in the early point of the sex friendship of Matthew and Stéphane is that Stéphane has a very sore and expressive gastrointestinal system. He farts constantly, filling casually French rooms with the scent of sulphur.

Stéphane is Matthew's youth and he's doing it better, because while teenage Matthew can only think about his own adolescence and notice missed chances, Stéphane is having an affair with an alleged museum curator from Seattle with a fake name and an obsession for Gertrude Stein's nephew. How many French teenagers can say that?

Memories haunt Matthew all the time, and in a place like Paris, he freely lets them take him over. Hanging out with Stéphane is the complete opposite. It only exists in the present, and it creates the future (yes, even desire for someone that doesn't create children in its wake *does* write the future, however blurrily and aesthetically odd to some).

When Stéphane mentions Tarkovsky, I almost fainted. When the simple lines of his body translate into the way he has sex, you know he's someone special—he's who Gertrude's nephew should have been. When he plays broken Pink Floyd on his guitar, first strumming and stopping and restarting, and eventually just plucking the same string as Matthew gets hard, you think that there was probably never a better sex scene written on earth ever. You can feel not only the smoothness of Stéphane's skin and of the head of Matthew's penis, you can smell the air, the breath, even the subtle bleachy scent of the semen. It's a remarkable feat, and it seems totally unfiltered by self-censorship or an editorial hand. This is, of course, not true. This novel is obviously finely crafted and you can feel this craftsmanship in the sentences, without ever seeming worked over. That is perhaps Stadler's greatness as a writer. He can make something special—hand-crafted, like an oil painting or a piece of hand-worked furniture, and the reader doesn't know it.

You could call it a homo *Lolita* (1955), but *Allan Stein* isn't satire like Nabokov's great work, so I don't think the comparison works. I read the two novels back to back, and beyond my preference for Stéphane over Dolores, I truly think Stadler's is the better novel. I think he describes the body better. I think he puts you there, when Nabokov tells you you're there. I know it's a stupid comparison, but Matthew Stadler is really up in the heights of the great writers, so he deserves to have his name in the same sentence as those whom we think of as our classic writers. If Stéphane were a girl (with no other details changed), I wouldn't have to tell you about this book, because it would be on your bookshelf already. It would be in your grandfather's library too. I miss these characters when I'm not reading them. I see Stéphane around Portland and I assume that Matthew Stadler does too. He's at Powell's, and at Stumptown, and riding his bike down Yamhill. He's inside us too.

BLAIR MASTBAUM is the author of the novels *Clay's Way* (2004) and *Us Ones In Between* (2008) and coeditor of the anthology *Cool Thing: Best Gay Fiction by Young American Writers* (2008). He attends Portland State University and lives in rainy Portland, Oregon. Quotations are taken from Matthew Stadler, *Allan Stein* (New York: Grove Press, 1999), which is currently in print.

GHOST DANCE
(2004)

by Douglas Wright

RICHARD CANNING

Joys impregnate. Sorrows bring forth.
—William Blake

This is one of two epigraphs to *Ghost Dance*, a dancer's memoir which won Wright the 2005 New Zealand Society of Authors E.H. McCormick Best First Book of Non-Fiction Prize, but remains little known outside his native country. This untypical autobiography is utterly idiosyncratic, utterly urgent, utterly beautiful . . . and utterly overlooked. Douglas Wright's career may be readily susceptible to *précis*. But the formal inventiveness, stylistic deftness, and—yes—utter integrity of *Ghost Dance* are hard to convey. They relate, however, to his many other talents. As a dancer, Wright proved capable above all of supporting complex narrative; he "wrote" it through his step. As a choreographer, he is (clearly) a born dancer. As a writer, he is fluent, to a terpsichorean degree.

Anyone seeking the essence of the male dancer's animus looks in vain in Nureyev's 1963 memoirs (a money-earner), or in Nijinsky's insane diaries (1936/99; obsessive but scarcely expressive). Wright's own dancing career—with the Paul Taylor Company in New York; later, with Lloyd Newson and London's DV8 on *Dead Dreams of Monochrome Men*; then from 1989, with his own company back in Auckland—is impressive. Its impact, though, was curtailed, as *Ghost Dance* relates, initially by something in Wright's temperament. After a time in Manhattan, his yearning for New Zealand's Arcadian idylls became overwhelming, though Wright must have known that such distance from the world's epicenters of cutting-edge dance, its audiences, critical coteries, and funding, might well do for his career (he was then in full flight as a performer). Indifference, narrow-mindedness, and hostility on the part of (much of the) New Zealand theater-going public and arts establishment made the inevitable transition to choreography scarcely less traumatic. Second was Wright's diagnosis as HIV-positive, the single circumstance which generates this book's energy, spinning it into each eddying, finely contoured digression: Buddhism, bird-watching, immune deficiency, distinguished New Zealand author Janet Frame, the London tube, a difficult adolescence, immune symptomatology, Vaslav Nijinsky, paganism.

There's a darker successor memoir, *Terra Incognito* (2006), whose account of the genesis of a new dance work, *Black Milk*, is among the most self-aware accounts of artistic genesis committed to paper—up there with Flannery O'Connor's *Mystery and Manners'* essays on writing fiction (1969). Its wrenching account of Wright's experiences at a respite center for those with HIV is among the truest reflections on the syndrome's enduring stealth.

Still, *Ghost Dance*, if not self-evidently the better book, is the more vital, open one, ranging across the peaks and insecurities of a whole life with insight, often devastating phrasing, and caprice. Old photographs, postcards, letters, and sketches litter these pages too, in a multiform technique also deployed in Carole Maso's (fictionalized) AIDS memoir, *The Art Lover* (1990). With the wrong eye for placement, the effect of these supplements could be all-too-predictable: catharsis; self-celebration; hubris even. With Wright, however, the imagery adorns, beguiles, moves, but never collaborates with the text. It's an aesthetic impulse that would instantly belong and make sense in a gallery, but is arresting between the covers of a book.

David Gere's *How to Make Dances in an Epidemic* (2004) has delineated how North American dance has responded diversely to AIDS; thus, it does not draw on Wright's choreographic experimentation. Rudolph Nureyev, of course, died of AIDS—but in denial. Only his drenched, near-cadaverous appearances at the last Parisian curtain calls gave his late work an "AIDS signification." Robert Mapplethorpe's self-portrait with skull is a more fitting encapsulation of the new aesthetic the syndrome imposed on a peer group of artists. One was Hervé Guibert. It seemed, through the 1990s, that nobody would equal the honesty in Guibert's self-flagellating engagement—in prose, and then in the video diary *La pudeur ou l'impudeur* (1992)—with HIV/AIDS. In the second "chapter" of the epidemic (post-treatment culture; loosely, post-1997), Douglas Wright's *Ghost Dance* alone has done so. (Gere relates poignantly how one gay man asked choreographer Joe Goode of his 1998 dance piece *Deeply There*: "Why are you making a piece about AIDS now?" Goode interpreted this as meaning: "We are in this respite from having to go to memorial service, so why am I making him think about this?")

Ghost Dance does something remarkable with Wright's diagnosis and progressively precarious health. He places these concerns center stage, but in the same gesture upstages them. This involves a principle of inversion, a discontent at the relationship between center and margin, which has been pivotal to Wright's choreography. It also, logically, relates to the innately topsy-turvy universe of AIDS—a world in which one ex-boyfriend, Warren, "was the one in a million recipient of side effects so severe they killed him," as Wright deadpans. *Ghost Dance* poses at the outset questions that undermine many dominant narratives. This early fatality leads Wright to wonder: "When does a side-effect become central?"

He confronts the retrovirus with all manner of responses. Everything is used by turns, it seems; everything except self-pity (though many circumstances prove pitiful indeed). You respond by thinking the unthinkable: it's as if it's taken this long for the syndrome to meet its rhetorical match; and in someone who never thought himself a writer, before HIV. *Ghost Dance*, in a sense, did an unintentional discourtesy to the newly cohering genre of AIDS memoir too. Wright gets it so *right* you start to distrust everyone else on this subject.

Ghost Dance also displays a most beguiling and worthwhile critical intelligence. For Wright is that rare thing: the prodigy who won't be schooled; the self-taught, polymath individualist. There's sometimes a predictable roll call here. But there *are* such people: Arthur Rimbaud; Raymond Radiguet; Pablo Picasso; Ronald Firbank; Charles Ludlam; Arthur Russell. Nijinsky—of key importance to Wright—was another; never so much taught as tolerated by his Petersburg tutors, and not so much promoted in terms of his technique as contained by Diaghilev and the whole *Ballets Russes* vehicle.

What Nijinsky did that was transgressive was the sum of all the things he couldn't or wouldn't do. Nobody can tell such people what to do. They're nature's instinctual rule breakers, propelling culture forward primarily by *not listening*. When they outgrow or transcend existing aesthetic protocols, it is never in ignorance of them. Their capacity for learning is limitless. But they also have an unusually strong instinct not to be weighed down by their knowledge.

So it is with Wright, a physical stunner as a drug-taking teenage bohemian dropout, but a bohemian vagrant nonetheless. Wright needed direction; perhaps encouragement; nothing else. A friend asked what he wanted to do in life ("Dance.") and why he wasn't doing it. Wright reacted the only way he could: with a vortex of self-propulsion. He put himself through the most punishing dance classes, at the fastest speed, just as Nureyev did, compelled to propel himself out of Ufa, then out of Petersburg, and so on.

I mentioned Guibert. It's surely intentional that *Ghost Dance* begins with a sentence reminiscent of the extraordinary opening of *To the Friend Who Did Not Save My Life* while also updating it. Guibert, in 1990, had thrown out the impossible conjecture that he "had AIDS" (had it, that is, and got over it). Wright's first chapter, "Invalid," reads: "It was after more than a decade of living with a disease once thought fatal I began to suspect that somehow, somewhere along the way, without noticing it, I had already died." So *Ghost Dance* opens with an equal but oppositional conceit: that the "voice" you read/hear is spectral. Wright's autobiography purports to go to, and come from, the one place "life writing" can never go—the place where life itself is exhausted.

Within a few sentences, he reports the "slow-breaking news of my possible reprieve." Even here reactions are never expected or commonplace. He resents this return of (relative) good health, and announces how he began "perversely, to secretly mourn a death I felt cheated of." We swiftly learn how hard the journey of a survivor might prove to Wright. He is (was?) utterly impossible, he concedes: "Face-to-face conversations with the rudely healthy felt at times like being gnawed at by rats"; "I longed for insults, any excuse to narrow my circle of friends." How many accounts of AIDS, or any illness, are capable of taking the writer's subject-position into account, even critiquing it? ("I became extremely touchy").

Wright's perceptive originality and remarkable turns of phrase endow each aspect of the by now rather dull, preformed AIDS illness narrative's trajectory with striking freshness: there's "ecstatic diarrhea"; a pill's name which "sounded like a concentration camp for Martians." Of his own body shape, induced by the treatments, he notes: "although my doctor was thrilled with my bloods, I looked like a pregnant stick-figure." *Terra Incognito* refers to Wright's occasional experiences of depression: it was "as if the shadow of a bird was flying right through me."

There's a DVD about Wright's dance career entitled *Haunting Douglas* (2003). Stage highlights are intercut with personal testimony from acquaintances and peers, plus more awkward exchanges with Wright himself. Rehearsal footage reveals a relentless, punishing approach to dance. His hunger for excellence is so unmediated that Wright as choreographer can't bring himself to attend his own premieres if the dress rehearsal reveals them as imperfect. (He watches soap operas in his dressing room, instead listening to the footfalls.) Still, just as he is clearly an inspirational choreographer, Wright could prove an outstanding teacher of creative writing. Take the start of "Raptor," *Ghost Dance*'s second chapter: "As I looked out over the landscape of my personal history I found that wherever I directed my attention, something was blocking the view." The blockage turns out to be his commitment to, and worries about Malcolm, stymied artist, ex-lover, and close friend. Wright does something necessary, simultaneously self-serving and altruistic: he invites Malcolm to go bird-watching with him. He cannot proceed without getting to the bottom of Malcolm, with whom "Raptor" directly, unfussily concerns itself.

Ghost Dance is characterized by a remarkable generosity of temperament—something vital to the art of the memoir, but seldom considered intrinsic to it. Aspects of Wright's self-staging as "difficult" make this repeated deference to others surprising. But it is there—most winningly when he feels "sorry" for the friends he gathers to reveal his HIV diagnosis. As they struggle to say the best things, Wright gently intrudes with this commentary:

> They were like actors who had forgotten their lines, trying clumsily to help each other fill the greedy silence. And it was my job to let them know they hadn't failed. This I tried to do as best as I could, in the same fumbling way.

Wright, whose own performance capabilities fast distinguished him from his peers, is also movingly empathetic toward other dancers' plight: the professional hurdles and disappointments. He compares the unselected hordes of talented New York dancers to "tireless mountain-climbers with the summit inside their heads, clawing for a toe-hold on almost sheer cliffs," marveling at their cheering him even as he eclipses them. The "it-could-have-been-me" instinct later informs an unforgettably laconic account of friends lost: "Jim died, Chris died, my older brother Phillip was killed on his motorbike, my cousin Christopher took his own life, and other friends died while they were still new." Wright reads this with mesmeric understatement to camera in *Haunting Douglas*.

Toward the end of *Ghost Dance*, he notes a new keenness for walking: "These days when I'm out walking I've started to see faint, overgrown traces of other less frequented paths and now I take them." The same curiosity informed his adolescent drug experiments, his reenvisioning (nothing less) of the possibilities in contemporary dance, and his capacity for sketching previously unstated facets of life with AIDS. Wright may joke that he's dead. I'm tempted rather to argue that he's the first, possibly the only writer yet, to consider from first principles just what "living with AIDS" means.

For one who has lived life globally and experienced it so greedily, it comes as a surprise to read, latterly, in *Terra Incognito*:

> For myself, I have no desire to travel anywhere physically, content with the magnolia in flower, art of all kinds, my mother, friends, the warring cats, and the "joy that comes in the making."

Like Derek Jarman, another multitalented artist displaced from his preferred discipline by advancing, AIDS-related debility, Wright acknowledged the relentless urge to create, answering it by determining to "make" something else—"a living garden to weed for my dead." (Jarman's garden at Prospect Cottage, Dungeness, endures today, as something of a shrine.)

Wright would be too self-effacing to promote his books as examples of spiritual revelation (nor, incidentally, are they ever apologies for a life ill lived). I'd be indifferent to any book described in that way. But *Ghost Dance* especially left me with two startling impressions: first, of having encountered someone of great integrity—someone necessary to one's own well-being; second, of having read, and learnt, something about grace—the ability, that is, to embody and evince the essentials of living a good life.

RICHARD CANNING is author of *Gay Fiction Speaks* (2000) and *Hear Us Out* (2004), which won the Editors Choice Lambda Literary Award, as well as two volumes in the Hesperus Press *Brief Lives* series, *Oscar Wilde* (2008) and *E.M. Forster* (2009). He has also edited two volumes of gay male fiction, the Lambda-shortlisted *Between Men* (2007) and *Between Men Two* (2009), as well as *Vital Signs: Essential AIDS Fiction* (2007; also Lambda-shortlisted). For 15 years, he taught at Sheffield University, England. Canning can be reached at simeslol@gmail.com. Quotations are taken from Douglas Wright, *Ghost Dance* (Auckland: Penguin, 2004) and Douglas Wright, *Terra Incognito* (Auckland: Penguin, 2006), both currently out of print.

BURNING DREAMS
(2006)

by Susan Smith

J. D. GLASS

"Everyone has to come out." So says Joe, just "average" Joe, to Paul, a man whose soul has frozen into grayness and who, in his instinctive reach for comfort and an attempt to reclaim his "old" life after the death of his father, finds healing instead in the Buffalo, New York home of a witch, her trans-man lover, and the young drag king who is now his ex-wife's lover.

Beginning in time where its predecessor *Of Drag Kings and the Wheel of Fate* (2006) ends, *Burning Dreams* is not a sequel in the true sense of the word, but is instead a new immersion into a richly woven tapestry of lives, people, and plot as we follow the progressions of the establishment of a new love, the progression of another, and the strength it takes to allow love to transcend death.

A major aspect of this tale evolves into a coming out for Paul: not as a gay man or even as a straight one, but as a full-blooded feeling human being, one in whom the richness of being and potential is fully realized.

Among a cast of characters, or rather, family members—a family created beyond the bounds of biology, instead shooting from the same root of love and respect—Paul wonders at the ease in which they all seem to be so strongly and uniquely individual: from royal Egyptia, the drag queen, to regular Joe—and privately thinks that none have had to struggle for identity, since each seems so much him-/herself. He learns, and we with him, quite differently, that each one has traversed through his or her own growing pains to discover, forge, and form identity, to "come out" and be exactly who they are.

In using the specific Buffalo, New York location—a character in its own right within the novel—Smith brings the right sense of place to her story, not just geographically, but metaphysically and metaphorically as well, since we adventure along with the leads to learn that who we are and who we can be is not limited to the body, the bonds, and the norms we are born to, but is instead a process of crossing and re-crossing borders, of revisiting old terrain and forging new trails; a constant unfolding journey.

There is also the examination of custom, costume, and construct, of how they interact, meld, mold, and change, hide or reveal primal essence, and the questions raised here are raised gently; with neither recrimination nor reproach, merely the gentle reminder that these are things we put on, accept, or discard, according to a host of dictates, both internal and external.

It is in novels like this, works where poetry masquerades as prose, where magic is quotidian and the ordinary magical, that ultimate human truths—ones which exist in disregard of external trappings—are revealed via fiction, and artifice itself is used as a direct path to archetypical ideal reality.

Emotionally, psychologically, philosophically, the revelations of this novel are universal to the human condition; the experiences within, while unique to the characters as they encounter them, are simultaneously recognizable to the reader as essential questions of being. As Paul discovers and becomes his soul's reality—ready to face who he was, who he has become and eager to discover who he will be—we, too, are drawn into a further opening of our own selves, should we be brave enough to take the journey.

J. D. GLASS is author of the novels *Punk Like Me* (2006), *Punk and Zen* (2007), *Red Light* (2007), *American Goth* (2008), and *X* (2009). She lives in New York. Quotations are taken from Susan Smith, *Burning Dreams* (2006), which is currently in print.